MW01095004

Returned

Also by Kimberley Griffiths Little
Forbidden
Banished

Returned

KIMBERLEY GRIFFITHS LITTLE

HARPER

An Imprint of HarperCollins*Publishers*

Library of Congress Control Number: 2016958597
ISBN 978-0-06-219504-3

Typography by Torborg Davern
16 17 18 19 20   PC/LSCH   10 9 8 7 6 5 4 3 2 1

First Edition

For Kirsten,
sisters are forever friends,
and I can't imagine my life without you

1

*L*ast night should have been one of bliss. After all Kadesh and I had been through—the loss of my family, the trek through the harsh desert . . . this should have been our night, the first as husband and wife in the marriage tent.

During the months of hardship and terror, I'd imagined us sipping wine and bathing in a marbled bath of bubbles. Lying in perfect luxury on a golden bed, together at last.

Instead, Kadesh and I were like lost children, orphaned by the sudden death of his uncle, King Ephrem, at our wedding ceremony, which had been irrevocably shattered mere hours ago.

"Come," Kadesh said, tugging at my elbow. His other arm went around my waist as he helped me mount my horse. We rode down the winding cliff path back to the beach where we had just sent off King Ephrem in a royal funeral pyre.

Those ominous lights we'd just spotted in the distance from the top of the cliffs had imprinted fresh horror on my mind. Strangers on the desert were never a good sign, but hundreds of lights on the desert spelled doom. Horeb's army was so close, so inevitable. There was no avoiding the war that was about to descend on us in all its wrath and fury.

Beside me, Asher, the Edomite prince, muttered, "No time left for planning or training. Horeb's armies will be here before nightfall tomorrow."

My horse brayed, as though the animal understood the gloomy words.

Kadesh frowned at the young man with disapproval. "Don't worry, Jayden," he said, trying to comfort me. "We're ready for them."

Despite his trying to calm my fears, I was beyond being worried. Within the next fortnight, Sariba would either survive or fall to its doom—and take the lives of everyone with it.

The crowd of mourning citizens and palace servants, guards, and king's soldiers began to disperse when we reached the funeral pyre. Shadowy figures drifted up the sandy beach back to the paths that led to the city above. Silent specters. Muffled tears.

While King Ephrem's pyre burned out, the last of the red flames snapped at the salty sea air, devouring the body of the king of Sariba.

A hot wind whipped at my bridal gown. I wanted to scrape

the horror of the night from my sight until my eyelids were raw.

The acrid smell of smoke and ashes chafed at my nose and throat. I was sure that no amount of water could ever quench my thirst again.

Gripping my hand, Kadesh lowered himself before the funeral pyre, pulling me with him. On my knees in the soft sand, while waves rushed along the shore, I bowed my head. Tears slipped down my nose, conveying my devotion and love to the kindly old king.

King Ephrem had welcomed me as his nephew and heir's betrothed, including my father into his household. We were part of his family now and he was ready to lay aside the safety of his kingdom and people in order to provide us shelter and a new home.

I was grateful for his love, but apprehensive about Kadesh's inevitable crowning. The sooner it happened the better when three threatening armies were now at the kingdom's doorsteps. His crowning would calm the citizens and show leadership and strength. But the man I loved was vulnerable, just as much as I was.

Kadesh's heart was tender, and too magnanimous. And, blinded in one eye as he was, he was not the perfect specimen of a fearless soldier and commander in chief. His physical obstacles might not endear confidence unto his army.

Reaching out to me from the blackness of midnight, Kadesh lifted my fist to his lips and kissed my fingers. We knelt in the sand, trembling and clinging to each other. "I give you all that I am, Jayden, daughter of Pharez. All my heart and all my protection, for as long as I take breath."

"We will fight together," I said, my voice catching. "Horeb now, and any future adversaries. We must trust each other implicitly. You must let me do my part."

"I'm not sure I'm ready for the latter." His mouth crooked into a small smile as he brought me close. "Dear God in heaven," Kadesh whispered into my hair, his hands cupping my head. "Help this kingdom. Help my people. Help us as their servants and leaders."

Swirls of fine sand rose and I closed my eyes. "Let's go home," I said softly into his ear.

Kadesh motioned for Asher to take our horses back up to the city, and then he and I walked together, our hands in a death grip, not wanting to let go. Our shattered wedding, King Ephrem's death, and the impending war overwhelmed us into silence.

When Kadesh and I staggered into the palace, my eyelashes were crusted with the salt of the ocean.

Servants rushed to attend us, bedraggled and dirty as we were. Wall sconces flickered with lowered late-night flames. We gulped down a goblet of water each, but the cool drink hurt my burning throat. All I could smell was ashes and death on me, my wedding dress, even my skin.

Waving away any more food or drink, Kadesh kept me moving past the columns and carpets of the entrance foyer, as though fearing I would collapse onto the floor. A fainting bride would never do in the public rooms with the eyes of the servants on us, despite the lateness of the hour and the few discreet guards on duty.

With Kadesh's arms around my waist, our fingers tightly laced, we maneuvered the hallways, the train of my wedding gown trailing dirt along the deep-cut carpets.

Kadesh pushed open the door to my suite, light from the hall falling across the floor.

All at once, my legs gave out, and I faltered on the threshold, reaching for the doorjamb to stay upright. Kadesh swung his cloak around me and lifted me into his arms, carrying me into the suite.

To my right came the sound of whispers and the soft closing of the door to the bathing and dressing area; my maids prudently disappearing at our unexpected appearance.

I pictured them waiting up for me, worried after the destruction of the wedding, the sudden death and funeral pyre of our king. Rumors were already spreading like wildfire over the sighting of the enemy armies bearing down on us.

At the moment we all needed rest, but my mind whirled with a thousand thoughts.

Kadesh strode across the room to my bed, tossing the extra pillows aside. Gently, he laid me down on the coverlet, the folds of his cloak still caught around my body. I was distantly aware of the shushing sound my ivory wedding gown made against my legs.

Kadesh knelt beside me and slipped off the gold sandals from my feet, allowing them to clatter to the floor.

I caught at his tunic with my fingers. The fabric was

smudged with ashes as well as dirt from the fight with the marauders who had attacked our wedding—and had shot an arrow into Chemish's back. We didn't know whether the King of the Edomites still lived or not.

"Any word from Asher about his father's condition?" I asked, my voice hoarse in the eerie stillness of the suite.

Kadesh shook his head, and my eyes burned with a fresh wave of grief. I choked it back, not wanting to break down. I had to be strong. Guilt might wrack my conscience at bringing Horeb to the doors of Sariba, but I could not give in to panic.

"Shh," Kadesh whispered. He rose from where he knelt on the floor and lay down next to me, curling me into his chest.

My fingers clutched at his back, pulling his warmth tight against me to stop the shivering. I didn't realize how cold I'd been until now. "Tonight was our *wedding*—" I began.

"Don't think of that, Jayden," he said softly. "It will tear you into pieces. The future is still there, waiting for us. I promise. Now you need to sleep."

I took a deep breath, keenly aware of his musky smell mixed with dirt and ash and blood. My limbs were limp and I was exhausted, but my mind continued to race with a hundred images. "There will be no more peaceful sleep until Horeb is defeated," I said in a broken voice. "Or we are dead from his invasion."

"Tomorrow will be a long day," Kadesh said, his eyes on mine. "I'll have your maids bring you a sleeping draught to help you relax." I shook my head, but he placed his hands on both sides of my face, staring deep into my eyes. "Tomorrow

Sariba will crown me as its new king. I must legally hold the throne before Horeb attacks."

"How soon will the armies descend on the city?"

"It won't be tomorrow, that is for certain. They're still half a day's journey away, and they'll need to set up camp, find water in the hills. Plan their first battle strategy. Remember, this land is foreign to them. They'll be sending out their scouts if they haven't already. The city will remain closed, our own army at the gates, our own scouts in the hills to bring news of their movements."

"Kadesh?" I whispered, his hair falling against my neck in the darkness. "I can't stay in my suite pacing the floor for the next many weeks, hoping you'll come home. I have to be at your side as your queen—even though we weren't married tonight."

His eyes flicked away and then back to mine. A deep sigh rose from his chest while he brought me closer. "I don't like you being part of this. I can't stand the thought of Horeb seeing you. Of hurting you again."

"Yet King Ephrem said *I* was to kill Horeb." My stomach churned when the words caught in my throat.

Kadesh pressed his lips against my forehead, his face hovering above mine. "Stay in bed tomorrow. Rest up for what lies ahead. Get your strength back."

"I am strong—"

He rose to a sitting position and let out a chuckle. "A girl who crosses the desert and takes on the Edomites will never be underestimated by me."

I gave him a small smile, wishing we were still lying together on the bed. I was cold, chilled, and terrified.

"I must go before the palace is filled with gossip about my presence in your room at such a late hour."

"What are your plans tomorrow?" I asked.

He lifted an eyebrow. "What are *your* plans tomorrow?"

"Actually, I intend to get my sister from the temple. She wasn't at our wedding tonight, even after I sent her an invitation. The High Priestess Aliyah stopped her from attending, I just know it. I must talk to her and convince her to move to the palace. It will be safer here. I—I don't even know if she's still alive. . . ."

"She is," Kadesh assured me. "You shouldn't leave the city, even to go to the temple. I'll accompany you."

"You have a war to prepare for. I won't waste your time."

"The forest between here and the temple might not be safe."

"If Horeb's army actually makes it that close to the city then we are all doomed."

"True. We'll face him in battle on the desert, between the frankincense groves and the foothills of the Qara Mountains. Far from the city gates. I plan to go out tomorrow with my scouts to see what we can learn."

"Wait until my return from the temple. I want to go with you."

"You are determined. We won't be riding out until nightfall. I want Horeb to think he's got a temporary reprieve. There won't be a sign of any of Sariba's scouts or soldiers. Silence from us—despite my secret convoy of soldiers already hiding in the foothills."

"Then we have quite a day ahead of us. Which means you must kiss me," I added softly.

"With all my heart."

He leaned in and gently kissed me, his lips warm and comforting. "Soon I can say that I am your queen," I murmured.

"To me, you already are."

"Being married to you almost seems like a dream now." I brushed away the tears leaking out of my eyes. "A dream that will remain elusive forever."

Kadesh gazed into my face, pensive. "After all this is over, I'm not sure the marriage tent is good enough for us. I want to take you to the place my parents would often visit when they needed a respite from royal life and duties."

"Where is that?"

"An ancient stone castle, or fort, almost two hour's ride from here in the mountains. It was abandoned and in disrepair, but my father fixed it up for my mother when I was young. They had many happy times and memories there."

I gave him a shaky smile. "It sounds perfect."

We finally broke apart. Kadesh's mouth was tight with grief, but his features were filled with an angry passion. "I vow to you, Jayden, that we will overcome the terrible deeds of this night. We will win."

"I believe you," I whispered to assure him. But did I actually believe that we could abolish three armies of Assyrian, Maachathite, and Nephish soldiers? To defend the city without the slaughter of innocent families?

Horeb's armies weren't our only worry, either. Kadesh had been away for a long year, recovering from the caravan raid and helping me search the city of Mari for my sister, Sahmril, while under siege.

Unfortunately, Aliyah—in her role as the temple High Priestess—had used that year to her advantage, gaining the trust of the city, showing off the fruits of the temple. With Kadesh's absence and King Ephrem's ill health, she'd had free reign to influence the army's leaders and Sariba's mayors and city council. Further, she had aligned herself with the Egyptians who were now living here and weaving their magical spells and charms. How dangerous that would prove had yet to be seen, but the knowledge made me incredibly uneasy.

"There's wisdom in your being crowned as soon as possible," I said. "To thwart any coup from your army—or Aliyah's influence. You must act quickly."

"I've been watching a myriad of thoughts moving through your head," he said with amusement. "You're weighing everything out."

"How can you tell?"

"Your eyes go distant. Then you take a breath and hold it while you're thinking. I always know when I'm about to get a barrage of ideas." He tightened his grip on my waist. "Please return from the temple as soon as you can tomorrow. You can't miss the king's crowning."

"*Your* crowning," I emphasized, running a finger along his cheek, my heart tugging at the thick white scar along his face from Horeb's sword that had gouged out his eye. "Who will do the honors of crowning you king?"

"Uncle Josiah, my closest relative to the throne. He's in line as my successor. When Uncle Ephrem was a young man, the High Priest Melchizedek from Salem crowned him king, but there's no time to get him here when the journey takes months."

"This will all be over long before then," I said soberly. "Horeb's men will likely be under orders to capture me and take me to him."

"I won't let that happen, Jayden, but if you stayed safely at the palace that risk lowers," Kadesh added pointedly.

"Many people will die over the next few weeks, all because of me. I can't sit idly by while everyone else takes all the risks. The High Priestess also wants to get rid of me and take you and your kingdom for herself. Death might be the easiest way, but who will try to kill me first, Aliyah or Horeb?"

2

The next morning I woke to darkness.

The hour before dawn hovered like a breath on the horizon. The city of Sariba lay in slumber outside my bedroom window, deceptively peaceful.

"My lady, it's time," Tijah, my handmaiden, whispered.

Fatigue gnawed at my bones. I shuddered to a sitting position and grasped the pillow, hanging on to it like a lifeline to sanity. I'd only slept three or four hours during which a mirage of images and nightmares had tortured me.

My mind replayed the sight of Horeb's raiders slashing through our guests with their swords, hacking draperies, overturning tables of beautifully prepared food. My wedding utterly ruined.

The shock of finding Uncle Ephrem dead behind the curtains of the dais, his heart failing him as he witnessed the horror of a group of foreigners bent on our extermination caused my heart to hurt with the pain of the great man's loss.

Finally, I thought about Asher sitting at the bedside of his father, Chemish, who had been shot through with an arrow, his life hanging by a thread. An arrow meant for Kadesh.

Kadesh, Asher, and the other Edomites had killed the intruders, pulling them off their horses—until one who was gasping for life confessed that Horeb had sent them. It was all I could do not to personally plunge my dagger into the mercenary soldier's heart.

"My lady, please," Tijah said, pulling me to my feet. "We must leave now if we hope to get to the Temple of Sariba before dawn. Prince Kadesh advised me that darkness will give us cover."

I dipped my hands into a basin of warm water to wash my face, wavering on my heels. I used the towel she offered and stared at her. "Are you sure we can get in through your secret way?"

A hurt look came over her face. "I wouldn't lie about something so important."

I laid a hand on Tijah's arm, recalling her knowledge of the temple tunnels and passageways. She could help me enter without detection. "I'm just worried that we'll run into one of those menacing Egyptian magicians."

Tijah's younger sister, Jasmine, stepped from the shadows of the dressing room, silently holding out a pleated emerald gown, her eyes luminous in the glow of the single candle.

Beyond her, hanging in the wardrobe, was my wedding

gown stained with mud and grass, ash and wood smoke still smudging the folds of ivory fabric.

Beauty to ashes.

The story of my life.

I stepped into the emerald dress, turning my head so the deaf girl could read my thanks on my lips. The girl gave me a tremulous smile and then busied herself buttoning up the back.

Smoothing the gown over my hips, I noted how the skirt dropped around my waist to fit every curve. The sleeves weren't loose, but folds of softness fell past my wrists. The plunging neckline set off a necklace of sapphires and topaz, while a heavy emerald dropped between my breasts.

"It seems silly to dress so extravagantly only to slink through the catacombs into the temple," I said, self-conscious at the luxurious outfit and jewelry.

Tijah's eyes darted to mine. "You must be dressed like a priestess in case anyone stops us."

Finally, my handmaids painted my eyes and brows in a midnight black kohl. Bloodred rouge on my cheeks and lips, my wedding curls still dusted in gold draping my shoulders.

I stared at myself in the sheet of bronze hanging on the wall, my figure shimmering in the reflection. I thought back to my home, and to Leila as a child. I still couldn't believe we were here after all that we'd been through. In Sariba, the High Priestess Aliyah was even more powerful and threatening than Armana of the Temple of Ashtoreth back in the oasis city of Tadmur. Leila was not going to leave easily or on her own. Aliyah was sister to the Queen of Sheba. She was a princess and part of the royal enclave and had a hold on my sister. She was previously Kadesh's betrothed, too. A fact I tried not to dwell on, but our relationship was too close, too personal.

While the girls put the finishing gemstone pins into my hair, I was trembling from nerves, my palms sweaty. Instead of a polished, refined appearance for the courts of Sariba, I appeared wild and unruly. The columned dress added five years to my age, and the makeup turned me into an Egyptian goddess.

The sight filled me with a sense of terror. I looked like a different person, not the simple desert girl I was in my heart.

"You are stunning, Princess Jayden," Tijah said, smiling at her handiwork. "We wish you were queen already."

I glanced in the bronze mirror one last time, lifted my neck, took a deep breath, and tried to feel confident. It helped that I had my dagger strapped to my thigh and my sling attached at my hip.

"I promise you that we will *not* be defeated."

Jasmine kissed my hand, understanding my words as she read my lips.

Tijah bowed her head. "Spoken like a true queen."

"I'm not yet a queen. And there is a very good chance I may never become queen. My life—our life—everything is precarious. We don't know what today will bring, or tomorrow. All we can do is be as prepared as we can and pray that goodness will win in the end."

I forced myself to impart confidence. Most likely, I would not cross paths with Aliyah at all—and I wanted to keep it that way. "Are you sure you want to do this, Tijah? You haven't told me about your past or your family's story, but the fact that you know a secret way into the temple tells me that somehow you're tied to the Sariba Goddess."

Tijah slowly nodded while Jasmine's eyes filled with sudden tears. "It doesn't matter any longer, but we grew up at the temple, and we'll do anything for you and your sister."

It was still dark outside the windows, but from a distance, a cock crowed loud and long. Wordlessly, we hurried out the door of the bedroom suite and into the hallway.

The reality was, depending on what happened at the temple, I might not ever come back. I was torn in two, desperate to bring my sister back home with me, but terrified of Aliyah's power over Leila, including the power of the Egyptians and their magic incantations.

3

*L*iquid moonlight dripped along the walls of the palace as I followed Tijah and Jasmine. The last of the moon lowered itself to rest upon the distant horizon.

I became like a thief, passing the chambers where Naomi, Josiah, their daughter Naria, and the rest of the royal family slept, making my way soundlessly through the halls blazing with lamps and candles.

The guards glanced at us quizzically but didn't stop us. We passed my father's bedchamber and then finally Kadesh's royal rooms.

Five hours ago, we'd lain on my bed together, in tears and grief. Now I pictured him wearing out the rugs on the floors of his suite with his feet. Or perhaps he was somewhere else entirely with his war advisors, talking earnestly through the night.

Tijah pressed a finger to her lips, and I tried to mimic the girls' stealth, not realizing that my sandals were making a shushing sound along the dense carpets. My heart drummed, pounding its way into my throat.

We turned left, then right, then left and left again. All at once, I bumped into Tijah who leaned in close to take my arm, guiding us through the side door to the palace gardens.

The hanging lights had been extinguished. Dawn hung on the brink and even the running fountains were stilled, waiting for morning.

Waiting for war.

The city was so dreadfully quiet. I swore that even from here I could hear the distant ocean kissing the shoreline.

I held Jasmine's and Tijah's hands tightly in mine so we wouldn't trip across the stone paving or stumble on the steps that led us off the palace grounds. I didn't know the layout like they did.

When we arrived at the stables, Asher had horses saddled and ready to mount. Walking past the stalls and stacks of hay, he stared at me through the gloom. His eyes swept over me from head to toe. "Are you sure you want to do this?" he asked.

I nodded. "I have to learn what Aliyah has done to Leila. The strange drugs the temple uses on the priestesses . . . I'm afraid Leila will forget I—we—ever existed. That would kill my father."

The Edomite prince nodded. His lips parted with words he wanted to say, but couldn't. We'd gone over my plan as we stood on the beach watching the flames devour our king, standing outside of Kadesh's hearing while he conferred with Uncle Josiah about the hundred pressing issues over Horeb's coming army.

"I have to rescue my sister," I said simply, but it was all I could do not to break down in front of him.

Asher's jaw worked, the muscles in his face twitching. "I don't like it, but I'd do the same if it were my sister."

"Please don't bring it up to Kadesh. He has enough to worry about and plans to make. Not unless—" I broke off.

I didn't have to say the words, *Not unless I don't return.*

It was obvious Asher knew exactly what I was thinking. "You know I don't like this," he repeated, as stubborn as I was.

"My maids can find Leila. They know the secrets of the temple."

Tijah spoke from the darkness. "Nobody else does." Quickly, she added, "Please forgive me for interrupting."

Asher waved away her apology. "A time of war has no need for etiquette—or silence about important matters."

Under the last of the glittering stars, Asher helped the girls up onto their horse. "I've given you the most gentle old horse King Ephrem owned, but be careful in the forest dusk."

Tijah said, "I rode when I was a child, a few times with my—" She broke off, and then added, "Jasmine is so tender, animals are never skittish with her."

Asher bent beside the second horse and laced his fingers together, indicating I was to place my foot there so he could hoist me onto the mahogany-hued Arabian steed. "No, Asher. This is Hara, your own horse. I can't take her from you."

"Hara already knows you from the journey across the desert. Besides, if I lend you my horse, it gives you greater incentive to come back home to us."

Our eyes met in the ensuing pause. "Incentive isn't the problem," I whispered.

Before I could turn around and run back to my rooms, I stuck my foot into his cupped hands, swinging my leg and dress over the horse's back. After settling into the animal's flanks, I grasped the reins.

Asher touched the hem of my gown, and I shivered. "I fear for you, not only because you're playing into Aliyah's hands, but because Horeb is on the plain in the valley of the Qara Mountains. At the temple up on the hill you'll be that much closer to him, and closer to danger."

Tijah wrapped the leather straps around her fists. "Nobody will see us. I promise, Prince Asher."

He pursed his lips. "That's a promise waiting to be broken. There's no predicting who you'll stumble across on the trail."

"I know a secret way into the temple because I grew up there."

Asher let out a low chuckle. "Even the servants carry secrets close to their hearts."

"I hope that lessens your worry," I told him, nudging Hara to follow Tijah away from the paddocks. Perched in front of her sister, Jasmine lay down along the horse, eyes closed, hands tangled in the thick mane, as though she was part of the horse itself.

"Asher—" I halted and then amended his name. "Prince of Edom," I murmured.

"Yes," he said, his eyes bright.

"How is Chemish this morning? What do the doctors say?"

He gave me a small smile. "I spent the night at his bedside, terrified at the letter I might have to write my mother, but he rallied two hours ago and gave my hand a faint squeeze. The doctors were able to remove the arrow from his chest, and it appears that the shaft didn't hit his heart or lungs."

"I'm so glad," I whispered, relief flooding me.

"He's weak from loss of blood, but the physicians are hopeful he'll recover. He's strong and he knows Kadesh needs his help."

"He'll be on that sick bed for weeks! There's no chance he could ever fight in this war," I told him.

"Don't underestimate my father."

"I'll visit him when I return from the temple," I promised.

Asher placed his hand along the length of my reins, making me pause. "Is there anything I can say to convince you not to go? You're going for your sister, but Kadesh doesn't trust Aliyah and neither do I."

Distaste crawled along my skin. Aliyah's previous words under the patio canopy several days earlier hissed again in my ears. My skin crawled with her strange touch. The insinuations she'd delighted to tell me about her betrothal to Kadesh were sickening. "I didn't trust her the moment I saw her."

"If you don't come back, Kadesh will never forgive me."

"I'll come back," I insisted. "Trust *me*."

Asher gave a snort. "I trust you both. I love you both."

His words shot at my heart. It was uncomfortable to hear his emotions spoken aloud because I knew his thoughts and feelings had a double meaning. Kadesh was unaware, and I intended to keep it that way. Asher's love for me would remain unknown to anyone else.

Silence drew out between us. Finally, I stared at him through the morning darkness, clenching the folds of my dress. "There's one more reason I'm going to the temple, Asher."

His brow creased in concern. "What is it?"

"Last night Aliyah stole my marriage contract. I saw her behind the dais. She fled during the attack, not caring that King Ephrem had collapsed before her. I raced to stop her but I wasn't fast enough. When I returned to the table, the marriage covenant papers were gone. I know she has them, and I'm furious."

Gripping the horse's halter, Asher's knuckles glowed white under the starlight. He nodded soberly. "I'm still your body-guard, Jayden," he said, using my given name. "Over the next several weeks, I will be your shadow. You need to be back to the palace before the sun is at its zenith. Uncle Josiah will crown Kadesh King of Sariba today—and you must be there. He needs you at his side, and the people of Sariba need to see you, too."

I was tempted to argue against his point. "My reception by the citizens of Sariba after the attack by the mercenary soldiers and their king's death leaves me in a precarious position."

"Don't overthink it, my lady. Prince Kadesh tried to marry you last night. That is enough for the people. Nobody can blame you when your own wedding was invaded by warriors and ruined."

"But Horeb sent those soldiers. They're *here*—because of me. I guess—" I stumbled, trying to sort out my thoughts. "Mostly, Asher, I don't want you to blame me for your father's assault. If we lose him, I'll be devastated."

Asher laid a hand on the horse's neck, dangerously close to my own hands wrapped around the pommel of the saddle. "We won't lose him. He has better doctors here than back home. Trust me now." He handed over the reins and then slapped the flanks of his horse.

My body jerked forward and the Prince of Edom melted into the shadows behind us.

4

We rode for an hour, and when my horse pulled up next to the other riders, a sudden tug at my arm made me jump. "You startled me, Jasmine."

The girl bowed her head in apology and beckoned me to dismount and follow them.

I glanced around at the lush surroundings of the rushing waterfall and a moment later the girls ducked behind the pouring water into the cave where Kadesh had taken me a few weeks earlier on our tour of the land of Sariba.

Moss crawled up the walls, and the narrow tunnel yawned into blackness. I shivered, a misty spray soaking my arms.

"Dawn is close," Tijah said, dropping all decorum when she snatched up my hand to pull me along the cave's floor. Moisture oozed from the stone walls, the air humid and cloying. "We need to get inside the temple before we're stopped by any guards. The gates don't officially open until later in the morning."

"But why are we going into a cave?"

Jasmine smiled as Tijah said, "It's a shortcut."

We formed a single line. My hands flattened along the walls where the cave sloped upward. I found myself panting, feeling the way with my fingertips—until I almost fell into some sort of hollow. A sudden rush of cold air and emptiness dashed against my cheeks.

Jasmine grabbed me by the waist and pulled me back.

"Is there a pit down there?" I asked, teetering in my sandals.

The mute girl shook her head while Tijah said, "No, merely another bend in the cave. But there's nothing down there."

A moment of silence followed her words. What was the truth—a secret cache of hidden weapons for Sariba's army? That seemed plausible and fantastical both.

"We *must* keep moving," Tijah admonished.

We pressed forward, winding along until we reached the bottom of a stone staircase. Without speaking, we climbed a set of endless steps until we came out into the opening of another cave set into a low hill.

I was out of breath—and tottered on my heels when I saw the Temple of Sariba rising before us in dazzling splendor. It was a palace of such grandeur and opulence I could hardly see the roofline. White walls sparkled as though embedded with gold flakes. Glazed mauve staircases wound about the massive arched entrance with a set of grand gold doors underneath the portico. Fountains shot straight into the air, even at this early hour.

The morning's dim light had grown hazy, the sun threatening to blast along the edge of eastern desert.

"Hurry!" Tijah hissed. She skirted the gardens and flanked the set of tiered steps that ended at the eastern doors, heading to a rear wall instead. A place where the shadows lay deep.

Jasmine pressed a finger to her lips, and then I spotted the temple guards rounding a corner, away from us, vanishing from sight. We twisted down a series of half staircases, and the gardens faded behind us. Just as quickly, we came to an old wooden door with brass inserts and bars running vertically.

Tijah tapped so faintly I wasn't sure the sound would penetrate to the other side, but a slot high above us slid open and then closed again. A breath later, the wooden door snapped open and we were ushered into a dank, smelly hallway.

"Where are we?" I whispered.

"The servants' quarters," Tijah said. "The basement of the temple. Aliyah never comes down here."

A moment later, we were assaulted by the smells of old food, body odor, and a drastic lack of fresh air. There were faint moans coming from within. It reminded me of the prison in Tadmur where Kadesh and I had rescued my father.

"What goes on down here?"

The girl didn't answer at first, only held my hand in hers as we walked the filthy stone corridors. "There's no one assigned to help down here, nobody to clean or tend the ill."

Growing alarm soured my stomach. I'd never seen this kind of poverty when I lived at the Temple of Ashtoreth in Tadmur. "What path would someone take to get down here from the halls and floors above?" I asked.

"There used to be a staircase on the underground floor where the kitchens and servants' bedrooms are located. But a few years ago it was covered up so nobody could get in or out. Food is now brought through the very same door we entered. Aliyah pretends these women—this place—doesn't exist."

Dread filled me when Tijah pushed open a door and we entered a large room filled with women, even elderly and infirm. The women sat listlessly at tables or lay on mats in the corners. Their dresses had turned to rags, and I shuddered at their tangled hair and blackened feet.

I pressed myself against the wall. "Who are these women and why are they kept here? I don't understand."

A mask seemed to fall across Tijah's face. "These women used to be priestesses of the Goddess. They've been banished to the dungeons of the temple because they are no longer viable."

"Viable?" I echoed.

Jasmine placed her hand in mine and pulled me across the room.

I halted on the cracked flagstones when Tijah crouched on the floor next to a woman who slept on one of the mats. She reached out a hand. "Mother," she whispered.

"What?" I broke off when tears slipped down the young girl's face. "This woman can't be your mother. She looks too old—"

Tijah's expression was unhappy but stoic as she bent over to kiss the woman's hands. "My mother is Erina. She'll have thirty-five winters next year."

The woman's skin sagged, drooping along her arms, her hair gray and stringy. Sores and boils scarred her arms and legs, and her mouth appeared unusually swollen. But behind the battered body, I could tell she had once been beautiful.

A hard knot of anger rose up my throat. I glanced about the room with its straw rushes strewn about in a feeble attempt to keep its occupants from sitting in squalor. "Where are the doctors?"

"Physicians come once a month," Erina told me quietly. She cleared her throat, but didn't speak again, holding her daughters tight while she rocked them, one in each arm.

"But *why* are you kept here if all these women used to be priestesses of Sariba?"

Her weary eyes met mine. "I was one of the temple's highest-level priestesses. I adored the Goddess—until I realized that I was being kept to manufacture children to give to the gods of Ba'al and Moloch for sacrifice."

"How many children have you borne?"

"Eleven."

"And your babies . . . ?"

"All of them were sacrificed to appease the gods and goddesses. I was forced to watch. And hold in my screams until I nearly bit my tongue in half."

"How did Tijah and Jasmine escape?"

Tijah spoke for her. "My mother was able to sell me into servitude. Jasmine was born mute, so the High Priestess claimed she wasn't worthy to be sacrificed. My mother was finally able to sell us both to the palace last year."

"You have no family that can help you, Erina?" I asked. "To live like this . . ."

"My parents were desert people. They disowned me when I went to the temple. I never saw them again. My brothers and sisters—I have no idea what has become of them." She sat up straighter. "I take responsibility for my life—"

"—but you were lied to."

"Life's choices are not without risk or consequences, are they?" Erina's tone held resigned irony. "I stay now to help the other women. Some in these dark corners are dying and they need someone to talk to and make sure they receive food."

I admired her for not turning bitter after being abandoned by those she had once trusted. "You have two beautiful daughters who love you."

Erina planted a kiss against the dark hair of the girls nestled beside her. "I count my blessings every single day."

Her words reminded me of my mother. I'd heard Rebekah say the same thing about me and my sister. Watching Erina with her daughters, my throat ached with loneliness. My mother would never meet Kadesh. Never see me married. So many times, I'd wished she could rescue me, heal the hurts, banish the evil that had fallen on our fractured tribe. She would have mended the rifts that had come between our family and never allowed Horeb to hurt me.

I knelt to take Erina's hand. "The temples have many dirty secrets, don't they?"

"I'm sorry to burden you, my lady."

"Never," I said. "I know the truth now, and the truth will set you all free one day. As Prince Kadesh's future queen, I promise you that."

A flicker of light filtered through the grated bars along the upper windows.

"Dawn breaks," I said. "We need to get inside before servants begin serving breakfast. I want you to come back with us to the palace, Erina. You need medical care."

Erina instantly protested. "I would never taint the palace of King Kadesh—or you, his queen."

"I'm not his queen yet," I said dryly.

"My daughters tell me he's madly in love with you."

I tried to shake off the heat rising up my neck. "You can't stay here."

"Oh, my dear, I've become a surrogate mother to too many girls. Besides, war is coming."

I flicked my chin upward. "You know what's happening, then?"

"I suspected things were changing when our old High Priestess suddenly died and Aliyah took her place. I knew for certain when the Egyptian magicians appeared a few months ago. News of a fierce army arriving on the same day as King Ephrem's death was too coincidental. Already there are priestesses packing to leave."

"Where can they go?"

"The hills," Erina said with pursed lips. "Our mountains of Qara."

"But Horeb and his armies are heading to the foothills between the frankincense groves and the mountains. Anybody who goes in that direction will be captured and killed."

Erina gave me a tight grimace. "But we know where the caves are."

I didn't want to argue with her, but I wouldn't have been surprised if Horeb had already camped a platoon inside the frankincense groves to prevent citizens from fleeing. We were surrounded by Horeb, the Assyrians, and Maachathites. There was little between them and the city. In every direction north of the mountains lay an infinite ocean of empty sands. It was impossible to escape using the beaches either. Kadesh had explained that except for Sariba, the entire coastline was cut off by towering cliffs that dove straight down into the surf.

We were trapped by geography and an army of blood-thirsty warriors.

Erina broke off eye contact. Her fingers tore at the broken threads of her dirty dress.

"Tell me the gossip, Erina. For the city's sake."

She bit at her lips. "People are saying that you brought death to Sariba. That if you hadn't bewitched our prince, we would still be safe and three armies would not be at our door-step waiting to slaughter us."

"I don't blame them for being angry. But know this," I told her, gripping her hand, "I will fight for all of you in this beautiful land. We will have the wits and courage we need to conquer this enemy."

"Please keep my children safe, that's all I ask." Waking

voices murmured from the room parallel to the one we were sitting in. The sound of a door opening. "Go! Don't be caught here," Erina cried softly.

Tijah clung to her mother, weeping large, silent tears while Jasmine slipped under her mother's wool blanket and curled under her shoulder. Before I could blink again, the girl's eyes closed and she was breathing deeply.

"Leave Jasmine," Erina said. "I'll bring her to you in the gardens when you're ready to return to the palace."

"We'll be gone on our horses within the hour," Tijah said, turning toward me. "Come, let's go."

My pulse throbbed with apprehension while Tijah, ever stalwart, led me out of the dismal gloom of the forgotten women's quarters.

5

We departed the same way we'd arrived, then entered the main temple through another outside door, finding ourselves in a windowless stone corridor. Wall sconces flickered, heat searing my cheeks.

Slipping through a bronze-plated door, we found ourselves in a marbled breezeway next. An odd gray color washed overhead, and I stared at the open sky above a columned portico.

"This way," Tijah said.

We darted down the smooth, polished floor, scurrying into an alcove when Tijah spotted a servant carrying a basket through a side door. The girl's hair was pinned up into a blue scarf, and she was yawning loudly.

Our skirts swept across the floor with hardly a sound. Quickly, we passed behind two guards talking before a window, gesturing toward the Qara Mountains. Their shoulders were stiff, fists on their swords and they were discussing Horeb's army potentially moving to the foothills where they could hide among the crevices and boulders and launch their attacks.

Two more doorways and a final staircase led to the floor above us where we walked a lengthy hallway until we reached the priestesses' quarters.

"This is it." Tijah's eyes were enormous in her pale face, and her lips trembled.

My heart banged against my ribs, I was so anxious to see my sister, but I pressed a hand to her cheek. "Everything will be all right, my sweet girl."

She soaked in my words, hopeful, but still afraid. "Hurry. We can't stay long."

I nodded and pushed open the door. A thousand butterflies fought to fly from my belly.

When the door opened, I was surprised to see the priestesses' large suites of rooms silent and empty. The beds were messy and rumpled, not smooth and pristine. No maids had come in to clean. The dressing rooms were a jumble, too. Clothes flung everywhere. Sandals tossed about the floors. Jars of lotions and rouge left open, a brush fallen to the floor. Trailing ribbons, a pile of earrings pawed through.

"The priestesses never rise before noon," Tijah said in a small voice.

"The temple hasn't been evacuated, has it?"

Tijah's eyes roamed the room, a frown forming between her eyes. "I have no idea."

I rubbed my hands together against the early-morning chill

coming through the fluttering curtains. "If the temple had evacuated, we would have encountered the citizenry coming down through the forest to the safety of the city—but we saw no one on the paths. Where would they have gone?"

Tijah trailed a hand along one of the bureaus as though the furniture could give up its secrets.

An idea flashed through my mind. "They're still here, and when we find the priestesses, we'll find Leila, too."

We retraced our steps down the staircase. At the bottom, I glanced into the dusky hallways. Through a window at the far end of the hall, a shot of gold on the horizon blinded me. The sun was rising faster.

"Show me where the halls and meeting rooms are located," I said.

Tijah beckoned me down two sets of stairs and then we passed through the massive gathering hall. A gigantic statue of the Sariba Goddess watched our every move.

Memories flooded me of the time I had danced with all the emotions from my heart—and nearly gave my body and soul to the Goddess of Ashtoreth. I could still conjure up the heady scent of roses, wine splashing in goblets, cinnamon breads, and the thrill of sensuality running like fingertips across my skin.

We headed toward the double doors to exit, and I paused. Something pulsed underneath my feet. The pounding of drums was low and throbbing. "Where's that sound coming from?"

The two of us turned in a circle while the floor shook beneath our feet. A length of draperies hung along the far wall and behind them was another set of carved doors, slightly ajar.

I peeked through the narrow opening, Tijah breathing on my neck.

The room was a smaller version of the great hall. Some type of ceremonial room with a life-size statue of the Goddess of Sariba front and center. She was, perhaps, even more beautiful than Ashtoreth. Large black eyes painted with kohl. A generous pomegranate-red mouth with perfectly shaped lips and high cheekbones. Flowing marble robes adorned her body, matching the length of sculpted black hair that fell below her waist and then melded into her gown—a gown carved with blooms of white lotus, scarlet miniature roses, and sprays of pale pink orchids.

The Goddess's face lifted to mine, as though the statue was animated by an actual soul. As though she sensed I was staring at her through the crack in the door. I sucked in air and tried not to meet the Goddess's eye.

While I watched, four and twenty priestesses fell down before the Goddess, holding golden vials of spicy oils in their open palms and raising them to the Goddess in adoration.

On either side of the statue, two altars had been erected. Behind the altars stood ten bald Egyptian magicians. The paint on their faces formed the shape of magical hieroglyphs. They wore leather aprons tied at their waists, and leopard skins draped their shoulders.

Their hands held up scepters crafted from polished frankincense timber and overlaid with gold and onyx, which gleamed in the ceremonial room. Someone must have fashioned them right here in Sariba.

A low chant accompanied the thump of three drummers sitting cross-legged in the corner. Their heads lolled to the side, eyes closed, as though transfixed by the music.

In fact, the entire room of priestesses and Egyptian men appeared to be in a trance. Candles of frankincense burned, smoke spiraling upward.

One by one, the priestesses came forward to the altar and took turns drinking from a golden goblet administered by one of the Egyptian priests of magicians.

My eyes flitted about the room, but I couldn't see Aliyah anywhere—or the Egyptian priest who had stared at me when our company had ridden into Sariba along the main thorough-fare after the long desert journey.

Their absence was unnerving and my fingers twitched with apprehension.

When voices came from behind us, I crouched among the draperies next to Tijah, putting a finger to my lips to make sure she didn't speak.

I sucked in my breath when Aliyah suddenly spoke in the alcove next to us.

"Will the spiritual transfer of the Goddess entering my body work, Heru?" the High Priestess asked in low tones.

"Egyptian magic always works, my love," a male voice replied. Chills ran down my neck. It had to be the High Priest of Egypt, that man with the menacing black eyes that had stared at me from the crowds the first time I entered the city. "When I speak the words of a spell or chant, they become real. Whatever is written—whatever is said—the gods make it so."

"That's what I'm counting on," Aliyah said with a note of pleasure. "After the ceremony the priestesses will believe that I am the Goddess incarnate. Whatever I say will be truth and fully obeyed."

"The Goddess is on your side. Egypt and the Priests of Ba'al are also with you. I've always wanted to see a mortal woman rise to divinity in this world. I'm honored that you chose me to be the priest to make it happen."

"You're so good to me, Heru. I knew you were the priest who could make this happen. After tonight, I will be the most powerful figure in Sariba. Prince Kadesh will have no choice but to honor me and make me his wife. The people of Sariba will demand me not only as their Goddess but as their queen."

I gripped Tijah's hand so tightly she whimpered. I mouthed an apology and pulled her closer.

"And isn't Prince Kadesh soon to be crowned, my lady?" Heru asked.

"Later this afternoon. Horeb's mercenary soldiers destroying that wedding last night . . . King Ephrem conveniently dying—both were strokes of luck."

"The Goddess provides," Heru said smoothly.

"Once her soul resides next to mine, the power of the royal family will also be mine," Aliyah continued. "There will be no stopping us from ruling this land. Our decrees will be carried into every corner of the earth, beginning with the kingdoms along the Red Sea and then east into Babylon. King Hammurabi will never know what happened."

"Don't forget that Egypt is already yours. I'm vizier to a

weak Pharaoh who allows me to do most of the ruling since the Hittites have taken control of the government. If you help him keep his throne, Pharaoh will gladly let our gold and riches flow to Sariba. The Goddess of Sariba will be High Priestess and Mistress over every minor goddess, from Isis to Ashtoreth and Bast."

"Very good," Aliyah said in a husky voice. "Are you ready?"

"I have one last question," the man asked. "There is one powerful kingdom that could potentially take you down. The kingdom of Sheba and the city of Sa'ba."

Aliyah's laugh was low and sensual. "My sister is queen of Sa'ba, and I am its rightful heir. She will be taken down easily, have no worries. She'll fall into line once I have Prince—rather, King Kadesh and Egypt under my thumb."

The Egyptian High Priest gave a grunt of admiration and then kissed her hand before departing the alcove.

Slowly, I let out my breath, my thoughts colliding.

A moment later, the Egyptian High Priest and Aliyah stood before the company of priestesses. The woman wore a dazzling red dress that draped her curves. Gold and silver bangles adorned her arms and neck. Elaborate earrings of onyx and rubies hung from her lobes. Her hair was dressed in magnificent curls streaming about her face, giving her an appearance that was both youthful and full of wisdom.

My fist clutched at the edge of the door when I noticed that Aliyah wore a peculiar tattoo on her forehead, a symbol created with whorls and hexagons.

A chill ran through me.

The temple priestesses formed a circle around the High Priestess when she stood before the altar where the magicians were chanting. With a sinking heart, I saw that every single girl had the same exotic symbol tattooed on her forehead.

"The seal of the Goddess," I whispered in sudden recognition. The seal was indicative of a significant ceremony. As an outsider, I had never witnessed any special ceremonies at the Temple of Ashtoreth in Tadmur, but Leila had once spoken of her initiation ceremony.

I glanced behind me and found Tijah shrunk into herself, wedged into the silken drapes that wrapped the corner of the great hall where we were hiding.

The ten priests dipped the end of their bronzed staves to each temple priestess's forehead. A peculiar white light blazed for an instant and then sizzled out.

Craning my neck, I searched for any sign of Leila. She had to be here, but the girls were dressed so alike, their hair unbound and draped about their hips. The noise of their bangles and ankle bracelets made a rattling sound that unnerved and distracted me.

My heart was in my throat when I spotted her. "Oh, Leila," I whispered, fighting against the urge to rush out from hiding. That would only jeopardize us both, but I ached to knock her over with an embrace.

Before I could take my next breath, my sister was kneeling before Heru. The Egyptian High Priest pressed his falcon-headed staff into Leila's forehead. A spark of light shot out and her body became languid, her limbs moving as though she were dancing in water. She whirled slowly on her toes, eyes closed. The other girls began to imitate her, and the room floated with dancing girls. Sheer silk dresses whirled about their legs, their bare arms glowing above their heads in the candlelight.

I was transported back to the grove of tamarisk trees the night I'd stumbled upon my sister dancing before the Goddess of Ashtoreth statue perched on a faux altar.

Each priestess's tattoo appeared to magically come alive, the whirling shapes shifting in intricate patterns on their faces.

My stomach twisted when Aliyah knelt before the statue of the Sariba Goddess to kiss her palms and bare, stone feet. When she rose, Heru held out his hand to her. Lifting the hem of her gown, Aliyah stepped up to stand on top of the altar, using the priest's grip to steady herself.

From this position, she spread out her hands as though to enfold every girl in the room to her bosom to keep them close in a show of her power over them. Aliyah's lips moved as though she were chanting a spell, but I couldn't understand the words.

The priests' voices raised in a shout of exclamation, and the pounding drums grew more intense while my sister began dancing, leading the girls in a frenzy of movement. An undercurrent of anticipation tinged the entire spectacle.

Leila wore a different dress from the other girls, a deep rose color in contrast to the rest of the girls' white dresses. Tattoos burnt a trickling gold color down her arms and along each finger.

I had arrived too late. If I wasn't mistaken, Leila had just been ordained the High Priestess of the Temple of Sariba. To take the place of Aliyah, who planned to use the Egyptian's magic to become the divine Goddess.

My throat constricted and my stomach hurt. Next to me, Tijah had her hands clapped over her ears, face bent over her knees. I wished I could carry her out of here, but neither of us could move from our hiding place.

The High Priest touched the alabaster head of the Sariba Goddess statue and then pressed his staff into the tattoo on Aliyah's forehead. Her body shook as though she'd become a reed tossed about in the wind. The room erupted into cries, shouts, and screams. Fearful and jubilant both.

The girls stared in awe at Aliyah as the magic began to take hold. In turn, they stared at the Goddess of Sariba whom they worshiped with their souls and bodies.

A sudden loud noise rent the air and an instant later, the statue of the Goddess cracked straight down the middle. The marble figure split in two, and pieces of stone flew off in every direction. The girls screamed, sinking to the floor to protect themselves from the airborne shards.

Instead of cowering for safety, my sister stood transfixed, enraptured by the sight.

Aliyah's eyes were on fire. She stared down at the priests and priestesses, her smile sharp and clever. "High Priest of the ancient magic!" she cried with a potency that carried the strength of a thousand rushing lions. "Your powerful spell has succeeded. I have been born anew! The Goddess's soul has transferred to me and I feel her divinity inside me. She encompasses my heart and mind in a beauty I hadn't dared to hope for. This land—and all lands beyond our borders will belong to me. All people will bow to me in worship and obedience."

I shrank back, horrified. She had actually done it. This was the reason the Egyptian magicians were brought to Sariba. They had transferred the soul of the Goddess into Aliyah's body.

She had *become* the Goddess. The most powerful person on earth. I had thought Aliyah was dangerous before, but now there would be no stopping her.

This was what the Queen of Sheba had warned us of. The queen was savvy to her sister's aspirations, and Aliyah had succeeded. The urgency to return to the palace to inform Kadesh pounded in my chest.

Aliyah laughed, exultant with the ecstasy of the moment. "Worship your Goddess, alive and powerful! I am ruler of all things. From the Irreantum Sea to the Great Sea. From Salem to Babylon and beyond every desert."

The priestesses broke into frenzied, joyful dancing. They circled Aliyah while she stood on the altar, kissing her feet, weeping and laughing.

"Oh, my daughters of divinity. You have been called and set apart in your roles as messengers of the Goddess. Midsummer's eve is upon us in three days' time and you must show your gratitude for the blessings of Sariba. On that night, we will thank the Goddess with the gift of a sacrifice. A sacrifice to keep our crops growing and our frankincense caravans moving across the desert. With a special offering, Sariba will flourish and become the most powerful nation on earth."

The High Priest Heru shouted to his men standing at the rear doors of the room. "Bring in the sacrifice."

Leila stepped forward, confusion in her face. My eyes darted about the room just as hers did. "But we don't have a sacrifice prepared, my lord," she said.

"Your Goddess has prepared the way, my sweet girl," Aliyah told her. "And you, as Sariba's new High Priestess, will have the honor of making the first sacrifice to the Goddess. I know that you love Her more than your own life."

She held out her hand, and Leila came to the altar where Aliyah towered over the room in all her fiery glory. Bowing, Leila kissed Aliyah's feet.

Two priests flung open the double doors at the back of the ceremonial room. An elderly woman entered carrying a child of about eighteen months in her arms. The High Priest took the child and then banished the woman, closing the doors on her despite her effort to cling to the beautiful child.

The magician placed the squirming child on the altar. In the candle's glow, I could see tears upon her eyelashes. My hands gripped the door I stood next to and I thought I would be sick.

"This final gift will take us into battle with the enemies of the Goddess," Aliyah said. "This beautiful child will be our sacrifice of love to the Goddess of Sariba."

Heru lifted the girl up in his hands and Aliyah leaned down to take her, folding her arms around the child who was now beginning to cry in earnest. She bestowed kisses on the child's cheeks and hair, and then turned to show her off to the priestesses with a triumphant smile.

My insides tore into pieces. I let out a choke. Black dots danced before my eyes and Tijah gripped my arms to keep me upright before I fainted.

The small girl in Aliyah's arms was the picture of perfect. Silky dark ringlets fell to her shoulders. The toddler's cheeks glowed pink with health and purity. Cheeks I had nuzzled in the camel litter while trying to feed her milk as a newborn to keep her alive.

Those lovely long-lashed black eyes were a replica of my mother's, the face a picture of innocence and confusion.

The girl was Sahmril, my lost baby sister.

6

"*No!*" I screamed. I shoved aside the draperies and lunged forward.

Urns of flowers and tapers of incense rattled on the tables. A single candle fell, and hot wax spilled, dripping down a sideboard laden with wine goblets and platters of rich food.

Stunned faces stared at me. Pushing my way through the priestesses, I scrambled to scoop up Sahmril, but the Egyptian High Priest was too quick and stepped in my path, fury in his face. Before I could reverse my course, he gripped my wrists like a bronze slave cuff.

Voices murmured around me, wondering who I was. Since I was dressed in a gown and jewels, designed to move about the temple as a priestess in disguise, girls wondered if I was from a temple in the land of Sa'ba or Babylon. Perhaps a special guest of Aliyah's for this important ceremony.

Leila pushed through the crush of people, striding forward to glare at me in annoyance for interrupting the sacred ceremony. "I know who she is, the girl who almost married Prince Kadesh last night. This is my sister, Jayden."

My sister scanned me from head to toe. Despite her attempt to put on a sultry air, I caught a glimpse of the real Leila behind the heavy makeup and Goddess tattoos. The woman before me was not the High Priestess of Sariba, but my sister. I reached out to embrace her, emotion pricking behind my eyes. *"Leila,"* I breathed.

She hesitated for a fraction, aware of so many eyes watching. I feared she would reject me, but stiffly, she moved forward and placed her arms around me.

A sob whimpered in my throat, and I hugged her back, pressing my face into her neck, trying not to burst into tears of relief. We were together at last. It felt like a miracle.

"It's been so long, Leila," I said into her ear. "I saw you kidnapped. I worried that you were dead. Or in slavery in Egypt."

"I'm very much alive," she said with her signature saucy grin under the jeweled headdress and veils. For that moment, we were sisters back in our mother's tent, dressing for my betrothal ceremony, teasing each other about the boys in the tribe. Laughing while she fixed the crooked black kohl around my eyes. "We both survived the death of our mother and the brutal desert crossing," she added wanly.

"I was so afraid for you when the Egyptians carried you out

of the temple at Tadmur," I told her, adding softly, "You—you look well."

Her eyes flicked to the side and then back to my face. "Is our father here in Sariba, too?" Her voice quivered ever so slightly. "I heard he'd been jailed for causing destruction at the Temple of Ashtoreth."

"Kadesh helped me rescue him from prison. He's as well as can be expected, but his bereavements cause him great despair. He mourns our mother, you, Sahmril—" I put a hand to my mouth. My eyes darted to Sahmril, frightened in Aliyah's treacherous arms. "Help me save her, Leila. I've been searching for her ever since the city of Mari burned."

Her forehead touched mine as she leaned in close. "Don't say another word. I only have so much power. Sometime we'll talk. I'll try to arrange it. But I'm the High Priestess now with a thousand duties and expectations—including the Egyptians and the Ba'al priests to take care of. And Horeb's armies have now arrived . . ."

Disappointment washed over me. Even though she'd been anointed High Priestess, it was Aliyah who still held all the power. Leila would have to do her bidding or be cast out from the temple. If she was lucky.

Two meaty hands clamped down on my shoulders. Twisting, I tried to see Tijah, but the priest pushed me to my knees. "Bow before your Goddess."

I let out a cry when Aliyah pivoted on the altar, smiling like a calculating lioness when she held Sahmril up for all to see. "Here is our sacrificial child."

"No! Please!" I tried to wrestle out of the priest's arms, but he held me tight. "Please give her to me. She's my sister. I've been trying to find her for over a year."

Aliyah ignored me, unaffected by my outburst. She could dictate doctrine and bend anyone to her will.

The people believed she was the Goddess and would obey her above anyone else. Above the royal family. Or Kadesh when he was crowned later today.

I was trapped in this room. Even worse, Aliyah could send me to the women's prison. With war brewing and the armies organizing for battle, it might be hours before Kadesh realized I hadn't returned.

When I came to the temple this morning, I'd imagined finding Leila in her room, my only task to convince her to come to the palace with me where she could be safe. I yearned to talk to her like we used to. To figure out how to be sisters again.

Instead, Heru, his bald head shining with perspiration, shoved me into a chair. Quickly he tied my arms behind my back, securing them to the chair's wooden slats. "Worship your Goddess," he commanded.

"You have no right to touch the future queen of Sariba."

Leila leaned in close, her silk dress falling over one bare shoulder. "Shush, Jayden, don't make it worse."

The tangy smell of wine was on her breath, and her eyes were glassy. Was she drunk or drugged? All the girls seemed to be falling into a trance. I was more frightened now than when she'd embraced me. "How can you be so calm? They're going to kill our sister, Sahmril!"

"It will be a beautiful thing, Jayden," she said. "Sahmril will be offered up to the Goddess of Sariba and the God of Ba'al to save us all. The gods will give Sariba victory against our enemies."

My stomach roiled. The room was hot, and perspiration dripped down my neck. "Listen to what you're saying."

"The Goddess came to life tonight. Her soul now resides within Aliyah. She's truly alive! She will be our queen, our protector, our savior. And now I am Her chosen High Priestess! I never imagined this honor would ever be mine."

"That's why you were kidnapped from the temple at Tadmur," I said slowly, all the threads coming together in my mind. "You were the perfect candidate—the sister of the future wife of Kadesh. A ploy to pit us against each other and take down the royal family."

Leila knelt before me, one finger sliding down the rope that ensnared my arms, her face an expression of woe. "You should never have come here. You're going to ruin everything. *I* have been crowned High Priestess of Sariba—a position I would never have had at the Temple of Ashtoreth."

Desperation swept over me, something I hadn't felt since I'd been stoned. Not even when I'd found my father in prison or Sahmril in the arms of adoptive parents in Mari. My little sister didn't know me any longer, and I had no idea how to help her remember her true family. I loved her desperately, but she had no idea who I was. "Leila, I've seen what's down in the temple dungeons. Once Kadesh and I marry, we will tear this temple apart."

Her lips curved into a sad smile. "You won't be queen for long. Nobody can compete with the brains and beauty of Aliyah. She'll reduce Kadesh to his knees, and he will beg her to come to his bed and be his wife."

I steeled myself against her words. I couldn't lash out at her. "Leila," I said more gently. "Aliyah will fail. Don't believe that she is actually the Goddess come to life. You are High Priestess in name only. She'll never allow you any power, even if she fools you into thinking so."

"You don't know Aliyah like I do," she spit out. "Or the power of the Goddess. Don't underestimate her, Jayden. She will tear you into pieces before you can blink an eye."

"This entire ceremony is a ruse to lure Sahmril here and destroy me."

For a moment, I was standing helplessly in the home of Thomas, the nobleman in Mari. His wife, Zarah, clinging to my sister, watching me from her garden with hooded eyes.

Thomas had remained stubborn, despite Kadesh offering him a bounty of gold. At that moment, I discerned that they loved Sahmril and had her best interests at heart. If they had sold Sahmril to someone else—like Aliyah—it was only under threat of death. Or because they were already dead at her hands.

"Sahmril's sacrifice is a great honor for our family," Leila said simply.

I struggled against the ropes, but they were too tight, the rough hemp scraping my skin. The dagger strapped on my thigh was too far to reach. If only Tijah could get to me, but she was pressed against the far wall, and I didn't want to see her hurt by coming to help me.

"Sahmril!" Her name escaped my mouth. She was my blood. The promise to my mother I'd carried for more than a year. The ache of my empty arms was overpowering.

Aliyah ignored my distress. "This momentous day has come to pass. I will rule Sariba. I will rule Babylon, and I will rule the seas and every city between. And we will do it with the help of King Horeb and his armies. As the Goddess of Sariba, I pronounce a blessing upon the armies who have come to help us. I have a meeting with King Horeb personally later today."

My jaw went slack, all my suspicions confirmed.

Two of the Egyptian magicians lifted Aliyah down to the green marble floor. Her deep red dress fluttered as though she were flying.

The company of magicians and priestesses bowed to her while Aliyah turned to Sahmril, a false smile on her lips. "Do you remember your sister, my precious?"

Sahmril's big dark eyes stared at me. She stuck two fingers into her mouth and shook her head, her baby fine hair flying about her face. Tears continued to run down her cheeks.

Of course she didn't know me. The last time I'd seen her she was just beginning to toddle on unsteady legs.

"Mama," she wept, her lips quivering. "I want my mama."

Aliyah pressed a manicured finger to her lips. "I'm your mother now, sweet girl. The Goddess is your protector. I will send you to heaven so that our land will flourish and we'll be protected from the evil within. Only you, an innocent child with an unblemished heart, can banish true evil. You will protect us all. Such a grand and marvelous thing. You will be remembered for redeeming this land and protecting us."

Caustic words flew from my mouth. "Look in the mirror, Aliyah, and you will see more than enough evil for the rest of your days—may they be short."

Aliyah's arms tightened and Sahmril's face puckered with fresh fear, her eyes pools of tears.

"Heru, please take her."

My sister turned her panicked face toward me when the High Priest stepped forward. "No! I want to go home!"

Tears dropped from my own eyes while I struggled against my bonds. "Take me!" I finally cried out. "I offer myself as sacrifice instead of Sahmril. Please let Leila take the baby to my father at the palace. Please let her live! I will die for the Goddess!"

Aliyah ignored my offer, turning instead to spread her arms toward the massive ceiling. "As Goddess of Sariba, I invoke the name of Ba'al," she cried. "Hear my words. Feel my soul unite with yours. Bless King Horeb's army after their treacherous journey. Spread our glory to the four corners of the earth by giving the armies of Assyria the power to kill with the potency of the beasts of the earth. May the Goddess rule to unite all peoples and nations!"

With cries of agony and ecstasy, the priestesses fell to the carpets to worship Aliyah.

All at once, somebody was behind me, tugging at my

wrists. I gave a cry thinking one of the Egyptians was untying me to put me on the altar and sacrifice me right then and there.

"My lady," Tijah whispered. "Hold still and I'll cut you free."

"What—how did you—"

"Shh!" In their prostrations, nobody was paying attention to us. A second later, Tijah's hand slid underneath my gown and grasped the dagger hiding there. In two quick strokes, she cut the ropes tying my hands. "We need to flee, my lady."

I shoved the dagger back into its leather strap and tugged at Tijah's arm to keep her close. Moving along the wall behind the altar, I didn't take my eyes off Aliyah as she called down the powers of her Goddess to give victory to her and my enemy, Horeb, King of the Nephish.

Planting our feet into position, Tijah and I shoved hard at the altar. The candles fell, sizzling in their golden tapers. Hot wax splattered across the long length of Aliyah's dress as the table crashed behind her, sending food and goblets of wine splattering.

The prostrate girls rose in confusion.

Tijah breathed out. "We're in trouble, my lady."

I grabbed her hand and raced through the doors, slamming them behind us while Aliyah screamed, "Guards, guards!"

Passing a smaller table outside the door of the ceremonial room, I kicked it over. A cluster of alabaster lamps cracked into a hundred splinters. Shattered pieces of ceramic urns scattered across the marble floors.

The chaos would slow them for only a few moments, but I was pleased at Aliyah's furious screams. I wished I could rescue

Sahmril, but I needed my own small army for that task. I only had a few days to figure out how to stop the sacrificial ritual. The full moon and midsummer's eve was three days from now. "I have time," I repeated aloud to comfort myself.

I should have left the temple premises without delay, but I wasn't going to leave without my marriage contract, which Aliyah had stolen yesterday during the chaos of my wedding attack.

Running past the Sariba Goddess's sneering, empty stare in the great hall, Tijah and I kept behind the draperies along the perimeter, then slipped out the farthest exit from the inner sanctum.

I stifled a cough, smoke from the incense burning my throat.

"My lady." Tijah's eyes were wide with terror. "I don't want to go to prison."

I squeezed her hand. "Do you trust me?"

She nodded, biting her lip.

"Do you know where the private rooms of Aliyah are located?"

Her eyes darted about, the urge to run strong, but the corridors would soon be overrun with temple guards. At least I was dressed as a priestess. That would help keep us incognito for a little while longer.

"We have to do this now," I urged her. "Aliyah has aligned herself with our enemies and will rule Sariba with an oppressive fist. I won't let her steal proof of my marriage to Kadesh. She plans to get rid of me and marry Kadesh herself."

7

We walked quickly down a parallel hallway, passing a spiral staircase. "Down below are the kitchens and servants' quarters," Tijah said, walking faster. Our breathing grew labored when we reached the next intersection of hallways and flew up two flights of stairs.

"Aliyah will be busy directing her guards to find us," I said. "She'd never think I'd go to her private rooms and search for my wedding contract."

We reached a landing three stories up. Through the windows, I could look down on the grounds of the temple. Early morning dew sparkled along the petals of the flower beds. Small fountains and emerald lawns wound along the hillside of the temple mount.

Aliyah's wing faced north. This morning the Qara Mountains appeared fierce. Gloomy with a bank of low-hanging clouds.

Soon our enemy's armies would be camped in its shadows. It was easy to imagine Aliyah standing here waving a red flag to tell Horeb it was time to march on the city.

"This part of the wing overlooks the roof of the story below," I said. "It's not as far as I thought. I find myself wanting a coil of rope."

"Rope?" Tijah echoed. "To climb down along the walls to the ground?"

I tried to keep myself from screaming with trepidation. "Only in case of an emergency."

"There might be maids inside," Tijah warned as we crept toward Aliyah's suite.

"I suspect that for her privacy, Aliyah's personal maids would have their own chambers. Probably there," I added, pointing to a door farther down the stone hall.

The latch swung open easily. Before stepping inside, I waited a heartbeat, but nobody came roaring out at us.

In a single step, I crossed the threshold, my dagger at the ready, but the luxurious suite was empty. Couches, chairs, and tables were laid out in attractive arrangements in a large, high-ceilinged room. Vases of roses and orchids dotted the inlaid tables, soaking the air with a heady perfume.

In the center of the far wall was a sumptuous downy bed with masses of pillows and bolsters. Sheer emerald draperies fell to the floor from a canopy railing. The swooping curtains appeared as billowing waves of green sea foam.

I ran across the burgundy carpets to the bathing room. Skylights in the high ceilings revealed that it was empty as well.

"I'll search the bedroom, you search the bathing room," I ordered Tijah. "Aliyah wouldn't put the marriage contract in the public offices where someone could stumble across it. The safest place would be in her personal suite."

Any commotion downstairs was masked by distance. Still, my heart pulsed in my ears and my hands shook when I opened each drawer in the wardrobes and bureaus.

Aliyah had exquisite taste. Her clothes were created from the finest silks, chiffons, and satins. Her dressmaker was extremely talented. The embroidery, jewels, and filigree had been stunningly sewn.

But the new Goddess of Sariba hadn't hidden any papers in her lingerie. I should have begun my search in her desk where thick stacks of papyrus and thin stone tablets included contracts, invoices, and deeds. I tried not to upend anything and make a mess, but there was no sign of the contract here either.

"I *know* it was you I saw after Chemish was shot," I mumbled as I whirled about the room, panic rising. Time was running out.

"I think I found it," Tijah screamed, bursting from the bathing area holding slightly crumpled papers. I couldn't read all the words of the Akkadian language, but I recognized the script with my name and Kadesh's. The empty lines where my father, Pharez of Nephish, and King Ephrem of Sariba were to have signed before Chemish fell by the deadly arrow of the invaders. I recognized the beautiful black ink. The gold seals. And, at the bottom, the places where our witnesses had marked their names, Asher and Chemish.

Clasping the marriage contract to my chest, I embraced Tijah.

"They were in a secret drawer of the bathing wardrobe."

"You clever girl," I told her. "How did you even think to search for a secret drawer?"

"Lady Naomi's maid who trained me showed me. Many high-ranking ladies keep their jewels and personal treasures in hidden drawers."

"You *are* a clever girl," a female voice spoke behind us. "Perhaps you'd like to come to the temple and work for me. I can pay more than the royal family grudgingly doles out."

Aliyah stood at the open double doors to the suite, her hands on the bronze handles, arms spread wide.

I clutched the marriage contract tighter and slunk sideways so she couldn't see me sticking my dagger into the belt of my dress for easier access.

"On second thought," Aliyah went on, "there's no need for you to move to the temple. When I become queen I'll be moving into the palace and I'll have my pick of any girls I want to attend me."

"I'd rather live with my mother in the temple dungeons."

Aliyah arched an eyebrow. "Oh, so you're *that* girl. Erina's daughter. The one she saved from being the sacrificial lamb.

Your younger sister—oh, what was her name, I've forgotten. She was first chosen to be sacrificed to the Goddess upon her birth. But then we learned that she was born flawed."

Tijah's face grew ashen, and Aliyah smiled, pleased that she'd wounded the girl.

I clenched Tijah's hand in mine to keep her from blurting out anything that would get her thrown into the temple dungeons.

Aliyah closed the outer suite doors and poured herself a glass of wine from a decanter on a table near the fire hearth.

"The ceremony with the Egyptian priests was merely to convince everyone that you're the most powerful woman in the world," I told her. "How can anyone argue with a goddess, right?"

"I'm glad you appreciate it."

"You misunderstand me. I can see through the charade. You standing on top of the altar addressing the audience as the Goddess herself—"

"Are you saying Egypt's magic is a sham?" Aliyah hissed at me.

"I don't know anything about Egypt other than the golden gods they prostrate to. What I do know is that you crave power so much you don't care how you get it."

"You don't know me at all," Aliyah said coldly, throwing her wine glass into the fire hearth with a crash of tinkling glass.

She was clearly irritated. How close to the truth was I? "You think you have Sariba's hearts and minds and souls, but you don't," I said quietly. "And this war with Horeb will prove it."

Tijah glanced at me, fear in her eyes. Perhaps I was going too far.

"I'm tired of listening to your judgments and pronouncements, Jayden of Nephish," Aliyah said. "Be warned. I have particular plans to obliterate you. And I will carry them out with the utmost delight."

I was done here, and we had to leave. I twisted to head for the door, but before I knew it, Aliyah wrenched my shoulder and spun me around. The marriage contract slipped out from under my arm. I floundered for it, grabbing at empty air.

Aliyah snatched up the contract and stepped out of reach.

"Those papers belong to *me*!" I cried.

"You sneaked into my room and stole them from me."

"I saw you behind the dais last night when King Ephrem died. The marriage papers disappeared into your hands. Your name isn't on the contract, so it does you no good. Besides, Uncle Ephrem is dead, so he can't even sign it." I was bluffing because Kadesh had told me that Uncle Josiah would sign in his stead when we were able to plan a new wedding.

"He was an old man and had been ill for some time."

"How fortuitous for you that he died at *my* wedding."

"It was. Quite. But make no mistake. I will have my own marriage contract drawn up for my union with Kadesh." Aliyah turned toward the desk, opening one of the drawers.

"If you're so sure of that then give me mine. They're worthless to you. Unless you plan to erase my name and add in yours."

"With your marriage papers in my possession it will be

more difficult for *you* and Kadesh to forge the missing signatures and pretend you did marry last night. This contract is incomplete and unbinding. And it will stay that way." A slender candle appeared in her hand. Before I realized what she was planning, Aliyah reached her hand up to the wall sconce above her head and lit the candle in the small flame.

With a shout, I lunged for her, but she had already put the candle to the papers. Fanning them quickly, she strode to the fireplace. The pages turned black, shriveling instantly. Aliyah tossed them into the glowing embers left over from the morning's fire.

I pressed a hand to my chest, my heart splintering into pieces. Now there was nothing. No proof. No royal insignia or stamp.

I'd been relegated to the status of a girl unworthy to capture Prince Kadesh.

"Oh, my lady," Tijah said, throwing a look of hatred toward Aliyah as she warned, "Temple guards will swarm this suite in moments and Aliyah will order our punishment."

I sucked in my emotions while Aliyah stood imperiously above me. "You don't have to worry about Kadesh's love or devotion any longer. The people won't blame you either. I will rally them to the Goddess, and to safety and peace."

Distant voices came through the doors of the suite and Aliyah gave a laugh. "My temple guards will meet you on the staircase if you attempt to go elsewhere in the temple. Return in three days for the midsummer night's eve ceremonies. I have so many pleasurable entertainments scheduled. You'll receive a personal invitation, of course."

"And I'll burn it with pleasure," I said, edging to the door, one hand on the hilt of my dagger.

Tijah called out from the hall beyond the door. "My lady! Guards, I can hear them below!"

I turned on my heel and followed her. The stone floors of the upper corridor were hung with paintings and draperies and wall sconces—and statues of the Goddess. I peered down the winding staircase, hanging on to the balustrade.

Marching feet came up from below, including the clanging sound of bronze swords. I hoped it was more threat than reality because Aliyah wasn't following us or screaming down the stairwell to her guards. She closed the double doors to her suite, and a bar locked into place. The sound was ominous. What other trickery would the woman use to torture me?

How would the guards even know we'd trespassed into her private suite anyway? She'd had no time to tell them. I took a deep breath, my thoughts racing to find a way out of here.

"Is there another way off the top floor?" I asked Tijah, relying on her knowledge of the temple floor plan.

She shook her head, eyes filled with alarm.

Returning to the corridor window, I saw the same flagstone patios and fountains three stories below. The walls of the temple were smooth. No balconies or window ledges to use for climbing.

"There's got to be another way down," I said. "What if there was a fire . . . what's at the end of this hallway?" Grabbing Tijah's hand, I pulled her along the hallway, turning to the right as the corridor wrapped around the temple's perimeter and ended at a door.

I pushed against it, and we hurried through, folding over the latch to bar the door against the guards who were trying to find us. Then I turned to marvel at the sight before me.

A private garden had been created on top of the temple's roof. Palm trees swayed along the perimeter. Life-size statues of the Goddess stood at each corner. A fountain sprayed, and the air was perfumed by beds of azaleas and exotic orchids along the brick pathways. Cozy furniture sat in groupings under pergolas for shade.

"It's beautiful," Tijah whispered, transfixed.

Racing to the railing, I reeled at the magnificent view. The rooftop garden sat on the southeast corner of the temple. I gazed at the ocean cliffs and the expanse of the city below the sloping hills.

Running to the northwest corner next, I spotted the groves of frankincense orchards, banked against the valley of the Qara Mountains.

I shaded my eyes, staggering at the sight of so many newly erected black-and-white tents in the foothills of those mountains.

My heart was in my throat. Too many tents to count. At least a thousand camels.

Hundreds of horses.

Horeb's armies camped and preparing for battle.

8

A crushing sense of doom weighed on my shoulders. The armies we'd seen last night on the desert at midnight had arrived in the Sariba kingdom, and they were real.

The boy I'd been betrothed to since birth had followed me, nipping at our heels like a hunting dog, hounding me. Horeb was here to fight until he sat on Kadesh's throne.

Emotion bit behind my eyes. I'd run away to the Temple of Ashtoreth and then to Mari with Kadesh to get away from Horeb's wrath and beatings. Banished from my tribe and homelands after he framed me for the murder of his father, King Abimelech, and my father's dearest friend.

But it wasn't enough for him. I knew the truth, and he was going to force me to become his wife solely to legitimize his place on the Nephish throne—a seat he'd coveted since he'd left his older brother to die after a raid.

With every ruthless act, Horeb had grown more powerful and more obsessed. He thought that marrying me—even after he'd tried to rape me—would bring stability to the tribe and my love. But he didn't know me at all. I'd never cared for wealth or jewels. I only wanted love from a good man—my family and peace.

During the long journey to Sariba, knowing Horeb was just beyond each horizon, I'd come to the conclusion that he was mad. His veins coursed with bloodthirsty ambition. His vengeance merely stoked his power. And now, so many innocent people would pay the ultimate price.

"My lady," Tijah said with a light touch on my arm.

I shook myself out of my reverie and blinked away the fear.

Shaking, I turned my back on the sight of those three foreign armies. My gaze swept over the city, deceptively peaceful from this higher view.

How were we going to get down from the roof of the temple? I'd been joking about rope earlier, but now I wished I'd actually planned for it.

My body thrummed with nerves. Down on the walkway below, a shadow came around a corner. I shrank down to a crouch. The figure was a young man, but not in guard uniform. Definitely not Egyptian. A priest of Ba'al? A gardener?

While I watched, the man ducked behind a half wall, avoiding the sudden appearance of a temple worker as though trying to remain incognito. I stared hard. The way he moved was familiar, his step quick, limbs slender.

"Tijah!" I hissed. "It's Asher!"

The curving pathways emptied and all quieted again.

"He can help us," Tijah said jubilantly. "I have an idea." She scurried to a rose bush and yanked at one of the branches covered in scarlet blooms, snapping it in half.

I scanned the temple grounds while Tijah tossed the branch over the parapet. The roses dropped to the walkway at the same moment Asher's foot came down on them. He glanced up at the sky, a frown lining his brow while I leaned over the parapet.

His eyes widened. "I've walked the perimeter three times to find you!"

"You should be at the palace."

"*You* should be at the palace. Come down."

"All exits are blocked! Aliyah's guards will be here any moment!"

Asher loosened a shaft of rope left near some gardening tools. "If I throw this up to you, can you secure it?"

"Oh, my lady," Tijah breathed. "I can't climb down that far! You're strong from riding camels your whole life."

"And you've probably scrubbed a few thousand floors. Asher will guide us down the rope. I trust him." I was sur-prised at how easily the sentiment came out, especially after the treasonous relationship he'd taken up with Laban on the desert journey. Asher had been young, blinded by his feelings for me, but he paid a severe penance to gain his father's and Kadesh's trust again. I knew his fierce loyalty was real.

We stepped back and, on the first try, Asher managed to launch the knotted leather rope over the stone ledge.

I tied two more large knots to use to secure our weight. We'd have to use our feet against the wall for leverage. "That boulder near the fountain will work to secure the other end of the rope," I said, using the knots my father had taught me a hundred times over the years of my life.

Running back to the ledge I called down, "Is there enough length left to reach you? Tug on it so I know it's secure."

The rope held without slipping. My eyes darted back to the door I'd secured. Fists were now pounding from the other side of that door that led into the dusky temple corridor. It wouldn't take them long to hack it down.

"You go first, my lady," Tijah said. "If the guards arrive while I'm stuck on the rope the Goddess will throw you into prison." I started to protest, but she cut me off. "I'm going to watch how you climb down and imitate it."

She had a point, so I finally relented and inched my way over the ledge, not looking down and bracing my toes along the wall. Within moments, I was panting with exertion and adrenaline, the muscles in my arms trembling to hold myself up.

"I'm right below you," Asher called. "Keep going."

Inch by inch I lowered myself while Tijah stared down at me with dread.

The sound of movement at the far side of the garden came to my ears. I tried not to let it rattle me, but kept going as fast as I dared.

A breath later and Asher's arms were lifting me off the rope. I jumped the last bit, landing on the path. Without thinking,

I pressed my face against Asher's chest, heart thudding with relief.

"How did you know to find us here?" I asked him.

"Too much time passed without your return, so I rode up the hillside."

"You'll need to coach Tijah down, she's petrified."

I paced the walkway while my handmaid crept along the rope, casting small cries of fear. I was thankful we were standing under a patch of trees to keep us hidden. Tijah's shaking arms weakened, and she fell the last bit with a small scream, but Asher was there to catch her.

"Guards above us on the parapet," Asher said tersely.

The sound of splintering wood came and then the door to the courtyard crashed open, followed by the shouts of the guards.

Taking off into an all-out run, we raced down the walkways and paths back to the dungeon apartments to retrieve Jasmine while the temple guards' shouts faded.

Asher carried the young girl in his arms as we moved through the tall grass on the hillsides, not speaking until we reached the cave and our horses. While Asher settled the two maids, I jumped onto mine, flinging my skirts, not caring that I was riding like a man.

Galloping down the forest path, we were within sight of the city soon. I was aware that we hadn't broken any laws by going to the temple, but we'd trespassed on a private ceremony and Aliyah's personal suite.

The woman was my enemy. The girl Kadesh had almost married. The girl who had seduced Leila, and burned my marriage contract.

I wished I could banish her from Sariba forever, but in three nights' time was the summer solstice and the sacrifices. I planned to be there and take back Sahmril before Aliyah could murder my young sister.

9

A strange atmosphere imbued the palace upon our return. Hushed servants, quiet halls, and guards conferring in terse words.

People disappeared down hallways that seemingly led nowhere, and a solemn mood accompanied the significant tension.

I followed Tijah to my room. All I wanted was to scrub off the heavy makeup and change into a simpler dress. But when we turned the corner to my suite, an older servant woman wearing a plain black dress stood outside the door.

"My lady, I thought you were still in bed!" Her glance shifted to the closed bedroom door and then back to us. "I'm Lady Naomi's handmaiden and she has requested your presence as soon as you are dressed and have eaten."

"I won't be but a few moments," I told her.

She gave a slight bow and moved down the hall without a single rustling sound of her skirts.

Tijah's eyes clouded with fear. "Will the palace be overrun with the enemy?"

"No. We have a better army, a bigger army," I said, as much to comfort her fears as my own. "No tears. Help me re-dress quickly."

My stomach was a jumble when Tijah deposited me at Naomi and Josiah's apartment. It wasn't quite noon yet, and I'd had nothing to eat or drink. I was hot and flushed, and my hands trembled badly. The mood of the palace was unnerving. The events that lay before us over the next few days filled me with a dread I'd never experienced before, not even during the most tense tribal raids during my childhood.

When the outer doors of Uncle Josiah and Aunt Naomi's suite flung open, Kadesh was there, his face pale. It was obvious he hadn't slept much.

"Kadesh," I whispered, barely getting his name out before he gathered me up in his arms. My toes left the floor, my hands around his neck, my face buried in his long hair. He held me so tightly I didn't know where my body left off and his began.

"Your skin is burning up," Kadesh said, setting me down. "Are you ill?"

"No, I decided to see how fast I could run up and down a mountain this morning," I said with a half smile.

Aunt Naomi came into view. "You do seem flushed. Bring Lady Jayden a glass of water, please," she instructed her maid.

Kadesh studied my face. "Only moments ago, Asher was

telling me about your scaling the walls of the temple to escape. I can't believe you confronted Aliyah, but did you see Leila?"

"She was anointed the High Priestess of the Goddess of Sariba." My eyes watered as I stared at him, and the knowledge banged at my heart again. "We *must* talk. In private. I have dreadful things to tell you."

"And I you," he added soberly.

Stepping closer, Naomi kissed me on both cheeks. It was the first time I'd seen her since the funeral pyre on the beach the night before. "Darling girl, I'm so sorry. Yesterday was appalling and shocking."

"I feel dreadful about Uncle Ephrem. The wedding attack, the armies camping out on the desert—I feel as though every horrible thing is my fault."

"Shh!" Naomi ordered. "I know what you're going to say, and I won't hear it. Ephrem was ill. The circumstances were vastly unfortunate. It was your wedding that was ruined. The day you and Kadesh have waited so long for."

"And Chemish, Asher's father—how is he?" I asked. As soon as we'd arrived back at the stables, Asher had left the horses with the stable boys and hurried away to the infirmary to see his father.

The Prince of Edom stepped out of the corner of the room where he'd been speaking with Josiah. "The loss of blood has slowed and his physicians say he will recover. If I know my father he'll be brandishing his sword ready for battle before the first war cry is sounded from the battlements."

I gazed at the room full of people I'd grown so fond of.

"None of you will let me take the blame, and yet I know the truth."

"You're the one who has suffered the most," Asher said quietly.

"But Sariba's suffering has only begun." My voice cracked, and Aunt Naomi turned me away from the servants and soldiers milling the room, guiding me to a quiet corner.

"Jayden," she said in low tones, "did you sleep at all last night?"

"Very little." Her tender concern and questions were so thoughtful while I tried to control my emotions in front of the palace staff.

"We are all devastated to see your beautiful wedding ruined."

"My wedding brought grief and death upon all of you. Chemish nearly killed, King Ephrem gone, Horeb shaming Kadesh with those mercenary soldiers. I've brought so much sorrow and death already."

"Nonsense." Naomi's beautiful brown eyes forced me to meet her halfway. "Jayden, don't ever speak this way again. I've never seen Kadesh so happy as when he sees you walk into a room. A joyful king and queen on the throne bring stability and makes the hearts of the people happy—which in turn brings peace. Nothing that has happened is your fault. And last night . . ." Naomi's voice stumbled with her own emotion. "You found Naria when all was chaos, and I was falling apart. My daughter is alive because of you. For that I will always be grateful."

Still holding my hand, Aunt Naomi turned back to face the room. I recognized King Ephrem's bodyguard—now Kadesh's protector—and his personal servant standing at the back.

The dining area sat in shadow, but the sideboard held trays of herbed bread and cheese cut into triangles along with grapes, slices of melon, and decanters of fruit juice. My empty stomach threatened to embarrass me with hunger pangs.

"Eat," Naomi urged, filling a plate for me. "Kadesh's crowning is about to be discussed, but everyone needs food first."

When she turned to pour cold water and fruit juices into goblets, I noticed her eyes swam with unshed tears. She was still reeling from the devastation of last night, too.

The draperies at the windows were lowered to keep out the glaring sun, but my eyes burned from lack of sleep. Across the room, my father sat in a corner chair, his fists palming the chair arms with a brooding air.

A plate of food appeared in my hands and I sank into a cushioned chair next to him. He set aside his partially eaten meal on a small table and then pressed a big, warm hand over mine, not speaking. My father had never been a man to fill silence with chatter, but his presence was comforting.

I swallowed a bite of buttered bread and glanced up at his face. Into eyes that held compassion for me.

He rubbed my cold fingers between his, and then brought my knuckles to his mouth for a quick, fatherly kiss, just as he used to do when I was hurt by a neglectful camel that had stepped on my toes, or angry with my sister. My eyes burned with melancholy and our idyllic past was gone.

"I'm sorry for the loss of your marriage celebration," he spoke, his gray beard wagging.

"Thank you, Father," I said, kissing his hand in return. "We're lucky nobody else was hurt last night."

"I never saw Leila among the guests or tables," he said. "Was she avoiding me?"

"I sent her an invitation, but Aliyah, the High Priestess, denied her attendance."

His back stiffened and his lips set in an angry line. "The temples never used to prevent family members from seeing each other for special occasions."

"Aliyah has a personal vendetta against me. I haven't wanted to talk about it, but she used to be betrothed to Kadesh."

My father gave a sharp intake of breath. "Your appearance here in her land is greatly unwelcome then."

"Kadesh broke it off with her long ago, long before we met."

He frowned, displeased. "It saddens me deeply that you might have interfered with a betrothed couple. But I have difficulty trusting any of the temple priestesses."

"Does that include Leila?"

He shifted on his chair and took a small sip from his goblet. "You know that her choices disturb me more than I can express. I went to prison for trying to rescue her in Tadmur."

"I know you did, Father," I told him softly. I paused and then added, "I went to the temple early this morning to see Leila."

"Is she back here at the palace?" The first sign of hope flickered in his eyes.

I shook my head, swallowing down the tragedy of leaving her behind again. "She was anointed High Priestess this morning in a ceremony with the Egyptian magicians and priests."

A groan escaped his throat, and he rose from his chair to stride to the window to hide his sorrow. I quickly followed him, plucking at the sleeve of his cloak.

"Please do not do anything rash. And do not mourn her. I promise that I will do everything I can to bring her back to us."

He shook his head. "Once ordained a High Priestess, she is bound to this temple for the rest of her life. There is no hope any longer."

"There is always hope—" I broke off, wanting to tell him about Sahmril, but I hated to destroy all hope. His small daughter was in the clutches of Aliyah who planned to use her for a sacrifice in three nights' time. I hoped to get her back, even if it meant offering myself, but with the High Priests and temple guards, the odds of success were stacked against me. "There is *always* hope," I repeated as much for myself as him.

His dark eyes filled with such anguish for Leila that it broke my heart. "Please believe me, Father. Never stop believing in me or Kadesh. Miracles do happen. You've always told me that."

His lips cracked slightly, and he gave a small nod. "Your mother is near, I feel her all the time."

I wrapped my arms around his waist, and he placed a hand on my head, bringing me close to his chest. I swear teardrops fell from his face to my hair, like so many drops of hopeful desert rain.

When I glanced up again, Uncle Josiah and Kadesh had come forward to talk to us. Josiah's robes were immaculate, long hair coiled into a rope. The gold-plated regal collar around his neck was embedded with black garnets. "We have urgent royal business to conduct. The crowning of Kadesh as Sariba's new king. With the passing of King Ephrem, I am Kadesh's heir and will have the honor of making my nephew king. At this critical time, we want the Sariba citizens to be united under King Kadesh. To not crown him as soon as possible creates uncertainty with war looming."

Josiah took Kadesh's hands in his, fingers thick and mottled by years of aging. His countenance held a love that I couldn't define with words, only feelings. His hooded dark green eyes were wise with awareness of the day's significance.

Emotion was plain on Kadesh's face. A haunted anguish he tried to blink away, but Josiah saw it. "My heart is weighed down, but I'm also filled with joy to know that you will take Ephrem's place on the throne. Your father's passing was much too soon, but you have all of his best qualities and will make a fine king." Josiah radiated a strength to Kadesh, and I was grateful to him for it.

Kadesh cleared his throat, eyes bloodshot from lack of rest. "Do you think Sariba is willing to accept a wounded, blind king—?"

Josiah held up a hand, noting the listening ears of the servants. "Deep in your heart you know the answer to that. Everyone in this room will follow you to their deaths to save you and this kingdom. Never doubt that, and your people will never doubt you." Stepping back, he addressed the room. "The crowning of King Kadesh will be in two hours' time on the steps of the palace promenade, in full view of the citizenry."

"I concur," Naomi murmured.

Josiah gave a signal to the herald awaiting instruction. "Alert the runners to proclaim the announcement on every street. The government officials, servants, and generals should gather in the Throne Room. After we assemble, I'll lead the procession to the public colonnade."

The herald stepped forward, eyes bright, fist grabbing the sword at his waist.

"And quickly," Josiah ordered. "We have a foreign army bearing down our throats."

$$10$$

The royal suite emptied as guards and servants followed
their orders.

Within minutes, trumpets blasted out the notes
of Sariba's anthem on top of the city walls, calling the people
to the palace.

Kadesh took my hand, and for a moment, we were the only
two people in the room.

"I *have* to talk to you," I whispered. "It's a matter of life
and death."

"Isn't that the sum total of our lives together—and we're
not even married yet?"

He was trying to get me to smile, but I had a hard time
lifting my lips.

"Come with me," he said, pulling me into his adjoining private office. We sat on the couch, and Kadesh laced his

fingers with mine, our eyes never wavering from our locked gaze.

"In a few days is the summer solstice," I told him. "The day of the temple sacrifices."

"I haven't forgotten. It is a day seared forever into my memory."

I disliked reminding him. It was the same day his mother had offered herself for sacrifice to the Goddess only two years ago.

"As much as I hate the summer sacrifices and the Sacred Marriage Rites, I can't stop it. I can't do anything about Aliyah until after this war is over. And if the temple rites help the people to have faith in our victory . . . I have to put that aside for now."

My voice faltered. "But Aliyah plans to sacrifice my sister."

He was startled. "Leila? One of her own priestesses?"

"When I arrived at the temple this morning, a secret ceremony was in progress. Leila was anointed High Priestess and the Egyptian priests turned Aliyah into the Goddess."

"What does that mean?" Kadesh said, alarm on his face. "I don't understand."

"Using their magic, the Egyptians called down the soul of the Goddess and transferred it to Aliyah. Aliyah's power is now supreme and invincible. It was real and absolutely chilling, Kadesh. I'm frightened to even be in the same room with her."

His expression was disturbed. "Aliyah's power is rising and I'm not sure what to do."

I gripped his fist in my lap. "Her treachery against you knows no bounds. She is in collusion with the Egyptian High Priest called Heru—and with Horeb. She's using him in the same way she uses anyone who can help her gain power. A divine goddess in human form usurps your position as king, and she cements her power over the city. She told me she plans to make herself your wife, and then you will die and she will be sole ruler. Both Goddess and queen. After all, she's already royalty as sister to the Queen of Sheba."

"But you know I'd never marry her. We've talked about this before. Long before I met you, I broke off the betrothal—"

"This is part of her revenge. I don't trust the magic of Egypt. All she has to do is get rid of me and that plan goes into motion."

"What do you mean?" Kadesh asked sharply.

"At the solstice celebration on midsummer night's eve, she plans to make a sacrifice of Sahmril."

"Sahmril?" He jumped up, visibly shocked and whirled about the room. "But she's with the Mari nobleman and his wife."

I shook my head. "She is already at the temple in Aliyah's possession."

"That's impossible," he whispered. "Are you sure it's Sahmril? I'm sure she's changed."

I rose from the couch. "I recognized her immediately. It's only been six months since we saw her in Mari."

Kadesh ran a hand through his hair, leaning back against the sofa cushions and staring at the ceiling. "With Horeb at our doors, Aliyah is trying to break my citizens. Uncle Ephrem banned her from performing sacrifices two years ago—after my mother took her life—"

"That's not her only intention," I said, sinking to my knees before him. I took his hands in mine and pressed my lips against his warm palm. "She wants to break you and me."

"Aliyah is sorely mistaken if she thinks this will bring me back to her."

"Her goal is to get me to leave Sariba. To break myself from you. She still wants you, Kadesh. Or she will kill me if I attempt to save my sisters."

He hunched over, his forehead resting on our locked fists. "Just before your return from the temple, I received word that Horeb's spies are infiltrating the perimeter of the city. Horeb's men killed two families who ventured beyond the frankincense groves. Families trying to hide in the caves of the Qara hills. The bloodshed is already beginning."

"Oh, dear God in heaven," I whispered in horror. "All the more reason to save my sisters, but how do I save Sahmril with hundreds of people at the solstice ceremony?"

Kadesh's expression was grim. "So many decisions to make and time has run out." His face was ashen from the burdens weighing at him. "The royal family is often called upon to make the greatest sacrifices of all."

"I won't let Aliyah win." My voice broke, but I forced myself to keep going. "Her sacrifice of Sahmril is not for the victory of Sariba but for *her own* victory. She's been building a coalition for a coup ever since you disappeared a year ago. Her greatest desire is to rule Sariba—with or without you."

He winced. "Tonight I'm going out with two of my scouts to scope out Horeb's camp. A meeting is planned tomorrow with General Naham that will last most of the day. All the captains, too. I'll arrange for soldiers to help you get Sahmril. They will have orders to stop any sacrifices." Kadesh shook his head, distracted. Horeb and Aliyah were already dividing us. "The sacrifices used to be held at dusk as the full moon was rising. You have two more days to plan."

It was a sliver of hope. Two days to plan while Kadesh was on the battlefield fighting Horeb's armies to the death.

Unease deepened on Kadesh's face. "You should never have gone to the temple this morning. It was foolish. Promise me you won't go anywhere else. Please, Jayden?" he added.

I took a breath. "I still want to go with you tonight. With the scouts."

"Absolutely not. It's too dangerous."

"I want to see the layout of Horeb's camp. After a year of running from him, I have to, Kadesh. I'll be with you. I can't be any safer than that, can I? This is my war with Horeb as much as it is Sariba's. We do it together. Not that long ago, Uncle Ephrem told me that I had to kill Horeb, which means I go to battle with you."

"Oh, Jayden, what have I gotten into falling in love with you?" His mouth quirked up into a defeated smile and finally, he nodded. "Wear black clothing. We'll ride part of the way and then go the rest on foot."

"Thank you." I pressed a hand to my heart. "If I could,

I'd tear those mercenary soldiers apart with my own hands for destroying our wedding."

Insight flickered across his face. "What else did Aliyah do to you?"

"She burned our marriage covenant. It's gone."

He made a growling sound and snatched up my hand, leading me to the door. "Then I can give you this now, Jayden. I won't wait to show you."

"What are you doing?" I asked when he pulled me up off the couch and across the room to fling open the doors to the suite. Pulling me with him, his fingers tight around mine, we marched up and down the corridors, practically running at one point.

Soon we were in another hallway, and then charging into another suite, slamming the doors behind us. Instead of carpet, the floors were laid with beautiful hand-painted tile, smooth as silk under my toes.

Painted murals stretched across the walls. Scenes of Sariba's horseshoe beach, the endless Irreantum Sea, the rugged mountains, and finally the lights of the city twinkling in an inky blue midnight.

Shoving open another set of doors, Kadesh led me into a series of royal private rooms I hadn't seen before. Masculine furnishings. Couches crafted from carved frankincense wood layered by dark green and burgundy pillows under an arched ceiling.

A stately desk and work area lay at the other end of the room. Shelves stuffed with parchments, scrolls, and tablets.

Another chair was affixed with a smooth tabletop for a scribe. I noticed a smattering of stencils in various sizes sitting alongside pots of ink. Carved stone writing tablets stacked along the floor.

Overhead, an alabaster lamp was lit by a hundred candles that gave light to the work area while the rest of the room rested under muted lamps and wall sconces.

A hallway skirted around one corner, most likely to a bathing area. On the other end a set of double doors no doubt led to a sleeping chamber.

I was stunned, transfixed by the opulence and beauty. And we were not alone. Servants rushed in from both ends of the hallway, and two guards stood at attention within and without the main doors. Beyond an array of wide windows, I spotted palace guards.

I stood unmoving, my ears roaring and my thoughts bumping against each other. "What is this suite, Kadesh? Why are we here?"

"It's my personal suite of sleeping rooms and private offices, away from the more public suite where I meet with my generals and the family for meals."

Lunging toward the desk, he rattled drawers, banging the chair, which sent a wall tapestry swinging. The chandelier of candles overhead reflected against his long black hair, and my heart ached.

Extracting a leather folder, Kadesh pulled a length of papyrus from it. He glanced up at me and then at his guards who didn't so much as twitch an eyelid. Returning to my side,

Kadesh took a lock of my hair and let it slip past his palm, the muscles in his face twitching with love and desire when he pulled me closer. "I'm giving you this. It's yours to keep until this is over."

I glanced down at the scroll he held in his fist. "What is it?"

"Our marriage covenant. A new one."

He held up the document and I recognized the same words from the paper Aliyah had burned only hours earlier. And there were the two black lines where my father and Uncle Josiah would sign as witnesses.

"I had it drawn up first thing this morning. Will you accept me with all my faults and shortcomings for the rest of our lives? Despite the fact that I can't marry you until after this conflict is over."

I nodded, blinking back tears. "Once, long ago, I told you that I would follow you anywhere. Your home is my home, your people my people."

We stared at each other with a solemnity that had never come between us before.

Kadesh folded up the contract papers and tied the scroll with a leather cord. Then he dropped to his knees, tilting his head upward to gaze into my face. "Will you keep this safe for our future?"

I nodded again, unable to speak against the tightness of my throat.

"And will you witness the crowning of the new King of Sariba?"

"After I change my clothes into something spectacular

befitting a future queen," I conceded with a quivering smile. "My king."

His arms wrapped around my legs and his face buried into my skirts, reminding me so vividly of the night he'd wept in despair after executing Laban. I was coming to realize how vulnerable he was. His heart was too forgiving, too good to hurt someone else despite the injustices they heaped on him.

"You know I can only do this knowing we are right with each other," he said. "We can't wed until this war is finished, but we must be united in every thought and act."

"And we are," I told him, shoving away my petty hurts. "You have the weight of the world upon your shoulders. The survival of your country. I can take on Aliyah."

I spoke the words, giving Kadesh comfort as much as myself, but inside I was terrified because I had no idea how to begin taking Aliyah down.

11

The trumpets were still blaring when we exited Kadesh's suite and made our way through the hallways back to my own bedroom. He bowed to me and then kissed my forehead before I entered my room, where Tijah and Jasmine stood waiting.

The girls had never worked so fast as when they prepared me for Kadesh's crowning ceremony. Wiping away the smeared black kohl from my eyes with a clean sponge, Tijah bent to reapply the liner with a practiced hand, sweeping the black lines outward from the corner of each eye.

When Jasmine handed me a bronze-plated mirror, I saw that what my grandmother Seraiah had told me only a few months ago before her death was true. The image of my mother stared back at me with determined eyes and heavy black hair.

Tijah placed the mirror on the dressing table, her expression without guile. "You're going to be the most beautiful queen Sariba has ever known, my lady."

We didn't mention the hanging threat of war. Occasionally I saw it in the flicker of an eye, but none of us wanted to think about it until after Kadesh was officially King of Sariba.

Palace guards escorted me to the portico entrance. The same polished stone steps Kadesh had stood upon the day we arrived a fortnight ago with the Edomite army. On that day, I'd been overwhelmed at the magnificent city, mortified at my bedraggled and dirty state astride my camel with a subdued Asher at my side. The same evening the Egyptian High Priest had stared at me from the cheering crowds with his gleaming bald head and malevolent staff, sending ominous shivers down my spine.

A different kind of anticipation emanated from the citizens for the crowning. Anxiety at the looming war, but relief to know they'd be guided by a king and general. My handmaidens trailed me, secretly thrilled to be so close to a royal ceremony.

Sea-green marble dressed the wide staircase that ascended to the gold-leafed foyer doors. Frankincense nuggets burned in brass urns, creating a heady perfume along with a wide array of roses, tulips, and orchids that spilled over monstrous ceramic urns on each step of the stairs.

I heard the murmurs of palace servants commenting on the pending crowning. They were relieved not to be bereaved of King Ephrem's heir at this critical moment. The enemy on the horizon was carefully ignored but not forgotten, a shadow on an otherwise happy day.

The gathering of people along the city avenue grew. I was already perspiring despite the breeze blowing in from the ocean.

I flinched when the trumpets blasted a series of sharp, crisp notes. The crowd quieted, and Aunt Naomi slipped next to me. Her eyes filled with reassurance. With one hand, Naomi clung to her daughter, Naria, so the child didn't dart away.

Normally, the crowning would have been performed in the throne room with invited guests and dignitaries of the city. Kadesh and his advisors, along with Uncle Josiah wanted there to be no mistake that he was alive and Sariba's new king. The public crowning was a show of strength and confidence. Especially with Egyptians crawling about the city.

Uncle Josiah was glorious in his royal robes. He wore a magenta and gold breast coat embroidered with gemstones, standing on a hastily constructed dais at the top of the stairs.

Sariba flags snapped in the breeze. The colors of the country's symbol were vivid on each banner: a frankincense tree with a halo of golden sun and azure-colored ocean in the background.

Another three booms from the trumpets heralded the entrance of Kadesh. Red rose petals were thrown into the air by palace staff, strewing his path as he walked toward Josiah.

Guard formations moved in rhythm, flanking the prince and bringing up the rear. Their robes were a striking black with magenta contrasts. Splashes of gold threads plunged down each coat.

Kadesh held himself rigid, his face sober. Beneath his striking posture, I sensed a deep abiding grief. This day had come abruptly, without warning, before anyone had had time to properly mourn King Ephrem.

"Believe," I murmured, speaking the words Kadesh had offered to me so long ago.

Aunt Naomi gave me a sidelong glance but didn't speak as she squeezed my hand.

A chilling clarity came over me. With Kadesh's crowning, I had to rise to the role of his queen much sooner than I had expected. It *was* up to me to grapple with Aliyah and the temple. I would have to deal with palace staff and problems, perhaps setting up a hospital for our wounded.

Now that Aliyah had both my sisters in her possession and Horeb wanted to kill the man I loved, I was fighting to save my family once and for all.

Uncle Josiah gave a booming welcome to the crowd, and a chorus of young people stepped forward to sing Sariba's anthem. A haunting melody celebrated the country's mystery and beauty, entwining itself around my heart.

My eyes darted about, praying no mercenary soldiers interrupted *this* ceremony. Soldiers stood along the perimeter of the city walls, even though I could only see a few from where I stood.

Swords and sabers at their waists, wicked daggers strapped to their thighs. Unlike the palace guards, the soldiers wore gray-green trousers and tunics, blending into the wall, scarves covering their heads and faces, alert and ready.

Uncle Josiah began to speak, telling great tales of long-ago wars against Babylon as well as of King Ephrem's wisdom and peace-loving soul. He commended our dead king to the care of that unseen God and then turned to Kadesh, the man who was now ruler and leader of this beautiful kingdom.

For a brief moment, I was back in my family's tent weeping over my mother's death. One minute she'd been holding newborn Sahmril, and the next she was staring at the tent roof, lifeless.

The crowd hushed when Josiah uttered the Oath of Kingship to Kadesh who repeated the words in a loud, clear voice.

At the conclusion, Josiah announced, "King Kadesh is now your servant and protector. We plead for a blessing from our God for Sariba's prosperity and safety."

A replica of the throne from the palace was brought forth and Kadesh was seated while Uncle Josiah anointed Kadesh's head with olive oil and then invoked God's power on him and the country of Sariba.

When Josiah finished, the trumpets burst with spurts of jubilation.

My heart rushed with love and pride. The journey we'd traveled the past two years passed across my eyes. Joy to have found each other but scars from a desert that both loved us and tested us.

Aunt Naomi wiped at her eyes while relief bubbled up my throat. "Kadesh is like the son we lost on the brink of manhood so many years ago," she confessed.

"Aunt Naomi, I had no idea. I'm so sorry."

"An accident on the desert. The desert is a place of refuge but also a place that can be deadly."

"You had no other sons or daughters?"

"I lost a daughter at birth before we finally received Naria."

Kadesh bowed before his people. The royal trumpets blared again while street vendors came out in full force with food and music. Even so, a company of palace guards moved quietly about the throngs of people on the streets and walkways, asking them not to linger too long. To prepare their homes and children and make sure they had stores of food and water if we ended up under siege.

My heart chilled. There was no place to escape. Only a lethal desert on all three sides of Sariba and an endless sea on the fourth.

It was safer to stay in the city, but how long could we hold out before Horeb executed a massive assault on our gates and walls?

I moved down the pavilion pavings, slipping around the dais to grasp Kadesh's fingers in my own. "My king, you should return to your suite and *sleep* until we leave at midnight with the scouts." I wagged a finger at him. "That's an order."

He chuckled at the term *king* and wrapped his arms around me. "You smell like home and heaven, Jayden. I wish you could sleep next to me," he whispered, his breath warm against my neck. "Then I could truly quiet the voices and demands inside my head."

I kissed his face, shivers running down my neck at the words of the intimacy I longed for, too. "The city is guarded.

If anything happens, General Naham will find you. But you'll be no good to anybody if you're falling over with fatigue."

He gave me a weary smile. "I will take your orders under consideration."

Uncle Josiah placed a hand on our shoulders. "Is there a place we can speak privately, the three of us? I have something to give you."

I sucked in a breath of surprise while Kadesh nodded and held out his hand to me. We walked together through the columned pavilion toward the palatial foyer entrance. The enormous palace doors, inlaid with amethyst and carnelian, were standing wide.

A fresh breeze swept across the polished tiled floors. Servants had brought trays of food and drink, which they placed on the foyer tables. I picked up a goblet of cold water, my mouth dry, nerves on fire.

We followed Josiah into a smaller sitting room furnished with magenta sofas and draperies. When the door closed, the outside world disappeared.

Kadesh's magenta and gold crowning cloak swirled about his legs as he strode down the carpet in front of the sofa where I sat. His stature and presence had already changed. The mantle of King and High Priest of Sariba had fallen upon his shoulders.

I perched on the edge of the couch twisting my fingers into knots.

Uncle Josiah spoke without preamble. "I have a letter that arrived this morning from the kingdom of Sheba."

"From the queen? Why didn't you give it to me earlier?"

Josiah smoothed down his short gray beard and placed a hand on Kadesh's shoulder in a fatherly gesture. "The note asked that I wait until after your crowning."

"The Queen of Sheba is a dear friend as well as cousin," Kadesh said. "One I have treasured all my life." He turned the letter over, taking note of the Sa'ba royal family mark, and then opened the scroll inside the leather pouch.

"My dear Kadesh,
If your crowning of Sariba Kingship has recently taken place, I give you my warmest congratulations—and deepest condolences on the passing of my dear friend and ally, King Ephrem. I hope I may also congratulate you on your marriage to Jayden, Princess of the Nephish. I await word on your news from Sariba with great eagerness, so please do not delay in writing."

Memory of that urgent conversation in the secret room at the palace in Sheba was seared into my memory. At the time, I didn't know who they had been referring to, but after meeting Aliyah I'd suspected it was her. They had talked about the threat of someone that might need to be neutralized. It was all the more complicated when I learned that Aliyah was the queen's younger sister.

"My warnings may come far too late—and I am actually writing this within hours of your leaving my palace—but I've recently learned that the marauders who live in our Sheba Mountains east of the city have been conscripted by the King of the Nephish.

*Horeb dispatched the mercenary soldiers ahead of his armies. I
will wear down my palace floors with my bare feet until I am
assured of your safety. This next is sad news and leads to my
final fear—the fear we have been trying to avoid. Along with
your enemy, an older couple was in their company. With a child
named Ramah."*

My sudden gasp was loud, interrupting Kadesh's reading. "She's referring to Sahmril! The couple who adopted her
named her Ramah, even after I told them her true birth name.
Horeb brought them all here with him? How did that happen?" My eyes blazed with anger. "This means Horeb and
Aliyah have met in person. Horeb gave her Sahmril for the
sacrifice. They are already in collusion."

Kadesh reached out to comfort me, disturbed at the news.
"This is worse than we thought," he said, continuing quickly.

*"I've learned through my city spies that the child is Jayden's
baby sister and the couple her adoptive parents, exiled from
the city of Mari when King Hammurabi invaded there several
months ago. They arrived in Sheba dressed in chains, kidnapped
by bounty hunters somewhere in the vicinity of Moab on their
way to Salem, using new names to escape detection and begin a
new life.*

*"I paid for their release and they are living here in Sheba
under my protection. But neither the bounty hunters, nor Horeb,
would sell the child to me. He took Jayden's sister with him across
the desert on the final trek to Sariba."*

A cry escaped my mouth. I turned to Kadesh, my legs wobbling. "Aliyah *planned* the kidnapping of Sahmril. She brought her here for a sacrifice to torture me and to plainly show her force and power. This exhibits how far her influence already reaches—across the nations of the desert kingdoms. We have our proof now."

Kadesh stared at me, stricken. "This complicates everything . . ." his voice trailed off, and I suspected he was thinking the same thing I was at that moment.

"My dearest Kadesh, this is all part of Aliyah's treachery. She intends to sacrifice the girl child. There is no longer any doubt that she is operating a secret treaty with Horeb. She intends to take control of your city and crown. She intends to crush you all. And now . . . you know what you must do."

It was the code phrase the Queen of Sheba had given to Kadesh two months ago.

The code to assassinate Aliyah.

Dropping the letter to the table, Kadesh strode to the door, and a servant whipped it open for him. Shouting for his scribe and one of the army lieutenants, Kadesh snapped Ephrem's kingly robes around him, making me jump.

Within minutes, a lieutenant raced into the suite followed by an elderly, wrinkled scribe who was struggling to keep up the pace.

"I want a decree posted immediately at every door and entrance of the palace," Kadesh told the scribe. "Aliyah, the

High Priestess of the temple, is banished from the royal residence, and all palace grounds."

The scribe blinked his eyes and pulled a small writing table close, his fingers flying as he opened up his pens and inkpots. Almost instantly, he was scratching letters into a tablet.

"But, Majesty," the lieutenant questioned. "The people will revolt. They rely on the Goddess for spiritual guidance, especially now with our enemy inside our borders—"

Throwing up an impatient hand, Kadesh's face tightened but he didn't explain his actions. "See that it's done. Within the hour. And then return. I have another task for you." Pointing at the scribe, he added, "Leave me, please, but your scribe tools will remain."

The man raised his eyebrows. "I can continue transcribing anything you wish, sire."

"Not now, thank you." Kadesh didn't speak again until the scribe departed, then he glanced over to me and Uncle Josiah. "Sometimes a king needs to write his own correspondence."

I stood silently while Kadesh sharpened the pen with a small knife, then swirled the tip in the ink and proceeded to compose a personal letter. When he finished, he blew on the ink to dry it. "I've written to the Queen of Sheba acknowledging her letter, and conveying the fact that, at the moment, I intend to ignore her recommendations until I have more information."

I plucked up the queen's letter from the table. "She didn't recommend a restraining order, Kadesh."

"When it comes to Sariba's citizens, I don't take capital punishment or assassination lightly. I have to fight a war that is much more imminent. I won't have my citizens rising up in revolt because I hung the High Priestess. I need their trust and cooperation. Or we shall all die together."

"But the queen is ready to move against her own blood! How can you doubt her recommendation?"

Kadesh's jaw set. He pulled me aside, his voice was low and tense. "The things I write are not done lightly. Don't question me in front of my advisors or servants."

"I suppose," I said carefully. "I have much to learn about palace protocol."

Kadesh nodded to the servant at the door. "Please get my lieutenant."

Thankfully, the silence between us wasn't long before the officer reappeared. Kadesh raised his chin. "I have a letter that needs to go directly to the Queen of Sheba. It's imperative that she receives it as soon as possible. In *her* hands and no others. Not her husband or a servant. Get our fastest rider and horse. He needs to deliver it in no more than a week with a reply."

"A three-week journey in only one?" I asked in astonishment.

Josiah answered. "A lone rider with a good horse who rides from dawn to midnight can accomplish it."

"Have him leave by the west gate at dusk," Kadesh commanded. "He can't be seen by the enemy."

The bronze medals clanked against the lieutenant's chest. "Very good, my lord."

The mood of the room was still tense after the door closed behind the officer and Josiah, but Kadesh came over to me despite the fact that my heart was hammering miserably. "I won't be afraid of Aliyah's power, but I also won't commit cold-blooded murder."

"I'll just have to provoke her into attacking me," I told him. "Then I'll have an excuse to fulfill the Queen of Sheba's wishes."

"Jayden, please—"

"No, Kadesh, I do understand," I said, my voice wobbling. "You have a better heart than I do. Despite the tragedy that befell your parents at Aliyah's hands, you forgive her."

His expression was fierce, a combination of anger and hidden pain.

"You believe in redemption," I continued. "You hope she can change or that we can stop her. Well, I will stop her. Perhaps I'm selfish trying to force your hand in order to save Sahmril." My voice cracked. "But I'll try to be the person— and the queen—you want me to be."

"The afternoon heat after the crowning ceremony is draining us all." Kadesh moved closer, and for a moment, we were the only two people in the room. "You need to eat before you faint dead away. And you need sleep," he added gently.

"As we all do." I paused. "I know you are king now with thousands of citizens to protect. I have to stop being selfish. I do trust you."

He kissed my hand as a palace butler approached, tall and erect in a suit of crimson and gold sashes. "Lady Jayden," he said, "you have a visitor. I deposited her in your suite with your handmaidens."

"Why not one of the public meeting rooms?" I asked, surprised at the liberty he'd taken to allow someone into my private rooms.

The butler inclined his head. "I thought you would like privacy, my lady. The young woman is your sister, the High Priestess Leila."

I started at his unexpected words. "Yes, yes, thank you. I'll go right away."

I made a move to depart, but Kadesh caught my hand. He cupped my face in his hands, gazing at me. "I have every confidence in you. And faith in my soldiers to help you bring Sahmril back to the palace."

I put my hands on his wrists, holding his eyes with my own. "That's my fondest dream, but you weren't at the temple this morning. The magicians have a hold on them all, and I'm outnumbered. Kadesh, there are terrible dungeons. Women held prisoner. Forced to breed children for sacrifice and then cast aside, ill and forgotten. My handmaids . . . their mother is one of them. I met her. I saw with my own eyes."

Visible disgust crossed his face. "When we win we'll tear down the temple and I will free them. I'll see you later tonight at midnight, correct?"

"I haven't forgotten," I replied as I ran toward the door.

12

mpatience ran through me, but I hurried down the corridor, passing servants and palace guards on their own hurried tasks. A moment later, I burst through my bedroom door. "Leila!"

She sat at the window staring out at the fountains; her slender figure perched on the edge of one of the embroidered chairs.

Jasmine and Tijah were serving sweets and pouring a deep amber wine.

They curtsied at my presence while I threw my arms around Leila, thrilled that she'd come down to the palace to see me as she'd promised. "You're here. We're together at last! After all this time. I can hardly believe—"

When she didn't respond, I slowly pulled away to stare into

her face. Her kohl was heavy, her lips stained such a deep red it appeared as blood.

I slid down and knelt before her. Leila had a faraway look in her eyes. "Is everything all right?"

At the touch of my hands, she smiled faintly. "Jayden, how pretty you are today. I'll try one of your sweets on this plate."

She spoke as if we were back home in our tent and getting ready for an evening with the women of the camp. As if nothing had happened since our mother's death. As if war wasn't on our doorsteps. As though Sahmril's life was not at stake. Her eyes were distant, and her spirit far, far away.

Instead of coming back to me, she'd drifted even further from reality. I could see it in her demeanor when she lifted my hand from the silk of her dress and placed it back into my own lap. The gesture told me that I shouldn't touch the High Priestess of Sariba with my human hands. It was all I could do not to cry.

"You look beautiful, too, Leila," I ventured at last. For months, I'd longed to see her, to fall on her neck and weep together for everything that we'd lost. To talk about our mother, and to ask her advice about our melancholy father.

I wanted to erase the memory of her dance that morning under the spell of the Egyptian magicians. They frightened me, but Leila had welcomed them, even though they had kidnapped her from the Temple of Ashtoreth and carried her across the desert.

Leila was part of the lure. The bait for me. To intimidate

me so much I'd run away from Sariba, which included running away from Kadesh.

When Jasmine set a tray of tea on the table under the window, I leaned forward. "What are you looking at, Leila? Please talk to me. I've missed you so much."

She gazed at the fountains and gardens, but now I discerned what she was watching so intently. In line with her vision, the spires of the temple glittered white under the afternoon sun.

My heart was so heavy I was weighed down by it. "The soul of the temple calls to you, doesn't it?" I asked her. "You're now tied to it permanently. Somehow, they've—*she's*—seduced you. You can't even pretend to be my sister anymore. Only the temple's devoted priestess." My voice choked, and I tried not to break down.

At last she turned her face, smiling serenely. "It's my calling, Jayden. All will be well. Have faith in the Goddess."

My hands shook as I poured the tea. "Tijah, may we have some sort of actual meal?" I was light-headed and my stomach gnawed with hunger.

"Of course, my lady," Tijah said, throwing hand signals to her sister. "We should have fed you before the king's crowning ceremony."

"There wasn't time," I replied, brushing off her apologies.

Moments later, herbed breads and roasted meat were delivered, including salad greens and fruit. I fixed a plate, but Leila shook her head, her face fixed with an odd serenity that was disconcerting.

"This is the first time you've visited me since I arrived two weeks ago in Sariba," I said, nudging her attention away from the window. "I sent a wedding invitation and was disappointed when you didn't come. I always wanted you at my wedding. Just like we planned when we were girls and daydreamed about our wedding gowns. Remember when we used to draw sketches in the sand?"

She sipped the hot tea. "It's a good thing I wasn't allowed to attend. I might have been shot with an arrow and died."

"They were aiming for Kadesh. And nearly killed the King of the Edomites, our ally and close friend."

"That's unfortunate."

"Unfortunate?" I practically spit the word out, my patience running thin. I bit my tongue, not wanting to anger her. Trying to compose myself, I asked, "Leila, why are you here? I'm surprised Aliyah let you come down into the city. And what about Sahm—?"

Before I could ask her about our younger sister, she said, "Speaking of weddings, I came to tell you that I am to be married."

I was shocked into silence for a moment. That was a statement I hadn't expected. "Are the priestesses even allowed to marry—or are you talking about one of Ba'al's clerics?"

"His name is Imarus," Leila said dreamily. "We fell in love during the long journey."

"One of the Egyptian magicians?" No wonder she was barely lucid!

"He's perfect for me. Our union will begin the day after the solstice. We'll be united during the Sacred Marriage Rite."

"So soon?" I asked, wanting to slow time down. Her news made me nauseous, and my drink spilled on my lap.

Jasmine bent over to mop up the liquid, a tiny frown between her eyes.

"Our marriage will help to unite Egypt's power with Sariba's."

"I didn't realize that a High Priestess could marry."

"It's a divine union, of course. We knew we were meant to be together on the night of the last Sacred Marriage Rite."

"Is this why you're here? To invite me to *your* wedding?"

"To attend, you would have to come to the temple and be part of the Sacred Marriage Rite, Jayden. Since your wedding has been postponed, you certainly could. The summer solstice will be a night of the utmost power and divinity. Especially after—" She broke off, her eyes inadvertently meeting mine.

I found myself wanting to shake her, to snap her out of the nightmare of her delusions. "You can't let Aliyah sacrifice Sahmril," I said, forcing my voice to remain steady. "She's our sister. The sister we promised to take care of when our mother died. I can't believe you would sanction this terrible deed."

A flash of pain crossed Leila's face. Deep down it bothered her, but she couldn't admit that her Goddess was asking for such an awful expression of obedience. "I can't tell her no," she said quietly. "I'm trying to believe that it will all be for the best. And who knows," she added, "perhaps Sahmril truly will end the war and bring peace. That would be a noble cause to give your life for."

"*I* would happily do that to save my people—if I believed

in your version of the Goddess—but Sahmril is a child. Her life is sacred and innocent. She knows nothing about what this means. For her, it will be torture. She has no *choice*."

Leila blinked her eyes and lifted her chin in an attempt to brush away my words. She couldn't face it, so she would deny it. Slipping a hand under her leg, she pulled out a finely etched writing plate with Egyptian hieroglyphs. "This is the purpose for my visit."

"You know I can't read it. I'll call a scribe to interpret."

"No need. Imarus taught me Egyptian during our long expedition. I'll read it to you."

My sister laid the tablet in her lap, running a finger along the symbols with affection.

"To Jayden, daughter of the Nephish
From Aliyah, Goddess of Sariba
The Goddess and High Priestess of Sariba officially invite
you to witness the summer solstice sacrifice in two days' time.
It will be a night you will remember for the rest of your life. A
permanent kinship with the Goddess will bless you and your
family forever."

"She sent an invitation to watch Sahmril sacrificed!" Grabbing the tablet, I threw it across the room where it hit the corner of a table and broke into pieces.

With a shriek, Leila staggered off the chair and crawled across the floor. Picking up the shards, she cradled them in her hands, trying to fit them together.

"How could you ruin it like that?" she moaned. "Imarus wrote this himself, and his handwriting is exquisite. Practically a work of art."

"Leila, what is wrong with you? How could you bring this to me?"

"You've been invited as a special guest because Sahmril has been chosen to honor the Goddess. Her sacrifice will bring peace and love to this land. *She* is the pure vessel. We're so lucky to have found her."

"Lucky?" I echoed. The nonchalant manner in which she spoke was horrifying. "Our sister was hunted down."

"Sahmril will help us win the war against the enemy armies. Think of the honor!"

I rocked back on my heels, trying not to become hysterical. "It's all a lie, Leila. How can you not see this? Aliyah has deceived you in so many ways . . . she wants to murder our sister and you are a willing accessory. Think of what you're saying. The child of our mother's womb! The baby we saved on the desert with camel's milk."

My older sister patted my hand. "It will all be worth it, Jayden. Trust me."

I couldn't continue the upsetting conversation, so I changed the subject. "Leila, I've never had the chance to tell you, but Father and I buried Grandmother Seraiah many weeks ago on the empty desert."

"I'm sorry to hear that," was Leila's meager attempt at remorse. I tried not to be offended at her lack of emotion at losing our beloved grandmother.

Speaking in fierce tones, I added, *"I refuse to bury Sahmril, too."*

Ignoring me, Leila held up the chunks of the tablet and squinted at the cracked lines. "You could ask your maids to glue this back together. It's not too terribly broken. If your girls placed the pieces just so, like this, it would be readable again."

"Leila, please." She was so detached, losing her grasp of reality. "Please stay here with me," I begged her. "Don't go back to the temple."

She glanced about the suite of rooms, the chandelier, the luxurious bed and plump pillows, as though waking up from a dream. "Oh, no. Soon the palace won't be safe. Nowhere in Sariba will be safe except for the temple."

I went cold. She knew, then, that Horeb's army had arrived in the dead of night and that they were here to potentially kill us all.

"Please clean up the broken tablet, Tijah and Jasmine," I asked the girls, my resolve hardening. "Grind the pieces into dust and have one of the servant boys take them to the cliffs and fling the remains out to sea."

"You can't do that," Leila protested, stuffing the pieces into her satchel to save them.

Wrenching the handbag away from her, I handed it to Tijah. She and her sister obeyed my command, but with a silence I'd never seen before. Tijah's face displayed her bewilderment at the odd conversation.

Leila rose and gripped my arm. "On the night of the summer solstice, arrange to arrive at the temple early so we can have a few moments alone. The three of us sisters together again, before eternity claims Sahmril."

Before I could respond, she pulled open the door and slipped through, the hem of her gown disappearing around the corner with the soft sound of silk.

Her last words left me stunned, and tears fell from my eyes. Pushing myself forward, I returned to the window and gazed unseeing at the pathways and fountains. I'd been so thrilled at her visit, but now I was left in emotional shambles. "You got it wrong, Leila," I said to the window. "The three of us sisters again—before Aliyah has Sahmril *murdered*."

Even though I'd lost my appetite, I crammed a few morsels of the bread and cheese into my mouth, then picked up a bowl of sugared berries. Fatigue was overcoming me, and I needed my strength for tonight. Only a few hours remained before the midnight rendezvous with Kadesh and the scouts to appraise Horeb's camp and ascertain any information that we could use to hinder them before the first battle.

Feeling cold by the thought of Horeb so close, I crawled onto the bed and wrapped a thick blanket around me. Before long, I was finally warmer. Images of my sisters as prisoners of the temple wavered before my eyes, but exhaustion finally clouded the world, and I fell into a stupor of sleep.

13

When I awoke, hours had passed. The sun had long set, and the room was dark. I stumbled off the bed, groggy, my cheeks burning from the heat of the afternoon.

I splashed cold water on my face and downed a goblet to quench my thirst before running a brush through my hair. After I changed into a dress I hadn't slept in, I left for dinner in Kadesh's offices.

We ate a simple late supper by candlelight while pieces of conversation between General Naham, Kadesh, and Uncle Josiah swept over me. They spoke of Sariba's number of troops, the daily practice drills, and various strategic formations.

"We need to keep the battles in the desert beyond the frankincense groves and far from the city," Uncle Josiah said across the table.

"It's a top priority," Kadesh agreed firmly. "Horeb's armies must be far from our citizens. Since we'll be riding out to meet him in battle, we need to time how long it takes us to go from the center of the city to Horeb's camp."

"Exactly, my lord," General Naham concurred.

"What we don't know is the actual size of Horeb's armies," Kadesh said.

"But tonight you'll learn a great deal," Josiah said, picking at his food. The lines in his face had deepened after the busy day and the crowning, and I suspected he would not be riding out with us.

I nodded in agreement, and General Naham gave me a particularly displeased frown. The man did not want me accompanying them to the desert.

"When I'm dressed in black, you'll never know I'm female," I assured the general, setting down my fork. Nerves had stolen my appetite again. "Now if you'll excuse me."

Kadesh rose from the table when I got up. "I'll see you in a few minutes," he told me.

Too soon, Tijah was helping me into a black tunic and breeches, pulling a black leather belt tight around my waist. Jasmine wound my hair about my scalp while Tijah pinned it into place.

Over my head went a length of black fabric, covering my neck, hair, and the lower half of my face. If I needed to, I could pull it up over my eyes, but the fabric was light enough that I could still discern enough to move about safely.

"Underneath this, your eyes won't glitter in the moonlight

and give you away to the enemy."

"True," I said. "Especially since the moon is more than three-quarters full. This next lunar week will be more dangerous for our scouts when they're trying to spy and remain unseen."

Before I knew it, Kadesh was at my door. Without speaking, he slipped his hand under my arm and we left the palace together for the stables. "Have you changed your mind?" he asked.

"Not at all. I'm going, and I want to be with you."

His hand gripped mine as we made our way to the stables where Asher was saddling horses. "I came down to make sure you ride Hara," he told me. "Of all the royal horses she knows you best, and you her. It would be unwise to ride an unfamiliar steed tonight."

I counted four horses. One for Kadesh, a highly recommended scout named Jonah, General Naham, and me. My stomach was in my throat when Asher helped me mount, and I wasn't sure that I might not get sick.

The last time I'd seen Horeb he'd pulled Kadesh out of Nalla's house in Mari and ordered his men to attack him. After dragging his body away, Horeb had tossed Kadesh's brown cloak at me stained with his blood.

I'd never forget the despair of that night, including the weeks hiding in the hills of Mari mourning Kadesh when I'd thought he was gone forever.

The memories sent goose bumps up my chilled neck. The stable doors opened and a small white moon sat at the pinnacle of a night shattered with stars.

General Naham's eyes were on me when I took the reins, but I ignored him and fixed my gaze on the task at hand. My thighs gripped the horse with new strength and my confidence surged.

We were a silent company, moving our horses quickly out of the city and up the hills in an easy gait, but not galloping to keep the noise down.

"We can't risk detection," Kadesh murmured beside me. "Horeb has scouts out here, too. Pray we don't run into any."

After a half hour's ride to the edge of the frankincense groves, we tied the horses up and moved forward on foot. A man in dark garb appeared out of nowhere, helping with my reins to tether Hara. He was shadowlike, a spirit of the gnarled trees and smelling pungently of the musky scent, silent as a ghost.

"One of the foremen of the groves," Kadesh said close to my ear. "He'll stay with the horses until our return."

We wasted no time in moving forward at a fast pace. I hunched my neck into my cloak, General Naham leading out. Keeping to the eastern sand dunes and salt shrubs, we could remain undetected while we skirted the main bowl of the valley.

When we crested the first rise of a dune, my breath caught. One league straight west from us were the lights of Horeb's camp nestled close to the Qara foothills.

Jonah grunted. "Bigger up close, eh?"

"Too close. Too real," I whispered, and General Naham glared at me for speaking, while Kadesh squeezed my hand.

Even though my mouth was dry and I yearned to take a sip from my water pouch, I didn't dare pause or lag behind.

I pulled the headscarf up, keeping it over my face as much as possible to muffle the sound of my heavy breathing.

The night was so still. Not a sound but the soft shushing of sand beneath our feet. The dunes and scrub, including a lone tree, were silhouettes of black.

We reached the foothills, now less than half a league from Horeb's camp, and slowed our pace.

Carefully, we picked our way through the rocks and boulders. Every few paces, Jonah, our tracker, held out a hand to halt our progress while he went ahead to make sure we weren't running into one of Horeb's men crouched in a crevice.

It was slow going, not wanting loose rocks to go sliding under our feet and create noise. The sand dunes had been much easier in that regard.

All at once, Kadesh stopped in front of me. The shadows were so dense I almost fell into him. I was blind. Holding my breath, I didn't dare move in the intense quiet.

I swore I could hear the faint rattle of the teapots from the campfires.

"Enemy guard post up ahead," Kadesh said, cupping a hand around my ear. He grasped my forearm and led me, one slow step at a time, into a niche behind a huge boulder. Crouching, I tried to catch my breath, but my heart was pounding so loud in my ears I swore the entire valley could hear it.

A few voices from the camp carried along the night air. Two men laughed over a joke. The embers of a fire crackled when stirred by a stick. But mostly our enemies were asleep in their tents.

No sign of Horeb, but obviously he'd be well guarded in a tent in the center of camp.

Up close, the camp was enormous and intimidating. I had no idea how to estimate the number of soldiers or animals, but the sight loomed ominous.

I sucked in air when I saw the shadows of several guard patrols walking the far perimeter of Horeb's camp. One such patrol stopped nearest to us and pointed to the boulders we hid behind. I didn't dare breath for several excruciating moments, holding my head down between my knees and shrinking into myself.

Kadesh was a statue next to me. General Naham and Jonah were in some other location, but I had no idea where.

The night grew even quieter, if that was possible, but now the sounds of the desert began to distinguish themselves. Tiny scurrying of mice or moles. A far-off wolf crying at the moon. Scrub brush branches whispering together.

And then I heard something I hadn't expected. The faint sound of water.

Kadesh relaxed the grip on my hand, and I slowly lifted my head, trying to make his dark figure out.

He lifted a finger to his lips and then rose to a crouched position, motioning to me that Horeb's perimeter guards had finally moved on. It was all I could do not to heave a huge sigh of relief.

We retraced our steps, Kadesh lifting a warning hand to

keep the slow pace so we didn't give ourselves away.

The trek back to the frankincense groves was longer and more tortuous. I was exhausted now. We'd been walking well over two hours in rock and deep sand, muscles taut, nerves on fire.

When we reached our horses and the shadowy foreman helped me into my saddle, I flopped over Hara's neck, dozing until we reached the stables again.

Nobody had yet spoken a single word. Whether due to fatigue or fear, I didn't know.

After the horses had been fed and groomed by the sleepy stable boys, Kadesh motioned to General Naham and Jonah to gather. In the dim glow of a candle, we sat on bales of hay, cold and overwhelmed.

"How close did we come to being discovered?" Kadesh asked.

Jonah shrugged. "There was a scout not too much farther in from where we stopped, but he was half-asleep on his sword. More guards up ahead, but they had no idea we were there."

Kadesh pursed his lips. "General Naham—your thoughts?"

The general glanced at me, obviously uncomfortable.

"Speak freely," Kadesh ordered. "Jayden understands what we're up against. Perhaps better than you do. She fought King Horeb personally. She outwitted him in the Mari hills and then rescued me in the Edomite caves."

General Naham stroked his beard, candlelight falling along the lines of his face. "Not one army, but three, including demonic Assyrians. There is nothing more to say."

I wavered on my seat. We were overwhelmed and outnumbered by brutal warriors.

"Do they have trained cavalry?" Kadesh asked.

The general nodded. "And archers."

Jonah spoke up. "I was able to climb a little higher into the boulders of the foothills to estimate the number of troops. My closest guess is nearly fifteen hundred."

Kadesh was thoughtful for several long moments. One by one, he caught our eyes in turn, as if to emphasize the gravity of the situation. "My first plan, then, is to send an epistle to King Horeb and ask for his surrender."

General Naham's eyebrows shot up. "Your Majesty—" he began, but Kadesh held up a hand to stop his interruption.

"The letter will be a ploy to put them on defense and make them nervous. I want them to think that *they* are outnumbered. These foreigners are not defending their homeland. Horeb has promised them riches, but nobody will fight a suicide mission."

Jonah's eyes were wide and staring between us all. "Good point. A wise idea."

"Intimidation," I said. "And it buys us time."

"Time to do what? More marching practice? Our army is as ready as they'll ever be," General Naham said.

"They can continue target practice and their sword-fighting. The problem is that the Sariba army rarely has had to go to war. Not exactly in our favor when we're dealing with professional armies of Maachathite and Assyrians."

Another moment of silence passed and then General Naham placed his hands on his knees to rise. "I'll meet you in the strategy room in the morning, King Kadesh."

"Wait," I said. "I have an idea."

"You don't know war strategy," the general told me dismissively.

"I'm not talking about a battle," I argued back. "When we were sitting in the boulders tonight, I thought I heard water coming from somewhere."

"You did," Kadesh said. "There are springs in the foothills. Those springs are one reason some of our people are escaping to the caves in the mountains. Many people keep their herds up there in the wintertime. Plenty of food and water."

"Are there any wells near Horeb's camp—or are they using those springs, too?"

Kadesh studied my face in the lamplight. "The last well on the desert route into Sariba is located about three leagues farther east. I highly doubt Horeb's men are walking two hours each way to haul water back to camp. They're definitely using our springs."

"What if we poison the springs?" I said quietly.

My suggestion was met with silence.

"Poison the springs," I repeated. "Make them sick. Kill them. It will bring down their numbers so we can fight them one on one more easily. Their advantage of outnumbering us will be diluted."

"And what about our own citizens?" General Naham asked. "How do we protect them? And how do you propose we poison a spring? Especially when the water will dilute the concoction."

"Send out word to our citizens to store as much water

as they can tomorrow. Do not allow their use until the king decrees it. The Temple of Sariba is well acquainted with herbal medicine—and poisons. The Egyptian magicians within our borders brought a supply with them. A fact I know. A poisonous plant like hemlock or arsenic, given in small doses, will make a person sick and doesn't kill them. At least not outright."

Kadesh let out a sound of approval. "It's a brilliant plan. We only need to get the poison and then administer it to the water source."

"I know someone who can get into the temple kitchens," I said, thinking of my handmaids with their quiet demeanors.

Jonah said, "We'll go tomorrow night."

"Or perhaps early in the morning," I suggested. "Then the poison has less chance to be diluted before they fill their water barrels for the day."

"It would be best if we could go directly to the large barrels of water right inside their camp," Jonah said. "No dilution in standing water."

"But that means going directly into camp," Kadesh said, shaking his head. "You'd be caught for sure."

"Let me figure that out," Jonah told him. "I'll wear a disguise to blend in. Act like I belong."

"That's why you make a good scout," General Naham said, looking more pleased than he had all evening.

"I have another idea," I said. "One I've been thinking about since the mercenary soldiers attacked last night."

"We'll arrange for an execution, Jayden," Kadesh said, reaching out to press his hand against mine in reassurance.

"The mercenary soldiers deserve death for the death and destruction they wrought at the king's own wedding last night," I said, my voice rising. "The dozen from last night are dead—by Sariba's soldiers—except for one. I almost thrust my knife through Basim, their leader's throat, when he lay gasping and bleeding. Now I'm glad I didn't. I think there's a way they can help us. Will you let me go to the prison block and talk to him?"

Kadesh stared at me, bewildered. "The prison? Absolutely not. It's no place for my betrothed—or queen."

I gazed back at him, not backing down. The more I thought about it, the more perfect the idea became.

Kadesh shook his head, grunting with frustration. "From the expression on your face, I won't be able to talk you out of this. But I will not allow you into a prison cell to speak with a known killer and our enemy—sent by Horeb himself to assassinate us."

"Then come with me. Let me do the talking, Kadesh, but I want you there as witness."

Kadesh let out a laugh, and even General Naham quirked his mouth into a smile. "Oh, you'll *allow* me to join you?"

"Exactly so, my love. I'll call on you in the morning when I'm dressed. Don't be late."

Kadesh shook his head. "You are impossible," he said softly.

Jonah rose to leave. "I await word about my next spying rendezvous in the hills, Your Majesty."

"We'll meet again with the captains tomorrow morning. At the moment, I have a letter to write to Horeb demanding his surrender. It will be delivered at dawn."

We were a silent group as we entered the palace corridors hours after midnight. All of us were exhausted from the hours of riding and walking, including the stress of nearly being caught.

Images of Horeb's sprawling camp flooded my mind. So many men. So many weapons. So much determined hatred.

General Naham followed Kadesh down to the royal offices.

"Come with us, too, Jayden," Kadesh said, taking my hand. I sank into one of the couches trying not to yawn.

One of the king's manservants rose at the sound of our voices and hurried in from his bed. "My lord, is everything well?"

Kadesh pushed his hands against the edge of the desk wearily. "I need a scribe. And quickly."

The man had begun to open his mouth and then shut it. "Very good, Your Majesty." He disappeared into the hall and the sound of hushed voices and scurrying feet met my ears while I lay on the couch in a half stupor.

"You need rest," Kadesh said. "I apologize for keeping you up. The trek by horse and foot was enough to exhaust all of us. After the past two days of wedding attacks and temple ceremonies and seeing your sisters, I can only imagine that you must be dead on your feet."

"Nearly," I said, closing my burning eyes.

"Please stay with me until this is on its way."

"Of course, Kadesh." He'd had less sleep than I'd had, and it was showing in his posture, the disheveled hair, and in the rumpled state of his clothing.

A moment later, a palace scribe was at the door.

"Come," Kadesh called out to the young man with his bag of tools and polished slate. "The night is racing onward."

The scribe settled himself cross-legged on the floor and spread out his writing tablets, powders, and stencils on top of a large square of white linen.

"To Horeb, King of the Nephish," Kadesh began.

The room went silent as both Kadesh and I realized that this would be the first communication between the two men in many months. Not since Horeb had tried to murder Kadesh.

General Naham cleared his throat, witness and confidante if Kadesh needed him.

"Keep writing," Kadesh said firmly. The young man bent to his work, dabbing at the damp ink and licking his stylus when needed.

"We know you are camped in our lands. Lands that do not belong to you and will never belong to you. We've seen your numbers and your weaknesses. To fight only means death. There are plans already in action that will make sure of your demise. I advise that you do not risk it. Surrender to me so that your men may live to go home to their wives and children."

Kadesh reread the document and then said, "Sign it, King Kadesh of Sariba."

When he finished, my fists were clenched so hard they ached.

"A bold move, my lord," General Naham stated. "Especially considering that we are outnumbered."

"All the more reason for boldness," Kadesh said simply. Despite his confident words I could see the worry in his eyes, the deep fatigue as he leaned on his desk. "Send a runner with the truce flag to deliver the message, General. Flanked by two guards. A small convoy, but not threatening. And return with Horeb's reply. He isn't allowed to stall on this matter. He either surrenders immediately or faces a deadly battle one day hence. We'll see how much his mercenary armies actually want this fight."

Kadesh stamped the message with his name and kingly seal, and then General Naham strode from the royal suite to enlist three horsemen as couriers.

"Now we wait," Kadesh said, slumping back into his chair. "And hope our men come back alive."

I moved toward him, placing my cool fingers along the hot skin of his neck. At first, he stiffened and then relaxed at my touch. Swiveling around in his chair, he pulled me to him, his face in my chest. "Oh, Jayden," he breathed. "How I long to make you mine."

"I am yours. Forever," I whispered, bending forward to kiss his lips. "No matter what happens."

He sighed and pressed his hands along my back while I stroked his hair. Worry and anxiety showed in his dark eyes. Finally, he raised his head. "Go back to your rooms. Sleep. I'll come for you in the morning to go see your prisoner." He gave a small laugh. "Though God in heaven only knows why you insist on such a crazy enterprise."

"You'll see," I assured him. "Soon, our army and Horeb's three armies will be more evenly matched."

14

In the morning a haze hovered over the city, brought in by the morning fog rolling in from the ocean.

Tijah and Jasmine dressed me like a queen. I had to sweep into that prison wearing full royal regalia to intimidate and secure what I wanted from our foreigner prisoner.

"You look astonishing," Kadesh said when he arrived at my suite, pulling me to him while the handmaidens giggled behind their hands.

It was good to see their smiles, but nerves danced in my stomach. Now that we were on our way, I was afraid my idea might fail. But when I thought of Aliyah penetrating the palace without our knowledge, I feared her more than the prisoner sitting in the palace jail. Basim had merely laughed at my ruined wedding, blood dribbling from his mouth while I held a knife to his throat.

"This paid soldier of Horeb's is fortunate you didn't gut him two nights ago," Kadesh murmured once we were outside, while gardeners and servants paused in their work to bow to us along the tiered patios and walkways.

"I hope he proves worth more alive than dead."

Following the stone walls, we came to the eastern rampart. This gate opened onto the city thoroughfare and was now permanently locked down until the war was over, but the locked gate wasn't our goal.

Kadesh and I took another staircase, seemingly down into the bowels of the earth.

At the landing, two guards saluted. "Your Majesty—my lady," they stammered.

"You've taken a wrong turn," an older guard said, his eyes shifting across our faces as he tried not to stare at my fine dress and jewelry.

"We're exactly where we planned to be," Kadesh told him. "Please let us pass."

The man's mouth opened and then shut. Reluctantly, he opened the door to the gloomy prison. Sour smells assaulted my nose, a mix of unwashed bodies and stale air.

Wall sconces flickered, pale light pooling on the floor.

Memories rushed back of the time we'd found my father in the prison of Tadmur; the horrible smells, the horror of seeing my father down in a hole and chained to the walls, standing in murky, foul water. He'd been ill and emaciated, and, in many ways he still hadn't recovered. Especially after we'd dragged him across the deserts to Sariba.

The prison warden rose from his desk. He tried to hide his surprise when he saw me, my gown trailing along the hard-packed mud floor. "My lady, you shouldn't be here."

"I'm not squeamish."

The man's eyebrows shot into his hairline and his figure bulged with muscles while his thick oiled hair had been tied back with a leather strap. "So you haven't lost your way, my king?"

"Not at all," Kadesh said. "We are here with a mission."

I glanced about at the ledgers on the rickety desk, the hanging lamp overhead. A bowl filled with nuggets of frankincense burned on his desk, tendrils of smoke hovering about the windowless room. Obviously burned to mask the terrible smell coming from the prison chambers.

"The prison appears small," I noted. "Do the citizens of Sariba keep the law that fastidiously?"

"We're a small city compared to others," the warden answered. "The people of Sariba are, for the most part, peaceful and happy. The temple helps when poor folks come on hard times."

I could barely hold back the words of contradiction on my tongue, but Kadesh touched my arm as if sensing that I wanted to blurt out my true opinions about the temple.

The warden cocked his chin. "For the most part these are holding cells for those who are caught breaking the law while they await trial. Sariba's main prison is on the other side of the city. Please don't try to find it."

His expression was indulgent, assuming I was a curious

female who needed an escort back to my suite. "How may I help you, Your Majesty? This is no place for the king and his betrothed."

"We want to see the prisoner brought here last night," Kadesh said. "The leader of the mercenary soldiers who destroyed our wedding."

The warden was visibly startled. "You mean the leader of the men who shot the Edomite king?"

"The very one," I said, interrupting.

"How is the Edomite leader, may I ask?"

"Chemish is still at death's door," Kadesh said quietly. "And now we have business with the prisoner."

The warden smoothed his hands down his chest. "Please, my king, you don't want to talk to him. He's a rough one. Any retribution you're planning won't go well. He doesn't even deserve a trial for what he did to you and our country."

"I appreciate your concern," Kadesh said placidly. "I assure you I don't intend to break any of our laws."

"My apologies, King Kadesh. I didn't mean—of course, you can do what you want. I will obey."

"The fact that we are here should stay between us. I promise the prisoner won't hurt us. At least not any more than he already has."

The warden bowed his head. "I've lived a long time and revenge never comes the way we want it to," he said. "And it's usually not very satisfactory."

"I call it justice," I mumbled.

"We won't be long," Kadesh assured the man. "I promise

that no backlash will come to you."

"Follow me, Your Majesty," he finally said.

Jangling a set of keys in his hands, he marched down a dim corridor. Two more narrow halls branched off in either direction. He took the left one. The walls were fashioned from cut stone. Dribbles of moisture drooled down the square blocks along with blackened candle wax.

I was aware of eyes on me as we passed. Prisoners sat in corners muttering to themselves or sleeping on mats of thin blankets. Two men talked quietly to each other across the narrow corridor, gesturing with their hands. The moment they saw us, they closed their mouths. Their eyes drilled into my back as we passed. A shudder skipped down my spine, but I was careful not to make eye contact while Kadesh kept me tight to his side.

No windows or fresh air graced this place, but at least these prisoners weren't chained up as my father had been in Tadmur.

I almost bumped into the warden when he stopped. He held up a candle, and the pale flicker of light shone beyond the brass bars of the very last cell. The marauder from the mountains of Sheba had been placed in solitary confinement.

"Got a visitor, foreigner," the warden barked, rattling at the bars.

The foreign man lifted his head, slowly, purposely making us wait. His black eyes stared through a curtain of dirty hair. But those eyes were intelligent. He knew immediately who I was.

"You're not wearing your wedding finery, Princess," he said with a grin.

Kadesh stopped to stare into the cell. "You're Basim," he said bluntly.

"Ah, I'm complimented, Your Royal Highnesses. You remember me."

I squared my shoulders. "As if we would forget within less than two days."

"Oh, it's after midday? But how would I know?" The marauder's mocking smile threw me off balance. His broad shoulders were like those of a giant and his mane of hair tangled by wind and sun, but he was well spoken. He could speak our language despite the distinct mountain accent. Men like him were bred for fighting. They had a blood lust. Hired for soldiering to whoever paid the best. No guilt or remorse.

When he came closer, I steeled myself not to step back from the bars.

"I think I like you, Princess," he said, showing a mouth full of white teeth. A man of the rugged mountains who kept his teeth clean was an anomaly.

"Careful, prisoner!" Kadesh said evenly. "If it were up to me you'd never lay eyes on my bride again. She is the only reason you're still alive."

He chuckled. "I knew she wanted to kill me—and didn't."

"You ruined my wedding to the king."

He pursed his lips. "Gossip says he wasn't king the night of the wedding."

"Were you trying to kill him?" I asked, coming right to the point.

"Which one?" He laughed.

I wanted to slap him through the slats, but I was fairly certain that would only get me a broken wrist if he managed to snatch my arm.

I had to admit there were qualities in him I wanted to use. I was here to prey on his lust for blood and greed for money.

"One of your men shot the King of the Edomites," Kadesh said evenly.

Basim lifted an eyebrow. "That's too bad. We respect the Edom city. They have fine, desert-bred horses and a fighting spirit. I have no quarrel with them."

"Which means one of your men is a terrible shot," I retorted. "Your men were aiming for King Kadesh, but that doesn't matter any longer. By the grace of God's hand, he lives and could order your death if he wanted to."

"But he hasn't ordered an execution yet. And your king is blind," he added, stepping backward away from the thick bars as if fearing a lash from a whip.

Kadesh jerked forward, but restrained himself. I sensed that it was all he could do not to choke the life out of the mercenary soldier.

"We can leave whenever you want to," Kadesh told me. "Just say the word."

I shook my head. I wasn't going to give up before I'd even tried. "You're only alive because *I* stopped Chemish's son, the Prince of Edom, from killing you."

A wicked glint sparked in the prisoner's eye. "I sit in my cell speculating about you. Am I alive because you are weak and cannot execute a foreign killer, or because you plan to make me a slave?"

"Neither." My throat was dry as dust at the idea of him daydreaming about me. "We have something better planned."

"Ah, I've somehow become valuable to you."

"At the moment your life is not worth anything. You were going to assassinate the King of Sariba and then report to Horeb about the details of our city and army."

"But you spared me," he said softly. "You've come to make me an offer."

"Tell me how many men came with you from the mountains of Sheba?"

"Why would I tell you that?"

Now I laughed. "I may be smaller than you, and a woman, but I'm a desert girl. I know gnawing hunger in my belly. Walking leagues a day. Riding until you can hardly move by sunset. Thirst so burning you'd claw your throat out for a spoonful of water."

Now he threw his head back and laughed. "Oh, lady, you have certainly risen from my previous estimation."

"May you attempt to rise in mine," I told him, stepping closer to the bars. "It's no secret that Horeb has gathered a large army of more than a thousand."

He shrugged, his eyes flicking between the two of us.

"If you can count your own men on both hands twice over I'd be surprised. Horeb used you to scare us. You're a pawn to be sent home with a few weeks of paltry wages. And for what? Death, dismemberment? Never to see your families again?

This war isn't yours, it's Horeb's. And it's a war manufactured by lies. When it's over he will rule you with an iron fist. If he keeps you alive at all."

The man's meaty hands curled around the bars, but he was silent now. "Doesn't matter," he said roughly. "I don't have a family to return to."

"Don't lie to me. A leader like you has had many women. But you are now faithful to one, the love of your life."

He was startled. I'd been praying my bluff would work, and my hunch had proved accurate. Even I could see that underneath the wild hair, sunburned skin, and sweat-crusted clothing, he would clean up to become a tall, handsome man with hardened muscles. Accompanied by wit and a keen mind.

"Perhaps I have met my match in the Princess of Sariba—nay, the *Queen* of Sariba."

"How many men do you have?" I repeated.

He smirked. "Fifty still alive in the hills. With trained war horses."

Kadesh asked, "Are you loyal to your Queen of Sheba?"

He lifted a shoulder as if he didn't care. "She rules with a fair hand. Leaves my tribe alone to live as we wish, but allowing free trade. City jobs when we need them."

"What if I told you," Kadesh went on, "that your Queen of Sheba is my cousin?"

He sucked in a breath and stepped back. "Horeb never said anything about that."

"Of course not," I snapped. "He wouldn't because it doesn't suit his purposes." I paused, allowing that knowledge to sink in. "You do realize what this means? You've declared war on your own country's ally."

His arms dropped from the bars. "I never—"

"If you value your life, tell me Horeb's plans," Kadesh pressed him.

"What is his strategy?" I added. "When does he plan on attacking? And *how* will he attack?"

A deep laugh burst up from Basim's chest. "You're a brazen princess. No subtlety or deal-making."

"I believe in truth. And I will do anything to save the people of Sariba from destruction and a tyrant like Horeb as king."

I glanced at Kadesh and he nodded at me, a tiny smile hidden by the prison shadows so that I alone saw it.

Basim's hands gripped the bar. "I swore an oath to defend King Horeb. Some of my men already died for him."

"You must have a death wish then, because more of you will die. Perhaps all of you."

"You clearly haven't seen the size or strength of Horeb's armies."

"We've seen," Kadesh said bluntly. "And Sariba has the upper hand. They love their country and have defenses you haven't even dreamed of."

We were bluffing, but we needed extra soldiers. And I had to believe, just as Kadesh and Naomi and Chemish and Josiah did, that we could win this war. We had to win this war.

"Horeb has completed a journey of thousands of miles with three well-trained armies to take Sariba for his own. He plans to rule the entire southern borders, the caravans, and the west.

He will rival the Babylonian Empire. He also plans to kill your maimed king—and take *you*, Princess, for his own. Horeb is not interested in striking treaties. He's only interested in wealth and power on the grandest scale."

"Do *you* have ambition?" I asked, lowering my voice to seduce him into listening to my offer

His eyes were wary, curious. I had him.

"Basim, leader of the mountain men of the kingdom of Sheba," I went on. "I hereby enlist you and your band of men to fight for the kingdom of Sariba. King Kadesh and I will double what Horeb offered you. And if your worth is proven quickly, you will receive a rapid rise in rank and position."

His teeth glittered in the gloom. "But what about my honor?"

Now I laughed. "You have none because you sell yourself to the highest bidder—but with my offer you can return with honor to Sa'ba and your queen and your family. You will live in luxury. Your wife will have jewels and gowns. You won't rot in a prison cell—or be executed ignominiously."

He winked at me and I tried not to look shocked. "Surely I can't be dying ignominiously, my lady."

Anger rose up my throat. "You joke, but I'm serious."

Basim crossed his thick arms over his chest. "Triple my pay and guarantee my honorable release and a return trip home with a frankincense caravan."

"Done," Kadesh said. "And your men will be rewarded for their loyalty and shrewd fighting."

He glanced between the two of us, as though determining

the truth of our words. "You drive a hard bargain, Lady of Sariba."

"And you are wise to accept it. Treason doesn't make a pretty death."

"When do I get out of here?"

"After I draw up the paperwork," Kadesh told him. "You can retrieve your men from Horeb's camp."

"Easier said than done with Horeb's captains watching our every move."

"I trust you can figure that out, Basim," Kadesh said without a shred of empathy. "You will sign your name to a covenant to fight for your country of Sa'ba as an ally of Sariba. The details of our agreement will be laid out. Warden!" he called.

Almost immediately there came the sound of a shuffling gait. A dirty cloak appeared. I suspected the prison warden had been listening to the entire conversation from the darkness.

"Asher, Prince of Edom, will return with the signed release," Kadesh said with finality. "You are officially conscripted into the Sariba army and will pledge your loyalty and fealty to me."

While Basim bowed to us, a glint in his eyes, I turned back down the stone corridors, the sound of scurrying rats in my ears.

Once outside, sunshine poured onto my head. Fresh air filled my nose. Kadesh and I didn't speak until we had climbed the staircase back up to the main grounds.

The moment we were out of sight of the prison doors, I collapsed onto a cushioned garden bench, pressing a pillow against my face. Sweat dripped down my neck.

"We enlisted fifty more strong men to the Sariba army," I whispered in awe.

"Your gamble paid off," Kadesh said with a laugh of admiration. "Your negotiating skills are impressive, my girl of the desert. You managed to back him into a corner. Threat of hanging for treason. The promise of riches. How else are mercenary soldiers hired?"

"It worked," I said, relieved to have helped Kadesh's army and this country I was coming to love as my own.

Kadesh gazed down at me thoughtfully. "That's why you stopped us from killing him last night. You were already looking to the future and how you could use the beast. Even now, I'm watching you rise to your position as queen."

"I can assure you that I'm more desert girl than queen."

"Then Sariba needs a desert girl for their queen."

"Oh, Kadesh." I sighed, leaning my head against his shoulder when he sat down next to me. Relief was making me exhausted again. "Basim's men have more horses than the animals the Edomites took down at the wedding. The animals with their owners can be part of Asher's cavalry."

"If they're not wild and unmanageable." Kadesh smiled at me. "I'll bet they live under shrubs and rocks in the mountains of Sa'ba. They probably eat scorpions and sand."

"And their women give birth while shooting game and skinning rabbits?"

"I'll wager that one day *you* give birth while wielding a sword."

I laughed at the image he created, but nausea quivered in

my belly. We had extra fighters in Sariba's army now, but it had taken all my strength.

We returned to the palace during a hot and stagnant midday. The silence on the grounds was eerie. Not even the fountains were splashing. The bed of irises and tulips seemed to wilt before my eyes, beaten down by the sun.

I needed a cold cloth and tea. And I needed to check in with Tijah and Jasmine about procuring those noxious herbs to poison the springs in the foothills.

Kadesh was pensive when we entered the palace. "I'm concerned we haven't heard anything from Horeb. The deadline I gave him has passed. I must speak with General Naham and make sure my scouts are still alive. That Horeb didn't have them tortured or beheaded."

I tugged at his hand, forcing him to look at me before he departed for his offices. "I want the chance for a future with you, King Kadesh."

His smile was rueful. "If you don't change your mind after all this is over."

"Never," I assured him. "I only hope that the Queen of Sheba is still on *her* throne when this is all over."

"I'm grateful the queen is a long ways from here," Kadesh agreed. "She's safer in her own land with her husband and family and army, even if she was unable to keep Horeb's army from advancing toward us."

We stared at each other, knowing that Aliyah coveted her sister's throne of Sa'ba as much as she sought the throne of Sariba.

15

W e parted ways at the royal offices at the same moment Asher appeared in the hallway. His face was gloomy.

"You don't seem well. Is it Chemish?" I almost hated to ask.

He shook his head. "He's slowly recovering. Mentally, he wants to leap from his infirmary bed and head out to fight, but the doctors are forcing him to stay quiet and heal, using sedatives so that he'll sleep."

I loved the picture he painted of his father, a warrior king of Edom.

"Except for the palace staff, everyone else is down at the training grounds. General Naham is overseeing final preparations, organizing the troops and patrols. Every man from sixteen years to forty-five has been enlisted, whether they've trained recently or not."

"It's so real," I said quietly. "Too real." I was hot and cold thinking about that first trumpet blast, which would signal the official start of war. The armies charging forward, the clang of swords, the shouts and moans of death. My breath hitched in my throat when I imagined the terrible scenes.

"You look exhausted, my lady."

"It's been a trying day, but Kadesh and I have had some success, and I was actually on my way to find you. I need a contract drawn up immediately, and I want you to take it to the prisoner Basim for him to sign."

Asher's eyes narrowed when he frowned at me. "I don't think I heard you correctly."

"It's true. Kadesh and I enlisted the mercenary soldiers to *our* cause. Fifty men with horses. Now go quickly and get a scribe. After Basim signs, give him a horse from the palace stables and send him back to his men."

"Horeb will soon realize that the marauders are deserting him."

"I'll leave that to you and Basim to figure out, but please send me a message when he leaves to return to Horeb's camp. If you go with him, disguised as one of his men, you can come back with information on Horeb's plans. Remember, Horeb doesn't know you at all. Take off any signs or uniform that show you are part of Sariba."

"Very shrewd, my lady." His mouth set into a thin line as he shook his head.

I studied him. "Don't keep anything back from me. Tell me."

"Yesterday morning when I was searching for you at the

temple I saw Horeb's camp in the foothills. I'd always expected to meet them outside the city in the desert where they had no provisions, and we could return each night to our homes. But now they have come in the middle of the night—arriving almost a week earlier than expected—comfortable in *our* mountains where there are springs of good water, shelter, caves."

"It is as though Horeb knew exactly where to go when they arrived . . ." I said soberly. "We both know it was Aliyah who passed along the information to Horeb. Will they be able to ransack our fields of food and the orchards?"

"Kadesh ordered extra guards, but small groups of guards are easy prey. Picked off like fleas if Horeb sends a convoy to steal from Sariba's resources. And, well, those mountains are special, important. At least, to Kadesh. I think that's why," Asher paused. "That's why he seems a bit curt at times. Horeb camping in the Qara Mountains treads on sacred ground."

We parted ways and I was left to speculate over what would bother Kadesh so keenly to think of Horeb trespassing there.

While Tijah helped me bathe and dress for dinner, I determined to ask Aunt Naomi. Jasmine attended me because Tijah had gone to the temple to procure poisons with the help of her mother, Erina. I imagined Jonah going out tonight, alone, biding his time until dawn's first light to administer the poison just before Horeb's chefs fetched their cooking water for breakfast. I hoped he managed to taint their water barrels as well.

Sickness or death of a portion of Horeb's troops would more evenly match the two opposing forces. I prayed that the idea would work—and that Jonah came back alive.

It was nightfall when Tijah burst into the suite, her cheeks flushed with the secret she was carrying in a bag hidden under her skirts.

"You got it?" I asked softly, watching her bright eyes.

The girl sank onto a stool and nodded. "My mother says this will work well. No smell, easy to discharge into the springs."

I nodded and put a finger to my lips. I didn't want any guards to overhear. A surge of hope swelled in my heart that this would give Sariba a chance at equalizing the armies.

A chance to stay alive a little while longer.

Later, in Kadesh's suite having dinner with his aunt and uncle, I studied my father across the table eating slowly, deliberately, but very little. He was thin, his cheeks hollow. The strong man I'd known my whole life was aging. He'd never been a gregarious person, but firm in his convictions, and immensely dependable. I'd always known of his undying love for me, even if we were at odds over Horeb's ambitions and character.

We just stopped talking about it.

"We've stopped talking about many things," I confided to Naomi as we sat tucked into a corner after dinner was over and the evening cooled. From across the room, I studied Kadesh while he spoke in urgent tones with Uncle Josiah, General Naham, and Asher who represented his father. Asher would lead the men of Edom when our troops assembled for battle. They had decided to allow the poison to work at incapacitating the enemy as much as possible before the first wave of battle. "My mother's death is a wound that never heals. He's lost without her."

Aunt Naomi's eyes flicked across the room toward Pharez who sat by the open window while a night of stars deepened. It was easy to see that he missed the desert. The longing in his eyes was unmistakable. All he wanted was to be out with his camel herd, his family, and his tribe.

He and I would never reclaim that life. It was lost to the desert sands forever.

Naomi took my hand in hers. "I hope that your mother's memories help Pharez get through the lonely nights. I can't imagine losing Josiah. Does your father know Sahmril is at the temple? Have you told him?"

Sorrow rose in my chest. "We don't talk about her. Not since I gave my sister to Dinah to nurse and care for. I let my parents down. I gave away my mother's last gifts to save Sahmril. I gave away our best camel, and still we lost my little sister."

"You must tell him," Naomi pressed. "He'll be heartbroken to learn that she's close, especially when she's in Aliyah's possession. He deserves that respect."

Naomi knew Aliyah had Sahmril, but she had no idea that the young woman planned to make a sacrifice of her to the Goddess. I hadn't had the heart to tell her yet, but I knew I should, and soon. I worried more about my father not knowing—or what would happen when he did learn of the fate Aliyah had in store for his little daughter.

"You're right," I finally said. "He deserves the truth. Tomorrow night is the solstice ceremonies. I'll tell him before I leave for the temple. Perhaps my intentions are misguided, but I don't want him running off and getting himself killed by Aliyah's guards if he storms the temple to retrieve her. I rescued him from prison once already, and it nearly killed him."

Aunt Naomi kissed my cheek. "And he won't recover, Jayden," she said softly, staring into my eyes. "He's endured too much, and he's getting older, which makes it all the harder."

Grief tugged at my chest. "I hate watching him deteriorate right before my eyes. If only he could see Sahmril before he passes from this life."

"Don't lose hope," Naomi added quickly. "He could be with us for many years to come. Now go to Kadesh and say goodnight."

My lips parted. "Will you answer a question first? Kadesh—Asher—they both allude to the mountains being special. Sacred. Why? What happened there?"

Naomi's eyes jerked toward mine. Clearly, I had startled her.

I lowered my voice. "I suspect it has something to do with the secret grief Kadesh kept hidden from me for so long."

Naomi bit at her lips. "Kadesh's parents are buried in the mountains. Asher and his parents were here when Kadesh's parents—" she broke off. "They had recently returned with a caravan to Egypt and stayed for the frankincense harvest. It's the only time I've ever met Asher's mother, Isra."

"She's lovely," I said pensively. "After my trek through the desert to find Kadesh, she took care of me."

Naomi glanced across the room at the men still in conversation.

We were purposely avoiding the circumstances of Kadesh's parents' tragic suicides. "I didn't realize that Asher's family was here at the time. It makes sense now. The reason Asher is so tied to Kadesh, and why he was adamant that Kadesh tell me everything a few weeks ago."

"They're buried in a beautiful sepulcher in one of those caves."

"Were Kadesh's parents sent off in the same splendid style as King Ephrem? I've never seen that tradition before."

Naomi's brow wrinkled. "The magnificent funeral pyres are reserved for kings and queens. It is a great honor and their deaths were . . . terrible. Kadesh's father was a hunter and spent quite a bit of time in the mountains. His wife often accompanied him. Despite her wealthy sheltered upbringing in Dedan, she loved the beauty of this world. Often, they would leave together for days at a time. Their own private retreats to the castle in the hills."

"I see it as a sign of their great love," I murmured, thinking how blessed Kadesh and I had been to be raised by such loving people. "I suppose it's fitting that they were buried in the Qara Mountains then. In the place that meant so much to them, close to the abandoned castle."

"Kadesh told you about that, then?" Naomi asked. "They were together in life and in death. When Kadesh's father discovered her body slumped over the statue of the Goddess, he went over the edge. He couldn't bear thinking of the pain she'd been suffering and it tore him to pieces thinking of her alone in a void of darkness. So he went to be with her. You can see why Horeb's army in those mountains especially pains Kadesh."

I nodded tightly, the lump in my throat growing. "I hope Horeb doesn't find their private retreat and raze it. Or use it for his headquarters."

Naomi shook her head. "Most likely not. It's too far from the open desert where the battles will take place."

"Small blessings then," I said softly. "But all the more reason to poison those springs."

Naomi lifted her eyebrows and I filled her in on the midnight scouting expedition and the plan to poison the water.

"It will work," I assured her, sensing her distress. She gave me a wavering smile and then I rose to slip my arm through Kadesh's as he stood at the strategy table in the adjoining sitting room.

"We're finished," Kadesh said. "You're going to bed. We're *all* going to bed," he added when my eyes widened to include himself in that directive.

In a low voice, I said, "I received the herbs from Tijah. I'll see that Jonah gets them before I go to bed. Will he go alone?"

Kadesh nodded. "Hopefully an early morning invasion will catch them all ill in their beds. This war could be over sooner rather than later, thanks to you."

"We shouldn't be overconfident, my lord," General Naham said, hand at his belt as he bowed to take his leave. "I apologize for eavesdropping, Your Majesty, but Horeb's army is immense, and there is no guarantee Jonah can administer the poison, or that it will work. But," he added, his eyes going to my face, "I will admit that the plan is a good one, so my acknowledgments to Lady Jayden."

That was probably the closest I would come to a compliment from General Naham, and I inclined my head in appreciation. "I hope Horeb rues the day he came to the Land of Sariba. Fighting within the boundaries of your enemy's country can hardly be a plan for long-term success."

"I agree," Kadesh said, lifting me to my feet to say goodnight.

Before I left for my bedroom, I kissed my father, holding his cold hands in mine. "Go to bed, Father. I need to speak with you, but tomorrow when we're both not so tired."

He pursed his lips, his eyes drifting from mine. "I've been pondering about what I can do to stop this war. War serves no purpose other than to create new enemies. There should be peace. If only your mother were here. If only we could have done our duties to one another."

His words pierced at my heart at the reference to my doing my duty by marrying Horeb. If my mother had been here this war might have been avoided. She might have helped to negotiate a union with Kadesh while maintaining good relations with Horeb and his family.

Perhaps I was giving her too much credit. Horeb had been determined to seize his father's throne and position long before the tragedies of the past year.

"Please don't blame me for loving Kadesh," I said now. "He

has been good to our family. I know you love Horeb like a son, but the boy I grew up with changed after his brother's death. For more than a year, he has been nothing but cruel to me. He attacked me, tried to murder Kadesh—"

My father jerked his hands up, palms facing me, shaking his head in agitation.

I backed away, and slowly bowed to show my respect. When I left the room, my eyes were swimming. I had to tell him about Sahmril, but I dreaded it.

"What kind of concoction did you get?" I asked Tijah when I finished dressing for bed.

"The belladonna was running low and wouldn't work as quickly anyway, so I pulled hemlock, which produces paralyzation until the victim suffocates. If Jonah uses it all we can only hope they will die within hours."

I shivered at her sobering words. "Has it already been passed on to him?"

Tijah nodded, and we dropped the subject as I pulled the linen sheets up over my legs and fell into a heavy sleep.

I became lost in the eerie darkness of a nightmare. My mind kept telling me I was asleep, but my body was running, running, running. Up and down strange corridors, stairs, and tunnels. Always turning in a circle. Never arriving at my destination.

All at once, I was jerked out of bed. My sealed eyelids ripped open. After two nights of little sleep, the fatigue was so bad it was as though I'd drunk three jugs of wine.

A flame flared and the ghostly face of Jasmine appeared,

her mouth working in an attempt to speak to me.

My head wobbled on my neck when I tried to get up. I had no idea what time it was. Had I been asleep five minutes or five hours?

"We have to hide!" came the hoarse voice of Tijah.

I untangled my legs from the sheets. "What's going on?"

The moment I spoke the words, a horrendous banging came from down the hall.

"My lady—no!" Tijah shrieked, yanking me back from the outer door of the suite. "Horeb's army is here! They're coming for us!"

My entire body crackled with sudden energy. "What do you mean?"

She began to shake uncontrollably. "They've invaded the palace!"

16

I raced to the door and flung it open. Hazy smoke filled the hallway. My night guards were gone from their post. We were alone.

"Is the palace on fire?" I stepped out, my neck turning back and forth from one end of the corridor to the other. One end branched off toward the foyer and the other toward the guest rooms.

There were echoing shouts, but I couldn't tell from which direction. When I raced back toward my suite, my feet ran over an odd patch in the hallway rug right before the threshold.

I bent down and ran my hand across it. The carpet was singed, clearly burned. But also damp, as if one of my guards had doused the rug with a bucket of water.

Cold drafts of air wafted in from the outer doors that were

open at the end of the corridor, and I shivered in my night-gown. Black smoke rose up along the high ceilings and I tried not to cough from the fiery taste burning my throat.

"*Where* are the guards?" I choked out.

Had someone tried to start a fire in front of my suite, or was it a spilled candle? Then I noticed that the wall sconces weren't burning any longer. Only one farther down, closer to the intersecting corridors, that cast a small glow.

"I'm not going to stay here and be ambushed. Tijah and Jasmine, hide in the wardrobe after I leave. Can the door be locked?"

"I have a better place, my lady," Tijah said. "Created for an emergency." She passed through the bathing room past the tub and pushed against the tiled wall in three different places. A narrow door slid open, exposing a small dark chamber.

"Does this secret closet go anywhere else?" I asked in astonishment.

"There's another door that connects to a guest suite farther down the hallway in case we ever need to get out a different way."

"Do all royal rooms have these?"

Jasmine nodded, her face pale, her dark eyes stricken.

Tijah followed me back to the dressing area. "What are you going to do, my lady?"

Ripping my nightgown over my head, I tossed it into the bureau, then yanked a shift from a hook in the wardrobe and pulled it on. The simple gray tunic was shorter so I could move about more easily.

I coiled my hair up on top of my head and jabbed a pin from the dressing table into it. My vision was now unhindered as I pulled my sword belt off the shelf and buckled it around my waist. My fingers shook with nerves and fear.

"Go!" I said, herding the girls inside the narrow space behind the wall.

Tijah's eyes were swimming. "My lady, you must hide with us. You'll—"

I placed a finger on her lips, our faces close. "We will all survive."

I pushed them inside, and my chest ached when I heard Jasmine's whimpering. After closing the door, I moved silently through the suite. We hadn't lit any lights, but the nearly fat, full moon bathed the window ledge in eerie light.

I scooted toward the door. Voices were coming closer.

My heart squeezed as I peered around the doorjamb. I had no protective clothing, no armor. If foreign soldiers were going to invade the palace, I needed better protection.

Shadows lurked far down the hallway, near the eastern doors, but I couldn't identify anyone. Sidling along the wall, I stepped slowly. At the intersecting halls, I nearly fell over a palace guard lying on the floor. I sucked back the scream that nearly shot out my throat.

Bending down, I touched his chest, and came up with blood on my fingers. He was dead.

Every nerve was on fire. I needed to go to Kadesh's suite. Behind me, in the hallway that led to the foyer, swords rang out, bronze against bronze in a sickening clash. I picked up my pace, terrified that I was going to run straight into a Maacha-thite soldier.

Soon I was flying down the hallway, turning right and then left toward the royal suite of the king. Hulking shadows were fighting down each bisecting hallway, the sound of fists and bodies slamming into the walls. I passed Aunt Naomi's suite and tried the door, but it was locked. I could only pray she and Naria and her servants were safe.

I shoved at the door to my father's rooms and burst through. My heart hammered so loudly I swore everyone from the kitchens to the lookout towers could hear it.

I raced about the suite like a mad woman, but the bed was empty. Not even slept in. The rest of the rooms empty.

Where was my father? Surely he wasn't fighting off an Assyr-ian soldier somewhere in the palace? "Don't die, Father, not like this," I moaned.

Hurrying, I kept moving toward Kadesh's rooms.

Right in front of the carved royal doors, four palace guards were fighting a group of foreigners dressed in black tunics. Kadesh's double doors had been flung wide open and the receiving foyer was pitch black. Not a good sign.

The distinctive white head scarves of the Maachathite tribe were wrapped about the foreheads of the men the Sariba guards were fighting. Flashes of metal sparked with every strike as they thrust and parried.

I slammed my head against the wall behind me when a Maachathite suddenly fell with a thud. A spurt of blood came up from his mouth, his eyes still open as he died.

The other two were taller and heavier than the Sariba men. Their backs were to me, fast closing in while the Sariba soldiers kept swinging their swords and moving them down the hall. Even so, the skill of the Maachathite men was impressive.

My eyes focused on the distant hallway I'd just crept down. More soldiers were fighting in that direction and parrying closer. I was caught between the two groups, grateful I was hidden by shadows but without any place to retreat to safety.

Where was the rest of the army? The entire scene made no sense.

No sight or sound came from the king's suite. Was Kadesh lying inside bleeding, dying? Had they assassinated him in his sleep? Was Sariba's king, my beloved, gone without warning, without any battle at all?

Even before I could cry out with grief, rage filled my belly. We were not going to lose the war by a skirmish with a few soldiers right here inside the palace. I slid my sword out from my belt and gripped it with both fists.

The struggling men breathed heavily, sweat and fear reeking. I moved backward, searching for an escape when one of Kadesh's guards saw me crouching against the wall. "My lady!" he cried.

A Maachathite soldier heard him and swung around. I could see the outline of his profile, so close to me. Instinctively, I raised my sword and brought it down on top of his head as hard as I could. The impact was fierce. My bones vibrated, and my fingers turned numb from the impact.

His body went limp. Within seconds, the Sariba soldiers

had finished him off as well as the other foreign soldier.

"My lady," the guard repeated, staring at me with a dazed expression. Before I could respond, they charged forward to help their comrades at the other end of the hall. I flung myself toward the royal suite, but before I reached it, a shadow passed swiftly inside.

I screamed, but the shadow completely ignored me, did not even flinch for a moment. Someone with a distinct objective. Insight flashed through me. The other soldiers were a distraction for *this*. For this man to reach King Kadesh and take him out.

My heart hammered and my ears rang. Recklessly, I leaped forward and ducked inside, clinging to the wall of the suite's foyer.

I wiped my sweaty hands on my shift and gripped my sword tighter. When I rushed into the study, the doors slammed against the wall. I held my breath, my eyes roving the room. Fat candles sat in glazed bowls, their flames low, keeping the room dusky.

Was I too late? No one seemed to be here in the main room.

Heavy breathing came from the interior of the bathing area. Kadesh *was* awake. And aware. He must have gone into hiding when he heard the alarm raised and the sounds of fighting.

I flew across the room, sword raised, ready to clash with the shadow I'd seen pass inside only moments ago. My breath was knocked out of me when I stumbled over the out flung arm of a palace guard lying motionless near the doorway of the bathing area.

The sounds of grunting and fighting came to my ears. Shafts of moonlight spilled onto the floor from the high windows, and the scene appeared in the silvery light before me. Kadesh was locked in a two-man battle, his sword held against the weapon of an assassin dressed completely in black, his face masked.

The two swung at each other with a strength and fury that was breathtaking. The assassin was an enormous man and highly skilled. I would never stand a chance against him. Despite my relief to see Kadesh still alive, it was disturbing to see the enemy's blade creep closer to his neck or ribs with every stroke.

All at once, the assassin jerked Kadesh's sword from his grasp and picked him up by the throat, slamming him into the wall. He pulled down his scarf, spitting out his message. "This is your reply to King Horeb's surrender. He will claim your bride and your throne. Even if it means killing every one of your citizens."

Kadesh's face was remarkably calm even as he gasped for breath. His black eye patch had been ripped off. The scar on his face lit up in the starlight. He grappled with the man's arm around his throat, kicking and shoving while he tried to keep from passing out.

"Horeb sends someone else to do his killing," he choked out. "He must be afraid to confront me himself."

The assassin laughed. "He's too wise to dirty his hands.

When you're gone, he will sweep in and claim it all. We all go home wealthy."

"That's Horeb's lie to drag you across the desert." Kadesh's eyes flicked to mine without giving away my presence. "Where are my guards?" he asked.

"Dead."

"If it's me you want then leave them alone." Kadesh was giving me time to reach him without the assassin knowing I was sneaking up behind him.

I slid my fingers along the edge of my sword to be sure it was in position, coming closer with each step while I reached for my dagger with the other hand.

Before my next breath, the assassin whirled about, hearing my footsteps, and my heart sank.

"Ah, the princess reveals herself," the Assyrian said with a barking laugh, dropping a half-dead Kadesh to the floor.

While the man still laughed, I flicked my wrist and threw the knife at his chest, sinking it into his ribs. His eyes shot wide with surprise. Before he could react again, my sword was out from my belt, and I plunged it into his heart with both hands on the grip.

The assassin's lips moved, and a gurgling noise spewed from his mouth as he slid to the floor in a heap.

From the tile, Kadesh gasped, swallowing as he tried to suck in air. "Jayden—"

I hurried over to him and knelt, checking the back of his head where he'd fallen. "Don't speak," I ordered him.

"I can't believe—" he began again.

"Stop it. You're going to have bruises on your throat. Let me get a cold cloth."

Within seconds, the royal suite was filled with guards and one of the army lieutenants. "The rest of the enemy assassins are dead," the lieutenant announced.

The men halted, staring wide-eyed at the dead man slumped on the floor in a pool of blood, his sword still in his grip.

"This one failed, too," Kadesh said weakly as I forced him to sip from a goblet of water.

Before I knew it, my legs failed me. I found myself lying next to Kadesh on the cool tiled floor, dizzy and disoriented, every limb shaking like a leaf in a fierce wind.

A voice spoke from across the room. "Dawn will be here in two hours." It was Jonah, the scout. "I'm ready to leave, my lord."

"Are there any others still in the palace?" Kadesh asked. "Did any escape?"

The lieutenant answered, "They're all dead. Six total. Five to kill the guards by your doors and set a fire to create a diversion, and the assassin to kill you."

"One of my guards is dead," I spoke up. "Down the hall from my bedroom door. I discovered him when I smelled smoke."

A flash of sorrow crossed Kadesh's face. "Those four guards—I was sending them down to you. The entire skirmish only lasted a few minutes. But I was caught by surprise when the sixth man sneaked into my suite as I was gathering my weapons."

Slowly, Kadesh rose to his feet, then helped me up, holding me steady with an arm tight around my shoulders. I tried not to think about the man I'd just killed.

"It's done, then," Kadesh said decisively. "Make sure the rest of the palace residents are fine. Dispatch new guards to every entrance and bedroom. Send a runner to the barracks to inform General Naham about what happened here. I request his presence as soon as he can dress. It doesn't look like anybody will be getting any further sleep tonight. I advise the household to pray the poisoned wells are successful to give us extra time to prepare. Hopefully, dozens of our enemy will fall ill and succumb to death."

He broke off when a lean older man staggered into the room, held up by two pale-faced servants while Kadesh's elderly body servant hovered behind.

My breath scraped at my throat. "Father!" I cried out.

"He'll be fine, but he needs to lie down," said the manservant moving to confer with the king while the others helped my father onto a sofa.

I knelt by my father's side and brushed a hand along his forehead. His color was as gray as a thunderstorm. He was breathing shallowly, but alive. "What happened to him?"

"I understand that he walked out to the desert tonight to try to talk to Horeb," Kadesh said. "The scouts surrounding the camp refused to take him to Horeb's tent. He was heartbroken. He thought he could talk reason with Horeb and stop the war."

"We're lucky he's alive," I murmured.

A knock came at the door and the general of Sariba's army entered. His headscarf was a deep magenta. Medals decorated his crisply cut coat, worn tight over a tunic and trousers. His belt held a long sword as well as two daggers.

Kadesh was curt. "How did they breach the walls, General Naham? I was nearly assassinated in my bed tonight. A spy of Horeb's lies in that corner in his own blood."

"Sire, they didn't breach the walls," the general said in a peculiar tone.

The room seemed to hold its breath. "How?" Kadesh demanded. "If not over the walls or through the city, do you mean—?" he broke off as understanding flooded his face.

General Naham nodded soberly.

Kadesh gave a loud, frustrated sound, running a hand through his sweaty hair. "This changes everything if they came through the tunnels."

I glanced between the two men. "Wouldn't they need to breach the walls of the city to reach any tunnels under the palace?"

Kadesh shook his head. "The tunnels twist under the mountains from the temple to the palace."

I nearly choked, realizing that he meant the same tunnels Tijah and Jasmine had taken me through from behind the waterfall to the temple. Which meant that Aliyah could use the tunnels from the temple straight to Kadesh's suite. "Why aren't they blocked off?"

"The tunnels can't be blocked off. They serve too many purposes—but they are supposed to be guarded at all times."

"I'm sure Aliyah had the guards killed," I said. "She knows the palace's habits and forces. How easy for her to escort Horeb's army straight to you."

General Naham said, "The foreigners infiltrated with a small envoy to ascertain how easy—or difficult—our defenses are to overcome."

"So Horeb's army isn't in the streets of Sariba yet?" Kadesh said coldly.

The general shook his head, watching Kadesh's face chiseled with anger. "Even as we speak, Sariba's army is on the walls of the city to protect it."

"Aliyah sent Horeb's spies through the tunnels to assassinate you, Kadesh," I told him evenly.

"If tonight's infiltration had been successful, the war would have been over before it even began. Aliyah had only to wait for a signal to enter the palace, find my dead body, and snatch the throne." Kadesh whirled on his feet, anger rippling out from his body in waves. *Just that easy.*

General Naham narrowed his eyes. "I believe tonight was merely a strike to intimidate us. Too bad Horeb lost his best spies on a suicide mission."

Kadesh lifted his chin and our eyes locked. We were thinking the same thing. Softly, he said, "The Queen of Sheba was right. And I failed to act."

"It's not too late," I told him. "I would gladly volunteer if you need an assassin—"

"No!" Kadesh said, his eyes widening at what I was implying.

"I've stood in her temple apartment," I said boldly. "I can even scale the wall," I added with a half smile.

Uncle Josiah's voice spoke from the doorway, where he had appeared from the shadows. "You may not be queen yet, Jayden, but I can't think of anyone more worthy of the role."

"The only reason Horeb's armies lie in wait to decimate us is because of me. People have already died. I will kill Aliyah, or I will kill Horeb. That is my responsibility. King Ephrem gave it to me. We both heard it."

Kadesh snapped a finger at his general. "Send a platoon to guard the entrance and exit to the tunnel. Horeb's soldiers will *never* come into the city again."

"And I will go out with Jonah to poison the springs," I added in a louder voice. "That plan *has* to work if Sariba stands a chance at living to fight again. We're outnumbered."

General Naham winced, glancing at the guards and servants standing nearby who didn't deserve to hear the odds we were up against. "Jonah goes alone," he said in a steely tone.

I interrupted. "Jonah will need backup. Someone to watch for the enemy while he gets to the springs. After this attempt on your life tonight, Kadesh, I want to go more than ever. I have to go while you assemble your army."

"That mission is far too dangerous, Jayden. I want you safely in the palace."

"And we've so recently seen how safe the palace is," I said pointedly.

Kadesh shook his head, clenching his fists in frustration. "General Naham, send two soldiers with Jonah," he ordered.

The General must have seen the look on my face because he didn't speak at first.

"A soldier can't move as quietly as I can," I told the room.

A voice—Asher—spoke from the back of the room. "She just took out your assassin, King Kadesh."

"I have to go. You need everyone here to prepare for the first battle. Let me do *something*."

"As if saving my life tonight weren't enough?" he said with a brief laugh.

"I have no doubt you would have killed him." I reached for Kadesh's hand, pressing my lips against his palm. "Most importantly, I'm a desert girl. I know how to move among the sand and rocks with stealth. I know how to become the wind or the rocks. Jonah and I will perform this task so that your first day of battle is successful."

Kadesh gave a sigh. "I can't seem to argue with you anymore." He lifted his head toward the scout, Jonah. "Bring back my betrothed alive and a gold coin bonus will be yours."

Jonah bowed deeply and the room seemed to exhale.

"Bury Horeb's dead. Clean up the blood. Then get some sleep before the night is completely over if you can," Kadesh said wearily to the guards still standing at attention, even as a cock crowed despite the darkness still engulfing the city. "We meet midmorning to finalize our attack for tomorrow."

17

When I returned to my suite to dress in my dark clothes again, my handmaidens had come out of hiding and were sitting on their beds in their nightgowns, Tijah whispering and Jasmine signing her thoughts to her sister with her hands. Seeing them together made me homesick, but I had to brush the nostalgia aside.

My fingers fumbled with nerves. I dreaded going back out on the desert, but I hoped with only me and Jonah we would be as unobtrusive as a salt scrub.

A knock came at the door and a messenger entered. "A message from Erina at the temple, my lady," he began.

Erina, Tijah and Jasmine's mother. It was highly unusual that she would send a message by courier to me. "Go on," I said.

"She wants to make sure her daughters are here at the palace, safe."

"Of course they are. You may reassure her of that."

The man went on to read off a list of names, and Tijah turned white.

"Do you recognize these people's names?" I asked her.

She nodded, her words coming out in jerks. "My aunt— my mother's sister—her husband and children—my cousins."

"What do these names mean?" I asked the messenger.

"The family was part of a group killed by the enemy on their way to safety in the foothills."

Tijah burst into tears. I took her cold hands in mine and rubbed them while she sobbed. Jasmine had read the boy's lips, and silent tears rolled down her face.

Horeb was killing innocent people. Not soldiers, not warriors, but citizens escaping to the caves they used for summer homes. Land they tilled for personal gardens, using the natural springs of the mountains.

"I'm so sorry," I said to Tijah, my arms around her. Jasmine buried her head in my chest, whimpering. I lifted my eyes to the ceiling, praying that Aliyah wouldn't take the same revenge when I thwarted her sacrificial ceremony.

When I returned from the poisoning mission, I would sleep a few hours and then make final plans to figure out how to save Sahmril from the temple sacrifice.

"You'll be safe here at the palace," I told my maids. "Naomi has invited you girls to have luncheon at her suite with her servants. Everyone needs to take their minds off the coming battles. If I'm not back in time, please go without me."

Jonah appeared at the door before Tijah could protest. "Are you ready, my lady?" he asked.

"I'll meet you at the stables in a few minutes." I returned to the dressing room and quickly pulled on the black pair of trousers I'd worn the night before for our scouting expedition.

A roughhewn tunic went over my head. A black sash knotted around my waist and then my sword belt. Dagger in a sheath on the side of my leg. Pulling my hair up into a knot on top of my head again, I covered it with a dark headscarf and then wrapped it about my neck, tucking the ends into my cloak.

Down at the stables, Jonah had horses ready.

We rode silently, passing hundreds of camels and goats out to pasture on the eastern plains of Sariba. Far from where Horeb was camped on the opposite end of the valley, and guarded against marauders from Horeb's soldiers. Sariba's caravan camels were protected at all costs. A bounty Horeb was probably salivating to plunder.

My legs ached by the time we skirted the temple. I'd done more riding the past few days than I ever had in my life, and I wasn't used to the saddle of a horse.

We continued east and took a path that cut across the bottom of the mountains. A circuitous route, but one that wouldn't lead us directly to Horeb's camp.

There was no time to walk. We had to get in and out quickly and then race back to the city, but pockets of trees and shrubs along the rise and fall of the earth helped keep us invisible.

When we came out from a dry river bottom, I gulped down a swig of water.

Less than half a league ahead was the camp of Horeb's armies, a familiar but ominous sea of tents and men.

Jonah's arm shot out to keep me at his side. "There are cooks and guards still at the campsites. We need to walk in from here."

We tied our horses behind a copse of bushes and climbed over the rocks, slipping through a ravine and approaching a series of yawning, black shadows—caves.

I pulled the scarf over my nose, speculating about whether I could find the caves that held the sepulcher of Kadesh's parents' bodies. A deep ache lay heavy inside my chest when I thought about his loss.

"Here," Jonah whispered, slipping inside one of the stone hollows.

Pausing only a moment to let our eyes adjust, we moved along the dusty floor. Soon we reached a stream of water cutting a path along the ground, which then disappeared into the rock.

"Where does the water go?" I asked, barely speaking above a murmur.

"This spring leads to three wells along the lower ridge of hills. The springs are the reason our enemy camped here."

"Will the poison affect the city's water supply?"

He shook his head. "Sariba's water comes from its own underground city springs, actually. Fed by the lakes and rivers you pass to climb up to the Temple of Sariba. The city is well situated with indoor plumbing because of natural cisterns underneath the tunnels. The cisterns are a constant source of water. In fact, these springs will dilute the poison after a few days, if not within hours."

"Why did Kadesh ask for the citizens to collect water, then?"

"I believe it was a precaution, and probably wise. Especially if the enemy invades the city or lays siege and cuts off the water supply."

"We should put all of the poison in then," I said decisively. "If it kills the Maachathites and Assyrians faster, so be it."

Jonah lifted an eyebrow as though surprised by my ruthless words, but he didn't speak, merely pulled out the package of hemlock he'd been carrying in his pack.

I knelt on the cool stone floor of the cave and helped him break it into pieces, grinding the flakes of herbs with my fingers to break it apart. The dark green herb floated away into the chilly water.

By the time we were done, I was anxious to be gone. Paranoia was setting in. Leaving the relative safety of the cave and returning to the desert where we might run into Horeb's scout was enough to immobilize me.

Without speaking, we moved to the entrance, a hazy dawn pouring in along the opposite wall from where we stood in shadow. Peering around the jagged rock to make sure we were alone, I finally moved forward and caught the reins of my horse—just as a man in a foreign uniform ran straight for me.

Before I could flee, he grabbed me and forced me to my

knees. I fumbled for my dagger, but he shoved me to the dirt and placed a foot on my chest, pinning my arms to my sides so I couldn't move.

The soldier, a Maachathite, laughed. "I saw your shadow, girl."

"I'm not a girl," I sputtered.

His chuckling turned to sudden, gasping gurgles when Jonah plunged his sword straight through the man's back, puncturing his heart and shooting forward through his chest. The spy's eyes froze, bright red blood dribbling from his nostrils.

"Get up, my lady," ordered Jonah. "Run!"

Scrambling to my feet, I untied my horse, swung myself up, and dug a heel into the animal's side. We took off at a full gallop.

My scarf whipped about my face, stinging my cheeks. Wind dried my eyes, bringing sharp gasps from my mouth. Jonah's horse kept pace with mine while I hung on with all my strength. The leather reins burned the skin of my hands, but I'd gladly let the halter tear off all my skin if it meant I returned to the palace safely.

Finally, I dared a glance behind but we were alone.

Once we entered the forest, we slowed to allow the horses to breathe. Their coats were lathered with foam, eyes rolling from the frantic speed.

"Good girl," I murmured to Hara. "We're almost home."

Birds chattered in the sycamores above us. As though we were a world apart and there wasn't about to be hundreds of men fighting and dying within sight of our location in a few hours.

A little while later I said, "That spy is dead, correct?"

"Yes. I just hope nobody finds him for a while. They could trace our steps to the mouth of the spring and deduce our mission. And ban the army from using the wells."

"If so, all of this will be for naught."

Jonah nodded soberly.

At last the eastern entrance to the city was within sight. Guards opened the giant bronzed gates and we galloped straight to the stables. After I slid off my mount, a groom was already nickering to my horse while I limped my way to the door, still gasping for air.

When I departed the stable, Jonah nodded to me without speaking. I watched him disappear into the streets, presumably back to his platoon. I knew nothing about him, only that he had heeded a royal call and fulfilled his duty.

I sagged against a post and sipped at my water pouch for a few moments before taking the side streets and heading back to the palace.

"Walk," I muttered, anxiety setting in as I passed empty shops and quiet streets. Everyone was in hiding. I didn't think I could stand enduring the hours awaiting the first battle tomorrow.

Even though my handmaidens and the rest of Kadesh's family were safe within the palace—the most secure spot in the city—I started to run.

18

After a quick wash, I dropped into bed for several hours. But when I woke, the sound of troops practicing under the direction of General Naham and the Sariba captains came through the window. Shouts and the thunder of horses' hooves, including the ringing of the metal forgers fixing swords and knives and fierce metal-tipped spears.

I lay in bed, my eyes burning, watching the sun rise toward noon. A moment later, I shoved back the bedding and staggered to my feet. Tomorrow night was the temple sacrifice, and I needed to get myself together, along with a few committed soldiers, to help me rescue Sahmril and Leila.

Raw nerves chewed at my gut while I took a deep cleansing bath, scrubbing away the dirt and sand from the night.

I also hoped Horeb's men were sick as dogs right now, but we wouldn't know how the poison had affected them until tomorrow's dawn, when they were crawling out of their beds and the Sariba army attacked with fury.

My maids and I were silent while I dressed. We were all thinking and hoping the same thing. "I'm going to Lady Naomi's suite. If I stay here alone in my room," I said, "I'll go crazy waiting."

My maids nodded, looking relieved at not having to entertain me or watch me pace the floors.

A quick brush through my drying hair and a pinch to my cheeks to get rid of the ashen color, and I went to find Aunt Naomi. I needed my mother badly. I wished I could talk to my father about Sahmril, but he would be heartbroken to hear of Sahmril's capture by Aliyah, especially after foolishly walking out to the desert to try and talk to Horeb.

Naomi was the closest thing to my mother that I had. She would be unbiased and perhaps have more experience with the temple rituals after watching Kadesh's mother sacrifice herself to the Sariba Goddess two years ago.

At first, Naomi's maids were reluctant to disturb her, but then her voice came through the door. "Jayden, please, come in!"

"I don't want to intrude," I told her as the door to her private bedroom closed behind me. A rush of orchid perfume wafted on the air.

"I've finished bathing." Aunt Naomi had one arm raised while her maid slipped a dress over her shoulders. "It seems so frivolous, doesn't it? Putting on jewels and glitter for dinner when an army sits on our doorstep preparing to annihilate us all?"

I glanced at the maids hanging on to our every word. "Could we speak privately?"

"Of course," Naomi said, nodding at her servants.

A few moments later we sat in her sitting room, hand-painted linens on the couches and bowls of fresh-cut flowers on the tables. Beyond the sheer curtains, the air was still, bringing the sound of battalion drills from the upper barrack yards.

Naomi brushed her damp hair from her forehead. "I shouldn't have said that about the enemy ready to annihilate us. My maids will be up all night worrying. But we'll be safe here in the center of the city."

"Horeb's troops would have to get past our entire army to reach us, but that's why I've come. I think we should have our rooms double guarded until this is over. Unless Kadesh has already ordered it. We believe we're immune to Horeb's army getting past our soldiers, but I was in the city of Mari last summer. The citizens there thought they were safe until King Hammurabi invaded and burned the palace down."

"Mari lies exposed on the river," Naomi said. "At least we have the security of the cliffs and hills. Much more difficult for an army to maneuver about. The fighting will be far away."

Knowledge of Aliyah's treason welled up. "Did Uncle Josiah tell you about the letter that arrived from the Queen of Sheba two days ago?"

Naomi shook her head. "A letter from the queen?"

"I met her when we passed through Sa'ba several weeks ago." I relayed the news of Aliyah's alliance with Horeb. "To make a pact with Horeb to destroy the very people who love and trust her is treachery of the highest order."

With a grave expression, Naomi smoothed the folds of her dress. "Is it truly that dire?"

I didn't want to answer her question, but I did anyway. "Yes, it is," I said soberly, and then changed the subject, trying to get my nerve up to tell her about the sacrificial ceremony. "I'm still unfamiliar with the palace's layout as well as the city, but Kadesh plans to take the fight away from the city. Even so, I think we should take every precaution here. I don't trust Aliyah."

"I don't know the woman very well. I've only ever seen her at state dinners, but I always found it peculiar that a woman who would inherit the throne of Sa'ba would work at the temple."

"You know the summer solstice ceremonies are being held tomorrow evening," I finally stated, lifting my eyes to hers.

Naomi reached out to clasp my hand. "Please don't go up there. It's much too dangerous to be away from the palace right now."

"I received a personal invitation from the Goddess herself."

Naomi's mouth set in an infuriated line. "The midsummer's full moon ceremony is the one thing I cannot abide about the temples of Ashtoreth and Sariba and Ba'al."

"I know," I whispered, plucking at the filigree of my dress as the words came out halting and stiff. "My little sister, Sahmril, has been chosen to be Sariba's sacrificial lamb."

"What?!" The shock on Naomi's face was unmistakable. "Aliyah would sacrifice your own blood?"

"She hates me. I stole Kadesh and the crown from her. My older sister, Leila, was ordained High Priestess three days ago, the morning after our wedding destruction. Relatives of a High Priestess are always a more powerful sacrifice, and Sahmril is the most beautiful, perfect child you ever saw, which makes her death even better." I stopped. The horror of it all knocked the air out of my lungs.

Aunt Naomi took my hands in hers. "We must stop it somehow. What can I do to help, Jayden?"

I shrugged helplessly. "I'm not sure. I have no idea what to expect. For now, please pray that I'll think of a way to save her." I unclasped my hand and rose. "One thing I do know. I need to sharpen my dagger and sword."

"Weapons won't stop Aliyah. You'll only get yourself killed by the temple guards."

"I don't have any other options. I'd rather turn Sahmril over to the nobleman and his wife who purchased her than give her to Aliyah."

"Aliyah took advantage of Kadesh's disappearance and Ephrem's failing health. She won people's hearts, making them fear famine and poverty if they didn't pay tribute and obeisance to the Goddess." She kissed my cheek. "I wish Kadesh's parents could have known you." She paused, her eyes filling. "His mother was my sister."

"I didn't realize that! I'm so sorry. Her loss has affected all of you in so many ways."

"As your own mother's passing," Naomi said with empathy.

"At first, I had thought Uncle Josiah was King Ephrem's

younger brother and would inherit the Sariba crown."

"No, Kadesh's father was Ephrem's brother and heir because Ephrem and his wife were unable to have children. Ephrem schooled Kadesh for this day. I'm so pleased to watch him crowned, despite the sober circumstances."

"King Ephrem seemed to have had uncanny insight."

Every time I thought of the dead king's last words to me, I grew chilled. That *I* needed to be the one to kill Horeb when the time came—so that no one could question the veracity of the claim and his armies could be convinced to lay down their weapons.

"From that sudden shiver, I suspect Uncle Ephrem told you something that frightened you."

"I think you lived here with him for so long you've picked up his talent of intuition. Or perhaps it's the mother in you." A fierce longing for my own mother washed over me and Naomi's eyes filled with compassion. "Where were you and Kadesh's mother raised?"

"We're all originally from Dedan, which is a close ally of Sariba's royal family. Binding the two families was highly favorable."

"We passed Dedan on our journey here. Kadesh told me that forts are being built to protect the caravans and provide supplies. How long have you lived in Sariba, then?"

"I came with my sister more than twenty years ago to be her personal handmaiden. I didn't want her to live in a strange land alone. Nobody ever expected Kadesh's parents to—" Naomi turned away to hide her sudden tears.

"I don't mean to bring back terrible memories."

"No, my dear, you've done nothing wrong. I try to remember my sister when she was strong and happy. The most beautiful and intelligent woman in the room. She and her husband would have made a grand king and queen. Just as you and Kadesh will."

I glanced down at my lap. "I'm afraid Kadesh and I are not always of the same mind."

"You'll grow together. It happens to all couples, and your marriage hasn't even begun. Don't think it's a bad omen. Despite Kadesh's wisdom and experience, trust your own heart. He'll listen to you. You may be right as often as he is. Especially in the case of Aliyah. A woman has instincts when it comes to other females." Naomi rose. "Now, come help me with a task I've been dreading."

I followed her out the door. Gently, she linked arms and we found ourselves at the door to King Ephrem's empty rooms.

"Josiah asked that I go through King Ephrem's personal belongings. I need to catalog his personal effects and clothing and make sure all is safely stowed and out of reach from potential thieves or marauders."

I glanced at her questioningly.

"Fine linens and jewels are too much of a temptation," the older woman said ruefully. "Kadesh will inherit the crown jewels, Ephrem's royal robes, and armor and weapons. Older clothing will go to the poor. After this war is over, Kadesh and Josiah will go through his possessions more thoroughly, but my husband asked if we would make a first attempt at organizing."

"It will help to pass the time," I said. Even so, my stomach was queasy thinking about what was to come the next night, and I was terrified that I'd be successful in rescuing Sahmril.

King Ephrem's elderly body servant had several chests on tables in the quiet room for us to go through. Before Naomi began to pick though the first chest of clothing, she squeezed my hands in hers.

"I know you're distracted and I feel guilty having you help me with this mindless task. What will you do? Is there a plan forming in your mind?"

"Leila suggested that I come to her first. That before the sacrifice begins we three sisters be together one last time before we say good-bye and send Sahmril off to her death."

Naomi recoiled at my words. "Jayden, I had no idea your older sister was so willing—so controlled by Aliyah."

"I'm thinking that perhaps I can make that meeting my chance to take Sahmril and escape before the ceremony."

"The temple will be crawling with Aliyah's personal guards—"

"And the Egyptian priests," I added.

Naomi strode to the open double doors and relayed a message to the guards on duty.

A few minutes later, a patrol of four guards appeared, and Naomi spoke with them while I continued to stack an entire chest with King Ephrem's bed and bath linens.

Aunt Naomi placed her hand on top of mine. "These are my personal palace guards, Jayden. I've requested that they give you whatever help you need. Come back with your sister. Both of them if you can."

I gazed into her face. "I'm so grateful to you. Kadesh is also sending a few soldiers with me. If all they can do is open up a path for me and Sahmril to escape before—" I stopped, unable to speak about the death Aliyah had planned for me, too.

When we finished three chests of King Ephrem's personal effects, we separated to prepare for dinner. Late afternoon light was already disappearing, shadows filling the corners of the gardens.

When Naomi embraced me, I clung to her, homesick, wishing this was already over. The anticipation for the ceremonies, and tomorrow's first day of battle, was going to kill me.

19

Dinner was a quiet meal, preoccupation for the first battle at dawn leaving little desire for speaking of mundane things. The setting sun cast shafts of red, like blood, along the distant mountains. An omen of what was to come.

I was having a difficult time eating anything. Finally, I pushed my plate away and lifted my eyes. Kadesh was watching me, his own dinner barely touched.

"You need to eat," I told him. "You need your strength for tomorrow. And more sleep."

Servants cleared the plates and bowls, pouring wine and strong, hot tea.

"Are you ready?" I asked, reaching for Kadesh's hand.

He gripped my fingers. "That's a question heavy with potential for both arrogance and regret."

"I'm worried about you."

"We're ready. I promise."

"And do you promise to go to bed early?" I asked. "It's been three days with little rest."

"Sleep while you plot to save your sisters? I have a final meeting with General Naham and our captains tonight. I hope to attend the ceremony tomorrow as well."

I glanced out the window at the deepening dusk. "You can't be in two places at once, Kadesh, and your army needs you. It's imperative that the first day of battle leaves Horeb crippled. I have Naomi's guards and yours—and Asher. We'll steal Sahmril away before the sacrifices even begin. It will all be over quickly and I'll be back at the palace with her before you know it."

When Aunt Naomi and Uncle Josiah departed for their own suite, I watched them leave with longing for it all to be over. It had been a long afternoon of pacing and thinking, despite the hours I'd spent with Naomi.

A sudden noise at the door startled all of us. The men jumped up from their chairs, pulling out weapons with a speed that defied my eyes. I slid my dagger from its strap and curled my fingers around the hilt.

The door burst open. Two soldiers dragged a figure between them, a slight dirty person with long strands of filthy hair underneath a black headscarf. The captive struggled against his confines. "Take me to your king!" the voice gurgled.

Asher came forward, one boot on the captive's arm. "You

are already before the king though you deserve nothing. Now bow you heathen!"

The guards pushed the prisoner down onto the floor. "We found him sneaking into Sariba with a patrol of men and camels."

"Spies of Horeb?" Asher asked.

Kadesh stared hard, not uttering a word before striding toward the trespasser lying facedown on the floor. Leaning down, he snatched the headscarf from off the spy and jerked the person's head up, kneeling on one knee to peer into the face.

The captive's hair fell in wild clumps, obscuring his features. With the blade of his knife, Kadesh carefully lifted the clump of hair away.

Big dark eyes stared back at him, and then the wisp of a smile cracked the dry lips. "My king," the voice croaked.

Kadesh jumped to his feet. "Lift him up!" he ordered. "Or I should say *she*. How her small caravan managed to slip past Horeb's camp in the middle of the night is beyond me."

I stared so hard my eyes seemed to bulge. There was something about the height, the figure under the bulky traveling clothes, the way the person held her head that reminded me of someone else.

Kadesh stretched out his hand and lifted the intruder to a standing position. The woman shook back her hair and straightened her shoulders.

The Queen of Sheba gave her first genuine smile.

"Your Majesty," I said, curtsying to the monarch while confusion raced through my mind. "However did you travel? Why are you—" I stopped, thinking it was probably best if I didn't call out the bedraggled and dirty state she was in. Desert travel was never pretty, but she was positively a wreck.

The queen seemed to read my thoughts. "I thought it best to disguise myself in case my envoy fell into the hands of Horeb's men."

General Naham cleared his throat. "Our scouts reported earlier that Horeb's armies are rather—should I say ill today? It appears the poison administered to their water supply was successful. We hope it's a blow they can't recover from."

"Poison," the queen repeated. "A clever ploy."

"It was Jayden's idea," Asher said, his face on mine.

"Good girl," the queen said, nodding her approval. "Ever since his armies came through my kingdom, I've been frantic to get to you. He's got nearly twice your numbers. Have you sent Horeb a letter yet?"

"My first one was answered with an assassination attempt last night." Kadesh leaned over his desk and handed a copy to the queen. "And here is a copy of the one I sent earlier this afternoon when we learned of the effects of the poison. We don't know exact numbers of ill or dead men, but would to God they all die by tomorrow morning."

The Queen of Sheba studied Kadesh. "You do know that's wishful thinking. Probably only the first couple hundred men got the most concentrated dose. As soon as Horeb realized their water source was contaminated he would have ordered his armies to cease drinking."

Kadesh gave a jerk of agreement with his chin, his jaw clenching. "I only want to spare my people the death of their husbands and fathers and brothers."

"Of course you do," the queen said soberly. "As we all do."

"Let me help you to one of the guest suites, my queen," I told her, coming forward. I nodded toward one of the maids clearing off the dinner dishes. "Please prepare a bath and a handmaiden to help the queen."

"I beg your pardon, my cousin," Kadesh said. "I'm still in shock that you're actually here. You've traveled a great distance at great risk. Is there something I should know right away?"

"Ever since I saw you weeks ago, I have been unsettled in my mind and heart. That was the reason for my letter to you. Even after sending the letter, I couldn't sit in my palace and do nothing. I had to come. After all," she gave Kadesh a tight smile, "Aliyah is my sister. And you are my cousin. I had to try to intercede, to help in any way I can. Sisters are a tricky business."

"Especially when they've recently declared themselves a Goddess incarnate," I said.

The queen's eyebrows shot up. "She's taken it that far? I understand that Ephrem has gone the way of all the earth," she continued soberly. "I had hoped to see him one last time, but I'm glad you are king, Kadesh, and that you were crowned immediately. You will do well with your new queen."

"Oh, my lady, I'm not queen yet," I said with a small laugh.

She looked at both our faces in surprise. "I see that we have a lot of catching up to do—and very quickly. Kadesh—"

She was interrupted by a messenger at the door.

"Have you got a reply from our enemy?" Kadesh asked, moving forward as the man, still heavily breathing after a hard ride, bowed and handed over a thin, smooth stone, wrapped in linen. "Thank you." He gestured to Asher to make sure the man was escorted out with extra coin in his pockets.

The room was dead quiet while Kadesh read the words. He looked up, anger etching his features. "Horeb of the Nephish has rejected all overtures and recommendations. He states that he didn't travel two thousand miles only to give up. He will never surrender as long as he has breath and Jayden and I still live. His final words are these: *My greatest ambition is not only to see your death and claim what rightfully belongs to me but to take your throne, your crown, and your title. This land, this people, this wealth will belong to me. For now and forever.*"

Kadesh's eyes found mine across the room. A look of a thousand sorrows passed between us. No matter what Sariba did, or how valiantly our people fought, Horeb would not give up. And he would have Aliyah with the power given to her by the Egyptian magicians as well as the control she held over the people to secure and retain Sariba's throne.

I watched the faces of the staff and guards turn pale. General Naham was furious, but remained stoic, awaiting his next order.

The Queen of Sheba's expression was taut. "It appears that your request for surrender has been rejected. The King of the Nephish dares to laugh at you. He is a man without any decorum for the rules of engagement or the rules of war."

"He has no moral code," I added. "Like any man lusting to conquer his enemy."

"No mercy, no prisoners," General Naham said. "Even in tribal warfare there is bounty to be split, losses to share, and a modicum of respect for the tribe you fight. All who survive return home at nightfall to peace. Not so in this case."

The queen took the letter and scanned the lines herself. She was intelligent enough to infer Horeb's underlying meanings—and the woman he aligned with. "Will you finish them off in tomorrow's battle, Kadesh?"

"He still has more soldiers then we do, a great many more. And the men who survived the diluted dose of hemlock will get over their illness to fight, too."

"What shall we do now?" I asked.

"General Naham, if Horeb dares to un-yield to reason, we will unleash all of the might of Sariba. Tomorrow we use all of our troops and a shock strategy."

General Naham slammed his hand against a table. "The rogue Nephish king proposes fighting until the death of us all. His arrogance knows no bounds. But know this. We will crush him and all three of his armies."

"I'm not going to allow him to pick off my army and the citizens of Sariba one by one," Kadesh said firmly.

"It's as we suspected," the queen said. "Is it not? His letter says it plainly. Winner take all. Horeb is here not only to grab Sariba for his own but to conquer all the southern and western deserts and cities. He wants to rule and own everything."

"With Aliyah at his side as his queen," I added. "They have plotted this together, just as you predicted, my queen."

"Tell me what you've learned about my sister," the woman asked.

"It's not good. She anointed my older sister Leila as High Priestess and is keeping my little sister in captivity as the sacrifice to the Goddess tomorrow. Aliyah has gathered the citizens to her, and with war and death on their doorsteps they're too frightened to defy divinity. Magicians are also here from Egypt with their sorcery and spells. Aliyah is convinced she has *become* the Goddess. I watched the ceremony myself."

"My younger sister is now the Goddess?" the queen said thoughtfully, an amused smile on her lips. "Aliyah is the real reason I'm here, Kadesh. After you and Jayden left Sheba, more information came by way of the mountain men in my hills."

"Basim and his soldiers," I quickly told her. "They destroyed our wedding three nights ago and we nearly killed him. But he now fights for us."

The queen took a sudden breath of surprise. "And who managed that feat?"

"Jayden did," Asher interjected from across the room.

I shook my head, embarrassed. "It's a long story, my lady. So much has happened since we last talked."

"I also have the best spies in any kingdom. When I learned that Aliyah hired Basim's men, I had to come. Which meant Kadesh hadn't done the thing I'd most recommended."

A shiver ran along my spine in waves of unease.

"Jayden, don't play games with me. I suggested that Aliyah

20

I returned to my suite and was able to sleep for a few hours after all the excitement of the Queen of Sheba's surprise appearance. Long fingers of sunlight crawled across the floor when I reached her guest suite the next afternoon. Anticipation gripped at my chest.

A moment later, I was bowing before the queen. She was dazzlingly beautiful, even after the long, frantic journey. Her sleek dark hair was pulled up on either side of her head with pearled combs. Garnet earrings brushed against her neck. Her flowing dress was a deep magenta, the bodice sewn with stones of amethyst, carnelian, and topaz.

"I wanted to see you, Jayden, before we go up to the temple because I think you need to understand more about Aliyah if you are to fight her. If we all are to fight her properly."

"Does Kadesh know what you're about to tell me?" I asked.

She nodded. "Our families have known each other for two generations. Kadesh's parents and King Ephrem were friends with my parents. We have been allies for a long time to protect the Frankincense Trail. In fact, the rogue mountain men outside of Ma'rib work for me. Thus, I was disturbed by the news of Basim working for Horeb. At first, I thought about arresting them all and letting them hang for treason, but when I sent my city soldiers, they had disappeared from the mountains. Only their women and children were still there—reluctant to admit except under great pressure—that their men had crossed the eastern deserts toward Sariba."

"They were sent into the city to destroy our wedding," I told her. "To instill fear. Until that night we didn't know how terribly close they were. It was unsettling, to say the least. And Kadesh almost took the arrow that pierced Chemish."

"Horeb must have had spies that brought word of your pending marriage, and he had to stop it. For you are part of his and Aliyah's plan."

"I've been well aware of that for a long time," I said grimly. "I have wished many times that they would go off and find their own corner of the desert to rule and leave the rest of us alone. But I know that's a foolish dream."

"Other than Babylon, Sariba has the most wealth, and its remote location makes it relatively safe."

"If Horeb succeeds, there will never be peace here again."

The queen pressed a hand against my arm. "Trust Kadesh. He has a plan. One that will temporarily devastate, but one that will work in the end. He will win this war with your help and confidence. Give it to him."

"I will," I promised, realizing that I had shown my own doubts and fear too often.

"You're concerned that Kadesh shows too much empathy," the queen said kindly. "That he wants to be loved and that will cause him to appear weaker than he should. But I have confidence that he will rule well and fairly, whether that's kindness or an iron fist that needs to be meted out."

My face burned. She was exactly right. "Kadesh has refused to arrest Aliyah. That shows his compassion, his willingness to give someone the chance to change their ways."

"Except that my sister grows more powerful, more hateful."

"Where does her anger and this need to control come from?"

The single lamp on the table next to her cast a column of light across the queen's glossy black hair, the jewels twinkling while she clasped her hands in a pensive gesture.

"I'm afraid it's a torturous history. Aliyah and I have different mothers. My father loved my mother desperately. They married young—it was arranged, of course—but my mother was infatuated with him and wanted to marry him. I was born between several miscarriages. After several years the loss of her children turned my mother melancholy, prone to bouts of solitude. She began to push my father away."

I could hear the strain and sadness in the queen's voice.

"I was definitely closer to my father, and perhaps that didn't help her mental state. It certainly caused her loneliness to grow more deeply. It's difficult not to feel guilty. My mother's suffering to bear children was like a betrayal on both our parts. My presence and affection wasn't enough for her, so I ran to my father for comforts and attention and schooling. Which only caused my mother to withdraw even more, convinced I didn't love *her*."

I tightened my fist in my lap, afraid of what was coming.

"One of my mother's personal advisors paid her more attention than my father and I did. They grew closer. He was the only one able to bring her out of her dark moods. The only one who could make her laugh. I used to stare down from my bedroom window watching them walk and talk in the gardens. For months, I watched the subtle tenderness, the physical touches of affection, the small gifts of roses, or an extra sweet. I was only nine or ten and I wanted to stop it, but I had no idea how to bring her back to us. Of course, I felt guilty, as though it were my fault. Especially when she finally ran away to be with the man she had fallen in love with."

Impulsively, I reached out to take her cold fingers. "How terrible for your father."

"He was the king and she was his queen. To run away with another man couldn't be tolerated. She was stripped of her crown. She chose exile rather than prison. In the middle of the night, she disappeared. Without saying good-bye."

"Did you ever learn where she went?" I asked.

She shook her head. "I never saw her again and spent the rest of my childhood creating elaborate scenarios of her returning home to me. When I grew older I worried that my father had had her followed and killed so that she couldn't bring shame upon him, but I couldn't bring myself to actually believe it. Then he married a woman far removed from Sheba. The daughter of a prince from the city of Damascus. Miriam was kind but young. A year later, Aliyah was born. I doted on her. I loved her. She was the sister I'd always wanted. Aliyah helped me cope with my mother's loss. But when she became older, it became apparent that Aliyah had a devious streak. She fought for her way, always wanted the best of everything, and then set her sights on gaining education and wealth. She was desperate to go to Babylon to study, so I finally sent her there to live with distant cousins, if only to stop our constant arguing. Then we learned that after her studies she came to Sariba to study as a priestess. A decision my father was *not* pleased with at all. He begged her to come home. He promised to meet her every demand. Her own mother couldn't stand up to her and Aliyah was so spoiled that she showed disdain to her mother and my father."

"I heard a story about Aliyah and the death of the previous High Priestess," I said.

The queen nodded. "We did, too. When Aliyah finally came home, we found her cold and hard. Calculating. She charmed the household but she was quite ungenerous. When our father told her that I was to have the crown after his death, she screamed and ranted. She said terrible things about me and called my mother a whore for running off with another man. She was convinced that since her mother was currently married to the king *she* should inherit the throne, and not me at all. She began a campaign to turn Miriam against him. My father was torn between all three of us. It was not in his nature to conspire and accuse, and to withhold love by blackmail."

"But your father's decree is law. And you were his oldest child and heir long before he married Miriam. Aliyah can't argue with that. How could she hate you for that?"

The queen gave a curt laugh. "With Aliyah she can argue for any reason at all. Only her opinions and desire matter. But something else happened that turned Aliyah against me even more, despite the day my father crowned me as co-regent when a sudden illness overcame him."

I frowned at her, confused as to what could have made the situation any worse.

"You see, Aliyah was in love with my husband—my betrothed. We weren't married yet, but Aliyah wanted everything that I had. My husband never returned her affections, but she accused him of it and tried to put a wedge between us so that I would leave him. She spun a story of how he had jilted her. Aliyah's biggest weakness is her talent to weave an entire life made up of falsehoods.

"When we married, she threatened terrible things: suicide, blackmail, all created by a thousand lies. She's convinced that she has been dealt with wrongly, that her rightful inheritance has been stolen from her. When she left to return to Sariba to attend to her new role as High Priestess she told me that one day she would be the most powerful woman in all the world— and she would do anything to achieve it and demolish me in the process. Murder, blackmail, war, it doesn't matter."

"And she has nearly succeeded," I said, stunned by the

queen's story. "If Kadesh had stayed here and married her, he would probably be dead by now and she would rule Sariba."

"I'm convinced of it as well," the queen agreed. "I'm sure she's furious that you interfered with the merchant soldiers of Basim, bringing them to Sariba's loyalty. Aliyah likes to think everyone around her is stupid and that she can outwit us. But I know her too well."

"You don't know me that well, my sister," Aliyah's voice came from the doorway.

I sucked in a breath and placed my teacup on the tray, missing it completely. The ceramic cup shattered on the floor, but I couldn't take my eyes off Aliyah. She was attired in the richest pure white gown, her hair a glorious mane of ebony and gold dust. She'd come ready for the temple ceremonies that night. Somehow she'd learned that the queen was here. Did we have spies in the palace? The thought was not comforting.

"How did you get into the palace?" I demanded. "Kadesh forbid you from coming here."

Aliyah swept into the room. "Just because the king can't keep a tighter rein on his locked doors and guards, doesn't mean I won't take advantage of his weakness. Kadesh is so gullible and you're an even bigger fool than my sister, Jayden. I'm the Goddess, or have you forgotten? A little spell, a whiff of herbal concoctions and the soldiers and guards become warm butter in my hands. They know their true queen, and they obey."

"Drugged citizens aren't stalwart followers," I shot back at her. "You can't drug everyone."

"But I've got a plan. Which is more than I can say for you,

desert girl. You are no match for me. And you, my dear sister," Aliyah said with a laugh. "What delusions you have thinking you can come here to persuade me to a different path."

The Queen of Sheba came forward. I noticed how carefully she was trying not to get angry. "Aliyah, you know I care about you. What have you done to your heart that you can kill without impunity? To carry out sacrifices—"

"That's the whole point you continue to ignore," Aliyah said. "The Goddess *is* my soul and that gives me all power. When we sacrifice something we love, the Goddess will bless her people."

"Your rule is one of fear, not love," the queen said firmly. "Stop this war with Horeb before hundreds more die, including Horeb's armies."

"Sariba's army isn't as strong as my new ally. It won't be long before Horeb and I are united and rule not only Sariba but *your* land of Sheba as well as Babylon, Salem, and Damascus."

"It will take more than Egyptian magicians hypnotizing your potential subjects. There are powerful armies in all those lands, including the people of Philistia. You'll need an army of a hundred thousand to claim their wealth and become their ruler."

Aliyah shook her head wearily. "I've heard it all so many times. From you. From our father. From Kadesh. Men are tiresome, especially royal men with egos as long and wide as the Nile. I only tolerate the Egyptians because they give me their magical knowledge and incantations; the methods to subdue."

"You will lead a lonely life," the queen said, and I could

hear genuine sadness in her voice.

"And you, my sister," Aliyah went on, "by coming here you signed your own death decree. You've double-crossed and stolen from me long enough. You stole Basim and the men of Sa'ba from me with Jayden's interference. You thwart me at every turn! And now you will be punished." In a low voice, she added, "I once told you that I would have your husband and Sheba one day. And *today* is that day."

Before the queen could utter another word, Aliyah brought forth a slender, glittering dagger from the folds of her gown and lunged.

The queen put up her hands in defense and Aliyah's knife sliced down her palms. Blood dripped in ugly red lines, and the queen fell back against the cushions of the couch. Disbelief flashed across her face followed by terror. She was unarmed and so was I. My weapons were back in my suite.

I screamed for the servants, but they were no longer in the room.

Aliyah's features were ugly as she sliced at the queen's dress, ripping it into shreds while the queen fought her off with wild hands, but Aliyah was taller and stronger, pinning her to the couch with her knees.

Finally, I lifted a heavy ceramic pot from a table and launched myself toward Aliyah to smash it over her head. It crashed into large shards, and, even though she was dazed, she didn't fall unconscious.

I continued to scream for the guards while wrestling Aliyah for the knife.

Booted feet finally came down the hall, and a guard shouted. Instantly, Aliyah stepped out of my reach, pocketed the bloody knife and raced through the door, disappearing in the opposite direction. As if she had turned to smoke, a sign of the sorceress she had become.

I sank to my knees, shaking while the queen moaned from the shock of the attack. Then I jumped up and got linen and water to clean up her hands. The blood was overwhelming.

"Do you need stitches?" I asked. "I'll send for the physician."

"The cuts aren't deep."

"I'll help you bandage them."

I worked quickly, cutting linen and binding the fabric around her hands. "You'll need some turmeric for infection and a sleeping draught to ease the pain so you can sleep."

The queen sat silently. We were both distressed by the sudden attack, but anger began to boil inside me.

I noticed that the tea tray had been knocked over during the struggle. The liquid still warm, staining the carpet, seeping away as the queen's life had almost done. I refused to see it as a bad omen.

The queen rose to stand at the window, and I followed her gaze toward the lights beginning to appear on the temple hill. "Despite my dread that we would need to assassinate or imprison Aliyah, I left my family and kingdom to try to persuade my sister of my love for her. Truly I hoped she could be saved, and that the worst might be averted."

"We always hope, don't we," I said softly, more to myself

than anyone. Despite my revulsion toward Aliyah and the horror she planned to inflict on my sister Sahmril, I could see why the queen and Kadesh hoped the young woman could be persuaded to turn away from her envy and desire for revenge

The Queen of Sa'ba turned away from the window and there were tears of hopelessness in her eyes. I'd never seen her look so vulnerable. "I'm going with you to the summer solstice, Jayden, and we have no time to lose."

21

It didn't take me long to dress again in the seductive gown from three mornings ago when I'd gone to find Leila at the temple and witnessed her High Priestess anointing. I wore jewels, perfumes, and freshly dressed hair. Despite the distraction of dressing, I couldn't stop thinking about Sahmril, and I ached to hold her in my arms.

The Queen of Sheba and I procured horses from the stables, and soon we were galloping up the slopes of the forest, taking the paths straight to the temple columns and gated archway, the platoon of Naomi's guards going before us.

Wild thudding reverberations ignited the night when we drew close. Throngs of people shouting and singing and dancing.

"Are you ready, Jayden?" the queen asked. Briefly, she pressed my hand in hers as we moved forward.

Holding myself regally, I tried to assume the same air of poise and self-possession while we took the outer walkways that circled the sumptuous garden pavilions. Even though the evening was warm, I shivered.

A sphere of gold sat on the horizon. The solstice moon. Glowing as though the sun shone through from the far side.

The moon was so bright the temple hardly needed the tall spears of flaming sconces situated about the perimeter. Or the candle lamps hanging from every tree. There were even lights up along the terraces outlining the glittering walls and the temple's spires.

"Regardless of the sumptuous festivities and dancing," the queen observed, "there is an air of tension and fear. The people are here because Sariba is outnumbered by an enemy they do not know or understand. They've already lost several hundred men—their sons and brothers and fathers."

I stopped along the outer wall, sucking in a breath. "I can hardly blame them for clinging to something they hope will help ease their pain—or insure their country's success."

Melancholy swept over me when I saw the distant light from Horeb's campfires sparking against the blackness. The people here in the temple pavilions could see the enemy dotting the landscape. The random lights sprawled endlessly. Troops as numerous as the sands of the Irreantum Sea.

Putting a hand on the edge of the stone wall, I tried to steady myself. How could we possibly defeat them? Right now I had to focus. "All I want to do is get Sahmril out of here and go home."

The crowd was dense with citizens already drunk on dancing and goblets of wine.

A raucous couple bumped into me, spilling red wine along my sleeve. They barely mumbled an apology before lurching forward to dance to the group of drummers.

The beat of those deep, rhythmic drums pulsed under my sandals. It reminded me of those soft nights in my family's tent dancing with my mother and sister and cousins. The sound of our camels outside the door while I moved to the rhythm of the desert's heartbeat, my toes digging into the sand and heat of its pulse. I'd never fully appreciated those happy years until my mother was gone.

The golden moon glowed hot. The priestesses and the women of Sariba shed their scarves, baring their necks. They danced, arms up to the sky, calling down the power of Ba'al and the Goddess.

Stiffly, I walked through the crowd, eyes darting about to spy the location of my sisters.

I signaled to the commander of Naomi's guards. "Disperse yourselves and see if you can find my sister the High Priestess Leila."

"Yes, my lady." The men quickly departed, moving in and out of the crowd, receiving glowering expressions from the temple guards and the Egyptian priests. I realized with a sinking heart that my handful of guards were no match for the swarm of foreign magicians and dozens of temple guards.

"*Where* are you, Leila?" I said aloud.

"If she wants to be found, she will," the queen said next to me. Her presence was a comfort, but waves of nerves and anxiety emanated from her, too. After Aliyah's attack at the palace, we were both much more frightened and intimidated by the spectacle before us.

"I fear that her suggestion about meeting and saying goodbye to Sahmril were hollow at best," I murmured.

"Your sister probably meant them at the time, but Aliyah will thwart any potential private meet-up. She can't risk your snatching Sahmril from the promise of a solstice sacrifice. Or persuading Leila away from tonight's purpose."

"I think you're right," I said, perspiration beginning to form on the back of my neck.

The Queen of Sheba observed the crowds. "Aliyah has whipped them up into a frenzy of demented hope for victory. But little do they know that it's not victory for their homeland of Sariba and King Kadesh, but victory for herself and Horeb's armies who sit within view of tonight's spectacle ready to crush us."

Satin curtains billowed about a vaulted tent, the focal point of the upcoming ceremony. A moment later I spotted Aliyah rising up on a podium. Her gown billowed in an unseen breeze, and it appeared as though she were flying through the summer night. She was stunning in a glowing white dress. Her black hair sparkled with gold dust shavings, thick dark curls falling luxuriantly to her waist.

"My people of Sariba!" Aliyah called to gain their attention. "Tonight we pay tribute to the gods and goddesses who are waiting to bless you. They desire to bless this land with fruit and meat. If you are faithful, they will give us victory over our enemies. Those enemies in our mountains who salivate to plunge their swords into our hearts and steal our lands and our wealth."

The crowd was so enthusiastic their screams and cheers nearly drowned out Aliyah's words.

"For victory!" the men shouted, raising goblets high into the air, wine splashing over the rims.

Aliyah spread her arms out as though to enclose them all inside a circle of adoration. "Your devotion to me as your Goddess fills me with a desire to bless you. But we know that we have to offer sacrifice—because sacrificing things we love to the Goddess brings forth blessings. The spirit of Sariba imbues me with the ability to grant your heart's wishes. We can conquer our enemies. We will send them home with their tails between their legs."

More laughter and more cheering surrounded me like a heavy tidal wave, making me ill. Where was Sahmril? And where was Leila? I paced the walkways, my neck aching each time I arched upward to scan the crowd.

"Patience, Jayden," the queen said beside me.

"They're not going to defeat three armies by drinking and dancing and falling into Sacred Marriage beds tonight," I said in an angry voice.

The crowd had quieted when I spoke so that my words were heard loud and clear. A sea of faces turned to me, curious, defiant.

Aliyah spotted me. "Our guest of honor has arrived. Come, Jayden."

The people pushed me forward, and I stumbled toward the pavilion dais. "Wasn't she part of that company of Edomites that arrived a fortnight ago?" a male voice questioned.

A disdainful female speculated, "Is *she* the one they say was supposed to wed King Kadesh? She's dressed more like a priestess, not someone our prince would marry."

The woman's words were true, and I had done so purposely to blend in. Now I felt self-conscious.

"Hold your head high," the queen ordered, gripping my arm as we stood close together on the pathway before the dais.

The voices continued, consuming me. "No, she's the Nephish princess betrothed to the leader of the enemy."

"This war is her fault."

"Our prince lost his mind wandering the desert."

"King Kadesh will save us."

Another person scoffed, "He's blind and maimed. We need the Goddess to save us."

My head spun at their scathing words. How could I blame them? In part, they spoke truth. I had brought the threat of destruction to this land.

Aliyah's next words were a balm. "*I am the Goddess of Sariba, my people. I've brought the power of the throne of Sa'ba, the magic of Egypt, and the soul of the Goddess to fruition within me.*"

The crowd bowed before her, sinking to the stone and manicured lawns.

Someone shouted behind me. "We need a sacrifice! A sacrifice!" The others took up the chant, and the roar gave me a headache, my stomach turning over with fear.

Aliyah bestowed smiles on her worshipers. "I have brought you the perfect sacrifice. One I have desired for a long time."

"Show us!" shouted the crowd. Some threw their goblets into the air. The drummers began a wild and frenzied drumming, while the temple priestesses formed a circle around Aliyah. They danced with abandon, tearing at their hair. The heavy makeup disguised their identities. I strained to recognize Leila, but I couldn't.

Aliyah gave a signal to her palace guards, and an enormous chandelier hanging over a second dais lit up with hundreds of candles, showering light upon a giant figure covered by folds of heavy draperies. A dozen priests of Ba'al surrounded the dais, and when Aliyah flicked her hand again, the priests of Ba'al pulled off the draperies.

Towering over the temple grounds was an enormous statue of the God of Moloch, the god of sacrifice for the priests of Ba'al. It was fierce, wings fanning out from its back, an animal mouth, and wide, staring red eyes aflame with light. The figure held out his arms in a beguiling welcome, each finger individually crafted, palms bigger than my head.

I'd never seen one before; I'd only ever heard descriptions. Someone whispered in awed tones, "It's the fire god!"

"Behold Moloch!" Aliyah shouted. "Regard your worshippers! We bow before you."

While I stood there, horrified, the people began dropping to their hands and knees.

The priests of Ba'al filled the hollow belly of the brass statue with kindling and logs. The priests lit the wood with a dose of liqueur and then threw their torches inside the pyre. Before I could flee, the fire roared, licking up the dry wood, sending sparks of yellow and orange up inside the statue.

The people scrambled away from the heat that poured off the towering statue, and I began to sweat great drops down my neck. Soon the bronze god began to glow. It was then that a movement beside Aliyah caught my eye.

The High Priest of the Temple of Ba'al opened a set of double doors behind Aliyah. With slow steps set against the pounding drums, the man brought forth the High Priestess of Sariba, holding her hand in his. She, in turn, was holding the hand of a young child.

The priestess was Leila, and the child was Sahmril.

22

eila!" I screamed. The crowd held me back, but I wriggled forward.

Confusion crossed my sister's face when her eyes rested on me, while a benign expression graced her lips. Sahmril had no idea I was shouting about her. I was merely a crazy woman, and the look of fear in her eyes tore at my heart.

An Egyptian priest pulled me away. Twisting in the man's arms, I finally managed to shove him off. It was Heru, the Egyptian High Priest who'd taken Sahmril from me in the ceremonial chamber a few days earlier.

"You!" I said, but he grabbed me again, pinning my arms behind my back. "Let me go!"

I craned my neck to see that two more priests had the Queen of Sheba held as well. We stared at each other, and my heart throbbed in panic.

Aliyah called down from her pedestal. "Let Jayden, Princess of the Nephish, come to me."

When she used my tribal title, the worshippers wouldn't see me as Kadesh's betrothed and their future queen. As someone to save for their king's sake. From their perspective, I had brought the threat of death and destruction. They hated me.

When I reached the dais, Heru shoved me to the ground, forcing my nose against the stone paving. "As Goddess of Sariba, you will bow to *me*," Aliyah commanded. "I will be queen of the southern lands. Queen of Sheba. And eventually Queen of Babylonia."

The worshippers wept, prostrated themselves, and howled for my demise.

Aliyah's eyes settled on her sister standing behind me. She laughed at the queen's bandaged hands, useless against the hold of her Egyptian priests. "Yes, my queen, you will literally hand over the kingdom of Sa'ba to me tonight."

"They're drunk!" I said, spitting at Aliyah's red painted toes. "Their wine goblets are drugged."

Aliyah laughed. "But they get to keep their goblets as a gift from me. And now I have a gift for you, sweet Jayden. Two gifts and a chance to redeem yourself before these good people. If I allowed my worshippers to act on their rage, they would tear you limb from limb for bringing the armies of the north here."

"I don't want your gifts."

"Oh, but you covet this one." She turned to one of her handmaidens, gesturing to a table overlaid with snowy-white linen. The girl clasped a box between her hands and walked forward to show it off to me.

I wept at the sight of my mother's treasured alabaster box. The beloved gift my father had given to her on their wedding day, and the one that my older sister had stolen away from our family tent so long ago.

"Open it," Aliyah ordered.

I stared at her, defiant, but finally lifted the lid. The last time I'd seen this box, Leila had hidden a wooden statue of the dancing goddess of Ashtoreth inside it.

I sucked in my breath. Now the box was empty.

"Your sister made a sacrifice. She gave up her idol of Ashtoreth to follow me, a goddess of greater authority and influence."

A familiar scent rose up from the box. The aroma of sandalwood, strong and perfumed. Along with the odor of burnt ashes. I shook the box and a pile of ashes lay in the bottom. The ashes of my sister's old and beloved statue.

Aliyah had forced Leila to burn the symbol of Ashtoreth to prove her obedience to the new Goddess.

"Go ahead," the woman said seductively. "Smell it again. Breathe it in. Deeply."

I stared at her warily. Was she poisoning me, tricking me?

Aliyah gave a throaty laugh. "Jayden, you now have the Goddess burned into your nostrils. Burned into your throat, your lungs, and your heart. You'll never get rid of Her. She will always be a part of you."

"It's merely a piece of wood," I scoffed, turning the box

over and dumping the ashes onto the ground. With my heel, I ground the figure's final remains into the dirt.

Anger flashed across Aliyah's face. "Bring forth the sacrifice!"

The enormous statue glowed a deep red from the fire burning in its belly. Sweat dripped down my chest and back.

"The sister of this heathen girl from the north will be offered to the great God and Goddess of Sariba!" Aliyah cried to the crowd.

Leila stepped forward, her voice an eerie melody when she pronounced, "Sahmril is kin by blood, and I give her willingly for the Goddess. A perfect life to bring forth new life for all."

"Leila, it's all lies," I tried to shout at her. "The only one giving up anything is the person who dies—for nothing. Aliyah should offer herself."

My sister gave an indulgent shrug. "But Aliyah *is* the Goddess. How can she offer herself?" Then she lifted Sahmril into her arms and crossed the lawns toward the High Priest of Ba'al, placing the beautiful girl with her dark sticky curls into the priest's arms. My breath hitched when he walked toward the fire god Moloch, chanting the sacrificial prayers. The other priests joined in, forming a line behind him.

Sahmril began to wail as Aliyah signaled the drummers to intensify their pounding. Flute players howled a high-pitched song, the notes straining into the black night.

The faces of the massive crowd turned upward to the god, light from the fire flickering across their features. The sight of the immense statue glowing against the night sky was so intense Horeb's men could probably see it across the desert.

Sahmril's crying was like a knife to my gut, ripping me in half. When the Egyptian's arms loosened for a fraction of a moment, I leaped forward, pushing the lesser priests aside to claw Sahmril from the arms of the High Priest of Ba'al.

There was stunned silence. The musicians stopped. And then I was running into the crowd trying to get away, tripping over the hem of my dress while I held Sahmril tight to me.

"Run!" the queen cried, urging me to escape.

Sahmril burst into tears. "Shh, shh," I tried to comfort her. "I'm going to save you—"

All at once, I went down with a thud on the soft grass, rolling to the side to prevent my sister from getting hurt. Before I could move, male arms lifted us both, and we were carried by a dozen priests before Aliyah.

"You dare to defy me, the Goddess," she proclaimed while I clasped my sister hard to my chest. Tears bit at my eyes when I breathed in the scent of her skin. There was no way to escape. We were surrounded by Ba'al and Egyptian priests and the altar where Aliyah stood in all her glory.

I strained my eyes to find the guards who had accompanied us from the city and finally spotted them. On the outer ring of Ba'al and Egyptian priests, Aunt Naomi's personal guards were being held at bay by temple guards, too many to count. The guards had been beaten badly, swaying on their feet, their weapons confiscated, their wrists tied with rope. I'd needed my own personal army to come up here to have any hope of leaving alive.

"Yes, I dare to defy you," I finally answered. "Because I will give the Goddess of Sariba a better sacrifice. I offer myself. But only on the condition that Sahmril returns to my father at the palace."

A smile crept across Aliyah's face. "Ah, indeed. Perhaps you are the more valuable sacrifice anyway," she said eagerly. Raising her voice to the crowd, the woman proclaimed, "The betrothed of Horeb has offered herself to the Goddess! A virgin. A girl with a pure heart. The ultimate unselfishness. I am most pleased."

Hands wrenched Sahmril from my embrace and her scream tore at my heart. Heru, the Egyptian High Priest, pushed me forward. Aliyah planted kisses on both of my cheeks, her fingers like claws on my shoulders while the priests handed Sahmril off to one another taking her farther and farther away from me.

Aliyah's violet eyes bore into mine when she gripped my shoulders in a vise that hurt. "And now I have everything I want," she whispered. "It couldn't have worked out more perfectly. You fell right into my plan, Jayden."

Before I could scream for help, I was lifted up into the air by four priests, each holding me by an arm or a leg while they carried me to the same altar upon which Aliyah had been standing.

The polished marble stone slipped along my back as the Egyptians laid me down. Hard, cold, and unforgiving. My hands and feet were tied to each of the four corners while Heru pressed a hard hand on top of my chest to keep me from writing. A shriek rose up my throat, and then died.

I was immobilized, staring upward into the stars, numb and cold. The longing for my mother intensified, my eyes dripping tears. I only hoped that she and my father would know that I'd done everything I could to save my sister. That I'd kept my promise.

My only regret was that I wouldn't be able to tell Kadesh good-bye.

23

W aves of heat pulsed from the brass statue of Moloch looming beyond the domed pavilion where I lay on the marble altar. I swore my skin was melting from the proximity.

From a great distance, the drumming began again. I could hear Sahmril still crying. "Give my sister to Leila," I pleaded. "We're doing exactly what you wanted, so honor your end of the bargain. Promise me Sahmril goes to my father. And that you will never see her again. Vow it, Aliyah!"

I knew I was a fool to trust her, but I had no choice now. There had been no time to steal Sahmril away in the crowd. No time to run hemmed in by guards and soldiers. It was either my baby sister's death or mine. But soon I would see my mother, and when I thought of that, I knew I'd made the right choice, despite all that I was leaving behind.

Aliyah's cool hands slid down my waist and upper thigh. "Ah, here it is. Your infamous dagger. It's no secret that you hide it on your leg."

I wished I could wipe the triumphant look from her face and shove it down her throat.

"Leila," Aliyah called, beckoning her to come closer.

My sister's face floated before me, her long hair soft about her bare shoulders, her slim figure delicate and beautiful. Her eyes gazed into mine, though I wasn't sure she actually saw me.

Tears leaked out of the corners of my eyes. I was angry at myself for thinking I could whisk Sahmril away before the sacrificial ceremony began.

The Goddess of Sariba held up my knife with its long, thin blade, the one I sharpened each night while my handmaids brushed my hair. "High Priestess Leila," she said. "You are the one who loves me most. Would you like to do the honor of slicing your sister's throat?"

I scanned the glittering jewel-like stars. There was no liberating angel to save me. I'd willingly offered myself in exchange for Sahmril's life.

When I thought of Kadesh, my throat swelled with grief. I would never feel his arms around me again; never hear his voice in my ears, his warm and heavenly lips on mine.

I blinked back the tears and self-pity, and tried to focus on the fact that Sahmril would live—even though she would never know me.

Leila hypnotically stroked my neck, and I shivered under

her glassy gaze. "Leila," I hissed, trying to catch her eyes with mine, forcing her to acknowledge me.

She shook her head. "It will be easier if you don't speak. I don't want to cut the wrong blood vessel and have you die instantly."

"Dear God, Leila, listen to me!"

A rumbling murmur began in the crowd.

My sister finally, reluctantly, looked at me. Fear lurked behind her eyes. She was afraid of acknowledging me. Afraid of defying the Goddess. Aliyah was now standing above me on the same altar of stone, calling to the skies. Shouting platitudes to her followers.

"Leila!" I said sharply. "*Promise me* that after my death you will run with Sahmril. I've given myself so that Aliyah cannot have her. Take her to the palace. Father is there, and Lady Naomi will care for her."

Leila shot a glance upward. "I can't defy the Goddess. I promised to follow her, to obey her in everything."

"If you don't take Sahmril away from here tonight, she'll sacrifice me and her both. How will you explain to Father that he lost two of his daughters tonight?"

She clapped her hands against her ears, shaking her head in agony. "No more, don't say anything else!"

The commotion was rising. I twisted my neck to see, but the writhing bodies, dripping candles, and the endless screeches of the crowd's bloodlust were too confusing.

"Where is the Queen of Sheba?" I suddenly screamed. I'd lost sight of her when I fell to the ground with Sahmril. Then

I saw that she was being held captive in the arms of three towering priests.

Her eyes were wide, her expression grim. "No, Jayden!" she called out to me. "Don't do this!"

I couldn't shout to make myself heard above the roaring crowd. I could only move my lips in a whisper and hope she understood. "I made a promise to my mother and I want to be able to face her after this life is over."

"Sacrifice her!" came the shuddering shouts again. I tried to squirm under the rope, but I couldn't feel my legs any longer.

Aliyah prodded Leila with her golden staff, a cluster of diamonds and emeralds forming the head of it. "Do it!" she screamed. "The Goddess is waiting!"

"Promise me, Leila!" I whimpered one last time, wishing I could hold *her*, my beloved older sister, one last time before I died. Above me, Leila raised the dagger, and then the Queen of Sheba was there, fumbling at the rope knots. "Let me be the sacrifice, Aliyah," she screamed.

"You're offering yourself to me?" Aliyah said, a smile floating over her mouth. "I had no idea it would be this easy. Two queens. Two powerful sacrifices in one. The Goddess is most pleased." She paused to look at each of us in turn. "How ironic that we are all sisters. Sisters are supposed to love each other, aren't they? Even when they keep secrets and husbands from the Goddess—as you both have done to me."

"No, it's ironic that the Goddess has taken our sisters from us," I said bitterly. "A sacrifice means nothing when the person is not a willing subject."

"You know nothing!" Aliyah snapped. "After tonight, neither one of you will have your kingdoms any longer. They will belong to me, as well as your husbands to do with as *I* wish."

Aliyah wrenched the knife from Leila's hand and, instead of coming for me, she raised the dagger up in the air for a single, terrible instant and then plunged the weapon straight into the queen's throat.

The Queen of Sheba's eyes widened in shock. Frantic words gurgled as she tried to speak. Her hand lifted to press against Aliyah's shoulders in a feeble attempt to push her away.

Aliyah's expression was cold and impassive while blood gushed from the queen's neck. The queen's eyes rolled back, her arms went limp, and then her body slumped over mine still tied to the altar.

"My queen," I screamed. "Stay with me! Leila, help her!"

My stomach heaved when Aliyah slipped the dagger from her sister's neck. She stared at the power she had wielded while spots of blood dripped along the front of her white gown. And then handed the knife to Leila.

I turned my head, weeping a thousand tears. "My queen," I whimpered, hoping there was a chance she still lived. I stretched my fingers to fumble for her cold fingers lying across my thighs. Holding her hand tight, I cried for the true friend she had become. A champion for Kadesh and me.

With her death, the southern countries and the Frankincense Trail would be in disarray.

"Go in peace, my queen," I whispered to the night sky.

With the Queen of Sheba's death, my murder was next.

I shook the tears from my eyes as a priest of Ba'al picked up the body of the queen and carried her off into the darkness. "Stop," I screamed. How dare they take her away? At that very moment, Leila turned to stare over her shoulder, her eyes flashing with new horror.

A stream of Edomite soldiers came into view. They cleared the crowd, pushing their way through the temple followers. People went sprawling, shouting drunken slurs, drinks shattering to the stone courtyard.

The priests of Ba'al and Egypt surged forward in an attempt to charge the Edomites, but they went down almost instantly, afraid of the large number of fierce desert soldiers.

"Stop them," Aliyah screamed. "Or the Goddess will curse you all!"

Her cries were in vain. The Edomites clearly outnumbered her guards and the Egyptians, circling them instantly.

As soon as the temple guards and priests were contained, a second company of Edomites marched straight up the pathway. At the head of the formation strode Asher and my father.

Leila dropped the dagger and staggered behind the altar.

"I'm here!" I screamed, straining at the ropes at the sight of Kadesh's beloved Edomites.

Asher had almost reached me when Aliyah jumped down from the altar. She stabbed a finger into the young man's chest. "Don't take another step or I will have you all sacrificed!"

She flicked a finger and the Egyptians sprang to life with their magical staves. All at once, the lamps and candles began to fly overhead, circling the gardens and fountains. Asher and his men ducked, narrowly missing a spray of sparks.

With both fists, my father crashed his staff to the ground. A sound like an earthquake rose from the depths of the earth. Leila was on her knees wailing when I caught sight of Sahmril, held by one of the other priestesses. The little girl had been squirming and finally pulled away from the woman and tried to run toward the parapet. "Stop your tears, Leila!" I ordered. "Get Sahmril before she gets hurt or lost!"

Remarkably, my sister obeyed, hurrying off just as Asher appeared before my eyes. "Jayden, are you hurt?"

"Just get the knife, it fell to the ground. My dagger! Hurry!"

He dropped to his knees to search at the same moment the Egyptians began to light their staves, preparing to throw flaming darts at the Edomites.

"I've got it," Asher grunted, sawing at the rope around my wrists and ankles. As soon as they loosened, I rolled off the stone altar and tried to stand but immediately sank to the ground. All my strength was gone, my legs turning to liquid.

Asher lifted me into his arms and carried me away just seconds before Heru, the High Priest, crashed his staff onto the altar where I had been laying.

The stone table split in half, and I marveled at the strengths the man possessed.

"Get Sahmril first," I choked out while the entire pavilion turned into a confusion of Moloch's roiling heat, torches, and screaming people fleeing the chaos.

I wobbled on the cool grass, wishing I could lie down while Asher rushed to retrieve Sahmril. He herded Leila over to where I finally sank, rubbing at my raw wrists.

I shoved my dagger back into the strap on my thigh, then pulled Sahmril into my arms, holding her close while she cried. "You're safe, sweet baby. I'm going to take care of you."

She put her face into my neck and sobbed, "I want my mama and papa."

A sharp pang came over me knowing whom she was referring to. "Leila, come with us to the palace."

The masked aura of the High Priestess washed over her like a facade. "You ruined everything with your Edomites. Sariba would have been safe if you hadn't stopped the sacrifice."

My heart stuttered at what she was inferring. "You would have killed me?"

She gazed upon Aliyah who was rallying her followers and screaming at the priests and magicians to reorganize. "Sacrifice is for the greater good. We need the goddesses' blessings."

"Then why doesn't one of the priestesses offer herself?" I snapped.

"Jayden," my father said, appearing out of the chaos. "We need to leave before Aliyah rallies her priests and finds another child to offer. Where's Leila?"

"She's right here," I said, whipping my head about, but my older sister was nowhere to be seen. Heru had obviously swept her away when the Edomites showed up.

"Oh, Father," I said. "I'm not sure we'll ever have her back again."

My father turned away while sorrow hunched his shoulders, but Asher heard my words and sent me a look of empathy.

"Leila made her choice long ago," I said quietly. "The temple is her home and we belong to a past life she cares nothing for any longer."

Asher gazed past the balconies to the foothills of the mountains. I followed his eyes and frowned. The lights of Horeb's camps were different somehow.

"It appears our enemy is on the move," he muttered.

"You mean they're coming to the city? Right now?"

He shook his head. "They wouldn't attack at night, especially when they don't know the city, but we'd better return to the palace right away."

"Please have your men retrieve the body of the Queen of Sheba," I told Asher. "One of the priests carried her off, but we can't leave her behind. She needs to be at the palace so we can mourn her and properly take care of her body."

Asher's brows were low as he directed five of his soldiers to find the queen, but he had no sooner uttered the command when Aliyah rose up to the dais once again.

Stretching forth her hands to the crowd, she said, "My people, my worshippers. Bring forth another child to fulfill the sacrifice."

Cutting through the crowds and commotion, the temple soldiers searched for a child to put on the altar. My stomach heaved. Aliyah was determined to have her solstice sacrifice. To wield her power in a public show.

"With the destruction of this sacred night," Aliyah shouted to capture their attention again. "I—the Goddess of the great land of Sariba—officially declare war on King Kadesh. We will cut ourselves from the foolish, malignant country of Sariba. King Kadesh is a traitor to bring strangers here to harm us. We will align ourselves with the powerful King of the Nephish and his Assyrian and Maachathite armies. With him we will have our victory!"

The worshippers' faces were rapt when they bowed to the Sariba Goddess, fearful at the death of the Queen of Sa'ba and the Edomite soldiers storming the ceremony, but hopeful that they would be spared from the horror of war.

It didn't take long before Asher and the Edomites had me safely enclosed within their ranks, including Sahmril and the body of the Queen of Sheba. We hurried away from the scenes of death, but behind us, the screams of a woman tore through the dismal night. I whipped around to look. A young child had been ripped from its mother's arms by the priests of Ba'al to fulfill the sacrifice on the burning arms of Moloch.

At the sound of the woman's ghastly shrieks, I went limp on Asher's horse. "Don't faint, Jayden," he told me. "Stay strong. We'll be home soon."

But after the horror of this night and Aliyah's lies, how would the people of Sariba ever trust Kadesh again?

24

e were a silent company as we rode down the forest path back to the palace. Waves of guilt smothered over me at the thought of being part of an innocent child's death.

My heart rattled inside my chest. Nausea churned at my belly. All at once, I leaned over my horse and threw up into the bushes.

"Will you be all right, my lady?" Asher asked quietly when I grasped the reins again and nudged at my steed to keep moving.

"Sahmril is alive," I said, watching my sister in the arms of my father. "That's all that matters right now."

My heart wrenched at the sight of my father's face wet with tears. We were all alive for now, but the queen had been murdered in cold blood. And another mother had lost her child tonight for absolutely nothing.

We rode into the rear gates of the city and up the narrow paths toward the palace in complete blackness.

"Has Kadesh ordered a blackout?" I asked.

Asher nodded, steadying our horses as our large group converged onto the city streets. Not a light to be seen, not a whisper of sound.

"The king gave orders for a nightly blackout until this is over. If Horeb grows bold enough to breach the city walls, Kadesh doesn't want to make it easy for them to move about."

When we reached the palace stables, servant boys ushered us in, closing the doors against the eerie night.

We hurried up the staircases to the palace. Once inside, I staggered against a wall, narrowly avoiding a table of fine vases and flowers. I was so tired I could have slept right there in a corner of the giant foyer for two days. But there were still tasks to accomplish before I got to collapse on my pillow.

"Let me inspect the room for your peace of mind," Asher said, accompanying me to my suite.

"Surely the palace is secure?"

"It's a precaution so I can assure myself that I'm doing an adequate job as your personal guard."

After what had happened tonight at the temple, I wondered if Asher was mocking himself. I could hardly blame him. I wished the queen had never come to Sariba. If she hadn't, she would be safely in Sa'ba with her husband and family. I choked down fresh tears, guilt threatening to swallow me up when the queen had offered herself to replace me as sacrifice.

The first thing I did when we entered was pull the thick

draperies across the windows. My handmaids rose from their beds and Jasmine hurried to light a lamp.

After Asher finished inspecting the bathing room, wardrobes, and dressing room, we said goodnight. "Before I leave I'll make sure a guard is posted at your door. Or I will stand guard myself."

I watched him disappear around a corner and then told Tijah, "I must go see the king for a few minutes before retiring. Don't leave this suite. If you need me, send a summons with one of the palace messengers."

I hurried down the hall, stopping a guard to send a message to my father to bring Sahmril to Kadesh's suite. After the chaos and destruction of the night, I wanted to see them with my own eyes once more and hold them in my arms.

Would the rest of the palace household think me brazen to appear so late in the evening at the king's private rooms without an official summons? Casting aside my insecurity, I crossed the foyer just as one of Kadesh's bodyguards appeared. "My lady, King Kadesh asks for your company, if you're up to it."

It seemed that he and I had the same thoughts.

When I was ushered inside, Kadesh rushed over to me. "Jayden! I've been pacing a hole in the rugs ever since I sent the Edomites after you."

I sagged against one of the columns in the vestibule and then sank against his chest while he held me close. "Your eyes are red from the smoke. You're pale, too. Shaking."

I tried not to give in to the terrible night, but the comfort of his arms was just what I needed. "I'm only worried for the citizens," I said. "For your soldiers and their families, and worried for you."

Kadesh said, "I heard what happened tonight. You volunteered to take Sahmril's place as sacrifice." Revulsion laced his voice and I took a step backward to stare at him. He was holding back an explosion of frustration—at Aliyah—and at me. *"Don't ever do that again."*

The anger in his voice was palpable, tangible in a way that hurt. "You've never spoken to me like that before."

"I never came so close to losing you." His arms tightened when he lifted me up off the floor, his face buried into my neck, breath shuddering.

"When I think back to how easily Aliyah sucked my mother into her web of influence . . . I think Aliyah has been plotting to overthrow Sariba's royal family for years. How swiftly she allied herself with Horeb, a complete stranger bent on invading Sariba to put themselves on the throne."

"I honestly believe that when she gets rid of me she will assassinate Horeb, take over his armies and then find a way to kill you in your sleep one night. Now that the Queen of Sheba is gone, she can rightfully rule there, too."

Kadesh's face twisted with grief. "My cousin's death is the worst blow today—and that on top of losing so many men on the battlefield. I'm in shock that she's gone. That Aliyah actually killed her own sister. How will I ever convey this news to her husband?"

"There will be time to compose letters," I said gently. "Or to visit Sa'ba yourself. Right now, the most important task is to win this war. I'm going to fight by your side. I'm going to wield a sword, along with Asher and the Edomites and the Sariba army to defeat Horeb once and for all."

Kadesh was vehemently against it. "If I lost you, I'd lose my will to win. That's why you have to stay alive."

"King Ephrem told me in no uncertain terms that I was the one to kill Horeb. Once that is done, his armies will fracture along with their will to fight. When Horeb is gone no one can question who the true ruler of Sariba is once and for all."

His mouth lifted. "I'm beginning to realize that you are your own secret weapon."

I leaned forward to give him a kiss. "You are a wise ruler, King Kadesh."

When his body servant entered from the rear bedroom, Kadesh said, "That's my cue. Stay another few moments. Help me try on my uniform. It's Uncle Ephrem's, but it might need adjustments."

"I've asked my father to come before he retires for the night. He should be here shortly."

"I'd like to see him myself," Kadesh agreed with a nod.

We'd no sooner said the words than Pharez came into view, Sahmril in his arms. Seeing the two of them together brought back all the memories of when she was an infant and my father would rock her on those terrible nights we crossed the desert and she was hungry or distressed.

I ran and threw my arms around them both. My father's beard tickled my cheek when I pressed my face into his neck. He was warmth and comfort and home, all at once.

"You saved her," Pharez said hoarsely. "My girl, my Jayden."

"Oh, Father, we're so very lucky. When Kadesh and I found her in Mari I never thought we'd see her again."

Sahmril wriggled in my father's arms, her eyes half-closed, sleepy. "Mama," she murmured against Pharez's tunic, ready to slip into dreamland.

"I know it's time to put her to bed," I said. "But I had to see you. I wanted to say goodnight." I lifted Sahmril from his arms and cradled her against me. "She's really here and safe—with us."

"And she needs a mother's touch," my father added, gazing at me. "You're all she has now."

I didn't mention the fact that Sahmril's adoptive parents were somewhere in the city, too. The Queen of Sheba had told me that herself, but there was time to deal with them later. "For now, I will count my blessings to have us all here together."

We didn't mention Leila. The ache of her decision to remain apart from our family hurt, but at the moment she was at least physically safe at the temple, even if she had chosen to abandon us.

Kadesh took Pharez's hand in his and gripped it. "I'm grateful to see *all* of you back safely at the palace. I was ready to tear the walls down after I sent Asher and his men off. General Naham had to hold me back from following them, convincing me that putting the king at risk was not a good idea."

"Your Edomite warriors dispatched the temple guards and priests with ease," my father said evenly. "I never thought I'd say it, but they have my honor and respect forever. I pray for

Chemish's full health and strength back soon."

Kadesh nodded, a real smile finally crossing his lips. "The physicians brought the news earlier this evening. He should make a full recovery. It's all the doctors can do to keep him down while he finishes healing."

"He wants to be with you and his son, Asher, for the battle tomorrow morning," Pharez observed.

"Having him get hurt again will do no one any good."

Pharez nodded, and we stepped back while Kadesh's servant came forward again from the shadows of the corner.

He was holding a great coat emblazoned with Sariba's symbol and magenta colors. Kadesh was already wearing matching pressed trousers and shirt. Royal insignia had been sewn on the shoulders and lapels. The servant hefted the uniform coat onto his shoulders, and Kadesh slipped his arms through the sleeves.

Next, the servant held out a deep red sash across his extended arms. He bowed his head to me, indicating that I should take it and adorn the king.

Wrapping my arms around Kadesh's waist, I placed the wide sash around his hips and tied it. Carefully I placed the knot, the sheen of satin shining in the lamplight.

"My sword will go here at this side, my dagger at the other." He paused, giving me a discerning look. "I don't want you on the battlefield, Jayden. Horeb's soldiers are twice your size and weight. One sword stroke and your head would be taken off."

"Then I will have to be quick and keep them dancing. Like Asher taught me." I studied the man I loved, elegant and commanding in the kingly uniform. "Do you intend to wear body armor? One sly sword stroke and *your* heart will be torn asunder."

"That will go under the uniform," the servant said quietly. "When I dress the king in the morning."

Kadesh lifted his chin. "We plan to meet at the barracks before dawn. Tomorrow is the day."

Tomorrow. I suddenly hated that word.

The servant undid the sash and coat. "I will take these to my wife for sewing," he said. "The sleeves need a bit of lengthening, and the coat taken in a touch. You're taller than King Ephrem, and more slender. It will be ready in a few hours when I awaken you." The servant bustled out the door with barely a whisper of sound.

Chills ran up my neck, knowing exactly what the servant meant. We were only hours away from the first battle. Dread snaked through my belly. I glanced up to see the weary lines etched on my father's face. "Sahmril is asleep," I said, transferring her warm body to Pharez's arms. "Do you want me to take her with me to my suite?"

My father shook his head. "Not tonight. I want her bed next to mine so I can know for myself that she's safe."

"I'll instruct my maids to bathe and dress her in the morning while I see the army off from the city gates. Tijah and Jasmine can play with her and help give her meals. Now go to bed before you fall over yourself," I teased him.

My father grunted. I kissed Sahmril's flushed cheeks and

stood at the door to watch the two of them slip down the corridor.

Kadesh's hands slipped up my arms to bring me close, sending shivers along my skin. "You can't leave before I get a goodnight kiss. We may not be in our marriage tent this week as we thought—" His voice grew husky, his eyes never leaving mine. "But I thank God you are safe and we're here now, together."

He bent down to bring his lips to mine, and my eyes burned with unshed tears at his gentleness. I closed my eyes, dreaming of the first time he kissed me at the hearth fire of my father's tent. The scent of wood smoke circling the stars. His rich exotic cloak enveloping me, melding me to him as though we had become one person, one heart.

But every time Kadesh touched me or kissed me these last few days, I hoped it wouldn't be the last.

"You're driving me insane," I finally murmured. "Tell me the army is ready. Tell me we will win. Tell me this will be over soon."

Sinking into a couch, Kadesh rubbed at his face. His hair was a tangle, and his face sagged. "It was a long, hard day of practice and preparation, but we're ready."

I knelt at his feet and laid my head in his lap. My stomach was ill from the events of the night and the queen's death. "I can't stand the thought of never seeing the queen again. To hear her voice and her wisdom. To emulate her as what a queen should be."

Kadesh pulled me up next to him and a wave of fresh grief came over me. "She was my true friend and confidante. I dread having to write her husband with the news. She should never have come here."

"I wish Aliyah had stayed in Babylon forever." The words were a childlike wish, but I spoke them fervently. "I should go to the queen's suite tomorrow and pack her things so nothing gets lost. After helping Naomi go through King Ephrem's personal effects yesterday, tonight is a nightmare I wish I could wake up from. I was so afraid of the queen when I met her in Sheba, but now I miss her dreadfully."

"Already you're taking on the duties of my queen, Jayden."

My heart rose into my throat. "Are we in any danger of another midnight attack?"

Kadesh shook his head. "We have a system of alerts set up. Sariba's army will sleep tonight with their boots on and one eye open."

I reached up to trace the scars surrounding his mangled eye. "You know I worry about you."

Kadesh took my hands in his. "I can see that you won't allow me any sleep until I tell you the truth."

"You know me well," I said, dreading what he would say next.

"We're vastly outnumbered. Horeb's army is more than fifteen hundred strong. Even with the Edomites and Basim's marauders, we only have a little over a thousand soldiers. We do have the advantage of protecting our home. Conquerors are never as motivated."

"Don't underestimate Horeb. He believes this land and its future queen already belongs to him."

Kadesh's dark eyes stared into mine, and I tried to read his thoughts, but tonight they were elusive. The thoughts of a king who would soon watch his comrades die in battle.

When I stood to go, Kadesh pushed himself up from the couch and gathered me in his arms. "This will be over soon, I promise."

"I fear Horeb won't give up until he is the last man standing."

"He'll be dead before then. And once he is, I will rally his troops in loyalty to me."

I put my hand to his face, memorizing his features and the touch of his skin against mine. "Spoken like a true king." I paused to kiss him one last time. "I'll see you from the wall of the gates in a few hours."

25

Wearing a bright red dress and a veil of white, I stood on the parapets that surrounded the palace while dawn crashed along the rim of the eastern desert. I hoped Kadesh could see my figure and know that I would be with him in every thought and deed during this first day of battle.

My palms clutched the stone edge while I watched Kadesh and General Naham finish their preparations in the staging area. Young men, barely a hint of facial hair, practiced their sword techniques while more than a dozen stable boys groomed and saddled horses.

Others filled water bags, ran errands, and sharpened daggers and swords for the lieutenants and soldiers. The commotion was loud, the air dusty. A mood of tension traced with a surge of odd excitement energized the compound.

The sun launched over the eastern horizon. Faint rays warmed my face, giving hope. No fog slipped down the mountains. It would be hot later.

It wasn't long before the mountain soldiers of Basim arrived. Despite the men's ragged beards and unkempt hair, their horses' coats gleamed with obvious care. Reins jangled the air, and the animals' powerful legs lifted in a distinctive gait.

The Sariba soldiers gave them wide berth, and even from here, I could see the exchange of glares and angry words. After all, these hired men had killed a few of their comrades, but even Basim had lost several of his own militia on the night of my wedding.

I watched Kadesh maneuver his horse to Basim. The two men spoke for a few moments and then Basim bowed his head in respect. When he lifted his face, the mercenary leader's eyes caught hold of mine standing at the tower gate wall. He stared at me from the saddle of his horse, and then briefly bowed his head in acknowledgment.

I held myself taller, in a stance befitting a queen, when I nodded in return. Trusting—hoping—that Basim would uphold his end of the agreement. The men under Basim were strong fighters and ruthless. Not easily overtaken. Knowing they were fighting for Sariba gave me a little more faith and lifted me from my despair.

My chin turned, seeking out Kadesh. He was a striking figure in King Ephrem's uniform. Back erect, he stood taller than most of his army. His regal bearing diminished the loss of his eye and the scars he bore, but he still suffered a deficit in his peripheral vision. I wanted to slip into the pocket closest to his heart and be his eyes and ears. His rearward protection.

"Come back to me," I whispered. If the king went down, we were all doomed. Nobody could take his place, not Uncle Josiah or General Naham. Horeb would quickly storm the city and declare himself the new king with Aliyah as queen.

A male voice interrupted my reverie. "Lady Jayden," Asher said, glancing down at Kadesh and then looking at me meaningfully. "I remember the night on the desert with Laban, when the traitor took a swipe at Kadesh's blind side. I plan to stay at his side."

"But without your father as general, you need to lead your Edomites into battle."

"My father is sitting up and vows to be on the battlefield with us by tomorrow."

I gave him a small smile. "With bandages and patches?"

"Even with bandages and patches. The bleeding has stopped, and he's eating well. Eager to kill a few Maachathites and Assyrians."

"I want you to kill a few Nephish, too, even though I've known many of the younger soldiers since my childhood. I can't think of their families back home without terrible remorse."

"No guilt, Jayden. No regrets," Asher said gently. "The Nephish banished you. Destroyed your family, your reputation, and framed you for the murder of your king."

I nodded, trying not to dwell on those terrible days. "I'm more worried about you and your soldiers' safety. The safety of Sariba's citizens. Families have been escaping, trying to find refuge in the Qara caves, and Horeb's spies kill them. Their blood is on my hands. How can Sariba ever honor me as their queen?"

Asher gripped my shoulders, turning me to face him. Morning light slanted across his dark eyes and the lock of hair that perpetually fell across his forehead. "Everyone's death in this war is Horeb's fault. Never forget that. Never."

I bit at my lips, knowing he was right, but it was difficult to put aside the guilt.

"Sariba will be victorious. Trust us. Pray for that."

I placed a hand on top of his, grateful for his friendship and protection. "Go with God's blessings and victory, Prince Asher."

He inhaled, trembling at my touch. "Thank you, my queen. With your blessings, I can fight fifty men and return to the palace tonight unscathed."

Asher bowed and then he was gone, while the weight of a thousand stones seemed to press upon me. I tried to take comfort from my last few moments that morning with Kadesh. Our kisses and Kadesh's refusal to speak any words of good-bye.

Thoughts like these would only get me weeping again, and I needed all my wits today—before the sun rose higher.

Aunt Naomi had requested my presence today, but I was putting her off for a few hours. I'd seen Uncle Josiah on a black gelding, ready to lead a platoon of archers with bows strapped to their backs.

All at once, an idea gripped me and I raced down the stairs after Asher back to the stables. When I arrived, I ordered, "Get me a fresh horse, please."

The stable boys stared at me as if I'd gone mad, but when I strode toward one of the horse stalls, they quickly went into action. When I swung onto a mount, I rode toward the northeastern desert beyond the temple. The army would be leaving within moments, and I intended to ride out with Kadesh as his queen.

General Naham frowned at me, visibly angry when he saw me appear. "This is no place for a woman," he said sharply. "This first battle is going to be vicious on my soldiers. They aren't used to fighting, despite their training. Watching their friends die will be brutal."

"This might not be a place for a woman, but it *is* a place for a queen," I reminded him.

A mix of emotions crossed Kadesh's face when I galloped toward him. "You should be safely at the palace with Aunt Naomi and the rest of the family," he said. "Please go. I can hardly stand to see you out here with three armies only a league's distance before us."

"Your army needs to see us together first. I will ride out with you. You are their king, and I am their future queen. They need to see our confidence and our loyalty to them and to each other. This war is only because of me and I won't sit inside the palace and wait—not when they are fighting and dying for me."

The outraged lines on his face finally softened. "Fall into place beside me."

All around us, the troops were moving into formation. Archers, foot soldiers, and then the cavalry made up of the

Edomites and Basim's men. The men wore full gear, their waists heavy with swords, daggers, and slings.

Kadesh and I sat before the army and he raised his voice. "My soldiers, my countrymen!" he shouted above the sound of the animals pawing at the ground. "We are your king and queen of Sariba! We stand together as one. We honor you for the loyalty and obedience you have shown to us. Go forth with courage and conviction. Remember that you are defending your wives, your children, and your homes from an enemy who would see every last one of you dead. They would steal your city, your shops and businesses, and farms and lands. They would rule over you and subject you to slavery and subjugation. Never doubt your right to live here peacefully. Never doubt our love and gratitude for you. We are not only your king and queen but we are your servants in life and in death."

The combined armies cheered his words, and then as one body, we turned our animals to face the open desert. Up ahead, the tents of Horeb loomed. The scouts had already seen us, and Horeb's troops were assembling. We wouldn't know their actual numbers after being ill from the poison until we were upon them.

Fear roiled in my gut. I couldn't seem to catch a decent breath.

"You have no armor, Jayden," Kadesh reminded me. "You will *not* be on the front lines. After we charge forward swing around and return home at once."

"I'll wait for you on the ramparts, my king," I told him. "My love."

Kadesh pulled me in for a fervent, hard kiss and Sariba's troops cheered again, along with spurts of laughter.

Silence descended again just as quickly. The morning air stilled while the early sun poured down upon our heads.

There was a quick intake of breath, and then Kadesh's voice roared the order to charge.

Instantly, the valley turned into a cloud of galloping horses and horrendous dust.

"I can *feel* the hooves inside the earth," I murmured aloud, and the sense of awe was overwhelming.

Sariba's cavalry broke off into two groups, skirting the main army to flank Horeb while Kadesh's archers stopped to set up their line, whipping out bows and their shields at the ready.

Screams rent the air as the first of the arrows were let loose, whizzing ferociously through the air and then thudding with precision into Horeb's soldiers.

Horeb's archers instantly launched a return volley, freezing me in place.

"*My lady!*" General Naham growled. "Get away now! Quickly!"

I tried to swallow but couldn't even speak. Finally, I wrenched my gaze away from the battle and turned toward the city, its walls a mirage in the distance.

Jonah appeared at my side. "This way," he added a bit more gently. "Our soldiers wear boiled-leather armor. They'll survive. The fight will go on all day. And tomorrow. And the next day. Our task is to prevent it from lasting so many weeks nobody is left alive. And my task right now is to see you home in one piece."

I wished I had leather or cloth armor under my tunic. I'd never been so vulnerable, but already, as I skirted the battle-field next to Jonah, men were sprawling on the earth in death. Swords glittered under the brittle summer sun, horses lying askew, taken down with their master still in the saddle. I bit down on my lip so hard I drew blood. Then I kicked the sides of my horse into a gallop.

Please, dear God, I prayed, head down over my saddle. *Please let Kadesh come home to me.*

When I approached the palace, I was shocked at the num-ber of people pouring into the outer complex and grounds. Frightened women with their children, older boys threatening to go fight beside their fathers and uncles.

Everyone was unnerved. Stories murmured all around me about those who had died trying to escape. Ruthless deaths by Horeb's army, intended to terrorize and demoralize Sariba. The brutality and mercilessness of it made me sick.

Thankfully, General Naham hadn't left the city defenseless. Part of the army surrounded the city walls in case rogue fight-ers attempted to invade while our army was gone. But Horeb's armies were larger, and leaving a contingency to defend the city shrunk Sariba's army that much more.

Wearing the deep red dress, I was self-conscious at bring-ing attention to myself riding through the city streets. The citizens stopped their tasks to stare at me. Shop owners, potters and weavers, the farmers, and the women at the wells.

I was still a stranger to them, but murmuring accusations rolled past like angry waves. Most of them had never seen war in this secluded valley of frankincense. Whereas I had grown up with tribal skirmishes on an annual basis.

I skirted the palace gardens and hurried to the east doors, taking the steps two at a time. When I pulled down my white headscarf, the guards immediately let me in, and I practically ran down the halls to my bedroom suite.

The same guard that had been on duty that morning was still at the doors of my suite. He gave me a brief nod while I slipped inside.

Two pairs of eyes stared up at me. Tijah rose from her mending beside the window, questions on her lips while Jasmine froze in her bed-making.

"It is done," I said quietly. "Our soldiers are gone to battle."

While I changed out of my good dress and scrubbed the dust from my face, Jasmine made a motion of eating with her fingers and left to retrieve breakfast from the kitchens.

I wasn't hungry, but not knowing what was going on at the battlefield gnawed at me.

Tijah fixed my hair and belted a sash around my dress. Then I spent the day pacing at Naomi's suite, making idle conversation, and staring out the windows from each side of the room.

"Shall we take care of the queen's quarters?" Aunt Naomi finally asked, worry in her eyes.

"I'm too distracted." I rose from the couch and slipped my sandals back on. "I'll be back in a bit."

"Perhaps a nap would do you good?"

I shook my head. "My mind is a jumble of worries and I can't sleep. I'm going to the parapet overlook."

I took the corridor to the east corner and then the outer stairs up to the wall. Gulping in fresh air, I gripped the ledge while the city spread out below me like a jewel. The red-tiled roofs and meandering streets with hanging baskets of fresh flowers were deceptively calm.

At the northern gates, guards stood on top of the walls in the late afternoon sun, Sariba flags rippling in the hot breeze. My stomach turned upside down when I spotted the army returning far in the distance.

A noise came from behind me and when I turned, Uncle Josiah was coming up the parapet steps. He took my arm. "Come, Jayden, let us go greet our king and his men."

We stood under the palace pavilion while the army of Sariba, including the Edomites and Basim's soldiers, clopped down the main boulevard.

A fragile dusk fell over the city like a curtain. Lights began to flicker along the avenues and roads until the cry for the blackout was called and the lamps were quickly extinguished. There were no cheering crowds. War was not something Sariba rejoiced in or celebrated.

Clinging to Josiah's arm, I watched the troops and horsemen head to the stables to relieve their animals. Then these good men would return home to embrace their wives and children, fill their bellies with hot food, and then sleep before dawn arrived again.

Bringing up the rear, the royal flags fluttered.

"I can hardly bear watching this," I said in a low voice. My eyes were dizzy and perspiration stained my neck.

"You must bear it, my lady," Uncle Josiah said. "This and so much more if you are to be queen of this land. There will be long caravan trips when you don't see Kadesh for months. Citizens who murmur against the royal family, poor crop years, and the encroaching sands of the desert to always fight back so it doesn't overtake our frankincense and homes."

"You frighten me, Uncle Josiah," I said, trying to keep my voice light.

"As queen you will be called on to do many hard things—and many wonderful things. From what Kadesh has told me, you are well acquainted with grief."

I gazed at him in silence, a mutual understanding and respect growing between us. When I spotted Kadesh in his royal uniform, the colors dimmed by dust and grime, I said, "But I've also been very blessed."

Picking up the hem of my dress, I ran down the stairs to the road. Briefly, I lost sight of Kadesh, but then he came into view again, surrounded by his guardsmen, the standard bearers bringing up the rear.

I choked down a sob and raced to his horse. "Kadesh!" I practically shrieked. Quickly, I swallowed my exuberance, knowing it didn't become my position, but the soldiers hid their smiles and tipped their heads toward me in respect.

Kadesh gripped my hand so tight I thought he'd crush it, and then bent to kiss my palm. "Your hands are chapped and there are fresh blisters. What were you doing today?"

"Scrubbing shirts at the local washing hole," I said, the teasing coming out so easily I surprised myself. I didn't want him to worry about me while he was fighting for the survival of his people.

He raised an eyebrow and I barely recognized him under the grime. "My scouts tell me that well over three hundred of Horeb's men were ill in their tents. Stricken by a strange flu."

I lifted my chin, suppressing a smile. We were eye to eye.

"Do you know anything about that, my queen?" he teased.

I lifted my shoulders in mock ignorance. "Our foreign water must not agree with them."

Kadesh let out a sharp laugh. "You clever girl," he murmured with admiration.

"Some soldiers don't know how to keep a secret. Kadesh," I added, "I want to fight with you tomorrow. Which means I need armor."

"The Assyrians will tear you to shreds in minutes, Jayden. I forbid you."

"But I want to be useful."

"You don't think you've been useful? I have Basim and an extra fifty extraordinary horsemen because of you. And over the past two days, hundreds of Horeb's men have been vomiting in their tents, or are now being buried in a mass grave. You are ruthless, my future queen."

Despite the hint of macabre humor, it brought me no pleasure to know that Jonah and I had poisoned so many men. My only consolation was knowing that these foreign soldiers were most likely unmarried men without wives and children. Whereas the men of Sariba left widows and orphans.

The ugliness of battle was strewn with dead and dying men. I imagine the grieving homes, the moans and tears of loss tonight.

Pain swam in Kadesh's face. He didn't say it, but Sariba had lost too many men today. I placed my hands against his cheeks and lifted my face to kiss him despite the grime all over him. "After you take care of your horse," I said quietly, "come inside for dinner and rest before you fall over faint."

"Am I a terrible king coming home to my own bed each night?" Kadesh asked. "We've left the rest of our army on the desert to camp tonight between the frankincense groves and the battlefield. It's too risky to leave the area open for Horeb's scouts and spies to infiltrate the temple grounds. Perhaps an even greater risk is if Horeb dispatches small envoys to slip into our forest to have them hide, waiting for an opportunity to scale the walls of the city and commit brutal acts against our citizens."

I nodded gravely in agreement. "It's better to have our army in between the city and the enemy."

Even so, I wouldn't doubt any sort of trickery from Horeb until he knew that every citizen of Sariba was dead or had bowed prostrate to the ground in obeisance to him as King of Sariba.

26

On the second day of battle, I found myself once more taking care of the personal belongings of a family member who had suddenly and tragically died in the last two weeks.

Naomi and I spent the morning organizing the Queen of Sheba's possessions and writing letters of condolences to the Sa'ba royal family. Letters that would be sent with Kadesh's letters when he had time to compose them.

We burned the queen's filthy traveling clothes and the bloodstained dress she'd been wearing when Aliyah murdered her at the summer solstice.

The queen had brought no personal maids with her, but her soldiers helped us lift and carry the trunks, their faces solemn, their demeanors tragically bereft. I sensed a deep abiding guilt underneath their heartache, as if they were responsible for bringing the queen to Sariba only to watch her executed.

I had no way of comforting them or telling them anything differently, but I knew their pain well; it was too close to my own.

Naomi had her scribe make a list of the few possessions, clothing, and weapons while we ordered her traveling chests re-packed. In reality, for the great queen she was, she had brought very little with her.

It had been a speedy and secretive journey to get here before the first battle began. She had traveled disguised as a man with her soldiers masquerading as a small pack of desert hunters. Knowing Horeb's armies were somewhere on the desert, the queen had felt it imperative to travel incognito and had miraculously avoided Horeb by traveling the last few days during the night. But as an ally and cousin of the royal family, it was a trek she was more familiar with than most who found themselves wandering the desolate terrain that skirted the empty sands.

The queen's camels and horses were being taken care of in the palace stables for the soldiers' return trip. Of course, Kadesh would make sure her caravan and envoy back to Sa'ba was worthy of a queen.

"Oh, that you had never come here," I groaned when I saw the small keepsakes she had brought with her from her children. A heart-shaped stone painted with flowers. A knotted string necklace with dried flowers from her homeland.

I laid the childlike treasures in our finest linen parchment and tied them with string, then laid them on top of the trunk before the lid was closed and locked.

"As far as we can tell, all is accounted for," Naomi said at last, dismissing the scribe.

By midafternoon, I was standing at the window of my room, straining my eyes toward the foothills of the mountains, catching sight of distant clouds of dust where the man I loved was locked in a fierce battle for the survival of our beloved country. A battle for his life, the life of his men, and the lives of every Sariba citizen.

My throat was dry, my eyes wide, because I could not cry anymore. It would be another terrible day of fighting, and I determined that I couldn't give in to desolation, not when the people around me needed me to be strong.

Before packing the queen's possessions, I'd spent the morning distracting my handmaids and Sahmril with stories about our baby camels and the details of our desert weddings, especially my cousin Hakak's beautiful wedding more than a year ago. I thought about the lost family of my tribe, relatives I would probably never see again.

A sudden, acute ache for my cousins—their smiles and laughter, the jokes and sewing nights, the evenings of dancing and gossip were gone forever. I could picture their faces. I remembered their beauty and generosity and the one-time loyalty.

Horeb had stolen them from me, too.

At the moment, I not only missed my mother, but I was desperate to hold the memories of my grandmother, Seraiah, close. I wished she were here to comfort me and my father. To rock Sahmril in her arms. To tell *me* stories of my father as a boy and the mischief he got into. For all Seraiah's wit and snapping black eyes, her son had turned into a stoic, mournful man, bereft of his land, his country, and the familial ties of the royal family of the Nephish.

A knock sounded at the door, and I started.

Aunt Naomi stood there, holding out her hands to me. "It's time, Jayden."

"I know," I said, sighing deeply. "I'm supposed to be an adult, but I wish I could crawl back under the bed covers and pretend that none of this was happening. I wish I could remember the queen as she was in all her beauty and wisdom."

"Taking care of her possessions is part of remembering her," Naomi told me, tugging me away from the window. "It's how we show her respect and love."

Reluctantly, I pushed away from the window ledge, wanting to watch and wait for Kadesh. "The melancholy weighs at me. The sickening waste of lives. The senselessness. All because of me. Perhaps I should have made different choices."

Fiercely, Naomi gathered me into her arms. "Your choices weren't wrong. They were yours to make. You have a right to happiness and peace as does everyone. Your choice never forced Horeb or Aliyah to make theirs. But they did, and now their choices force all of us to live with terrible consequences— and choices we should not have had to make."

"But the consequences are no less hard to bear," I said.

"That is certain," Naomi agreed sadly. "Now let's go pay our final respects to the great Queen of Sa'ba."

The queen's soldiers stood at attention outside the room where her body lay in state. She would have no formal embalming. None of her queenly robes, crown, and jewels that she deserved.

Waves of anger pulsed over me at her death. Such a senseless, incomparable tragedy. Such a waste of a noble ruler. A woman who had helped to keep the peace of the desert kingdoms after her own parents' sad lives.

Our skirts rustled when Naomi and I entered the quiet, windowless room. It was hot and stuffy, the worst room for a body recently deceased, despite the frankincense and perfumes she had been anointed with. We were past the summer solstice now, and the summer heat was becoming unbearable in the afternoons.

"We must move her to a room with windows on both sides for a cross draft," I said immediately. The words were out before I'd consulted with Lady Naomi first, but when I glanced at her she nodded her approval.

"I agree, Lady Jayden," she said, loud enough for the Sa'ba soldiers to hear. "Kadesh and Josiah will want to pay their respects tonight."

I lowered my voice. "We also need to discuss the future for her body. Do we have a funeral pyre as we did for King Ephrem?"

"We don't need to make that decision right now. Talk it over with Kadesh. You'll make the correct decision on that course. For now, let's focus on the queen."

A soldier stepped forward. "I'm the queen's captain and I'd like to dictate a letter to the queen's husband in Sa'ba and dispatch it immediately."

I shook my head. "No, I forbid you until we speak with King Kadesh. He is her cousin. He'll write the necessary letters himself."

The man bowed. "As you wish, my lady. We'll stand guard so that nobody has access to the queen until the King of Sariba directs us."

"Thank you. I'm grateful for your loyalty and discretion."

I stepped across the tiled floor toward the bier, emotion choking at my heart to see the queen laid out in death. I turned cold, my head reeling and my chest throbbing.

Two nights ago, I'd scrubbed at the Queen of Sheba's blood on my hands and clothes for an hour. Ever since, food had tasted like sand.

I'd never forget the wounded expression on Kadesh's face when he saw the bloody queen carried back to the palace after Aliyah had killed her. His mourning broke my heart into small, sharp edges.

The small room was lit by candles placed on four corner tables. There were no overhead sconces or chandeliers. A table laid with finely stitched magenta-dyed linen draped to the floor in soft folds, overlaid with a snowy-white triangle.

Lying in state was the Queen of Sheba in the finest dress she had brought with her. A dress meant to be worn at an elegant royal banquet. One she had never had the chance to wear. It was deep blue like the ocean, blue as the garnet jewels fastened to her neck and ears.

The queen's long black hair had been washed to a glossy sheen by Lady Naomi's personal maid, an older woman experienced in life and death a hundred times over. Her hair was now overlaid with a net of amethyst and carnelian.

She was as beautiful in death as she had been in life, her attire the scent of lilac and frankincense. Bouquets of roses and orchids lay in baskets about her feet, breathing some semblance of life into the mourning room.

I reached out to touch the queen's cold fingers, placing my palm on top of her folded hands. The gashes Aliyah had given her along her palms were still there, forever unhealed, but no longer bleeding.

"Aliyah broke her sister bond to you, my queen," I whispered. "My heart is broken for you, for all of us who will mourn you from this day forward. Kadesh will be kind to your husband and children who wait for your return."

A shiver crawled down my spine. I wanted to shake her awake, to see that serene smile one more time. If only I could beg her to come back to us. All the deaths I'd known my whole life had been sudden and unexpected. Beginning with Horeb's older brother Zenos, dead after a raid with the Maachathite, leaving Leila lost without her betrothed. My mother's dead babies, and then her own sudden death giving birth to Sahmril, Uncle Ephrem's collapse at the wedding, and now a queen I admired. A woman who had been my friend. A woman I'd looked to as a role model and friend.

"Oh, my queen, what is noble? What is right and wrong anymore?"

"The same virtues that have always been right," spoke Kadesh from the back of the quiet room.

My head jerked up. The sight of him brought an onslaught of tears to my eyes. Tears I'd been fighting all day as I rushed across the room to fly into his arms.

We embraced and walked back to the bier together.

"Nobleness is love for your family," Kadesh said. "Fidelity in your soul. The goodness of one's country. Devotion to the true and living God. But sometimes, to protect the good we have to do away with tyranny and fight for freedom. Even if we lose our lives in the process."

Dusk descended upon the city. The fighting was over for another day. "But you're here now," I said, clinging to him. "You're alive."

"I promised I would come home to you every night. And I intend to keep that promise."

"The Queen of Sheba lost her life trying to stop her sister. I fear Horeb will give me no other choice either."

Kadesh lifted my chin and gazed into my eyes with his bottomless pools of darkness. I leaned against him, falling into those eyes, into him. He pressed me close, and I wrapped my arms around him.

"Jayden," he said. "Horeb has already given us no other choice. He had many chances to stop the hate and war, and every single time he's chosen oppression, greed, and power."

His words strengthened me while I took a deep breath and stepped toward the dais for the final time. Was the queen's presence still among us? I hoped she was listening and hadn't already moved beyond our world.

"Good-bye, my queen," I whispered, smoothing a hand along the rich textured fabric of her sleeve. She was younger in death than I had realized because she had been so formidable in life. "I will be forever indebted to you."

I bent over and kissed her cold cheek, tears slipping down my cheeks, and then I stepped back to allow Kadesh to say his farewells.

27

nother day of fighting passed and I was about to
leap out a window from nerves.

The loss of life was devastating. Every family
had been affected, and the mourning in the city was an agony
of weeping and wailing. I stood at the windows of the palace
gazing down at elderly gravediggers walking up and down the
city streets with their shovels and red-rimmed eyes.

When Kadesh and General Naham arrived at the end of
each day's fighting, there were few words and little eaten or
spoken between them.

No matter how much I enjoyed playing with Sahmril and
singing the songs of home, I couldn't stay in the city any
longer.

I'd moved Sahmril into my room and slept with her curled
in my arms. Thomas and Zarah, her adoptive parents from

Mari, were right here in Sariba. Ready to snatch my baby sister away from me again. A letter had arrived after midsummer's eve, asking for her, but I hadn't responded yet.

Each night when I pulled the blanket around her against the cool night, I fought my internal battle of not wanting to share her. "I can't give you up now that I've found you," I whispered against her hair. "If they take you, I'd never see you again. You belong with me, with your father. *We* are your family."

For the first time since I'd rescued Sahmril from Aliyah's sacrificial ceremony, the little girl turned in her sleep and put her arms around my neck. Her dark eyes fluttered, half-asleep, half-awake.

"I love you, Sahmril," I told her. "I've loved you from the moment I held you in my arms on the day you were born."

She stared at me with those big dark eyes of my mother's, and I didn't know if she understood what I was telling her, but I suspected that she did.

I tried to tamp down the memories of that terrible day. "Your mother is my mother. You and I are sisters, and I promised I would always take care of you."

Her eyelids closed, and she was soon asleep while the moon sank.

Before the sun rose on the third morning, I instructed Tijah to dress me for battle. She had scrubbed the trousers and my black tunic so it was clean again. The previous evening I'd sent a message to Asher asking for armor. He had brought it reluctantly, his eyes conveying his unhappiness that I was planning on going to the battlefield that day.

The armor he'd produced was crafted of thick cloth and sewn together in multiple layers. When I tied it around my chest, I realized that the pieces had seen previous battles if the tears and nicks were any indication.

A knock at the door sounded and when I opened it, a palace guard held out a thick, woven helmet from the armory.

"I wish I had boiled leather armor for you, my lady," the guard said, his eyes roving over my newly sharpened dagger and sword, a magenta Sariba sash tied firmly to my waist where my sling hung.

"Me, too," I said, praying that I wasn't making the mistake of my life.

After kissing my sister and maids, I was surprised to pass Uncle Josiah on my way to the north doors. He stopped to take in my unexpected appearance, even as he bowed.

"You recognized me so easily in my disguise as a soldier?" I asked.

He grinned in return. "I've lived a long time, my lady. If you insist on being with the troops, go with my blessings." He laid his big, warm hands on my head, and the touch was a comfort. "Fight with your heart. Do not doubt your love for this land and its king. I will see you on the battlefield shortly."

When we reached the stables, Asher led me outside to the open-air paddocks. "Jayden, I don't like this at all. If Kadesh learns I gave you armor he'd—"

"It's too late for that," Kadesh said behind him.

I cleared my throat. "I understand that the Edomites and Basim's mountain men are going to be your shock troops this morning. I want to go with you and give them my support and gratitude."

Asher shook his head, his lips a thin line of unhappiness. We stared each other down for several long moments.

"I can't spend another day pacing the palace, knowing I could kill a few Assyrians," I said, feeling rebellious.

"I don't envy the enemy who gets in your way," Asher finally said, giving a brief tug at my sling before mounting his horse.

Beside Kadesh, General Naham ordered the line-up of troops and horses. Dust rose as we left the compound and headed up the hills of the city.

I fell in between Asher and Kadesh while Basim, flanked by two of his men, passed us to fall into formation on the left side of the Edomites. Basim didn't appear surprised to see me. Rather, he tipped his head toward me, recognizing me as easily as Uncle Josiah had.

An hour's ride later, we were in sight of Horeb's camp.

Sariba's army had left even earlier than the previous morning, hoping to catch Horeb by surprise. Dawn slanted across the valley in strips of gold and red.

"Can you see anything?" I asked Asher.

Nerves tore at my gut as we drew closer. I placed a hand on the hilt of my sword, running through various sword moves in my head.

"Steady, my lady," Asher said, as if seeing the panic on my

face. "Horeb's men are ready for us—as many as there were the last two days. His ill men must be healthy again, unfortunately."

He was right. "So many of them," I whispered, observing the perfect formation of troops as far as I could see.

He glanced at me. "It boosted our morale to not lose more men, but losses still take a toll. Many men are weary and grieving. Or overconfident in their eagerness for revenge, which can often be worse. That's when mistakes are made."

"Asher," I said, turning to stare at him. "What aren't you telling me?"

His eyes flickered away. "Horeb's army has a secret weapon that we do not possess."

My chest rose. "Aliyah," I breathed.

"She was here this morning—with Horeb. She's their talisman. Their hope. Their Goddess."

Kadesh spoke up, visibly reigning in his anger. "There was a ceremony this morning with the magicians from Egypt. Including a human sacrifice of one of his horse handler's. A son of one of the captains."

Asher watched me steadily. "Yesterday, Aliyah rode out at Horeb's side on a white horse. A sword raised in her fist."

His words painted a picture in my mind. I envisioned Aliyah in all her glory. Black hair flying in the wind, strands streaming across her face. A stunning dress billowing about her figure, luring the men to follow her. To die on their swords for her.

"They're trying to intimidate our soldiers," I said. "Did she actually fight?"

"Of course not," Kadesh said grimly. "It was merely to show us that Sariba's Goddess temple has sided with the enemy. General Naham is worried about desertions now. Or rather, our soldiers fighting for Horeb instead of Kadesh. After all the deaths our army has suffered, the citizens are even more afraid of angering the Goddess. They are beginning to believe that they sided with the wrong king and forsook the Goddess at their own peril."

"People should realize she's a traitor to her own people," I snapped.

"She makes a pretty convincing traitor," Asher said.

I glanced at him sharply, but his face was sullen. He had accepted the odds against us, and the consequences, whatever they would be. A bite of emotion ate at my heart.

"I didn't mean for that to sound like—"

"I don't doubt your loyalty to Kadesh," I assured him.

"And my loyalty to Kadesh's queen," he added. "I would die for Edom and my people, but I will also die for Sariba's sovereignty."

"And freedom," Kadesh added. "Without the freedom given to us at birth, we are merely slaves to tyrants like Horeb and Aliyah."

We went silent for the last half league, but my heart stuttered inside my chest. I hadn't been this close to Horeb in months. His large camp was intimidating. When they caught sight of us coming up the final rise, we watched his army assembled into professional ranks almost instantly.

"Despite our hope to catch them by surprise their spies

already saw us, and reported," Kadesh said, his voice rising with frustration. He shouted to his general, "We must go faster."

A signal came from one of the trumpets. The pounding of the horses' hooves grew louder as we picked up speed. My belly tumbled with every second, and already I was dripping sweat inside my clothes.

The Edomites broke into two formations, one going south and one to the north. General Naham sent two of his captains with the group to the south. I followed Asher to skirt around the north end of Horeb's camp.

All at once, Kadesh gained on me. "Please, Jayden, try to stay back. The Assyrians are twice your size and their hatred just as venomous. Despite our own losses, the army of Assyria lost almost as many. The poisoning we did especially incited their hatred for us."

I attempted a smile, shouting over the noise of the galloping horses. "So I'll let you handle the Assyrians."

His long hair blew like a flag in the wind. "That's why I love you. But if any of our enemies suspect you are Sariba's queen, they will kidnap you, and I shudder to think what they will do to you."

I nodded, fully aware of the danger, and then our horses broke away. Fifty Edomites at full speed on their splendid horses was a sight to behold. I choked on the dust from the grinding hooves, despite the scarf covering my face.

"Shock troops," Asher yelled when we rounded about on our enemy's archers. Lining up behind their shields, they began launching arrows in the direction of our foot soldiers. The sudden blood-curdling cries of the Edomite men when they charged was eerie and unexpected.

The Maachathite archers were as rattled by the screams as I was, rallying frantically to get their first arrows up in the air.

Kadesh wheeled about on his horse before the cavalry, galloping up and down the lines with a speed that overwhelmed me. "Draw your swords!"

And then we were in the fray.

"Stay at my side!" Asher yelled, drawing my horse close to his. "We'll work together!"

My sword came out of its sheath like water slipping over a riverbed. Its edge glinted in a sudden ray of brilliant dawn, and my heart was in my throat at its deadly beauty. Sitting low on my horse, I swiped at one of the standing archers, giving him a blow that knocked him off his feet.

With a single stroke, Asher finished him off, and the man fell to his knees, keeling over, a sheath of arrows spilling to the earth. The man next to him seized the arrows, crouching behind a shield.

Before he could notch one of the tapered weapons into his bow, Asher and I took him out with a blow on either side of his neck.

All around me came the clash of swords, the bitter grunt and cries of men fighting hand to hand. Many Edomites carried axes. Other Sariba soldiers were skilled in spear throwing, for which I was grateful when I found myself nearly taken down by an Assyrian warrior. After swinging about with our swords on our horses, a sudden slash razed across my arm. A heartbeat later, the Assyrian fell to the ground when a spear pierced his neck, but I had no idea who had just saved my life.

After several more blows, my arms ached. My bones shuddered each time I swung the sword with one hand, gripping the mane of my horse with the other. After three more swings, I couldn't stand the pain and feared I'd shatter into a hundred pieces. Straightening, I utilized both arms, but sitting higher on my horse also made me more vulnerable.

"Stay down!" Asher ordered, delivering the death blow to another archer. "We're pulling back now!"

I clung to my horse's mane while we retreated in a frenzy of men and animals and dust.

Miraculously, the shock strategy had worked. Many archers were dead or wounded. A few arrows rained about us, but we deflected and galloped south in the direction of the city. At least the temple and the lower forest stood between the fighting and the city.

When we pulled up at a safer distance, we turned around to stare over our shoulders. The shock troops to the north were having success, too.

"There weren't as many archers today," Asher said, confusion in his face when he searched the horizon.

The fields filled with foot soldiers now fighting man to man. Free from the threat of screaming arrows raining down from the sky.

Kadesh pounded up beside us. "The fighting will go on for hours, and I won't stand idly by." His words had the edge of acute frustration. "So many times we've tried to deal a resounding blow and push them back, but they're too experienced, too hardened."

Several Edomites had just lost their lives from the expert archers, their beautiful Arabian horses wounded or roaming the desert.

I stole a glance at Asher, his face pale.

"You've done well with Asher," Kadesh praised me, reaching out to grip my hand in his. "It's after high sun."

Hours had gone by already. My stomach was hollow with a peculiar pain. I jerked the reins of my horse, moving closer. "What is it, Kadesh?"

"Horeb's numbers were up today, unfortunately. Some of his men must have recovered from their illness. My men are stressed to keep up. Although Basim's group hasn't had a single casualty yet. With thanks to you, my love."

Kadesh pulled at the leather harness of my horse, bringing me closer. We were eye to eye, my leg locked tight against his.

I gave him an optimistic look despite my sweaty hair and blood-splattered cloak. "I hope my true character will remain noble in the future, dear sir."

"Have no fear on that score." He lowered his voice so that Asher couldn't hear us. "Our marriage covenant as King and Queen of Sariba just became much more real."

"We will keep the faith together," I told him.

"I'm trying," he said, but his eyes were devastated at Sariba's losses.

"Kadesh," I said, "I need you to stay strong. You have to. You can't give up. Not only for me and my family but for those men out there fighting and dying. For your father and mother and King Ephrem."

"You should have stayed at the palace," he told me now.

"The battlefield is worse than I expected," I admitted. "Which means, I will continue to fight with all of you," I said. "So our soldiers don't lose hope."

Kadesh's mouth tightened. "Stay close to Asher. Circle around to the northeast along the low-lying boulders and get a report from Basim about the fighting there. I'll be here on the west with General Naham. Return *here*."

I saluted him. "Yes, my king."

All at once, he pulled me to him and kissed me. "Now go before I change my mind."

After a gulp of water from my leather skin, Asher and I raced toward the foothills. Basim's men were bloodied and fierce. The sight was unsettling.

"Come this way, my lady!" Asher shouted, beckoning me to follow him.

Even I could see that some of the marauders from Sa'ba were in trouble. Horeb had sent in fresh men, and we were losing this skirmish. After everything I had promised Basim, I couldn't let him lose his men.

We raced forward and employed the same strategy as in the morning, working as a team to keep Horeb's men at bay. Hot sun poured along my shoulders and sweat streamed down my face. With every stroke of my sword, I tasted grit in my mouth.

A Maachathite galloped toward me and I screamed for Asher, rising up on my horse to grip my sword with both fists.

I swung and the clang reverberated so harshly I thought I'd broken my arm. My sword fell into the dirt, and, before I could steady myself, I was falling. The ground rushed up to meet me, and I landed with a cruel thud.

I lay still, trying to suck in air. My lungs seemed to have seized up. The sounds of battle disappeared with the roaring in my ears. I stared up at the sky, gulping against the pain in my lungs.

Sunset slipped along the valley floor of the Qara Mountains like sand through an hourglass. The man who had knocked me off my horse must have thought he'd killed me because he'd left me where I'd fallen.

I lifted my head cautiously. Basim's men had drawn the enemy deeper into the center of the valley. My horse was placidly eating grass, but stood too far away. I dared not call to him or walk out to retrieve him while the falling light blinded me.

Groaning, I rolled over and tried to sit up to get my bearings. I needed to head for the boulders and caves and walk back to the city. And I needed to move before any Assyrians spotted me.

Getting to my knees, I tried to stand but my legs wobbled and I fell over again.

Taking a breath, I attempted to rise once more—just as two sets of arms grabbed me on either side and hauled me to my feet.

28

Two men from my old tribe gripped me so tight I swore their hands had turned into a vise. Words gurgled in my throat, but I coughed up more dust than coherent sentences.

"Prisoner of war." They laughed while one of them picked up my sword and stuck it inside his waist belt.

"That sword is mine!" I protested, but they ignored me, dragging me along the ground as they took me in the opposite direction of Sariba.

The tents of Horeb's armies loomed, becoming more distinct by the moment.

Soldiers moved about. Returning from the battle zone. Building fires, tending to their weapons, carrying water, grooming horses.

The stutter in my chest turned to such a painful pounding

I feared I might have heart failure.

"Where are you taking me?" I demanded.

"To the King of the Nephish," came the curt reply.

The thought of being in his presence terrified me more than fighting his foreign soldiers. I couldn't believe I'd allowed myself to get captured. Where was Asher? I'd lost sight of him and worried that he'd fallen in battle. If he died, I'd never forgive myself.

The camp swam before my eyes, but the enemy territory had suddenly stilled. The clatter of dishes stopped. The tasks ceased.

The two soldiers handed me off to another pair, and these men hauled me so fast along the rocky path my shins scraped along the stones as I scrambled to stay on my feet.

"It's a woman!" someone shouted. "Sariba is so weak their women are fighting!"

Jeers and rude language surrounded me. I shut my ears, praying that I would survive.

I was shaking by the time we came to the main tent. Horeb's personal guards lined the perimeter, and one of them parted the doors, shouting, "Tell Horeb we have a gift for him!"

The next moment I was shoved inside. The interior was dark, and it took a moment for my eyes to adjust.

My arms hurt from being bandied about, and I rubbed at my shoulders, trying to rid myself of the lingering imprint of their touch.

"What gift is this?" Horeb was closer than I expected, his bulky shadow looming directly in front of me. There was a note of surprise in his voice, followed by a low chuckle. "A very *nice* gift to end my day of battle," he added, reaching out to cup my elbow with his meaty hand, and then catching my fingers with his to pull me closer. "A day of battle in which I kill my enemy's army and then sliced the King of Sariba into tiny pieces."

I shuddered while he stared into my eyes, willing myself not to flinch.

Horeb had fully become a man over the past year. He was taller, wider, even more muscled than I remembered, his hair long and ragged and wild. The girls of my tribe used to swoon at a glimpse of him striding about the camp. He was as handsome as ever, but there was a calculating coldness in his eyes brought on by years of raids and ambition fueled by the belief that his father preferred his older brother Zenos. That belief drove Horeb's every waking thought and action.

"What do I owe the pleasure of a visit from my betrothed? My Nephish princess."

Horeb drew his sword. Circling me, he tugged at the clasp of my cloak, releasing the ties so that it dropped to the ground about my feet. "I hardly recognized you in your battle gear. You even wear body armor. I'm impressed. But I find it amusing that the King of Sariba has you fighting with him. A sign of weakness, indeed."

The other men in the tent laughed, and I sucked in my breath, gripping my fists so tightly it hurt.

"You've changed, Jayden, my love."

"Don't call me that," I said in a low, hard voice.

His eyebrow lifted as he spun around. "Ah, is that what the heathen dictator calls you?"

I stared at him coldly.

"So you got lost during battle," he said, his lips pursing as he mused on my predicament.

"After I took down a few of your men."

"You're still a fighter. Remember our night by the pond?"

"Anybody will fight back when they're attacked," I countered.

"You risked death to fight so close to my camp and headquarters."

"*You* trespass the kingdom of Sariba. Besides, I don't think you'll kill me. That's not why you traveled thousands of leagues to get here."

"Don't be so sure." He came closer, his breath on my face. "I do believe you've come to surrender to me. The question is, will you surrender to me in all things?" He smiled wickedly.

I ignored the insinuations. "I didn't surrender at all. But you must stop this war if you don't want your men to die."

He clucked his tongue. "But Jayden, you know I will win. And then you can become *my* queen of Sariba."

I tried to breathe and remain calm. "*If* I did agree, would you spare the lives of the city's citizens? Will you spare the lives of the royal family?"

He had me exactly where he wanted me. His countenance filled with gloating. "My terms are these: You declare Sariba's surrender. I ask for Kadesh's head. You give it to me. I send my armies home with the bounty of this land. I stay as Sariba's king and live in wealth and ease the rest of my days. See how easy that is?"

I pressed my lips together, uncomfortable with so many listening ears. "May we speak privately, King of the Nephish?"

Horeb grasped my arm and pulled me closer. I shuddered at his touch, and the smell of his skin brought back a rush of horrible memories. "It's been a long time since we've seen each other, Jayden," he said huskily, his tone softening for a moment. "You're even more beautiful, and now you're a warrior woman, too. I've always known you would make a formidable wife and queen for our tribe. And I was right."

"You're changing history now." I tried to take a step backward, but caught my foot on a pile of coiled rope stacked along the edge of the tent and nearly tripped. I had to endure this—and find a way out of here. "Call off your guards," I commanded. "You and I have known each other our entire lives. Where am I going to run? I'm surrounded. You carry all the power here."

Horeb smiled and poured two goblets of red wine, handing one to me. I took one tiny sip, only enough to wet my dry throat.

"Now do you feel better?" he asked.

I tried to continue making eye contact without showing my terror. "You are king of a growing tribe. You have power and honor and riches, an army at your beck and call. Why do you sacrifice their lives? Why don't you form an alliance with the Assyrian and Hittite nations and rule the northern deserts?"

He gulped down his drink. "Because I want the power King Hammurabi has. And I want you. Kadesh has to die because I need the wealth of the frankincense lands to accomplish my goal. We'll be king and queen of the desert kingdoms. It's a heady feeling. Quite a feat I've performed finding the secret frankincense lands, don't you think?"

"Because Laban, the Edomite traitor, led you. And then you only had to follow our tracks from the land of Sheba."

His brow pulled together, dark and angry while his arm lifted to throw the goblet across the room. I shuddered at the loud crash it made against the tent pole.

"Horeb," I tried again. "Our fathers were brothers in every sense. They loved each other. Surely you don't intend to kill Pharez. My sisters are here and vulnerable—"

"Your sister is High Priestess of Sariba. She has her Egyptian lover. Why would I care about her?"

"If you've aligned with Aliyah, and she wants to make you her king, why do you need me?"

"The northern tribes care about blood leadership and vows and covenants, Jayden. You know that, and that means you belong to me. We are the rightful heirs and kingship of our tribe. I'm only aligned with Aliyah because she can get me the obedience of Sariba—and now she can help get me the kingdom of Sa'ba."

"Then you know that she killed her sister, the queen, last night?"

"It was all part of our plan. So why would I stop now? I have everything within my grasp. And then, like God's miracle, you fall right into my camp. Offering yourself."

"You're delusional if you think I'm here to offer myself to you, and you greatly underestimate Aliyah. You are merely her means to rule as queen of all lands and kingdoms and the Frankincense Trail. You're only a pawn in *her* game. The sacrificial scapegoat. A token. A fool."

He laughed, however, I'd seen a flicker of uncertainty in his eyes before he turned away. "No woman will get the best of me."

"Aliyah has the Egyptian magicians helping her. She's using the power of the Goddess to control the people, to bend them to her will and obedience. How can you fight the power of that kind of magic?"

Horeb snorted, waving away my words. "If I have to annihilate every city between here and Babylon I will do it. You have only begun to see my power."

"Listen to your own words. You are a man who would rather destroy the very country you desire rather than see it slip through your fingers."

"Then so be it. I won't be made a fool. I *will* win."

"Horeb, my cousin," I said, forcing my voice to mellow, "we have a history, you and I. Our families have known each other all our lives. Our fathers were loyal to each other until the end. I loved your mother, your sisters, Hakak and Falail and Timnath." Tears filled my eyes with a sudden outpouring of memories.

"Tears, Jayden?" he said softly, grinning at me.

"I miss them. I wish I could meet their husbands, see their

babies. I hate being so far from everyone I used to know and love. Even your mother, who cast me off after your father's death, was like a second mother to me. When my mother died, Judith was the one that comforted me. Wept with me. I'm the one who knew you as an innocent boy, playing stick games and tending camels. Teasing me, outracing the other boys. And you did the same with your younger brother, Chezib."

Horeb turned away, the muscles in his jaw twitching with emotions I couldn't name. Was he merely remembering, or was I only making him angry?

"I believe that boy is still inside of you," I said now. "A boy who longs for home. For peace, for a family. You won't get any of that with Aliyah. She will cast you off as soon as your army is wiped out. Even now this fight is draining you, weakening you so she can go in for the kill."

He whirled around, but didn't raise his voice. "You're wrong, Jayden. And if you want to stay alive, you will be *my* queen of Sariba. My men will kill Kadesh, it's only a matter of battle days. God brought you here to me because your future is with me. I know it now."

Before I could speak again, he snaked his arm around my waist and pulled me tight against his chest, bending over me to crush his mouth against mine. I couldn't breathe. I pushed against him but his weight was like the stone columns towering along the temple hallways, heavy and immovable.

Tears dribbled from my eyes, and yet he stayed locked against me. "I—can't—" I tried to speak to catch my breath.

His rough hand brushed my cheek. "There's no need to

cry. We're going to have a magnificent life together, exactly as our parents planned so long ago. This is why you're here. Because you know it in your heart."

"Horeb," I said softly. "I didn't come to you willingly, and you never had my heart."

I was still locked in his arms while he brandished his dagger, laying the blade between my breasts and curving the handle so that the point of the knife pricked at my tunic. "I could cut your heart right out of your chest, and then it would belong to me forever."

Before I could respond, he took a length of rope and knotted my wrists together. Thinking quickly, I held them in a position so that the knots wouldn't be too tight, but he wasn't worried about me actually escaping. His men were everywhere. Horeb held all the advantage.

Posting two men at the door to the tent, he left, saying, "I'll return after I speak with my captains. If she tries to escape, knock her out and come find me."

I didn't have much time. Under cover of the dim light of the tent, I fought back my panic and worked to get out of my bonds. The rope gave only slightly, but I was able to lift my elbows and move my hands higher. Grunting, I slipped a finger into my waistband and retrieved the piece of linen I'd tucked inside.

It was a painful process, but I managed to use my fingernail to punch a hole at the corners of the linen fabric and insert the narrow strips of leather I'd also hidden in my waist sash. I tied the ends into knots, sweating, my fingers slipping with nerves.

Finally, I slithered one of the small stones hidden inside the crudely fashioned linen pad, tightening the strings in preparation for throwing the stone. Horeb's guards had taken the sling tied around my waist and out in the open for anyone to see, but they hadn't thought to search me for hidden leather straps and stones.

Now I waited for his return.

29

My wrists were chaffed by the time I finished preparing the makeshift sling.

I went through the motions of using the sling in my mind. A single swing and then the quick, hard throw to propel the stone at my target—Horeb's guards. Over and over I pictured it so I was ready, just like Asher had taught me out on the desert during our long journey. The only problem I had to overcome was how to get out of the rope binding. Somehow, I'd get the guards to loosen the tie and then use the sling on them before they realized I had it.

The sounds of dinner preparation continued outside. Pots clanging, the crackle of fires. The candles on Horeb's desk dripped wax, mimicking the drops of sweat dribbling down my neck.

All at once, a series of war trumpets sounded, and I jumped

in my chair. What did that mean? The end of the battle? But surely it had long been over.

A moment later, Horeb thrust aside the tent doors.

"Your betrothed and king is on the plains. A search party is attempting to rescue you. A kiss for luck, my sweet Jayden— including the promise of our marriage bed."

"You've lost your sanity if you think I've been waiting for you to arrive in Sariba to save me."

He brushed aside my words. "Too bad I have to keep you tied up, daughter of Pharez. I desire a proper embrace before I go kill your maimed prince, but it will have to wait."

His face came down on mine and his lips pressed hard against my mouth. I tasted the salt of his sweat. I tried not to heave as his hand slid from my lower abdomen up along my chest. Images of the night he attacked me at the oasis rushed back again and I almost gagged.

"Victory is mine, my future queen," he said.

I wanted to wipe my mouth to rid the taste of him. "Please stop this war, Horeb," I pleaded. "You don't need to slaughter the families of Sariba. That will gain you nothing but hatred and contempt if you want to rule them one day."

Horeb rose to his full height, ready for battle again with swords and daggers at his waist. Ready to go find Kadesh and kill him once and for all. I *had* to get out of here.

He gave me a mock bow, and then he was gone. The shouts from outside the campsite faded. I pictured the scene of Horeb and Kadesh clashing yet again. Sariba couldn't survive many more days of fighting.

I worked at the knots, glad I'd spent so much time on the desert with my father who had taught me so well.

All of a sudden the sound of trumpets came again, yet it was getting darker by the minute.

"Guards!" I screamed.

The same two soldiers snapped open the tent. One of them said to the other, "Go check what's happening beyond the camp. Those trumpets aren't ours. I'll stay here, but if Sariba's army is within our camp return immediately to tell me."

The first soldier disappeared at the exact moment I tore off the last of the rope and reared back, whipping the sling overhead. The stone hurled across the tent with a quiet snap. The rock hit the guard smack in the center of his forehead, and he went straight down, slamming into a chair before he hit the ground without a single whimper.

Elation filled me. Immediately I wedged a second stone inside the sling in the event that he rose to his feet, but the man wasn't moving. There was a breath of silence, and I lunged across the tent, stepping over the guard.

Pausing at the door, I surveyed the camp. A few hired cooks were taking care of meals and wouldn't be armed with much. Another handful of guards lined the perimeter, but were looking out toward the desert rather than back at camp.

Every nerve tingled, but I had the advantage of dusk now. Moving slowly, I skirted the tent, searching for an opening that wasn't as heavily guarded while I found three more stones for my sling. My grip tightened around the leather straps, holding one of the rocks in place in case I needed to use it quickly.

Keeping low, I headed to the boulders of the mountains, hoping I could find the cave to the spring. When I flung myself toward an opening in the rocky foothills, a black horse reared directly in front of me, its legs scrabbling at the air. I fell, dropping the stones for my sling, my knees slamming into the ground.

"Get up, Jayden!" a male voice yelled.

The world around me whirled, and then I recognized the horse, Haran, Asher's steed.

Gripping the reins in one hand, Asher reached down with his other arm, seized me under the armpit, and jerked me up onto his horse in front of him. I fell backward, grabbing at his forearms so I wouldn't lose my balance.

Asher kicked the horse's sides and swerved away from the oncoming Maachathite guards coming at us full speed. A spear whistled through the air, and I ducked against the horse's neck, the weapon falling short by a mere fraction.

My heart was in my throat while Asher skirted the battlefield and sprinted toward the city. The camp was soon a distant mirage, but the desert was littered with dead soldiers.

The distance to the city gates was interminable, but we finally arrived. Asher pulled back on the reins and jumped down while I slid off the back. He gripped my arms, seething. "What were you thinking walking into the enemy camp? Have you gone insane?"

I jerked his arm from off me, glaring at him. "I didn't walk into Horeb's camp—I fell from my horse and was taken by his men."

"You're lucky he didn't kill you!"

"It's not me he wants to kill," I spit back. "It's Kadesh and you, and everyone else I've grown to love—" I broke off, chest heaving while I tried to regain my balance. The world wobbled, mostly my legs.

Asher rubbed at his dirty face. "Did you learn anything from him?"

"I took the opportunity to try to stop this war. I tried to save my family, my friends, and this country. It's *my* fault people are dying. What if I had offered myself in exchange for his vow that he would stop fighting? Would that change things?"

Asher stared at me as if I'd lost my mind. "You offered yourself to Horeb? We never asked you to do that. If Kadesh knew about this, he'd string me up a tree and let me rot. As it is, I've been searching for you for hours. I failed in my duty."

"You didn't fail. I failed. Again."

"There's no reasoning with King Horeb," Asher said soberly.

Silently, I held up my hands in the moonlight. My wrists were raw and bloody.

Asher went pale. "He did this to you?"

"No, I managed to get out of the ropes he used on me. And then I took out the guard with a sling I made out of a piece of fabric and string. They took the one you helped me make."

Asher let out a sharp laugh, his chest heaving. But there was admiration in his eyes, alongside fear for me.

"I think Horeb will survive this war," I said quietly. "And he'll take me anyway. King Ephrem tasked me with killing him, but I have no strength against him. He's too big, too powerful." A single tear leaked from my eyes at the futility of it all.

Asher ran a weary hand through his hair. He was filthy and blood-stained from the day's battle. "You need to trust Sariba's forces. You need to trust Kadesh and his strategies. They've been defending the frankincense lands and its wealth and secrecy for hundreds of years. They have a strategy for a final outcome. But it can't be implemented until Horeb's forces are cut in half—and I think we are nearly there."

Clarity came slowly. Kadesh had alluded to Sariba's secrets, but I'd been distracted by fear and Aliyah and the queen's murder.

"You need to listen to me," Asher said evenly. "And you need to see something. Follow me." We walked out of the stable and up the set of stairs by the northern gate tower.

I took the stone steps to the parapet. All was darkness in the valley, except for the faint fires of Horeb's camp. A cool breeze bathed my face, and I shivered. Only an hour ago I'd been inside Horeb's tent.

My legs shook, and Asher reached out a hand to steady me. "I need to get you back to the palace."

"Where's Kadesh?" I asked, panic pressing against my ribs. "Horeb left me tied up with the express purpose of hunting him down and killing him. Now that the forces are shrinking, it will be easier for him to search out Kadesh and take him out—with the help of a platoon of his own soldiers. That can't happen again."

Asher reached out a hand to steady me. "My lady, he's alive.

Kadesh is well. We were all heading back to the city when I discovered you missing. Yes, the final fight of the day was terrible, but when Kadesh discovered you were still out there somewhere, he was beside himself. But the fighting got so bad we had to retreat and get him off the battlefield."

I sagged against him in relief. "But how long are we safe? The casualties are worse every day. How long can we go on before Horeb's forces truly do wipe us out?" I caught Asher staring up at the temple, its golden lamps shining on the hill. "Aliyah waits like a spider in her web, for Horeb to bring Sariba down so low that we surrender and she and Horeb take over."

"That's why I brought you up here," Asher told me. "Because one of the secrets of Sariba is right before your eyes." He pointed straight ahead. "To the east. What do you see?"

"Camels. Hundreds of them," I replied, gazing at him quizzically.

"No, thousands. And when you own *thousands* of camels, you have a secret weapon that Horeb probably hasn't thought of yet."

"What are you talking about?"

"Kadesh and General Naham have been discussing using them, but I don't want to speak out of turn. There is much to be planned if our king and general make the decision to implement the camels as a last resort. But be assured that we have a plan."

His words were confusing and ominous, but I was reassured to know that our king and general were discussing further strategies.

Asher helped me down the steep parapet stairs, and it wasn't long before we were entering the palace foyer. Within moments, we were at the royal suite. I burst inside and raced toward Kadesh. "You're alive," I cried, trying not to weep while I laughed with relief.

"*You're* alive." Kadesh clasped me against him and fiercely kissed me. "You were in Horeb's camp. I almost lost you. I should never have allowed you to come to the battlefield. It's my fault." He paused. "You and I will have words later."

"Yes, we will," I agreed soberly, gazing across the large table where he'd been going over the day's battle strategy and casualties with General Naham and Chemish. Asher's father bent over the war plans table, his brow knit in consternation.

"Chemish!" I cried, my voice choking. It had been over a week ago when he'd fallen at my wedding from the arrow sprung from the bow of Basim's men. "You still have bandages wrapping your back and arm," I chided him. "How can you possibly fight?"

"Sore muscles heal," Chemish said with a smile.

"What about arrow holes?"

He lifted an eyebrow. "I've been working my herbal medicine magic, but it's slow these days."

"Perhaps it needs more than a week," I pointed out affectionately.

"My queen, I will be in the battle tomorrow and nobody is going to stop me. We need every capable man."

"Your doctors may tie you to your mattress, but I most certainly will not," I assured him. "Tell me what the day's news is.

And I'll need a salve, Chemish, for my raw wrists, if you have any to spare."

He inspected my hands and arms, grimacing at the chaffed and torn skin. "I have plenty, my lady."

After applying the ointment and wrapping linen around my wrists, we bent over the table spread with the map of Sariba and the positions of Horeb's armies.

"Despite poisoned soldiers and days of shock troops and battle," Kadesh said, "the news isn't getting better. Horeb lost a hundred soldiers today and Sariba just as many."

I'd learned that servants and scribes walked the battlefields each evening, writing down the dead men's names before removing the bodies. The logistics of war revolted me. Lives gone—for nothing, only greed, power, and dominion. Each generation the cycle of war began again. Over and over it perpetuated the same conditions, the same bloodthirsty men through the ages.

Kadesh sank into his desk chair, studying the numbers. Nobody spoke for a moment. The truth of the numbers was staggering. When the king lifted his face, his skin was gray, his expression both vulnerable and furious. I swore he hadn't slept in a week. "How can I ask my people to sacrifice so much?" he asked quietly.

"They will lose much more than this if Horeb rules this land," Chemish said. "We need to find out if there are any seeds of discontent in his troops. See if we can lure anyone over. Tempt them with caravan riches."

"In two days' time, we will use our camels," Kadesh said.

"No later than that time frame. Or we have truly lost."

There was an intake of breath from General Naham. "But Your Majesty, the risk is great indeed."

"I'm well aware of that, but we are already past the point of no return. We have no choice."

"Should we poison the water again?" the general asked.

Kadesh shook his head. "Those springs will be well guarded by Horeb's men. Any food or wine offered will be rejected as well."

"Surely there's something else we can do," General Naham said, pacing the floor.

"We've used shock troops, archers, every weapon and strategy we can in open desert warfare."

"They'll never be lured into the rocks of the mountains," Asher added wisely.

"The Assyrian and Maachathite armies are too powerful," Chemish said. "They've always had the advantage of size and sheer numbers from the moment they arrived."

"Would that the desert sands had swallowed them," I said softly. "But we're beyond wishes."

Kadesh stepped away from the strategy table. "We've done well," he said, standing erect before the room. "We've been able to cut their numbers down, but we're still outnumbered. If we continue to fight as we do each day with our swords and spears, we will continue to die, until Sariba's last resort is too late to carry out successfully."

General Naham's voice was strained. "Already there is murmuring in our ranks of surrender rather than leave our wives and children to suffer the torture and slavery the Nephish King will inflict upon them. At this point, we have no other solutions, my king. I will follow whatever you think is best."

Kadesh rubbed at his face, staring unblinking at the battlefield sketches on the long table, and then moving toward the windows to gaze out upon the city. "There is risk in either choice. To fight in hand-to-hand combat and go down in dozens every hour, or use the camels in a final attempt to bring the enemy to their knees—and get them to surrender to us."

Chemish moved toward Kadesh. "I agree with you, King Kadesh. Despite the danger, it is the only way to have a chance at survival.

"Please tell me," I pleaded, staring at each man in turn. "What are you talking about?"

Kadesh turned toward me, his voice softening, but laced with an icy vengeance. "We're going to create a camel stampede, Jayden. We'll run our camels straight into Horeb's camp, before they're ready for the day's battle. Before they have time to prepare."

I sucked in air. "But isn't that horribly dangerous for our army, as well? Stampeding camels can't be stopped or controlled. Once they go . . . we could all die."

"That's true, but this strategy has been in the back of my mind for weeks in case this day ever came. The day when we can't fight Horeb's soldiers two to one and hope to survive."

"I've heard my father talk of it. Warning me away from large groups of wild camels ever since I was a child."

"Exactly, my lady," Asher said, his eyes meeting mine across the table.

"It can actually work?" I asked. "To take out Horeb's army?"

"Yes, it will work," Kadesh replied. "Once most of his armies are dead, we can demand their surrender once and for all." He turned to General Naham.

"Get the camel herders organized and your foot soldiers prepared. I want my lead camel riders in front. Tight, compact formation."

Chemish lifted a hand. "Allow me to be your strategist in this endeavor. I run your caravans from Edom to Salem and Egypt. My horsemen are excellent camel riders as you well know, my lord."

Kadesh kept his face steady on the King of the Edomites. "Are you positive your health is up to this?"

"I'm tired of sleeping and taking my medicine. I'm better rested than all of you, and I'd love nothing better than to get rid of a few hundred Assyrians within an hour's time on the battlefield. Safer for *our* soldiers and more deadly for the enemy."

"But only if the camels will run full speed, as one body," Kadesh warned. "Not even a horse is safe from the impact of a camel's weight at full speed."

"I've seen herds of feral camels go after a man who isn't watchful and careful," Asher spoke up.

"Chemish," Kadesh said. "Enlist the help and expertise of Jayden's father, Pharez. As an experienced camel herder, he can advise us on the best methods to set up the motivation needed to get the camels galloping together in one large group. I think we should build fires near the dunes where we keep the animals," he added. "Camels are terrified by desert fires and that will set them running."

"That would work well," Chemish agreed. "Leave the details to me and Pharez."

"Is tomorrow too late to prepare?" the general asked. "Our men are spent after today."

"Yes, the camel herders and Pharez need tomorrow to organize the camels and prepare the fires. But we can't let Horeb become suspicious if we don't show up for battle. We don't want them marching toward the city. Not yet, at least."

"Not yet?" I echoed.

Kadesh's eyes flickered to mine and then away, but nobody answered my question. "We need a day's preparation, but it means that more of Sariba's men will die before we can carry out our plan.

"Chemish, take Asher and any camel handlers you need. Laying out the plans will take most of the night and they'll need all day tomorrow to round up the herd and organize the animals into groups for riding."

Chemish bowed. "It's already done, Your Majesty."

Kadesh stepped forward to embrace the man he'd known his entire life.

Emotion pricked my eyes at the sight of these two men who so obviously loved and revered each other.

I spoke up, but my words wouldn't be met with acceptance.

"I will ride next to my king. No more being on the outskirts to be captured."

"You don't know what you're saying, my lady," General Naham said, obviously bothered by my presence. "This will be the most dangerous strategy yet. There's great risk of dying under the legs of stampeding camels."

"That's true," I conceded. "But I'm a camel herder first, like my father, and I've been riding and training with him since I was small enough to sit on a single camel's foot and hang on."

The image brought a smile to the men.

"Jayden, no—" Kadesh started to protest.

"We'll ride side by side, my king," I told him firmly. "Since our troops are down in number, you need as many riders as you can get. I wonder if my father will want to ride as well. He'll be a great asset, but I know he's distraught over this war."

"Yes, he will ride," said a deep voice behind me.

We all turned to see my father at the entrance to the suite. He held himself tall and rigid like a desert man, but his beard grew whiter each day. Time and weather and grief had taken their toll on him. Despite that, he stood before the group of king's advisors, a man in a strange land, far from his homeland, and I was so proud.

My father's eyes caught mine. He gazed at me with love, and my eyes burned with affection toward him. I went to his side and he took my hand in his, pressing it tight. Comfort swelled inside me, and I was grateful that he was here to give aid to the Sariba soldiers' daring plan.

"After Horeb's men suffer the plan we have in store for them, he will have to respond to my latest letter requesting his surrender," Kadesh said. "He will finally yield to Sariba once and for all."

"I will pray it is so, my king," Uncle Josiah said from the shadows of the suite.

I understood their sentiments, but I'd spent the afternoon in Horeb's tent. The memory of his lips against mine was sickening. His boasting and lust sent chills through me. He wasn't going to surrender, no matter if we trampled and killed every single one of his fighters.

30

W aves of endless camels crossed my vision every time I closed my eyes.

The day of preparation was intense. Nobody spoke openly about the camel stampede, but the palace staff and servants were more subdued than usual. Tension was thick, and with the incoming reports of the day's battle and fresh casualties, it became apparent with every passing hour that the camel stampede was Sariba's last chance for survival.

After so many days of fighting, even Horeb's foreign armies backed off before sunset. The kingdom seemed to breathe a sigh of relief. There were too many graves to be dug on both sides of the war.

My father was gone all day with Chemish and Asher. Meals were brief and informal. The men didn't return that night, sleeping at the Sariba camp instead so as to ward off any enemy spies and keep watch over the camels.

When the moon slipped low on the horizon, I blundered out of bed in the dark. My eyes were red and scratchy when I donned a simple dress and headscarf, but I was already late.

I hefted my freshly sharpened dagger into its sheath, then adjusted my sword and tied the sash tighter. My heart was beating rapidly. Today's events would prove to have dramatic and devastating consequences. I could only hope that today was also the end of the war.

The last of the moon before sunrise bathed the palace grounds with a silver glow, but most of the activity was out of sight on the desert, past the forest and the temple.

Hurrying down multiple staircases, I raced across the royal complex to the horse stalls. Waking up a sleepy stable boy, I had him get a horse ready for me, and then took off as fast as I could.

The horse and I were both heaving by the time I headed east out of the city where Sariba grazed its enormous herds of camels.

The finest purebred camels were kept within an enormous fenced-in area—a fence I couldn't even see the perimeter of—while the rest were allowed to forage the fertile valley at will, camel herders tending them round the clock.

By the time I reached the high plain, the clamoring multitude of camels became my guide. Moments later, lamps came into view out of the darkness, held aloft by a few Sariba soldiers.

I stopped short, astounded by the sight of camels stretching as far as I could see. There must have been several thousand. The animals brayed and spit and grumbled with such a commotion I was tempted to cover my ears.

"Where's the king?" I asked one of the soldiers hurrying by.

"Somewhere in this sea of camels. He and the Edomite king are organizing us into lines and rows. A tight, deep formation. We have enough men to ride about five hundred camels. The hope is that another thousand will follow."

I pictured a sea of towering camels, twice as high as any horse, their large padded feet galloping across the harsh terrain with ease.

The man gave me a crooked smile. "Camels and riders a league across."

"Are the camels trained enough to follow a group and a leader?"

"These are Sariba caravan camels," he said without reservation. "The best bred and trained in the desert world. Once they start galloping, there will be no stopping them."

The image of thousands of speeding camels was both terrifying and thrilling. I pushed through the crowd while Edomite captains shouted orders to the men already astride their animals.

Slowly, lines began to form. I didn't recognize anybody with their headscarves covering much of their faces, but when I pushed closer to the front of the massive ensemble I saw Kadesh conferring with Chemish.

I ran toward him, eager for his comforting touch on my arm. Before I could reach him, out of the darkness, someone swung a small lantern close to my face.

Asher glared down at me. "After what happened with Horeb yesterday, I can't believe you're here. You need to stay safely at the palace."

"I heard the plan last night, as you well know, Asher. So yes, Kadesh knows. He may not approve, but it's my choice and you need all the riders you can get. I am his queen, and this war will be fought and won by both of us."

"You do realize that many of our men could die horrible deaths today. Not only Horeb's foul soldiers. This strategy is dangerous for Sariba's army. A stampede is rarely used. Only as a last resort when troops are falling faster than we can replace them. We'll be riding so fast some of our own men will fall from the camels. Camels will stumble, break legs, and potentially trample the men galloping in from the lines behind."

A shiver quaked down my spine. Planting my feet in the shifting sand, I tried to steady myself.

"Please go back, my lady," the Edomite prince said. "Jayden," he added more quietly. "I couldn't bear it if you were hurt, or worse."

"Go tell your commander that I've arrived, and Kadesh and I will ride out together. Seeing us together will give the men courage to run toward the danger—and succeed. We *have* to win. There's no longer any other choice."

Frustration sounded in his throat. "No—" Asher spun in the dirt. The muscles in his jaw twitched, but he paused to hold himself in check. "I need to round up my men into formation. I'll convey your message to my father."

I let the air out of my lungs. "You are becoming a leader," I told him gently. "I'm proud of you, Asher, Prince of Edom."

He bowed. "My lady, I pray to God that I see you after it's all over." His voice broke, and I could tell emotion had overcome him.

"I'll see you afterward," I agreed with as much confidence as I could muster.

The faintest gray washed the black night sky. The first sign of the approaching dawn.

Quickly, I ran to find Chemish and get an assignment for a camel. I could tell he wasn't too pleased to see that I was ready to ride with them, but he wouldn't argue with me in front of the entire army.

Finally, Chemish ordered one of his captains to find me a good, steady camel. "One who shows no fear or apprehension," he told the man. "The Queen of Sariba will be riding with us." Then he turned to me. "Once we're in a full-out gallop, the camels need to keep moving. They cannot stop, not for anything. Any hesitation dooms the animal and you."

I swallowed past my dry throat. "Yes, my lord."

When a tall, muscled camel was led over to me, I smoothed my hand down its long neck, but the animal didn't flinch. Our task was more difficult because we were strangers. "Trust me, my beauty," I whispered to her.

The captain told me, "If you aren't nervous or afraid, she won't be either. She's used to carrying strangers. This one is one of our best caravan camels."

I brought her head down between my palms while I stood

on tiptoe to gaze into her eyes. "Then we will ride confidently into the fight." Her long eyelashes blinked, holding mine, but she didn't even twitch.

My father appeared and touched me on the arm. "This camel reminds me of Shiz," I told him.

"I was thinking the same thing," he said, his eyes moist as we reminisced about the camel we'd lost to Dinah in exchange for Sahmril's life so long ago. Shiz had been my personal camel since her birth. The baby camel used to follow me around camp and kept me warm at night. My heart had broken to give her up to the selfish Dinah.

"The King of the Edomites says there is no talking you out of this foolhardy venture," my father said, eyeing me.

I clenched the camel's leather halter. "I can't watch the final battle from the ramparts. This is my country now, my people, and my future husband. I have a role to perform with honor and unconditional love. How can I not do anything else?"

My father placed a warm hand on my face. "I've raised the daughter I always wanted, then. Your mother would be immensely proud of you."

"Thank you, Father," I said, hugging him tightly.

The captain who had brought the camel helped me onto her back. I settled my legs around her wide girth, tightening my belt to secure my sword and sling, touching the dagger at my thigh to give me confidence.

That day when I'd used Kadesh's frankincense nuggets to purchase the knife seemed like a whole other world now. But the same fears were real. I'd bought the dagger in self-defense against Horeb, and once more I was confronting my former betrothed.

There was one thing nobody had discussed. That once the stampede was over, there would still be foreign soldiers alive. We would have to fight them on the ground and close up. That part frightened me more than the stampede. I knew how to stay on a racing camel, as well as a camel that got spooked. During my childhood, I'd learned to never let go no matter how daunting the terrain or the camel's temperament.

My pulse pounded in my ears. The formation was filling in.

Distant lanterns revealed dark-swathed Sariba, Edomite, and Sa'ba soldiers sitting motionless on their camels, waiting for the signal. Row after row of them, unmoving, quiet, not a single spoken word. A knot moved up my throat. Their solemn determination was almost eerie.

"Your queen is here," I told Kadesh when I moved into place beside him.

His head whipped around, alarm in his face. "Jayden! I'd hoped you were too exhausted and that your maids wouldn't wake you. I came too close to losing you two days ago. I'd rather know you were safe in the palace."

"But I couldn't be safe waiting for you, my love," I told him. "I've been riding camels longer than I've been able to walk. I can't remain at the palace awaiting word of your death. If you fall, I will be at your side, holding you in your last breaths."

He took my hands in his, gripping hard, his black eyes steely on mine. "If I can't talk you out of this, then don't you dare move a hair's length away from me. We ride tight together, all of us. There's less chance of falling and breaking our necks. Or being trampled. No breaking away, not for any reason."

"We are prepared to ride!" Chemish shouted up ahead.

"Come with me, my queen," Kadesh said. I followed him to the front lines and we turned to face the regiments of camels and shadowy figures sitting astride their animals.

The men's surprise was tangible when they recognized me at their king's side. There was a shift in the air. Reverence, confidence, a mood of fortitude and determination.

Gray light gathered along the hills, and Chemish gave another signal from his animal.

Behind the formation of men and camels, a row of lanterns brightened the scene. A platoon of Sariba men carrying lamps poured oil and fire along the dry grasses behind us.

Sparks leaped in the shadows, and the flames spread quickly, crackling through the underbrush. The camels began to fidget, shying away from the heat and growing flames.

The crackling noise turned them skittish. The camels were edgy and jumpy, wanting to flee, but held tight in formation by their masters. The noise of their agitated braying grew louder.

With a sudden cry, Chemish and Kadesh and the other captains slapped the rumps of their animals, yelling a strange, delirious cry. It was unsettling. A breath later, the entire battalion of men screamed and shouted until the noise of men and animals was deafening.

A blast of heat from the fire washed up and over me.

Perspiration broke out along my forehead. I pulled my scarf up over my face. Glancing along the line, I saw each man's disconcerting black eyes, their identities hidden by head wraps. A few of the Edomites gave me a brief nod and I nodded in return, grateful for these devoted men.

Kadesh pulled out his sword and raised it high. "For Sariba!"

As one body, the men, packed tightly on all sides, brought forth their swords and held them aloft. "For Sariba!"

"For life," I breathed. A surge of swords and shouts enveloped me. Emotion rose in my chest. Adrenaline in my thighs. My grip tightened when my camel tried to break free and run. We held them back, waiting for the exact moment to send the animals leaping forward with enough motivation to run and not stop for at least half a league.

Tiny embers popped along the field under our feet. Each sizzle created an ominous, threatening noise.

"Wait for it," Kadesh warned, holding up both arms to force the army to wait, to remain motionless until his signal. Timing was everything.

The fire spread and grew larger, a wall of flames and heat.

Just as the camels were about to bolt and break formation, Kadesh brought down his sword with a glittering flash of bronze.

The signal to *run*.

The animals were off at an insane speed. A shriek escaped my mouth.

We were so close, Kadesh was barely half an arm's length

away from me. "Stay *on* your camel. At all costs," he yelled. "Whatever you do, don't fall off!"

I nodded, my arm muscles shooting spasms I was holding the reins so tight. I gripped my camel with my legs. I didn't have to guide her at all. The camels would follow each other to the ends of the earth—or until they collapsed.

Like the incoming tide of the sea, the sun soared above the horizon at that very moment, bathing the valley with yellow light.

The stampeding camels galloped faster. I'd never felt anything like this frenetic speed, the sheer terror and majesty of pounding across the desert.

Camels without riders began to sweep past, almost daring us to catch them. Clods of dirt spit into the air. The cloud of dust and smoke climbed as high as the camels' bellies, engulfing our legs.

Horeb's camp grew closer. Shadows of men rising from their tents in the hour before dawn began to clarify into outlines. I tried not to think about what we were about to do, but it was impossible to shove it from my mind. Many men were going to die today. Men who would never see their wives and their children again.

I shook cold tears out of my eyes. These soldiers had made a choice to bring war to Sariba, steal its wealth and take the lives of the people. I would not give way to remorse for these men who didn't care if they killed every last one of us.

I thought of my mother's compassion for others, her selflessness, and kindness. I would probably never be like her.

Dread of the unknown usually caused me to turn inward, not outward.

Most of all, I wanted to stop living with fear. I wanted Horeb to find his life in the old lands of our people, in the stark deserts and oasis at Tadmur. He could be king. He could have all that he wanted if he would stop trying to possess me.

All at once, the sun shot over the horizon. Warmth folded its rays over me. Horeb's camp lit up in the golden light. Close now. Too close. We'd caught them at their breakfast, dressing, taking care of their horses.

Their mouths were slack-jawed, eyes baffled. Dazed by the sight of us.

Before terror filled their faces.

For a moment, I stopped breathing—and then we ran straight over them.

31

amels are nearly double the height of a man and with the weight of three horses they created the perfect stampeding animal. I knew that if we packed hundreds of them together, Horeb's armies stood little chance.

Soldiers began to run from their campfires and tents, stumbling over gear and stakes.

The sound of a thousand galloping hooves was deafening. I wanted to plug my ears, but I didn't dare loosen my fists on the reins. Indeed, I gripped even tighter when we began to crash over tents and fire pits and brass pots and saddle gear.

My camel barely flinched despite screams all around us as we tore at a frenzied pace through the campsite. Spears launched from Sariba soldiers sailed through the air, taking down men as fast as the camels were running.

Next to me, two camels went down in a sudden crash when

they trampled Horeb's soldiers. From the corner of my eye, I saw the men jump off and try to avoid the camels coming up from behind.

It wasn't much longer before our core formation broke apart as men and animals tumbled and fell onto one another.

Leaning close to my camel's neck, the reins became sharp needles jabbing into my palms. I gritted my teeth and held on, knowing it was life or death.

"Jayden!" Chemish yelled in my ear, although I couldn't see him, my focus on the melee before me was so great. "Your sword!"

My head whipped up. An enemy soldier was racing toward me on his horse, a sword leveled at my throat. Instantly, I pulled my sword and swung frantically. The Maachathite tried to grab it away. We tussled for a moment, swords clanging, but I lifted my arm and brought the weapon against his shoulder with all my strength. I knew the blow wasn't enough to knock him off his horse, but before I could blink, the man disappeared behind me, cut down by Chemish bringing up the rear.

Glancing around, I realized that the stampede was in disarray. Sariba soldiers were fighting the enemy from atop their steeds or from the ground if they'd fallen and were still alive.

Men lay strewn everywhere.

Tents were trampled into shreds. Camels were down with broken legs, horses mangled.

To my left the remains of a fire pit oozed along the ground, its stones and embers scattered. My pulse throbbed hard along my temple.

The Edomites who had been thrown off their animals scrambled to mount their camels again, often fighting against one of Horeb's men for the animal.

Dazed, but still astride my slowing camel, I glanced down at myself. I was entirely covered in brown filth from riding inside a cloud of dust. My teeth were gritty, my throat dry as sand.

When I heard my name shouted, I whirled about, pulling hard at my camel's neck to see what was happening behind me.

"Archers!" It was Asher, wheeling behind me. "Stay low!"

The Assyrians had organized on the far side of the camp and were launching arrows into the stampede. Immediately a dozen camels went down.

Bending low to avoid a direct hit, I prayed my animal wouldn't suffer an injury.

But still the stampede continued, destroying everything and everyone in its path.

I blinked back grit and tears while the greater part of the company continued to race through the camp. It wasn't long before I found myself beyond Horeb's camp. It took another half league to slow down the camels and calm them enough to stop.

The agitated animals turned in circles, their eyes wide with fear and adrenaline.

Somehow, I'd managed to follow Kadesh out of the fray, and Asher drew close when we reached the rocky foothills. I stared at the two men with ripped tunics, faces with so much grit they were almost unrecognizable. I noted that Kadesh had a bloodstain along his arm.

"How bad is it bleeding?" I shouted above the madness we'd left behind at Horeb's obliterated campsite.

Kadesh shook his head dismissively. "It's only an abrasion. We managed to keep more than half our camels in one piece. Only about fifty of our men are dead or wounded."

"What do we do now?" I asked.

"There are still Assyrians and Nephish alive," Kadesh said in a hard voice. "Our men are fighting hand-to-hand and we must return to help them." He raised his voice, signaling with his arm to the men still on their camels that had managed to stay together in a makeshift group. "Swords out! Charge!"

My gut leaped when my camel jerked forward to follow Kadesh. I placed a hand along her neck, awed by her strength and intelligence. Before I was mentally ready again, we were back in the middle of the enemy camp again. And the sight was beyond gruesome.

Spread along the sloping sands were hundreds of Assyrian, Maachathite, and Nephish bodies. Each soldier still wore the uniform and colors of his individual tribe, tunics askew, swords buckled under mangled, lifeless forms. The onslaught of more than a thousand camels charging through camp was more than anyone could survive.

My stomach was in my throat. But had Horeb survived?

Kadesh wheeled around to me. "Jayden, return to the caves in the foothills. You shouldn't witness any more of this."

"I want to remain with you. Where are you going?"

"I intend to take Asher and find Horeb—either his dead body or arrest him if I find him alive."

I nodded shakily, finally closing my eyes to the scene of death everywhere I looked.

"It's almost over, Jayden," Kadesh said, trying to comfort me. "I'll send Basim to take you back to the city, but for now get away from the soldiers still fighting about the camp. It's much too dangerous for you to be here in the middle of it."

Reluctantly, I turned my camel around, marveling that my camel knew exactly where to take me in the rocky foothills to hide. Soon we were ensconced behind a curtain of rocks, safe from the remaining troops of Horeb's armies.

Gulping down deep breaths while I perched on a boulder, I tried to calm my hammering heart. The sound of skittering rocks made me jump. When I whirled about, my ankle twisted on the loose shale. An instant later, Horeb loomed like a deathly specter before me.

"*Horeb,*" I breathed. "Where did you come from—how did you get here?"

I turned to run but his hands clamped down on my shoulders. He pushed me down to the ground and I stared up into his miraculously unsoiled face. A face without dirt or scrapes or any sign of struggle or fighting.

"You weren't even there," I said hoarsely. "You're *clean*."

"I recognized the sound of a stampede long before my foreign men did."

"How did you get to these caves?"

"I'm not a fool. I left my tent when I saw the fires and the charging camels."

"You watched the entire assault from behind these rocks?"

I tried to grasp what he was telling me. "You left your men alone?"

"There wasn't much I could do to stop it. Their fate was out of my hands."

"You could have warned them . . ." my voice trailed off. I was sickened by his pure selfishness and lack of integrity. "You lured three armies into the desert to fight for you, and you left them to die in the stampede, knowing—seeing—it was coming."

"My queen," Horeb said, snatching at my hand to bring me to my feet. "You and I can now claim ourselves King and Queen of Sariba. We have only to get your father to draw up the marriage contract and spend a week in the marriage tent to make it official. It's all very simple now."

"You're insane," I whispered.

Laughing triumphantly, Horeb pulled me against him, sweat and leather scenting his skin. He stared down at me. "Jayden, you're rather dirty after your stampede attack." He tugged me along a narrow trail, knowing I had no recourse but to follow him. "Every time your foreign lover attempts to best me, you fall into my lap. The gods' eyes are upon us. They've chosen our union."

He spoke in even tones, as though trying to confuse me with a show of feigned kindness, but I knew that he could turn on me in an instant. If Horeb killed me, Kadesh wouldn't even know I was dead among the foothills. Not until he returned to the palace and I wasn't there.

Before I could reach for a weapon, Horeb sliced through

my waist sash, catching my sword before it fell to the ground. I shrieked when he lifted my skirts and ripped away the dagger hidden there. With a strong arm, he threw my weapons far down the small ravine of rocks where they clanged away out of sight. The knives were useless to me now.

Next, he slid his hands up and down my limbs and hips to make sure I had no other weapons. "Please, Horeb," I pleaded. "Let me get my camel. We can't walk back to your camp."

He shook his head. "We're not going back yet. We'll wait until Sariba has departed with their dead."

"My mouth tastes like dirt. I need my water pouch."

He eyed me and I crafted my expression to be as innocent as possible. All I had to do was incapacitate him for a few minutes to get away. I could never fight him on my own, even though he'd stolen away from his camp before he had a chance to put on armor. The stampede had been effective, if gruesome.

"Get your water," he said gruffly, standing over me to watch my every move.

I nickered to my camel, heart thudding against my ribs so hard I swore the entire valley could hear it. My camel trotted over, and I reached for my water pouch, taking a long draw while my other hand stole inside my supply knapsack where I'd fastened my sling.

Hope surged as one of the smooth stones I'd packed slipped into the sling's pouch as easy as water. When I returned the water pouch to my knapsack, I maneuvered the leather strings of the sling and began to whirl the weapon above my head.

All at once, I snapped the sling, and the stone sailed across the rocks, hitting Horeb squarely in the forehead.

He let out a cry of surprise, but it was cut off when he fell forward, hitting the ground with his knees. But he didn't go down. I hadn't knocked him out; I'd only make him more angry.

Time seemed to stop. I watched him blink his eyes, dazed, and then he hauled himself to his feet, an angry red mark on his forehead. I'd been so eager to take him down, I hadn't managed to get the sling at the highest speed it needed to incapacitate him.

Quickly, I dug into my knapsack and fumbled for another stone, but Horeb roared and charged me, taking me down to the earth so fast it knocked the wind from my lungs. I gasped for air, throat burning.

"That'll teach you to attack me."

I kneed him next, and then we were grappling on the dirt, rocks slamming into the back of my head, sun scorching my eyes. My arms and legs burned as I fought and kicked and tried to wriggle away, screaming all the while.

It was the oasis pond attack all over again. Horeb tore at my dress and then pressed his thumbs into my throat to make me pass out and stop fighting him.

Black dots swam before my eyes as I fought for air. Over and over, I kicked him, flailing my fists against his torso and shoulders. "Horeb—please!" I gurgled.

I was losing strength, but it suddenly came to me again that he wasn't wearing any armor. I stopped kicking and reached out to bring him closer. A smile came over his lips and his body lowered to mine. At the same moment, I slipped the dagger out of the holster on his hip.

My words squeezed between my gritted teeth. "I'll stop fighting," I told him. "Let—me—breathe!"

I forced myself to relax, and then Horeb loosened his stranglehold. I didn't wait another moment. I shoved his dagger between his ribs as he lay on top of me, straddling me with his knees.

Horeb gasped in shock and pain. Before he could fully grasp what I was doing, I wrenched the knife from his chest and thrust it into his neck. Blood spurted in a gush of red, spattering my own face and neck.

"Jayden—" He tried to speak, but his whisper cut off with a gurgling sound when I shoved the knife in farther.

I was still half-pinned beneath him, but he was quickly bleeding out.

I heard someone screaming over and over again as I slowly heaved his weight off me. My skin was slick with blood and tears and when I glanced down at myself, it became quite clear that I was the one hysterically yelling.

Finally, I pushed his head off my lap and scrambled away on my hands and knees. Horeb lay sprawled in a pool of red, his blood trickling into the hot sand.

The sound of my own moaning frightened me. I was like a wild animal. My camel nudged at me, biting at my shoulder to get me to rise to my feet, but I couldn't seem to move.

The horror washed over me. Horeb's death was on my

hands, my arms, raindrops of his blood splattered across every shred of my clothing and skin.

I'd killed him.

Despite the blood seeping into the sand and the awkward angle of his legs, my mind couldn't seem to take it in.

Horeb was dead. *He was dead.* He couldn't hurt me any longer. He hadn't killed Kadesh. He wasn't King of Sariba. He wasn't King of the Nephish any longer.

No more running. No more nightmares. No more terror.

My shrieks turned into whimpers.

I turned away, sobbing with revulsion and relief. Still holding Horeb's knife in my fist. Gripping it with all my strength.

I opened my fingers, and the handle was stuck to my palm with his blood. Hastily, I dropped it, wanting to throw up.

Heaving over the sand, sweat pouring off my face, I recognized the dagger as a gift from Horeb's father, Abimelech. A gift he'd received in his twelfth year from the same father Horeb had murdered when he learned that Abimelech planned to give the Nephish throne to me and Kadesh instead.

I crawled toward a flat rock, gripping the rough edges, but I could not get my body to stop shaking. Rocking back and forth, I wished for endless buckets of water to take away all the blood and dirt and sweat.

"My lady!" a voice called. Instinctively I crouched behind the stone to hide, not recognizing the voice, ready to run. Then I spotted Basim and two of his men. They galloped up on their horses. I was so relieved my legs gave out, and I sank to the dirt.

Basim's eyes roved over my bloody appearance, my tangled

blood-matted hair, my empty sword sheath and missing dagger. "What happened, my lady? Are you hurt?"

I shook my head, unable to even speak.

The barrel-chested man dismounted and dropped next to me, his eyes examining my body for any life-threatening injuries. An instant later, he saw Horeb lying across the sand in a pool of red.

"I killed him. I killed Horeb." A tear slipped down my face and, unexpectedly, Basim reached out to wipe it away with a gentle finger.

"Kadesh sent me to find you and take you back to the palace, but he believed you were on your camel at the edge of the camp. I've been searching for you. The rest of the foreign soldiers have surrendered to us."

"I saw them—so many men—tumbling and dying."

I closed my eyes, thinking I might just lie here for a while. It seemed easier than trying to stand.

"Come, my lady, I need to get you home." Basim lifted me up and set me on his horse. I gripped the leather halter so I didn't slip off. One of his other soldiers rode my camel back to the stables. My hands ached, my wrists were still bruised, and every muscle in my body seemed to have turned to water.

"How many of our men survived today?" I asked.

"Most of them, my lady."

"What will happen to—to Horeb's body?"

"I left one of my men with him. He'll be taken to King Kadesh who is directing the aftermath of today's battle."

We were quiet as we walked, and then I asked, "I trust

you believe you made the right choice in your jail cell the day I visited you."

His eyes flickered over to my face. "I underestimated Sariba's defense systems. And I underestimated its king and queen."

"Not yet queen," I murmured, slipping in and out of a haze of exhaustion.

We passed the temple, and, at the bottom of the forest hill, we finally approached the walls of the city. "The Sariba army is safe?" I asked again, knowing I probably wasn't making much sense.

"Battle-scarred and some wounded, but they'll be fine. Eager to return home when the foreign camp is cleaned up and burned. In a few days, the sands will be clean again. It will be as though the war never happened."

He was trying to wash away the horror of this war, but I knew better. The pain of our soldiers' deaths would never fade, especially for those who had lost husbands and fathers. But at last it was a war that was behind us. And now Sariba could begin the small steps toward recovery.

"And where are the bodies of our enemy?"

Basim's hooded eyes were grave. "The desert battlefield is not a pretty sight, my lady. Our army is mostly recovering bodies, not rescuing them."

I suppressed a shudder. "Has there been any sign of Aliyah? I assume the women of the temple are safe?"

"All is well at the temple, but I have no information about the goddess women," Basim said, knowing I was asking about my sister Leila.

"I need you to investigate her whereabouts. She hasn't been seen since the night of the temple ceremonies. No, that's not true. Kadesh told me she was on the battlefield with Horeb on the first day."

He nodded. "Yes, my lady."

"Oh, and Basim. Do you know where my father is?" I began to swing my leg off the horse, anxious to find everyone.

Basim stopped me. "My lady, I'll escort you into the city."

"I need to walk." Despite my trembling limbs, I craved the steady ground beneath my feet.

Understanding crossed Basim's face when he nodded. "As you wish."

The terrain flattened when we approached the city. At the northern gates, I turned to my mercenary soldier, unable to keep the tremor out of my voice. "I'm sure you're anxious to return home. The land of Sa'ba needs you after the death of your queen."

"Before King Kadesh left for battle this morning, I requested his permission to be the one to take the news back to my king, the queen's husband, and her children."

"Of course. As our ally, Basim—and her countryman—you should be the one. That will give you an opportunity to answer her husband's questions and attend to his grief. The king and I will send mourning gifts and personal letters . . ." My voice trailed off. I was completely out of my league, comforting soldiers, giving instructions, taking care of wretched, heartbreaking tasks.

For a queen who loved her people, I didn't think it would ever be easy.

I lifted my head, the sight of the beautiful city calming me. I was no longer a girl on the run, uncertain, frightened. Doubting every thought, each decision, with an erratic future.

"Perhaps there is a way to take the queen back home and not have to dispose of her body here in Sariba," Basim suggested.

I turned to meet his eyes. "What do you mean?"

He gave me a tender smile, incongruous on the visage of a hardened warrior. "There are Egyptians here in Sariba, are there not? The Egyptians know the ways of long-term embalming, and they have access to all the frankincense they need."

"You're right," I said with fresh admiration. "Taking the queen home would be the best gift we could give her family. Please, as soon as you know where King Kadesh is, tell him I must speak with him about this. The funeral pyre will be canceled. There are hundreds of other bodies to be burned tonight, and graves for their bones to be buried somewhere in the mountains of Qara." I tried to swallow, but the day's trauma had left my mouth dry, my chest hollow. "But deep inside the mountains, far from our own people's homes and tombs."

Basim lowered his head respectfully. "This way, my lady," he said, steering me through the gate.

We walked until we saw General Naham standing across the

sloping ground, a breeze ruffling his hair. Chemish crouched beside him and a wave of nausea almost knocked me over when I stared down at the bloodied body of Horeb.

I swallowed hard and asked, "How did you get him here so quickly?"

"Basim's man brought word to Kadesh, and he ordered his body taken from the desert and brought here before vultures dragged it off. The king has plans for it."

The royal uniform Horeb wore so proudly was shredded from our fight. Bruises crushed his skin, and his eyes stared unseeing at the blue skies above us.

The boy of my childhood, my former betrothed, and the man my father had loved as a son was finally dead. It was real. I didn't have to fear him any longer. I was free. I was living a new dream in a new world now and I was having a hard time taking it in.

With a single motion of his hand, Chemish closed Horeb's eyes and then rose to his feet. "It is finished," he said quietly.

I wavered and sat down on the grass with a thud, trying not to sob, my breath catching hard in my chest.

Basim knelt beside me. "My lady, please rise. You should be in the city, not out here, with the bodies of our enemy."

Like a father, he gently took my hand in his rough one. Basim escorted me through the clamoring chaotic streets. Soldiers were cleaning themselves at the town plaza, dumping buckets of water over their heads. Some people were celebrating our victory while solemn women clutched children to their breasts. It was a mass of confusion on the main throughway and along the wide palace stairs and portico.

Whispers scuttled around me like spiders in my ears. I was relieved the war was over, but I still had a long ways to go to fully win the people's hearts. Perhaps I had a chance now—if Kadesh had survived.

I was desperate to see my sisters. The temple had been untouched by war, but I could imagine the sober mood among the priestesses and Egyptians. Was Aliyah hiding her head, or was she already out recruiting King Hammurabi of Babylon or King Idrimi of Damascus to her ambitious cause?

I spent the next two hours with my maids, who bathed me, washing Horeb's blood from my crusted hair, and massaging my sore limbs. My wrists still hurt from the bonds of Horeb, bruising now in purple and green mottled colors.

My filthy bloodstained clothes were taken to be burned and I could finally stop gagging.

When word came that Kadesh was back at the palace, I tore through the halls, slamming doors, until I found him in his royal rooms and ran into his arms.

There were no words to express all that had happened that day with the stampede and Horeb's death. We held each other, the room spinning with emotion and relief and a euphoric sensation of liberation.

"There's something I have to take care of," Kadesh finally murmured. I released him reluctantly, but he wasn't that far away, only across the room at his desk.

A servant bent to offer me food, but I shook my head.

My clean hands and clothes were almost dreamlike, too. A

world apart from what had happened earlier. Dusk settled over the city while I stared, unseeing, through the windows.

Restless, I stood up to pace the room, touching a vase, clutching a piece of linen curtain. I stopped behind Kadesh's desk, desperate for a way to fight the demons left over from the surge of thousands of camels slaughtering men under their feet.

Kadesh turned to me, his face haunted. "I'm almost finished," he finally said, gesturing to the ink brushes and tablet.

"I can't stop my mind from obsessing over the details of the stampede. Will I ever get the terrible images out of my head?"

He rubbed his hands along his face before gathering me into his arms. "I wish you hadn't been there. I wanted to protect the girl I love. The woman who will be my wife when this is over."

"But I will also be Sariba's queen," I reminded him, brushing my cheek across his jawline, my lips close to his. "And today, your men needed us both."

A scribe entered the room, and we broke apart.

Kadesh directed him to recopy his notes and add the official royal lettering and the engraved stamp of King Kadesh in the soft clay.

By this time, Chemish had arrived and inspected the letter.

"Any words of wisdom?" Kadesh asked the old warrior.

"After today's bloody battle, I don't see how Aliyah could reject this. You're offering her and her Egyptians a chance at redemption, including supplies and water and fresh camels to see them back to Egypt."

"But my terms are that Aliyah departs from Sariba forever

and never returns. If she does, she'll be arrested and imprisoned."

"It's generous. More than any other invading army would receive."

After dispatching the letter, Kadesh fell into an armchair, laying a hand across his forehead. His servants plied him with food and drink, but he barely ate a few mouthfuls.

Instead, he ordered the lamps dimmed and me next to him on the sofa. I curled into his side while his arms went around me. His fingers stroked my hair, and I couldn't recall a single time we'd ever sat quietly together. We'd always been traveling, with a roomful of people, hiding our love for each other—or hundreds of miles apart.

We watched the moon float above the window, the desert stars like silver drops of molten liquid.

"And now we wait," Kadesh whispered. "For the answer that will bring an end to this madness. If Aliyah doesn't respond and acquiesce by tomorrow, General Naham is under orders to invade the temple and arrest her and her coconspirators."

His words should have brought me comfort. To never see Aliyah again was all that I wished for, but I knew deep in my heart that Aliyah would go down fighting to her last breath. I dreaded that a temple invasion by our own army might be the result, and that Leila could be hurt in the process.

32

The next morning I determined to take care of something I'd been putting off. Sahmril's adoptive parents, Thomas and Zarah, had been staying at one of the palace guest houses during the duration of the war, and I couldn't ignore them any longer.

Every day Sahmril and I had grown closer. I'd spent hours with her when I hadn't been on the battlefield. Being with the daughter my father thought he'd lost had given him new life and purpose. He gazed adoringly at Sahmril each time she entered a room, smiles lighting his grizzled face for the first time in months.

Despite my determination to accomplish the task at hand, my steps were slow that morning. Aunt Naomi met me in the hallway of her suite and we embraced for the first time since I'd returned with Basim from the battlefield.

"Jayden, my girl! You're safe, praise the living God."

She clasped me again, and then looked me in the eye. "You are a remarkable young woman. Josiah told me all that transpired yesterday, and it's a miracle our enemies are dead and you are safe."

"I know it happened," I told her. "But I'm still trying to convince myself it's real. Where are Uncle Josiah and Kadesh this morning?"

I hadn't seen any of the royal family since the previous evening. After the letter Kadesh had sent to the temple demanding Aliyah's surrender and banishment, the unsettling fear in my gut was growing instead of dissipating.

"Josiah is overseeing the cleanup with General Naham. He told me that envoys will accompany the next caravans to take word of the war's results to the tribes of the Nephish and Maachathites."

A chill came over me when I thought about Aunt Judith's reaction to Horeb's death. She would despise me until she took her last breath, but what would my cousins think—Horeb's sisters and younger brother, Chezib? What truth or lies did they know about me and the events of the past year?

"Will the Nephish tribe survive after all of this?" I wondered, speaking my thoughts aloud.

Naomi smoothed out the frowns along my forehead. "Jayden, don't trouble yourself. You are part of Sariba now."

"But will the rest of the people here ever feel as you do? Or will they now despise me for taking away their husbands and fathers?"

"Give them your love, your kindness, and your service and they will know that this war wasn't your doing."

"I know you're right, but my stomach is unsettled. Sa'ba is in a precarious situation."

Naomi nodded. "Prepare yourself for a trip with Kadesh to help provide a transitional period while they mourn their queen. Your presence can give that land comfort as well as stability."

I mused on her words and advice. She was right. When the aftermath of the war was cleaned up and Aliyah taken care of, a trip to Sa'ba was in order to help stabilize both kingdoms. And we would have Basim and his fifty warriors to accompany us. I glanced up at Naomi with a half smile. "Can Kadesh and I get married first?"

"Oh, my girl!" Naomi said. "Yes, and I'm already a step ahead of you. I have a meeting with my servants and the palace staff to begin the preparations immediately. We've all waited long enough."

"You never did say where Kadesh is," I reminded her. "Only Uncle Josiah."

"Kadesh ordered the capture of the enemy's horses and the burning of their camp. Then he planned to ride to the temple to speak with the Egyptians about embalming arrangements for the queen. After that he planned to demand an answer from Aliyah. Josiah said the king was not happy when he left the palace this morning after not hearing from her."

"I was afraid she would have to be forced—" I broke off

when Jasmine and Tijah ran in from the foyer.

Jasmine buried her head against me, silent tears trickling down her face. "I'm ordering your mother to come here as soon as possible," I said. "The widows and orphans in the city need her tender heart and skill, but her daughters need her most of all. Now take me to Sahmril. Is she napping? And where is my father?" I added.

Aunt Naomi spoke up, her words reluctant. "I'm afraid Sahmril is in one of the private sitting rooms. The nobleman and his wife arrived this morning, demanding to see her."

Her words were like a punch in the chest.

"Jayden, please," Naomi said. "Stay calm."

She was too late. I was already running down the hallways and through the foyer, pushing open the doors to the various sitting rooms bathed in morning light.

In the third room, I stopped short. Sahmril was lying with her head upon the shoulder of a woman I'd only seen once before in the city of Mari. A woman who had stared defiantly at me through the windows of her great house that overlooked a lush pond and gardens.

Thomas straightened as I entered, his hand immediately reaching for his wife's in a show of solidarity against me.

I lost all breath, and my composure wilted.

"Mama," Sahmril said happily, snuggling into Zarah's arms. She gave Thomas an adoring look. "Papa," she told me, pointing to him.

"Sahmril—" I couldn't speak her name without my heart

breaking. I sucked in the tears, trying to stay in control in front of these strangers, but my emotions were strung like a rope to its breaking point.

I stepped forward, forcing a happy smile so Sahmril wouldn't be afraid.

Zarah and Thomas stiffened at my presence, their faces sober.

I knelt down, my skirts sinking to the floor. I was a wreck, physically and emotionally. Every part of my body hurt, and my head still ached after Horeb slammed me to the ground. But none of that mattered when I saw my little sister. The hurt in my heart swelled to even greater proportions. "Sahmril, my darling girl," I said softly.

"Jayden," she said with a giggle. After a week together, she knew me so much better now. I reached out a finger to stroke the soft skin along her arm. I touched her dress, the red silk ribbons in her black curls.

"You will always be the sister of my heart, sweet Sahmril," I said. I choked back the burn in my throat, tears streaming from my eyes.

"No cry," my little sister said, dimples breaking in her cheeks as she patted my face, trying to get me to laugh.

"You're right," I told her. "No more tears. We're happy now in this beautiful land." I kissed her cheeks and smoothed a hand over her hair, then lifted my face to Thomas and Zarah. "Have you heard the news of the Queen of Sheba's death?"

"This country has seen great difficulties the past few weeks," Thomas said in his quiet voice. "You have lost many loved ones and just finished a dreadful war. We empathize having recently survived the Babylonian war on our city last year."

"My father, Pharez, and I, have only recently been reunited with Sahmril. My father needs to be with her. These past two years have been devastating for him in more ways than I can begin to tell you."

"We've been talking," Thomas said, glancing at his wife. "We learned much as we traveled with the queen from Sa'ba to King Kadesh's kingdom. We were ungenerous when we first met you both. And now, after having a child for the first time in our lives we realize the heartache it was to take your sister from you."

"Is there another way?" Aunt Naomi said from the doorway. I hadn't realized that she'd followed me and now her voice was serene and diplomatic. A voice of calm. "Is there a way to bring peace to both families? Sahmril only knows you as her parents, and yet she and Jayden have formed a bond—not including their blood bond. Jayden has fought for months to keep her mother's deathbed promises."

"We do empathize with that," Thomas said. His face was somber, but not unkind.

I swiped away the tears on my lips. "Please stay and make your home in Sariba. You may stay in the guest house for as long as you like. And please come to the palace every day. Kadesh and I welcome you to our kingdom. Sahmril can enjoy both her families."

Thomas lifted his chin. "Thank you, my lady, that's very considerate. We've been vagabonds since Mari burned, and running from dire fates across empty deserts for too long."

Zarah stared at me, and then dropped her eyes to her lap. "Thank you," she said, her voice so soft I barely heard her. "I understand you are to be married to the King of Sariba."

"One day soon, I hope," I said, forcing myself to remain serene. "Very soon. We've waited a long time."

"We wish you every happiness," the woman told me, and I believed her sincerity.

After our meeting, I went to visit the wounded soldiers in the infirmary. There were so many of them, and every physician in the city was on hand working.

By afternoon, my path had yet to cross with Kadesh's. I had so much to tell him, but he'd been busy with General Naham and his captains, as well as enlisting the Egyptians about embalming the queen. There were also the remaining soldiers of the Assyrian and Maachathite armies to deal with. I could only imagine he was beyond exhausted in the aftermath of the past several weeks.

After an early dinner with Sahmril, my father, and the nobleman and his wife, I wrapped a shawl around my head and shoulders, hoping to stay anonymous while I marched up the hill to the temple. I needed to find Kadesh and see if Leila was there and well. I hadn't learned a thing about my sister's fate.

At the eastern wall of the city, I was surprised to see scores of people moving through the gate, headed up the forest paths to the temple mount. The sound of their voices floated on the cool night air.

I followed the crowd, and when we reached the upper

temple courtyards, hundreds of lights blazed through the trees. A riot of sound and noise as people gathered at the place of sacrifice.

I halted, my stomach in my throat.

The priestesses of the Goddess were weeping and wailing at the temple gates. They were a stark contrast to hundreds of Sariba citizens jeering at the terrible sight that lay before us all.

King Horeb and the leaders of the Assyrians and Maachathite armies hung from the temple gates. Proof of Sariba's victory. Proof that the war was over.

Their brass armor had been stripped, their heads cut off, and their bodies fastened to the walls of the Goddess and Ba'al.

I shoved the nausea down my throat.

Someone bumped into me and I turned to ask, "Where is the enemy's armor and swords?"

"They put it all in the house of the Goddess," came the answer. "The king has decreed that their defeat be published in every land."

Down below in the city, the trumpets of Sariba blasted notes of triumph and peace, but up here at the temple, all was chaos and fighting. The hanging bodies of our enemies did not bode well for trying to get inside the temple and find Leila. I decided to wait until someone could accompany me, or until it was safer. I'd have a scribe deliver a letter asking her to come to the palace.

Unsteadily, I walked back to the palace alone, passing restaurants aglow with lights. Something about all of this didn't feel right.

My bedroom suite had been freshly cleaned. The only thing that was missing was the presence of Sahmril playing with Jasmine, her giggles as the two of them built towers out of blocks and rocked their baby dolls to sleep. I'd agreed to Sahmril staying with her adoptive parents that night, but her presence was sorely missed.

After my maids were asleep, I roamed the suite restlessly. Dozing in a chair by the window, I dreamed about Horeb pinning me to the earth, his mouth on mine while blood gushed from his chest and neck.

I woke in a sweat and stood at the window to cool my hot face. Going to the door, I found a guard pacing the floor in the outer hallway. "Is there any word from the king?"

"No, my lady," he replied.

"Please leave a message with his servant that I must see him. No matter how late it is."

I shut the door and leaned against it, sick with worry. Opening the door again, I said to the guard, "Please have someone find Basim and bring him to the palace to meet with me."

Unable to wait, I threw a robe around my shoulders and strode down to the foyer. The grand foyer was lit with dozens of sconces and burning lamps. Guards spoke quietly in the anteroom, discussing the week's battles, a topic I did not want to think about anymore.

I moved into a sitting room, unable to bear my own thoughts. Perched on the edge of a sofa, I stared into the lamp's flame until a noise came at the door.

"My lady, it's well past midnight," Basim said, fully dressed and armored as though he'd never gone to bed.

"Tell me what you know about Kadesh. His suite is empty, and I'm about to jump out a window from nerves."

"I've returned from the temple with a few of my men. A soldier relayed your message and I went to investigate the king's itinerary so I could allay your fears."

"Basim." My voice shook, and my hands were like ice. "I was at the temple and saw the bodies hanging from the walls. I saw people celebrating and the priestesses in mourning. That alone has made me terrified. They should be cowering in fear after Kadesh's decree."

"Your instincts are valid. The High Priestess finally granted me an audience. She was accompanied by an Egyptian priest."

"You mean my sister Leila?"

"She wouldn't give me any details, but handed over a letter for you. I was on my way here when I got your summons."

"Leila knows I can't read. Can you?"

"I'm a warrior, not a scholar, my lady, but I've ordered a palace scribe."

Indeed, even as he finished speaking a scribe appeared at the door. He bowed, appearing uncomfortable when Basim towered over him. The scribe held a thin stone tablet with the seal of the Goddess embedded at the top.

I broke into a nervous sweat. "Read it, quickly!"

"It's short and simple, my lady," the scribe said, his eyes scanning the lines. "It appears that King Kadesh went to the temple in search of the Goddess Aliyah to arrest her for treason and the murder of the Queen of Sheba."

"So Aliyah is being held in the city prison awaiting trial?"

"No," the scribe said solemnly. "It appears that the Goddess was not to be found."

My heart fell to the floor. "What did Kadesh say to this news?"

The scribe glanced between me and Basim. "The king was not to be found either. Only this note given to me by the High Priestess Leila. It appears that Aliyah has taken him somewhere. Kidnapped him."

"What do you mean *kidnapped*?" I echoed. "That makes no sense." Except that it did make sense. "The woman had to have witnessed the devastation of Horeb's armies. She has to know that he's dead and his foreign generals as well. She could probably see the burning of their camp from the temple balconies. After all, their heads hang from the temple gates!"

Basim's eyes were on mine. "Kadesh's disappearance keeps the city disrupted. Without the king's leadership, the people can't heal from the war's destruction."

My chest ached with despair, but my mind was flying with frightening thoughts. "By taking Kadesh captive she forces her will. Threatens him to do her bidding. If she took the Egyptian High Priest with her to perform their marriage—she could easily declare herself co-regent of Sariba. Dear God in heaven, I have no claim. Do you see what this means?"

"She has wasted no time in continuing to bring about her ambitions," Basim agreed gravely.

"Even if Aliyah forces Kadesh to marry her they need to

return to rule. Unless," I jumped up, every nerve on fire, "she sent someone to assassinate me while Kadesh is gone."

The scribe shook his head. "Her instructions are explicit. Jayden must find King Kadesh, alone. No one can go with her, not the generals or Asher, Prince of the Edomites. Or Basim from Sa'ba."

I stared helplessly at the two men. "Why does she want me to find him—and where would she have taken him?" As soon as the words were out of my mouth, comprehension swept over me. "She's taken him to the abandoned castle in the hills. The one that belonged to Kadesh's parents."

"I won't let you go alone to walk into her trap and die." Basim said.

The scribe set the letter of instructions on the table. "If Jayden doesn't show up alone, Kadesh dies. And the Goddess will set an assassin upon her."

"I'm leaving immediately," I said.

"This is extremely dangerous, my lady," Basim said. "You're walking into her trap. She'll kill you both and get exactly what she wanted all along. Only this time, you took out Horeb for her."

"Aliyah should have been arrested after she murdered the queen."

"I agree, but it was deemed a lawful sacrifice on the night of the temple ceremonies."

"Then I'll change the laws as soon as we get Kadesh safely back home."

My chin rose when Uncle Josiah appeared in the doorway. "An old man doesn't sleep well when he feels the household stirring," he said soberly.

"You've heard then?" Basim asked.

He tugged at his beard. "Aliyah sees her power waning. Bringing her magicians here gave her power for a period of time, but with the death of the enemy she's losing influence with her Egyptians. The foreigners have their own scheme, and Aliyah has now come to comprehend that she fell right into *their* trap. Egypt wants the temple and its priestesses—priestesses they brought here and trained and influenced."

"My sister Leila plans to marry one of those priests," I murmured.

"They will turn the temple over to their powerful God Amun, the god of darkness," Josiah said. "Once they have the temple *and* the people *and* the king, they will give the frankincense trade to their Pharaoh. Egypt is rising in stature and wealth. All they had to do was send a few of their magicians to use Aliyah against herself."

I dropped to a crouch, staring at Basim, pondering this sudden twist of loyalties and deceits regarding Aliyah and her precious Egyptians. "Who could have guessed that we should have arrested the Egyptian priests as well? My sister has been a pawn, and I am the bait for Aliyah to snatch Kadesh and put herself on the throne as fast as she can before her High Priest Heru takes her out."

"It's more complicated than that," Josiah said. "Aliyah believes she is the Goddess and can wield magical abilities.

Little does she know that the Egyptians have played her for a fool with their ceremonies and magical tricks."

I crossed the room to Uncle Josiah and he wrapped my cold hands in his. His eyes seemed to see into my very soul, reminding me of my grandmother Seraiah's intensity and inner wisdom. His gentle soul poured like warm water, giving me comfort. "Faith in yourself, Jayden, and faith in Kadesh will be enough. The blessings of the God you know is enough, daughter of Pharez," he added. "Trust in the Goddess that gives *life* not death. That endows with *love* not hate or subjugation. She will give you what you need to bring Kadesh home."

I rose to prepare myself to leave, but Basim's worried face made me pause. He went down to his knees in a display of obeisance. "Basim, when you arrived at my summons, you said that you were already on your way here. What were you going to tell me?"

"I took a small envoy of my men out into the desert and we searched for your missing weapons." The mountain man folded over the fabric of a package he'd been carrying. Laid out on the cloth was the dagger I'd purchased for myself in Tadmur—and the Damascus sword Kadesh had given me. The weapons Horeb had flung away from me. I picked up the sword in my fist, tears pricking at my eyelids. "I wasn't sure I'd ever see these again, Basim. I cannot express my gratitude enough, thank you."

"Unfortunately, my lady, you need them again tonight."

Not an hour later, I was dressed with a calmness that defied my own fears. I'd secured my sword, dagger, and sling to my belt. Pulling my hair back, I clipped it up on top of my head with a jeweled band to keep it out of my face. "The jewels are frivolous," I said, reaching out to put a hand on Tijah's shoulder.

She gave a helpless shrug in her nightgown, fear glistening in her eyes. "Jeweled hair finery is all we have in the dressing table at the moment. And the jewels mean you *will* be queen one day."

When I reached the stables, Basim was there preparing my camel, Shay.

"You know me well," I told him.

"Your camel can find her way in the desert. She won't abandon you in the Qara Mountains," Basim said as he slapped the animal's rump. He stared at me with flinty black eyes, his large frame towering over me. "Come back to your people," he said. "I'm not leaving for Sa'ba until you return."

"Is that a promise?" I called when Shay trotted out from the camel barns, but when I glanced back over my shoulder, the mercenary soldier had already disappeared behind me in the early morning mists.

33

I maneuvered the twists and turns of the mountain trail, leaving behind the frankincense groves and desert where Horeb's armies had camped for the last fortnight. Remains of the opposing armies and the battles had left scars on the earth, now blackened by the burning of the camps.

Three armies gone. Forever. A grim outcome.

When I reached the hollowed crumbling structure, my heart was jammed into my throat. The old castle looked similar to an ancient fort at the edge of the empty sands from eons earlier. A hideout when Kadesh's ancestors had first begun to establish the frankincense trade, when rogue tribes from the empty sands roamed in and out of the valley.

I approached slowly, relieved that I'd brought candles and flint with me. The empty windows gave off a foreboding atmosphere, as if they were eyes watching me.

Lifting her legs in agitation, Shay jerked in small steps about the exterior while we walked the perimeter to get our bearings. Four stories crafted with stone. A structure filled with rooms and hallways.

The crumbling site appeared deserted, but I knew better than to trust appearances. After all, in the land of Edom, dozens of soldiers spilled out of the caves like ants rising from the underground.

Close to the front gates, a falcon careened through the air, diving at me as if preparing to attack. I screamed and jumped off Shay to duck beneath her belly. The falcon screeched, its black eyes ringed with yellow. The bird stared at me with an alarming gaze that was disturbing.

"Go back to where you came from," I yelled.

The great bird continued to circle me, swooping closer and then zooming away to provoke me.

I allowed Shay to roam the area where a few clumps of shriveling flowers would provide her with something to eat while I explored. "Don't leave," I ordered sternly. She merely raised her long neck and batted her eyelashes.

Carved doors that used to be grand and imposing now rusted on crooked brass hinges. I slipped past with a final glance back at Shay who stood placidly chewing her supper.

Dirt and rubble littered the stone floors, large rooms empty of furniture or carpets. I stepped carefully, the foyer echoing as I walked the adjoining empty salons and smaller sitting rooms. A massive staircase with splintered railings took my breath away, curving away into upper darkness.

I lit a candle and held it, my dagger clutched in my other hand, at the ready in case I encountered a vagabond—or worse—a lethal Aliyah.

Despite my hunch, the castle appeared to be empty. No sign of life anywhere, but I wouldn't leave until I searched the entire place.

I took the first step, holding my candle high. No windows lit the stuffy stairwell, but once I reached the second floor a series of small windows were set into the thick walls.

Masses of sticky cobwebs adorned the corners, dripping like filigree down the walls. It had been at least two years since Kadesh's parents had stayed here.

The second and third floors were a maze of rooms with cold, blackened fireplaces, and broken stone lying along the floors. A few minor pieces of furniture had been left, but I assumed most had been taken back to the palace upon their deaths.

The silence was eerie, until a second falcon charged through one of the wide windows. The bird circled, diving at my head but not actually touching me. The eyes were the same as those of the earlier falcon. Too intelligent for a normal bird. Too focused on me.

"Am I trespassing in your home?" I said, forcing my voice to remain light and nonthreatening.

Another terrifying screech echoed, the creature's mouth opening and closing rapidly in a repetitive movement. Holding my hands to my ears, I fell back against the wall. I ran from room to room, trying to stop the bird from following me, but it kept darting in and out of windows so fast my head spun.

"Do you like my wild pet?" a voice whispered along the upper floors. That sensuous, lush voice was unmistakably Aliyah.

At first, I didn't respond, purposely slowing my walk to figure out where the sound was coming from.

She *was* here. In this castle. My instincts had been correct, but how had she managed to bring Kadesh all the way here? He would never have agreed, unless he'd been forced to by Aliyah's High Priest Heru. The Egyptian was a powerful man, with powerful concoctions for drugging someone. My skin prickled knowing the bald-headed man with his frightening eyes and falcon-headed staff was nearby.

I sped out of one room and into another, but the hallway seemed to twist in the opposite direction. I stepped over to the staircase to gaze down into its depths and then lifted my head to stare upward.

I ran to the next floor and the direction of the stairs changed again. An illusion or fatigue?

I wasn't sure of my own mind any longer.

The sky outside the windows darkened and a wind rose, blowing dry scrub along the ravine. I leaned out over the windowsill to take a breath and then whirled when a light tap on my shoulder startled me. My heart pounded so hard I thought it would burst. "Kadesh?"

Nobody was there. I lit two more candles and placed them on the floor of the landing. The wax cylinders stayed aflame for a few moments, wavering with small strokes of yellow. And then all at once they snuffed out.

Craning my neck, I could see up through the spiraling staircases into the next floors above me, but if I was on the third floor now that meant there were five floors, not four as I'd first supposed.

Sinister darkness enveloped those upper landings. I didn't want to go up there, but I had to.

Once again, I was carrying a candle that barely cut the darkness and my dagger as I dragged my way up the next flight. At least the falcon had disappeared into a hidden eave somewhere and I hoped it died there.

When I reached the final landing, I stared back down at the endless stairs below. My legs shook with vertigo, so I grasped the banister—the only thing keeping me from falling straight down.

"Jayden," another whisper came from overhead, but from what I could see, I was utterly alone.

Slowly, I gazed up at the timbered ceiling, almost afraid to look. A body was hanging from one of the beams by a length of rope. A man with shoulder-length dark hair and an exotic rich brown cloak.

I screamed and my candle went flying. Hot wax spilled across the dirty floor and the candle sputtered out. Fortunately, the last of the full, golden moon was rising, streaming light into the large upper windows.

Horror gurgled in my throat when I stared at Kadesh, rope tied around his torso to keep him away from me on one of the roughhewn crossbeams. His legs dangled lifelessly and I choked on my own fear that I had arrived too late. That Aliyah had already killed him.

Sucking in air and forcing my fear down into my belly, I called out, "It wasn't enough to murder your sister. But General Naham, King Chemish, Basim of Sa'ba—they all know what you've done, Aliyah. And you will hang for murder and treason."

"Not if they die first," Aliyah said, a laugh in her voice now. "My priestesses have their orders and their poisons. By tonight, I will be Queen of Sariba and Queen of Sheba. I've already sent letters to King Hammurabi of Babylon conveying the events of the last many months. He's ready to be my ally and collaborator in uniting the tribes and cities under one rule—mine."

"And what if he rejects your proposal?"

"I've spent a long time forming friendships with the other Goddess temples and Hammurabi's enemies. As soon as I say the word the man is gone, and Babylon is mine."

"All you need to do is get rid of me," I said bitterly, never taking my eyes off Kadesh who hung so still, his head drooping.

Before I could speak again, Kadesh's fingers twitched and I let out a gasp. He was still alive. Perhaps Aliyah had merely drugged him. After all, she still wanted him. To be his queen was still her dream, until the city accepted her as the stronger ruler and no longer cared if their old king had a sudden illness or accident. An assassin assigned to one of the caravan trip and Kadesh never returned again.

I moved forward, and a row of candles lit up with a distinctive sizzle. The lights had been placed on top of the decaying wooden railing that surrounded the open pit of the staircases. Aliyah materialized behind the candles on the far side of the railing. She'd been there all along, her voice crawling along my neck, invading my mind.

Her face was pale in the candle's dim flames, her lips gray. Her rich red gown from the Goddess ceremony a week ago was now in shreds. Her hair a wild nest of black curls standing straight out from her face.

Her eyes were alive with a violent darkness. Chills crept along my spine. The young woman I'd been afraid of ever since I'd arrived in Sariba wasn't well. The Goddess's spirit had taken hold, and had not been kind. She was consuming Aliyah with each breath.

With a seductive laugh, Aliyah said, "You aren't stupid after all, Jayden. Yes, you will die today. I plan to perform another Egyptian ritual. Heru is out in the desert gathering the firewood we need. While you slowly die during the ceremony, he will help me take your spirit and vitality and consume it for my own."

Her words should have terrified me, but I'd heard the threats before, ever since the day I'd first met her. Her malevolent Goddess didn't have the power over me that She used to. One stroke of my sword and Aliyah would be gone. I only had to get close enough. "And how do you propose this takes place?"

Before she could answer, the sound of boots scraped across the stone floors below. I shrank against the filthy walls. Was I about to face the monstrous Heru? It would be impossible to fight them both.

I pulled out my sword, my eyes flying to the windows, and then to the ground far, far below. The sheer walls held no balconies or ledges for escape.

While I was appraising an escape method, my sword was yanked from my fist. Aliyah laughed, her form gliding away with my weapon. She was like an apparition, moving about the railings. I lunged at her with my dagger next, but the weapon met only air and clattered to the filthy floor. Before I could pick it up, a sudden gust swept it through the slats of the staircase railing. I watched my knife fall past five stories of stairs to the bottom of the old fortress, hitting the floor with a distant clang.

I was now unarmed. The footsteps sounded louder on the stairs, coming closer every moment. "Kadesh!" I screamed, hoping he would wake from his unconscious state.

His legs jerked again, and the hem of his cloak fluttered. His hands were bound behind his back, and he had no way to release himself. Even if he could release himself, he'd drop instantly and die from that height.

A shout came up the stairwell, and someone was calling my name. Before I could move again, Asher leaped up the last level of stairs and I ran toward him, never so glad to see him in all my life.

"Asher! How did you know I was here?"

"I intercepted Basim and he told me you were headed to the mountains," he whispered, keeping his voice low. "When I saw your camel outside this old fortress, my hunch was correct. Nowhere else in the city could Aliyah attempt to intimidate you or Kadesh into bending to her will."

I grasped his hands, but Aliyah was moving about the upper chamber, her wild hair floating on an unseen breeze.

"Where's Ka—" his voice cut off when I directed his gaze upward. "It appears I should have left Sariba earlier," he said between gritted teeth.

"I could say the same," I replied.

Asher stared up at Aliyah whose long white fingers trailed across the railing.

"Now I have you both," the woman said.

"But you only get one of us," I reminded her. "You said so yourself."

Her eyes narrowed. "To save Kadesh, Jayden will offer herself to me by throwing herself into the stairwell. Don't you remember making me that promise at the temple, Jayden? You said you would sacrifice yourself to keep your family and Kadesh safe. Now we're here to collect your debt."

Anger surged through me like fire in my gut while Aliyah continued in her maddening pompous tone.

"A freely offered sacrifice carries great power. Your love will release Kadesh and imbue me with all the traits I need to rule. I will be both loved and feared. A stunning combination for a queen, don't you think?"

"My weapons are gone," I confessed to Asher in a low voice, keeping my grip on his arm, terrified that Aliyah would suddenly snatch me away.

"There must be a way to get Kadesh down," Asher said. Together, we moved across the upper landing to inspect the pulley and ropes holding the king up near the timbered beams of the roof.

Aliyah threw a knife, narrowly missing Asher. "Stop where you are and obey me."

A strange resolution formed in Asher's features. The expression caught at my heart, and I was worried about what risks he would take to save Kadesh. The young Edomite prince would do almost anything, and I didn't want it to come to that. There had to be another way.

"No, Aliyah, you will die this day," Asher told the woman. "For war, for murder, and for treason. The Goddess temple will crumble and fall with your death."

A laugh escaped Aliyah's mouth. "You are all so naïve. Nobody can best the power of the Goddess within me!"

Grasping a staff from an old table, Aliyah threw it straight across the railing at us like a spear. Asher whipped out his sword and knocked out the staff, sending it right back at Aliyah who had to duck to avoid a direct hit in the throat.

With a scream of fury, Aliyah charged at Asher and tried to knock him down the stairs, but he fended her off. When his grip on his sword slipped, the priestess managed to gain control of the hilt, sending the sword sailing down through the stairwell where it landed on the floor below with a clang of bronze.

My throat burned with fear. All of our weapons were now five floors below us.

"Without a weapon," Asher said, "there's no way to cut the ropes and get Kadesh down."

"But she can't win," I said with despair. "Not like this, not after everything." I sagged against him, and Asher's arm went around me. I stared up into his face. "I will gladly die so Kadesh can live and have a chance. Sariba needs her king. He and I are not married, and I hold no crown."

Asher's face hardened. "You can't give up, my lady."

We stared at each other for a long moment, and then Asher turned his head toward Aliyah. "You need a sacrifice to convince you to bring Kadesh down from that rope? Will that fulfill your supposed magic and curse?"

"Oh, but it's a curse that includes a great blessing. As soon as the requirements are met, Kadesh will wake up from the sleeping potion I gave him when he came to the temple last night. He will live and then, Prince of Edom, you may help your new queen—me—bring him home again. It's very simple."

"What if I offer myself as your ill-gotten sacrifice, Aliyah?"

Her eyes burned with a malicious light. "You would sacrifice yourself for both Kadesh and this girl, a *princess* of a tribe that no longer exists?" Aliyah paced the floor, sweeping the hem of her dirty gown along the stone squares. "A most interesting offer since a willing sacrifice is that much more powerful. With your sacrifice I have the chance to rule forever."

"*No!*" I said, shoving my hands at Asher. "You will *not* do this! There must be another way to stop her."

"Time's running out," Aliyah said evenly. "When the moon sinks below the zenith of the sky, Kadesh will die and I will be Queen of Sariba. The sacrifice must be tonight."

"Don't believe her, Asher!"

"She speaks truth," Asher said sadly.

"What are you talking about? You need to go home with your father to your mother and your family. Go home to the girl that waits for you in your future. You do have a future, I know it."

He took my hands in his, his brow knitted together.

"I see your thoughts, Jayden, my queen, but I've had so many faults and transgressions over the past year. Someone else will make a finer king, perhaps my younger sister will be the next Queen of Edom. There is no girl in my future."

"You can't say that," I contradicted.

"There has only ever been one girl I've loved."

"No!" The word choked in my throat and I pounded on his chest with my fist. "We need to figure out a way to do this."

Asher's face was pale. "We have no weapons, and Aliyah has Kadesh drugged with her poisons, the High Priest waiting in the wings to kill us if we try to fight her."

I shook with anger and helplessness. "Aliyah can't win, Asher, she *can't*. We cannot allow it."

"She won't," he said with a sad smile. "This is it. Now. We can beat her once and for all. I have loved you, Jayden, daughter of Pharez. It was wrong for me to have loved the woman who belongs to my dearest friend. This is a chance to redeem myself. By doing this, I'll set you and Kadesh free forever."

I fought back the rising tears. "No, Asher, please stop saying these things. There has to be another way."

"Trust me," he said, speaking low so that only I could hear. His forehead lowered to mine and the back of his hand brushed gently against my cheek.

My lips parted to speak, but nothing came out. *This* boy. This crazy, foolish, selfless boy willing to sacrifice his life for Kadesh and me.

"You have always been there to protect me," I told him. Gazing deeply into his eyes, I lifted my face to press my lips to his. His skin was feverish with love and fear, but his arms came around me and I pressed myself to him, giving him the wish of his heart.

He kissed me for a long moment of utter stillness, and I was acutely aware of the pounding of his heart beneath his tunic. It was a kiss meant only for him, a token of my affection for his friendship and protection the last many months.

When we broke apart, I said, "I will never forget you, Prince of Edom. Go to God, Asher. Go in peace."

He gave me a soft smile and then bent over my hand to kiss my palm.

Aliyah mocked us from the top of the stairs that separated us. "How precious, you two. If I'd only known—"

"Let's make a run for our weapons," I started to say, but I never finished my sentence.

Before Aliyah could continue taunting us over the kiss I

had just given to Asher, I watched as the Prince of Edom flung himself around the railing, grabbing the priestess with both arms and then jumping into the blackness of the empty stairwell, taking her with him to their deaths.

It happened so quickly Aliyah never had a chance. The woman's screams reverberated off the empty chambers all the way down to the bottom of the fortress.

I closed my ears to the terrible thud of their bodies and then sank to the floor, dissolving into grief. My heart broke into a thousand pieces at his incredibly brave act. "Oh, Asher," I moaned. "I'm sorry. I'm so terribly sorry."

Tears streamed down my face while I rose to my shaky feet and tried to light a fresh candle to hunt for my sword.

On each floor, I searched through the debris, finally finding my sword and dagger lying in the dust. Grabbing them up, I raced back to Kadesh and studied the pulley's knots to release him. Sawing at the complicated knot, it finally loosened enough so that I could turn the crank to bring him down safely.

It seemed to take forever, but Kadesh finally slumped to the floor, his cloak folding around him in a heap.

I lifted his body into my arms, cradling his head in the crook of my arm. "Kadesh, wake up!" I cried.

He stirred and I pressed my lips against his forehead, his blind eye, his scars, and every part of his face. My heart pulsed so hard I thought it would leap straight out of my chest, but he didn't wake. Surely the drug would eventually wear off. I knew Aliyah hadn't poisoned him. It was only a strong sleeping draught to bring him out here to this castle, unable to fight her.

Rocking him in the twilight, I waited, bathing his face with cold water from my leather water pouch. Finally, Kadesh's eyes fluttered open, and he blinked against the candlelight. "Is Horeb dead?" he whispered, reaching up to tangle his fingers in my hair. A sob caught in his throat, and then he buried his face into my neck, bringing me down on top of him. We embraced so tightly my arms trembled.

"Yes, Horeb is dead," I assured him. "Aliyah is dead, too. It's over, Kadesh. It's truly over."

This time, I was the one to help Kadesh lift himself up onto Shay. He was weak and almost incoherent. I tied him to my waist with rope so he didn't collapse and fall off the camel.

We rode quietly through the ravines and hills of the mountains as dawn lit the new sky.

34

After several more hours, the lights of the city came into view, including the dark waters of the sea beyond. I left the edge of the desert and pressed my thighs against Shay's belly, urging her forward.

By the time the gates of the city were in sight, Kadesh began to wake more fully from his drugged state. "Home," he said, twisting around to grasp my hands.

I untied the rope between us, and we slid off Shay. He wrapped his arms around me, and I laid my head on his chest. His heart was steady and sure, and I stopped fearing any long-lasting effects of Aliyah's sleeping potion.

At the moment I could hardly do more than weep from exhaustion and relief, but I needed to send Basim back to the castle to retrieve Asher's body so we could give him a prince's burial. I thought about his parents, Chemish and Isra, and my heart physically hurt inside my chest. Our shared kiss was a secret I'd hold inside for the rest of my life.

"The war is finished?" Kadesh asked again. "Tell me what happened."

"We have plenty of time, my love," I said, tracing the fading scar along his cheek. "Right now there are a lot of people who want to know that you are alive. Once we're home I refuse to let you out of my sight for the next month."

Kadesh brushed at my hair, cradling my neck with both hands. "You're real. I feared so many things—"

"Shh," I whispered, putting a finger to his lips. "We can talk about all of it later. I'm dead on my feet, but it's finally over. And I want to marry you as fast as possible. Uncle Josiah and Pharez need to sign our new marriage covenant. It's waiting for us in your suite, remember? Chemish is waiting for you, as well as Aunt Naomi and General Naham—and your new commander, Basim, who will escort the Queen of Sheba back home to her people."

"Oh, Jayden," he said, gathering me up in his arms. I blinked back the emotion biting at my eyes, not wanting to break down when he seemed so fragile after his ordeal with Aliyah.

"What of Asher?" Kadesh asked, pulling back to look at me. "Please tell me he survived the final battle."

"The final battle," I echoed. "The battle with Horeb's armies or the battle with Aliyah?" My throat constricted. What could I say? I needed to tell him the whole story, but how?

His face filled with sudden sorrow, instinctively discerning that I had bad news. "Oh, Jayden, no, please no."

I pulled Kadesh against me, stifling a sob. "Asher offered the ultimate sacrifice for both of us," I whispered at last.

Kadesh dropped to the earth, his hands covering his face in grief.

I knelt with him as the early morning sun broke over the mountains. "Asher died nobly with a pure heart. He died to save you and me. He sacrificed himself because it was the only way to assure Aliyah would never threaten us or the kingdom of Sariba again. He died loving you to the end, and loving Sariba. When I think back over the past year, it's clear that Asher would do anything for us—and he did, over and over again."

Two days after rescuing Kadesh, I finally had my entire family under one roof.

After Aliyah's death, Leila finally came down from the temple in response to my pleading letter. Our reunion was both joyful and melancholy, but my sister did not want to talk about the young woman she had followed and revered, even though we hadn't seen each other since the night of the solstice sacrifices.

Today I was glad to see her in the royal apartments playing with Sahmril, the first chance they'd had to be together.

Leila had crafted a ball from scraps of fabric and yarn, and Sahmril squealed as she ran from corner to corner trying to catch it. When she giggled, the sound of her laughter was infectious. I wished my mother could see how precious she was. How alive she was. That we were here, all together after so long.

When I entered the room, Sahmril jumped into my arms and I buried my face into her silky dark curls, kissing her cheeks and tickling her belly. Soon Tijah brought out a plate of sugared fruit for a snack and, while Sahmril ate, Leila and I sat before the window staring out at the city below us.

"It's been a long time since we were together like this," I said. She gazed back at me, and then said simply, "I'm still going to marry him."

My heart turned over to hear her say that. I reached out to stroke her hair, her elegant shoulders soft underneath the temple silks she wore.

"Your Egyptian lover?" I asked. "Is a High Priestess allowed to marry outside of the Ba'al priesthood?"

She pressed her pomegranate-red lips together. "The priestess cult is disbanded temporarily. I will probably move back to Tadmur or perhaps live with my husband in the city of Thebes in Egypt."

"I've heard grand things about that capitol city."

"You know I always wanted to go to Egypt," she said, bringing back those long-ago sisterly conversations.

"I'm sure you'll love it," I told her, despite the fact that if she did go to Egypt I'd probably never see her again. Instead, I turned to memories from the past. "Remember how we used to ride in the camel litter across the desert and talk about all the things we wanted to see and eat in Egypt. Visit the Pyramids. Watch the street dancers. Eat exotic foods."

"I remember," she said quietly. "Would you believe me if I said that sometimes I actually miss those days? Only two years ago, but a lifetime after all that's happened to our family."

"You don't miss traveling the harsh desert, but I think we both miss the innocence of those simple, uncomplicated days. The peaceful nights with our mother. Listening to her sing, sitting in Father's lap while he told stories." My throat closed up, and I stopped.

Leila fingered the necklace at her throat. "I'm sorry for not fighting the Goddess when she wanted to sacrifice Sahmril. I was caught up in my position as High Priestess. I wanted to impress Aliyah, to be like her. I was desperate and stupid. Will you ever forgive me?"

"Of course I'll forgive you," I said, swallowing down the heartache. "You were under her spell. You're my sister. Sometimes we fight and disagree, but mostly we know we'll love each other forever. No matter what happens."

"Our lives have taken such drastic turns," she mused. "You became a warrior and a queen of a beautiful country."

"You will always be welcome here, Leila," I told her. "And I'm not queen yet. Three more days. The gardeners and palace staff are working overtime to get everything ready. Exactly the same as it was a fortnight ago." I wagged a finger at my older sister. "And you had better not leave before the royal wedding."

"I'm going to give you your wedding present early," she said, jumping up to fetch something from across the room where she'd hidden it. A carved chest came out from under a blanket.

I opened the lid and dropped to my knees on the carpet. "This is Mother's carved chest," I said, my voice catching. "Her gowns and linens and household items. The pieces we grew up with, the pots we cooked with. And the loom we practiced our stitches on." I marveled at their intact state. Dresses folded just as I remembered them. I pulled a bright yellow dress out and buried my face into its soft folds, the perfume of my mother rising from the fabric. I closed my eyes and tried not to weep.

"Imarus allowed me to bring them with me from the Temple of Ashtoreth in Tadmur. I didn't want them getting stolen."

"I thought they were lost forever."

"And this," Leila added. "Your favorite. She brought out another box and reached inside.

"Mother's alabaster box," I cried, pressing my nose to the richly carved lid with its intricate design. "Thank you, Leila, thank you. You know how much I treasure this."

It was the greatest gift she could have given me. The last missing piece of my mother. The alabaster box symbolized the beauty and love she brought to her family, beginning with the love my father had for her.

Before dinner, we visited my father who sat in a heavily cushioned chair before the windows. He took Sahmril in his arms, his voice cracking each time he spoke her name. When he smiled at her, she tugged on his beard while he stroked her curls.

I watched them together, and the lump in my throat grew so large I couldn't say a thing.

My father brought out a doll that he'd fashioned from wood

and clay, and Sahmril clapped her hands, bringing the doll to her chest in delight. The two of them proceeded to play a game of peek-a-boo while Sahmril giggled, splaying her hands over her face in an attempt to hide.

After a while, I could tell that my father was getting tired. Leila took Sahmril to the window to point out the various landmarks while the sun began to set, casting pink and purple rays through the sky.

I ached to see him so old and frail, worse even since the news of Horeb's death. He'd taken it badly, always holding out hope for reconciliation. I could see that his heart had torn into pieces, and he was giving up on life, despite his joy at seeing Sahmril again.

"Jayden," he spoke now. When I glanced over, he was staring at me intently. "Thank you for finding your sisters. For honoring your mother's promises."

I held back my emotions, feeling silly to cry in front of him. "Of course," I whispered. "I love you."

"And now, will you fulfill another promise for me?"

"Anything. You know I will."

"I don't know how much time God will give me yet, but I want to lie on my death bed assured that you will teach Sahmril the ways of the desert." He gripped my hand tightly. "Teach her how to be a daughter of Pharez. A child who loves the desert. How to ride a camel without falling off. How to wield a knife to cut an herb for medicine, or tend a newborn calf without getting her fingers bitten off."

I smiled at him through watery eyes when he lifted his

face toward the window and kept it there for several long moments.

"What's there?" I asked him, confused about what he could be searching for. "What do you see?"

"Rebekah?" he finally said, his voice hoarse with age.

"No, it's Jayden," I said, biting back the ache in my chest when he spoke my mother's name for the first time in months. "I'm wearing one of her shawls."

But he wasn't actually looking at me. He was looking for her somewhere in the distance. "She comes to my dreams."

"She does to me, too, Father," I told him, pressing his hand against my lips. "I miss her dreadfully."

With a sigh, he sank back against the pillow I'd stuffed behind his head to make him more comfortable.

We were quiet for the next several moments. I gazed through the window as storm clouds moved across the mountains. Moving my chair closer, I laid my head on his knees, my cheek resting in my folded arms. No longer did the past weigh us down. Instead, it was bringing us together at last.

His big hand fell on top of my head, and he stroked my hair. When I glanced up again he smiled, and a rush of relief came over me. My father would be there, standing at the wedding dais to sign my marriage contract.

My wedding to Kadesh took place three nights later when he'd regained his strength. Blessedly, the scars of war were already beginning to fade from the battlefield.

The palace staff created the same magical night that had

been destroyed weeks earlier. The celebration was fashioned to erase all the war and death that had happened in between. It was a night where Horeb and Aliyah didn't exist any longer.

The food smelled even more heavenly, and the rich swaths of drapery along the dais were even a richer purple color than before. The fountains sparkled brighter, the hanging lamps glowing as if lit by the moon itself.

The palace grounds were packed with the city council, noblemen, army captains, and citizens who brought with them an atmosphere of hopeful festivity and optimism. They yearned for a new king and queen. A future that wasn't tarnished by the horrible events of the past many weeks.

"As long as there is hope, all is not lost," I murmured when Aunt Naomi inserted my earrings and clasped the matching necklace of rubies about my neck.

She leaned down to kiss my cheek and, while I loved her dearly, I mourned that the Queen of Sheba wasn't here to celebrate with us.

"It's hard not to be weighed down by what our country has just endured," Naomi said while Tijah finished my kohl and rouge and lip color. My handmaidens tried to hide their giddy smiles over the excitement of the wedding, but I could see them in the copper mirrors hanging around the dressing area of Naomi's suite.

"My heart aches for the mourning so many of our citizens are enduring while we have a wedding celebration," I said, glancing up at Aunt Naomi's face.

Naomi shook her head. "The country wants you married.

We need the stability this wedding will bring. They rejoice to see you both alive."

"Kadesh and I have determined to visit every family of our fallen soldiers and give any aid or comfort we can."

"That's a wonderful plan. The king and queen personally reaching out to them will give consolation and comfort. Now that our enemies are banished, we *can* return to peace."

"Outward scars heal and disappear faster than those we carry inside."

"You have lived under fear for so long, dear Jayden. Give yourself time. You and Kadesh finally being married will go a long way toward banishing the horror. Returning to each other and returning to the new life you've waited so long to claim will bring you both inner peace and joy."

I nodded, biting at my red lips. "My old tribe has gone the way of the sands blowing across the desert. When I was young, my father used to laugh at me because I tried to catch the wind. I could see the wind pick up the corners of the tent or toss my toys about or turn over a pot of supper when a storm was coming, but it was always out of reach, an invisible joke on me."

"You're creating a new homeland here with us," Naomi said. "There is no greater blessing at the moment. And now," she added, "if we don't finish your hair and get outside, the wedding will begin without us."

"Did you see the marriage tent, my lady?" Tijah asked, applying the final gold glitter to my curls.

"I toured it earlier today. I think it's even more beautiful now than it was before, if that's even possible."

"This time," Naomi reminded me, "there will be no imminent war hanging over you to spoil your time together. No worries; only each other."

When I walked down the flower-filled paths to the wedding dais in my ivory lace dress that Aunt Naomi's dressmaker was able to repair, I saw smiles on the guests and palace staff. I was relieved to see Leila who was restraining Sahmril and Naria from running wild in their new party dresses, clutching baskets of magenta roses and orchids.

Imarus stood behind my older sister, his hands on her shoulders while I headed straight for Kadesh who waited for me at the dais.

He was devastatingly handsome in his royal uniform and gilt-edged black cloak, that distinctive mysterious smile in his eye. The noble face and beguiling man I fell in love with when we crossed the desert so long ago.

It was an evening such as this one, on the night of my cousin Hakak's wedding, when we no longer held back the desire we had for each other. The night Kadesh had enclosed me in his rich brown cloak and kissed me for the first time.

Now Kadesh reached out to take my hand in his, bringing me to his side as we stood before the dais and our people.

Uncle Josiah and Pharez presided over the proceedings together, signing a fresh copy of the marriage covenant with a flourish of ink, the chief palace scribe's chest puffed out in satisfaction.

I was keenly aware of Asher's absence. My eyes pricked

at the memory of his sacrifice. I could hardly look at Chemish without enormous guilt over Asher's sacrificial offering of himself, our kiss and hearts entwined in the final moments of his life. Despite the King of Edom's assurances, I would feel responsible for the rest of my life.

When Chemish came forward, my stomach tightened. I tried to keep my composure when he placed his hands on my cheeks to kiss my forehead and whisper congratulations.

"Dear Chemish," I began, but he put a finger to my lips to stop me.

"My son was your bodyguard and Kadesh's loyal friend. Of course, he would race across the desert to find you. He lived the last months of his life with nobility, and for that I will always be proud."

Even so, the King of Edom's eyes were filled with a grief I wouldn't fully understand until I held a child of my own in my arms.

"I promise you," I told him. "Kadesh and I will visit your wife, Isra, in your homeland as soon as we can." We also planned to stop in Sa'ba to pay our respects to the Queen of Sheba's family. It was a visit I dreaded, but I wanted to meet her husband and children so that I could personally tell them of the sacrifice she had given to Sariba and to me.

"Be happy, Queen Jayden," Chemish said softly when I embraced him. "I wish a long and fruitful life for you and King Kadesh."

At the dais, Uncle Josiah held his hands over mine and Kadesh's, speaking words of blessings. "Go forth and be happy," he told us. "Love your people, but most of all love each other for now and eternity."

After we signed the marriage contract, cheers erupted throughout the palace grounds and Kadesh kissed me in front of the packed pavilions. There was hearty applause and then drums and harps broke out in joyful music. The heady scent of exotic summer flowers perfumed the air. Lavish food would be served all night until dawn.

My father embraced me, and Leila and Sahmril hugged me tight, as well as the rest of the royal family and my handmaids.

We stepped off the dais and a hundred people showered us with a thousand more congratulations. Chemish kissed my cheek. "Now we are allies and friends forever." Words choked in my throat. How blessed I was to find forgiveness within this great man.

Kadesh's arm went around my waist and he kissed me again, scooping me up into his arms to spin me around while my dress billowed about in a flash of sparkling jewels. My stomach soared into my throat, the lamps a whirl of light behind my closed eyes.

The crowd cheered at his exuberance. The night rang with joy and laughter.

"And now," Kadesh's voice came in my ear as he brought my toes back down to the earth. "Our marriage tent awaits us, my love."

"Are we allowed to disappear from our own wedding party?" I whispered against his lips.

"We can, and we will," he assured me in a low husky voice.

We moved through the crowd to the tent on the far side of the palace grounds, secluded by trees and a bubbling stream to mark the perimeter. We turned to bow and make our final farewell to the guests. After the last of the cheering died away, Kadesh and I gazed at each other, hands gripped tightly together.

Suppressing laughter, we ran through the garden pathways, past benches and fountains to the entrance of the marriage tent. "We never got a chance to eat our own wedding dinner," I teased Kadesh.

"Servants will bring us food and drink, but for now you are mine." He lifted me up into his arms and carried me across the threshold. Roses and orchids bloomed about the marriage tent, sweet and heady.

When Kadesh set me back onto my feet, we fell into each other's kisses. Husband and wife, King and Queen of Sariba.

"My mysterious frankincense boy," I murmured into his ear.

Kadesh kneeled before me to kiss my palms, just as he did that first time in the canyon so long ago. The touch of his lips made me burst out of my skin, and when his mysterious dark gaze met mine, I was lost to him forever.

"You're tied to the mysterious southern lands for the rest of your life," he told me when he poured a handful of perfect golden nuggets into my hand. "Frankincense tears for my love."

"Your home is my home, your secrets my secrets," I whispered, moved that he remembered the gift he'd given me that night on the desert when I feared I'd never see him again.

Rising, he swept his rich exotic cloak around me, enclosing us together—and suddenly I recalled the sound of the fire hearth crackling on that dark moonless night when he declared his love for the first time.

His heart pounded against mine, and it was as though we had truly become one person, one soul for the rest of our lives.

Through the window, my eyes flicked upward to the hill beyond the city. A hill now empty of temple lights marring the view of the horizon and the mountains. Tonight, the moon hung like a ball of gold just for us.

Later that night I danced the dance of the seven veils of womanhood for my husband, just as my mother had taught me.

Author's Note

I can't finish the last book of the Forbidden trilogy without sending a little love note to my readers around the world. Thank you for being my companions into the distant past of four thousand years ago when a girl like Jayden might have lived and loved while surviving the dangerous Mesopotamian deserts. Thank you for all the beautiful reviews and letters that you send by email and snail mail that brighten my days so much.

I wrote lengthy author's notes in both *Forbidden* and *Banished*, which answer many readers' questions about the time period, tribal warfare, family life, culture, camels, frankincense, and Goddess temples, so I highly recommend reading those.

It horrified me to read about camel stampedes in the Middle East, where wild camels will suddenly race across the desert in groups of hundreds or thousands, ultimately trampling anything that gets in the way, and often killing innocent bystanders. I knew this had to become the final epic battle among Jayden, Kadesh, and King Horeb's foreign armies. The multitude of camels used by the caravans of the ancient Frankincense Trail provided the perfect setting for just such a battle tactic.

The Frankincense Lands are an intriguing place because of their mysterious, lost history and their location on the bountiful fertile coast of the Arabian Sea, bordered by the Empty Quarter of endless sand dunes. Frankincense was used anciently at dozens of temples, for medicine, and for embalming. Currently, medical research centers around the world are having astonishing success in using frankincense to treat various forms of cancer.

A map of the ancient Forbidden lands and cities, as well as book club guides and curriculum-centered teachers' guides, can be found on my website: www.kimberleygriffithslittle. com.

Pinterest boards about belly dancers, the Middle East, as well as my trip to Jordan, Petra, and the deserts of Wadi Rumm can be enjoyed here: www.pinterest.com/kimberleylittle.

ACKNOWLEDGMENTS

A thousand thanks and all my love to my husband, my three sons, and my daughter-in-law, who all brainstorm, critique, and help with so many aspects of my writing career, including holding down the fort when I'm traveling to festivals and school visits.

I'm grateful to my writer and nonwriter friends who have cheered me on when the journey gets tough, and been so generous to read all my books. It truly means the world to me, so thank you!

Jayden's personal journey is both physical and emotional while mine is the brainsucking mental variety, especially when I'm throwing whole chapters away and would rather be gorging on movies and cookies. I've loved Jayden's story and these characters for well over a decade, and that love drives me to keep going despite the desperate cookie-binging days.

Thank you so much, Tracey and Josh Adams, my wonderful

agents whom I adore. My gratitude is difficult to enumerate and express, but I'm so happy you're with me to keep me sane, cheerful, and optimistic.

Loads of gratitude go to my wonderful editor, Karen Chaplin; Rosemary Brosnan; and the entire team of copyeditors and artists at Harper who lovingly and creatively guided the Forbidden series along its book production journey. The covers are magnificent and I've fallen in love with every single one. Thank you, Karen, for championing this trilogy over the last five years since that thrilling phone call when you signed Jayden up for this particular journey.

A final thanks to the adorable Connie Griffin at Bookworks in Albuquerque for organizing all the book launch parties over the years, as well as the long, chatty talks. Thank you, Mark and Morgane Walton, for the fantastic evening at Weller Book Works in SLC, including dinner and hours of talking afterward. Friends and books are definitely a match made in heaven, and I've been blessed to have an abundance of both in my life.

READ
THEM ALL!

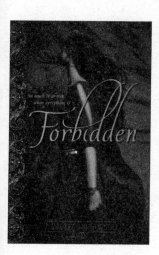